FREAKY WITCHES
A MYSTIC CARAVAN MYSTERY BOOK SEVEN

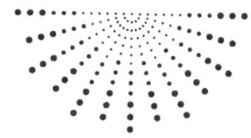

AMANDA M. LEE

WINCHESTERSHAW PUBLICATIONS

Copyright © 2019 by Amanda M. Lee

All rights reserved.

No part of this book may be reproduced in any form or by any electronic or mechanical means, including information storage and retrieval systems, without written permission from the author, except for the use of brief quotations in a book review.

❀ Created with Vellum

ONE

"So ... witches?"

My boyfriend Kade Denton slid me a sidelong look as he gritted his teeth and gripped the truck's steering wheel more tightly. A kaleidoscope of emotions flitted through his eyes, and I could feel the nervous energy practically oozing from every pore.

"Witches aren't so bad," I said hurriedly. "Besides, I'm not sure if we're dealing with real witches or fake ones. The information has been hard to pin down because the stories are really ... out there."

He flicked his eyes back to the rather rough expressway we were traversing — apparently Michigan had continuous problems with roads — and shifted his hands to get a better grip. "I'm pretty sure I don't like witches."

He said the words with such authority that I couldn't help but smile. "And what witches do you know?" I asked gently.

"Well ... there's the witch who tried to kill us by making living dolls. If I remember correctly, she had fake dolls that were murderous, too. There're the witches who almost killed you in Utah. Oh, and the witches who turned that poor woman into a wendigo and almost killed us two weeks ago."

A muscle ticked in his jaw and I knew that was the instance really bothering him. I wasn't sure how to soothe his obviously frazzled nerves.

"Technically the people in Utah weren't really witches," I said finally. "That was a whole big thing that's better left in the past because we're unlikely to fight that sort of monster again."

"And the woman who sent the living dolls after us?"

"She was definitely a witch, but she had other things going on, too. I don't think you have to worry about living dolls going after us in Michigan."

"You said it's a town full of witches," Kade argued. "There were several witches in the last town — and they spanned generations — and you saw what happened."

Ah. Now we were getting to the heart of the matter. "I *did* see what happened," I confirmed, allowing my gaze to drift out the passenger-side window. The foliage was thick and lush in this part of northern Lower Michigan. We were about to turn off the freeway and point ourselves west, heading for a small town called Hemlock Cove, but Kade's mind was clearly still in northern California.

In some ways, my mind was back there, too, with a woman who was supposedly a monster. She wasn't, though. She'd managed to maintain a sense of self despite the atrocious things done to her. In the end, it was the purported humans who moved on us — and paid the price — while the monster fought to save the innocent. It was a humbling experience, and I was still dreaming about the final battle.

As for Kade, his aversion to the situation in Eureka was for completely different reasons. He was upset because he'd finally used magic he didn't know he had. He was the son of a powerful mage, so I always thought it was inevitable that Kade would manifest. The way his father Max watched him made me believe he felt the same way. Kade, however, didn't consider it most of the time. Sure, the possibility was always there, but he chose to believe he wasn't magical because nothing had ever popped up.

And me, Poet Parker, the resident fortune teller for Mystic Caravan Circus, I believed it was probably inevitable ... although I couldn't tell him that because he was still freaking out about using his magic to save us during a tense standoff almost two weeks earlier.

I would've thought he'd adjust to the realization relatively quickly. I expected a few days – maybe even a full week – of moping and whining. The fact that he was still struggling two weeks later, turning shrill whenever one of our co-workers brought up the subject, didn't leave me feeling warm and gooey.

"Kade ... ." I wasn't sure what I was going to say, but the notion of babbling until I made him feel better immediately died when he shot me a look.

"I don't need constant hand-holding," he said as he pulled off the expressway and immediately started lowering his speed as we crested a hill and moved into Grayling, Michigan. It was a mid-sized town for this area (which wasn't saying much), although we were told that Gaylord (one town over) had better stores to choose from. The shopping would have to wait until after we'd unpacked in our new digs.

"I thought you liked holding my hand," I teased, instinctively reaching over and grabbing the hand resting on his thigh. Something sparked between us, as it always did, and I saw him relax a bit at the tactile comfort offered.

"I like holding your hand ... and other stuff," he teased, his eyes lighting with mirth as I grinned. "I just ... don't know that I want to talk about this right now."

He'd been saying that for the better part of two weeks as we made our way across the country with a caravan of circus workers and equipment. I'd let him get away with it until this point. However, I was no longer sure coddling him was the right move.

"Maybe I'm not going to give you a choice," I said finally.

Kade arched an eyebrow. "And what do you mean by that?"

"I'm worried," I replied simply. "You're one of my favorite people in the world, and I'm worried. You've been withdrawn since it happened, and it's starting to give me a complex. If you don't want to be with me any longer ... or here with us ... ." I trailed off, my heart aching.

"Don't you ever think that," Kade hissed, his eyes going dark.

Thankfully we were stopped at a light so he could ignore traffic to his heart's content. "Is that what you think? I don't want to leave. Not you or the circus, but especially not you. Don't think that."

I held my hands up in surrender. "Okay. I'm sorry." I turned my attention back to the window as the truck started moving again. I could feel him watching me, but couldn't bring myself to turn back and face him.

"I'm sorry, baby," he said quietly, waiting until we'd moved past the town limits to speak again. "I didn't mean to shut you out or anything. I've been trying to get a feeling for what's going on."

"And you don't like it," I surmised.

"I'm afraid of it," he clarified, taking me by surprise. "When it happened ... when the magic flared to life ... it was like losing myself. You know what a control freak I am. I don't like losing myself."

Despite the dour curtain hanging over the truck, I couldn't stop myself from laughing. "You are a bit of a control freak."

He reached for the hand I'd pulled back a few minutes earlier and gripped it tightly. "I'm sorry if I've been hurting you. That was not my intention. I just ... can't wrap my head around this."

And that's what worried me most. "I don't think you're going to be able to wrap your head around it if you don't talk about it," I said quietly. "It doesn't necessarily have to be with me. I'm not a mage, so I don't understand everything you're going through. Max understands. Maybe you should talk to him."

Kade slid me a sidelong look, his fingers remaining linked with mine. "I'm not ready yet. I'm sorry. I know that's not what you want to hear, but I'm simply not ready."

I absently scratched my cheek as I regarded his strong profile. He was ridiculously handsome, like, criminally so. He had jaw bones that looked as if they were carved from marble and eyes that made me go weak in the knees (although I would never admit that to anyone, least of all him). Most importantly, he also had a good heart.

"I don't want to push you," I said finally. "That's not my intention. It's just ... I don't like feeling separate from you."

He flinched at the words. "I didn't realize I was pushing you away that hard. I'll do better."

"I don't want you to react in a way that's not natural for you."

"I'll do better." He was firm. "I've been afraid to touch you at night when we sleep." It was as if he was reading my mind. We shared a trailer, one his father bought for us as something of a bribe. It was beautiful ... and we absolutely loved it for the first few nights we got to enjoy it. Since then, however, he'd been sleeping as far away from me as possible. It was a small crack in the foundation of our relationship, but I worried it would turn into a crevasse.

"If you don't want to share a bed ... ."

"Don't say that." Agitation rolled off Kade's tongue hot and fast. "I do. I'm just afraid that my hands are going to catch fire again in my sleep and I'll accidentally burn you or something."

He was so earnest I knew it was mean to laugh, but I couldn't help myself. The chuckle that escaped my throat was low and husky. The accompanying glare from him was cold.

"I'm sorry." I held up my hands. "I'm not laughing at you."

"It sounded like you were laughing at me."

"I just ... was laughing at the situation," I clarified, and meant it. "I would probably do the same thing out of fear because it would kill me to hurt you. The thing is, you've had this power inside you the entire time. You've never hurt me. In fact, the power only manifested because you wanted to protect me.

"I know you don't believe it, perhaps can't believe it, but you don't have it in you to hurt me," I continued. "You're going to be okay. But you need to talk about it. And you need to practice."

"Maybe I don't want it to ever happen again," Kade challenged. "Have you ever considered that?"

"Yes." I nodded without hesitation. "I'm sure that's true. I don't think you'll be able to stop it, though. Whenever one of us gets in trouble, the magic will be whispering in your ear to get loose and you'll let it loose because you're a hero."

"I don't feel like a hero."

I smirked at his discomfort. "You're *my* hero and you did a good job with the Falk ghosts. You have to trust yourself. I trust you. Everyone else trusts you. You're the only one who doesn't trust what's building inside. Maybe you should figure out why that is."

He let loose a heavy sigh. "If I promise to think about it, can we let it go for a little bit? I just need to think."

"Sure." I took pity on him and massaged the palm of his hand. I needed to change the subject, for his benefit as well as my own. "Have you ever been to Michigan?"

Relieved that we could talk about something else, Kade relaxed. "No. I've heard good things about it. You've been here before, right? You grew up here."

"Never to this part of the state," I replied, my eyes busy as the trees grew larger. "I've been to the Detroit area and even mid-Michigan. I've never been this far north."

"And why are we going to a new location?"

"A place called Hemlock Cove is having a huge festival," I replied. "I guess they always have festivals. I saw their schedule, in fact, and I think they have like forty-two a year."

Kade snickered. "That's a lot of festivals when you consider there are only fifty-two weeks in a year."

"I know, but apparently that's their shtick. My understanding is that the town used to be called Walkerville. Then, a few years ago, they changed the name and rebranded as a paranormal vacation destination."

Kade was obviously dubious because his eyebrows hopped. "What is that supposed to mean?"

"They're a witch town," I explained. "Everyone in town pretends to be witches. I guess they have a cauldron store ... and themed bakeries ... and other magic stores. Our scout warned me specifically to stay away from the porcelain unicorn lady."

"Is that a euphemism for something?"

"No. Apparently there's a woman who sells nothing but porcelain unicorns. She hired us, though, so I don't think I'll be able to stay away from her."

"That's kind of a bummer."

"Isn't it, though?" I grinned at him, something he returned, and then turned back to the packet of information I'd collected for this job. "The thing is, we've heard rumblings about this area for years. While the town is mostly filled with humans pretending to be witches, supposedly there is a group of women who are real witches pretending to be normal humans pretending to be witches."

It took Kade a moment to follow my line of thinking. "That's a little ... ."

"Funny?" I supplied for him.

"I was going to say weird."

"I think it's funny." I leaned back in my seat and stretched out my legs. "How much longer?"

"About twenty minutes. You have plenty of time to finish telling me about the real witches."

"I don't know much about them," I admitted. "I only know the rumors. Supposedly some very powerful magic has been wielded in this area, and it didn't start recently. If there are real witches here, this has been their home for a long time. Max said he's been hearing about it for, like, fifty years."

"So ... you think it's true that there are real witches?"

"I don't see why not." I lifted my eyes to the vista. "This is a beautiful area. It's remote, though. Witches could hide here for a long time without discovery."

"If you've heard the whispers, then they're clearly not avoiding discovery."

"Yes, but we're a unique magical convergence," I explained. "We hear more than normal people."

Kade was thoughtful as he slid me a look. "You're excited about this, aren't you? You're not worried in the least that we're going to run into real witches — just like the last bunch — and have to fight our way free."

"We're monster hunters," I reminded him, opting for pragmatism. "We fight monsters. If the witches here are monsters, then we'll fight them. It's as simple as that."

"It doesn't feel simple to me," he muttered under his breath.

"Not all witches are monsters," I said softly. "There are more good witches than bad. In fact, the vast majority of witches are really hippie chicks with a nature fetish. It's rare to find a witch with real power."

"Do you think we will here?"

It was obvious that he was nervous. I could've lied to make him feel better, but that didn't seem fair. "I definitely feel magic here," I said finally, my heart giving a little lurch as his lips twisted. "It doesn't feel like bad magic, though."

"So you say." Kade was officially grouchy. "I don't want to be attacked by witches again. Why can't we fight something else? This is Michigan. It seems to me, with all the Bigfoot legends, that we should be fighting shifters. Why can't we fight shifters?"

I smiled. "Shifters are as dangerous as witches. Sometimes they're even more dangerous, especially if you manage to stumble over a pack."

"Well ... I wouldn't know. It seems we're most often taking on witches."

"I think that's perception." I dropped the packet of information on the floor and unlatched my seatbelt so I could slide over the middle cushion and snuggle closer to him. If Kade was surprised at my sudden appearance at his side, he didn't show it. "I'm here to help if you need me." I was quiet as I rested my cheek against his shoulder. "You don't have to do this alone."

He sighed. The sound was long and drawn out, as if he was suffering and it took everything he had to keep from exploding. I expected him to yell, or at least pull a Bossy McBossypants and tell me to fasten my seatbelt because it wasn't safe to drive without one. Instead, he kissed my forehead three times in rapid succession.

"We'll get through this," he said quietly. "I'm sorry I haven't been paying enough attention to you."

I balked. "That is not what I was saying. I don't need attention."

He chuckled at my outrage. "I guess I'm not the only one with buttons to push."

"Ha, ha." I poked his side. "I just want you to know you can talk to me."

"Do you think I don't know that? You're the one person I can always talk to. The thing is, I don't know what to say. I don't know how I feel ... or what to expect. I simply don't know."

"You could tell me that so I'm not left wondering if you wish we hadn't moved in together."

"Don't ever think that." Kade was firm as he shook his head and pressed his lips against my forehead a fourth time. "I'm fond of you, too, and am happy living with you. That won't change."

"You're just afraid to touch me."

"Not when I'm awake. I am a bit fearful something evil will crawl out of me in my sleep and hurt you."

"We could always put an enchantment on you to make sure that can't happen."

Kade looked intrigued. "Is that really a thing?"

I searched his hopeful face and nodded. "I can make that happen."

"Oh, if you could do that, I would be so grateful. It doesn't have to be forever or anything, but just until I'm sure I won't hurt you in my sleep. I'm so terrified of that, you don't even know."

I could actually feel the tension unknotting as he relaxed a bit, which made me realize he was more keyed up than I'd imagined. "I'll take care of it. We'll keep it on the down low."

"Thank you." Another kiss on the forehead. He relaxed quite a bit as we drove, and I melted against him. It was nice to have a few moments of quiet together. We needed it, and once we hit town, we would be too busy to engage for several hours.

I was so lost in the quiet comfort of the moment I almost missed it when Kade's body stiffened. The sound he made in the back of his throat didn't allow me to ignore whatever it was getting his dander up.

"What?" I asked, instantly alert.

"Look at that." Kade pointed toward the woods to our right. There, as if she didn't have a care in the world, an elderly woman strolled toward the trees.

"What do you think she's doing?" I asked.

"I don't know, but she has a shotgun, a combat helmet and a whistle. Why would you need a shotgun and a whistle?"

That was a very good question. "I don't know. I'm more interested in her leggings. I think that's a dragon on her ... you know. She would have to bend over for me to be sure. It seems to be breathing fire in her ... nether regions."

"Oh, why did you have to point that out?" Kade whined. "I don't want to see that."

"If I have to see it and know what it is, you have to see it."

"Yeah, but ... ." Kade forgot what he was about to say as the woman disappeared into the woods. "Do you think we should tell someone that there's an old lady wandering around the woods with a gun?"

I shook my head. "This is Michigan. I think that's a normal occurrence."

He didn't look convinced, but he leaned back in his seat. "You're probably right."

"I'm sure it's fine. I mean ... what sort of trouble could a woman with a whistle and a gun find?"

2
TWO

The Hemlock Cove fairgrounds consisted of one main drag and a field at the far side of the town. We parked, a steady stream of vehicles flowing onto the property, and I hopped out of Kade's truck to study the layout with an experienced eye.

"This makes me nervous," a voice offered from behind. Raven Marko, our resident lamia and House of Mirrors enchantress, moved up next to me. She looked as concerned as I felt.

"It's definitely different," I agreed, rolling my neck until it cracked. "I don't understand how a town this size is funding a full circus. I mean ... it's basically one street."

"And only thirty businesses," Raven noted. "That's including the library, the newspaper office, the police station and the stables over yonder." She gestured toward a huge barn and livery yard about a block down. "This seems extremely odd. Are you sure we got full payment?"

"We got the appropriate down payment," I clarified. "They don't pay the final amount until the day we leave. They passed all the financial checks, though."

"It still doesn't make sense." Raven narrowed her eyes. "I think we should make sure this is on the up and up before we start unpacking."

I hated to agree with her — mostly because we irritated each other quite regularly and it was like ceding the first battle of this stop without a fight — but I was too tired to put the work into unpacking if this wasn't going to work out.

"You're right," I said after a beat. "Our liaison owns the unicorn store. I'll head over there while you guys stretch your legs. Don't bother unpacking until I give you the okay."

"I'm fine with that." Raven flopped on the ground. "You'll find me here when you return. Those cross-country drives are murder, by the way. I hate them."

"Yes, but none of the drives scheduled for the rest of the year will be nearly as long, so now we can say it's out of the way."

"I hate it when you're a glass-half-full person."

I patted the top of her head condescendingly. "You'll get used to it."

I started across the road, and wasn't surprised when Kade fell into step with me. "Are you serving as my protector?" I teased.

He grabbed my hand. "I'm head of security. That's my job."

"I doubt she's a witch. She sells porcelain unicorns, for crying out loud. No self-respecting witch would go that route."

"Actually, that would be the worst sort of witch, wouldn't it?"

He had a point. Still, I was more than capable of taking care of myself. Of course, he was still recuperating from the last bout of witches. If he wanted to stay close, I wasn't about to argue. "I guess you can be part of the team."

He lifted our joined hands, pressed a quick kiss to my knuckles, and then released me. It was an oddly sentimental reaction. "We're always on the same team," he said. "Let's get this done. We have hours of unpacking ahead of us and then I could use a good night's sleep ... just as soon as you do that enchantment thing so I can't hurt you."

Something occurred to me. "Have you been sleeping at all over the past few weeks?"

He ignored the question as we reached the store, instead holding the door open so I could step inside. "Ladies first."

I wanted to push him on the issue, but now wasn't the time. Instead, I pasted a bright smile on my face as I entered the store ... and then did my best not to wretch at the mish-mash of cutesy tchotchkes and souvenirs. It looked as if a giant eight-year-old girl had exploded and the unicorns were the remains.

"May I help you?"

I jerked my head to the counter, where an elderly woman stood. Her hair was perfectly coiffed, not a strand out of place, and she wore a pink shirt that reminded me of a stomachache aid. "Hello." I squared my shoulders and stepped forward. "My name is Poet Parker. I'm looking for Margaret Little. My understanding is she owns this place."

The woman's eyes darkened as she looked me up and down. I was dressed in simple yoga pants and a T-shirt — comfortable travel clothes are a must — and I distinctly sensed suspicion sparking in the air around her. "And why are you looking for her?"

"I'm with Mystic Caravan Circus," I volunteered. "We just arrived and I want to make sure we're in the correct spot before we start unpacking."

"Oh, of course." The woman exhaled heavily, relief palpable. "I'm sorry. I'm Margaret Little." She wiped her hands on her hips as she moved around the counter. "I thought maybe you were part of a practical joke or something — you know how that goes. I'm sorry I was less than genial. I've been having difficulties with one of the residents and thought there was a chance she sent you."

That was odd, to say the least. "Oh, well ... ."

"We're not here as part of a joke," Kade offered. He introduced himself and shook her hand, ignoring the way her eyes roamed his handsome face. He had an interesting effect on women — it didn't matter the age — although he often ignored it. "We just want to make sure everything is in place."

"It is," Margaret confirmed, bobbing her head. "You got the paperwork I sent?"

"I did." I pressed the tip of my tongue against the back of my teeth, debating how far I should push things. Finally, I decided it was best to ask the obvious question. "It's just ... this is a small town. We've never been in a venue this small."

"And you're wondering if we'll have enough visitors to pay for it,"

Margaret surmised. "The answer is ... yes. Don't worry. We have a festival launching in a few days. My understanding is that it takes you that long to get everything set up properly."

"It does. Do you really think you can fill the circus for an entire weekend?" I couldn't quite fathom that. "I don't mean to tell you your business or anything. We're simply used to larger venues."

"And we're used to festivals," Margaret pointed out. "I know the town ... and what it's capable of providing when it comes to tourist numbers. We're having an absolutely huge festival this weekend. Witches from around the world will be here."

I felt Kade stiffen beside me but he held it together. "Witches from around the world?"

"Yes. It's a huge witch festival."

"What kind of witches?"

Margaret made an odd face. "Honey, there's only one kind of witch."

Something told me she wasn't one of the real witches masquerading as a fake that I had to worry about. "Well, as long as you're sure," I hedged.

"We're expecting ten-thousand people this weekend," Margaret gushed. "Every inn in the area is sold out. Every inn in neighboring towns is sold out. There aren't even any rooms available in Traverse City. That's how many people are coming."

The city name meant nothing to me, but she seemed impressed. "It sounds good. I didn't mean to question your business acumen or anything. It's simply a different location than we've ever visited for business purposes."

"Of course. You're used to metropolitan areas. I promise you'll see something impressive when the festival kicks off. Some of the witches have already arrived."

Unable to stop himself from asking the obvious, Kade leaned forward. "And what makes them witches?"

I saw the fear cascading through him, and it made my heart lurch. Margaret wasn't a keen observer of the human condition, and she misread his expression. "I don't like witches either." She patted his hand, causing me to smile as she winked conspiratorially. "I'm part of the 'only good witch is a dead witch' contingent, but everyone coming thinks he or she is a witch. There's nothing to worry about."

Kade slid his gaze to me, genuine mirth lurking in the depths of his eyes. "Okay, well ... that sounds great. We should probably head back to the fairgrounds so we can get as much unpacked this evening as possible."

"That's smart." Margaret's smile was back in place. "I'll come by to check on you later, make sure you don't need anything."

"Actually, we could use a market," I said. "We need to buy food."

"The nearest market that will have the amount of food you need is in Gaylord," Margaret volunteered. "You can eat at any of the restaurants for free. That was negotiated into your contract."

I'd obviously missed that tidbit while perusing the documents. "That's good to know. Thank you so much for your time."

"Don't mention it."

I waited until we were outside, safely out of earshot, before speaking again. "I was wrong about her being a witch."

"She seems a little ... intense," Kade said. "She's not so bad."

I had a feeling she was going to be a righteous pain in the behind before it was all said and done, although there was no reason to bring that up ... at least not yet. "Let's get unpacked. I'm already exhausted. By the time we finish I'm going to pass out on the ground."

"We can do it." Kade's mood was brighter than it had been in weeks. "I think we'll like it here. It's quiet, relaxing. We probably won't even find trouble in this spot for a change."

"That would be a nice change of pace, huh?"

"Definitely."

TWO HOURS LATER I was starting to wish for a monster simply to get a break from the tedium associated with unpacking.

"I'm not sure I like this," my best friend Luke Bishop announced as he moved to my side. He was a shifter — and infatuated with being the most interesting man in the room — which meant he was high maintenance. I was so used to it I barely noticed.

"You don't like what?" I challenged.

"This." He gestured toward the layout. The heavy equipment was a day behind us and wouldn't arrive until the next afternoon. Our personal trailers were already arranged in neat rows, essentially forming three and one-half walls to close us in. It was a layout we'd designed to protect our secrets, and that somehow seemed even more important now that we were trapped in the middle of Witchland.

"You'll have to be more specific," I said. "What don't you like about the layout?"

"The fact that we're so close to town." He pointed toward our row of trailers. "You and Kade are right at the front there. Anyone passing by might see what you're doing."

"I guess that means we're going to have to lay off the kinky sex, huh?"

The look Luke shot me was withering. "Please. You're not inventive in that area. I'm guessing he's a strict three-position guy. I'm sorry for that." He patted my arm.

It took me a minute to realize what he was saying. "Oh, must you always take it to the lowest level?"

He nodded without hesitation. "As a matter of fact, I do. That's my superpower."

"And here I thought it was irritating your co-workers."

"That's an offshoot of my superpower."

"Good to know." We stood in silence for a moment, both of us staring at trailer row. "I thought it was best for Kade and me to be at the front so we can head off anyone if they try to cross the boundaries. This set-up is definitely weird, but I'm hopeful the town will be empty tonight so we can erect the dreamcatcher."

The dreamcatcher was a magical net I erected with Raven and two of our other powerful circus friends, the pixie twins Nixie and Nadia, so we could lure evil creatures and trap them for easy eradication. You see, Mystic Caravan is more than a circus. We're also monster hunters.

"Do you think we'll need the dreamcatcher here?" Luke asked. "It seems like a quiet area."

"An area that is thick with stories about real witches," I reminded him. "Plus, I don't know about now, but years ago there was a huge shifter population."

"The shifter population is located in mid-Michigan now. They moved."

"Maybe it was because of the witches."

"I guess that's possible." Luke slung an arm around my shoulders. We were unbelievably close, and had been since we'd met. He would always be my best friend, and even though he was initially worried that my relationship with Kade would displace him, I knew it would never happen. We were stuck with each other for life.

"We have to be careful." I kept my voice low. "That unicorn woman will be watching for odd things."

"How can you tell?"

"It's just a feeling. When we first went inside she thought we were there as part of a joke someone was playing on her. I'm guessing she's not well liked in this town."

"Small towns have their merits, but they're filled with people spying on one another. That's always something to worry about."

"Yeah. I ... ." I tilted my head when I caught a hint of movement behind my trailer. "Did you see that?"

Luke was busy studying his cuticles. "See what? It's too bad they don't have a salon in this town. I could definitely use a manicure. We're going to Detroit next, right? They'll have good manicure places."

I ignored his fixation with his nails. "That." I pointed toward the woods directly behind the trailer I shared with Kade. "There's someone over there."

Luke followed my gaze. "Perhaps it's the unicorn lady."

I had my doubts about that. Margaret didn't seem the outdoorsy type. I slipped from beneath Luke's arm and headed in that direction, something calling to me. I was almost to the trailer when a figure stumbled out of the woods, and it was someone I recognized.

"You're the lady with the whistle," I blurted out.

The woman, a smile that reminded me of the evil clown from *It* on her face, took a moment to look me up and down. She had a shotgun slung over her shoulder and her combat helmet was slightly askew. "I go by many names," she said finally. "Who are you?"

"Poet Parker." I answered automatically. Lying was a waste of time. Even though I sensed something about this woman, something I couldn't put a name to, she seemed friendly enough. "I'm with the circus."

"I always considered joining the circus," the woman said. "I fancied myself an acrobat. Do you have acrobats?"

I nodded dumbly. "In the main tent as part of the big show. The main tent doesn't arrive until tomorrow."

"Maybe I still have time to be an acrobat," she mused.

"Aren't you afraid you'll break a hip?" Luke challenged as he moved up beside me. He seemed more amused than worried. There was something almost comical about the woman's appearance.

Her face remained blank. "Why would I break a hip?"

"You're old."

She narrowed her eyes to dangerous slits. "Do you want me to show you how old I am?"

Something told me that was the last thing Luke wanted. "He didn't mean that in a rude way," I interjected quickly. "He simply thinks he's funny."

Luke was affronted. "I *am* funny."

I ignored him. "Is there a reason you're in the woods?"

She nodded. "I'm playing a little game with a friend of mine. Perhaps you know her. Margaret Little."

Things clicked into place. "You're the person she worried was playing a trick on her. She thought you sent me when I stopped in her store earlier."

The woman snorted. "I wouldn't send you if I was plotting against her. I've got my own arsenal of sarcastic youngsters to employ.

Although ... ." She broke off, thoughtful. "I'm guessing you have some hidden talents."

The way she said it set my teeth on edge. "I was just about to say the same about you."

"I want to go back to this acrobat thing," Luke argued. "Have you been trained as an acrobat?"

The woman waved her hand dismissively. "Please. I could be an acrobat professionally if I wanted."

"Aunt Tillie!"

The new screech came from behind us, and when I swiveled I saw a blonde exiting the newspaper office, bellowing.

"Uh-oh," the woman muttered, shaking her head. "That's not good."

I arched an eyebrow as I turned back to her. "Are you Aunt Tillie?"

"Tillie Winchester." She extended her hand, which I had no choice but to shake. The second our fingers touched I felt a rush of power that almost knocked me backward. "And you are?"

Did she feel that? I couldn't be sure. She remained calm, as if this were a completely normal conversation. She was either the best actress in the world or oblivious. "Poet Parker. I'm the fortune teller."

Tillie brightened. "We're definitely going to have things to discuss."

"Aunt Tillie!" The blonde screeched again.

"Whatever happens, you haven't seen me," Tillie hissed, moving back toward the woods. "When she comes over here, play ignorant. She just wants to boss me around. I'm sure her mother put her up to it."

I opened my mouth to ask who the blonde was, but Tillie was already gone.

"Who was that?" Nelson "Nellie" Adler, our cross-dressing bearded lady who was really a dwarf from another dimension, hurried to my side. "Was she a threat?"

I searched my heart. "I don't think so. She was definitely something, though."

"Yeah, she was." Nellie's grin was so broad it threatened to swallow his entire face. "She was awesome. We need to find her again."

Nellie was something of a headache — and I had a feeling Tillie was as well — so I wanted to prevent that meeting of the minds. I wasn't sure it was a possibility. "Don't worry. I think she'll find us when she's ready."

"Awesome! I think I'm in love."

That was a frightening thought.

3
THREE

The blonde didn't head to the grounds, instead standing in front of the newspaper office and staring for a long time. She didn't look particularly suspicious, but she gave us a wide berth, which I found interesting. Most people are drawn to the circus because they have questions or are naturally curious about the animals they thought we had tucked away in the tents at the back of the grounds.

The blonde was different. She stared directly at me before offering a wave and disappearing inside the newspaper building.

I found her intriguing.

"What happened over here?" Kade asked as he moved toward us, curiosity etched across his handsome face. "Did something happen? Nixie said there was a strange woman over here."

"She wasn't strange," Nellie argued, his gaze still on the woods. "She was ... awesome."

"I'll need more information than that."

"She had a combat helmet and a gun," Nellie volunteered.

"It was the woman we saw entering the woods when we were driving into town," I explained. "Her name is Tillie Winchester." And she's powerful, I silently added. The power I felt soaring through her was impressive. The last thing Kade needed to hear about was a powerful being. He was in the best mood I could remember in the past two weeks. I didn't want to eradicate that mood.

"And she's a goddess," Nellie said. "I'm telling you right now, I think we should ask her to join us. She'd be a big draw."

"Because she has a shotgun?" Luke asked dubiously.

"Because she's ... awesome. Did you see those leggings? I'm dying to see what that dragon is protecting."

I made a face. "She was, like, eighty."

"So what? Dwarves like older women. That's a known fact."

I didn't know that. "If you want to romance her, go nuts."

"Thanks for your permission, Mom," he said dryly.

I ignored the dig. "Let's finish setting up and then make dinner. We have more than enough food to get through tonight. Tomorrow, we might have to make some decisions regarding the food situation. Margaret said we could eat at the area restaurants for free, but that might become cumbersome at some point."

"We'll worry about that tomorrow." Kade stroked his hand down the back of my dark hair. "Are you okay? You look ... off."

"I'm fine." I plastered a smile on my face. "I'm thinking about the dragons for a different reason, that's all, and it's giving me waking nightmares."

He matched my smile. "I'm sorry I missed it." He gave me a quick kiss, which made Luke and Nellie groan in unison as they pushed past us to return to work. "I kind of like this place," he admitted. "It's quiet. You have no idea how much I need the quiet."

I did know. That's what worried me. "Hopefully it will stay quiet."

"Yeah. Come on." He tugged on my hand. "Let's get the food area set up and then we can start talking about dinner. We have steaks and corn, right?"

"Your favorite."

"You're my favorite." He winked at me, his playful personality back in place. "The steak and corn are definitely a close second, though."

. . .

DINNER WAS A FESTIVE affair. We had a good time cooking and enjoying the various glimpses of Hemlock Cove's resident fake witches. Raven pointed out a woman with short green hair as she crossed from a store named Hypnotic toward the stables.

"She's definitely a fake witch," she said as she munched on a piece of cake. "No real witch would have green hair."

"That's true," I said, dusting off my hands. "It will be dark soon. As soon as we're relatively sure the town is clear, we'll put up the dreamcatcher and then go to bed early. It's been a long trip, and we're going to have even more work to do tomorrow."

"Sounds like a plan." Kade slid his arm around my back as we sat at one of the communal picnic tables. "I've been watching the town. Most of the stores are already closed. I took a walk down Main Street earlier. Most of them close early on Mondays and Tuesdays, and then stay open later as the week progresses. We need to do the dreamcatcher tonight."

"We will." I briefly rested my head against his shoulder. "We'll set up sentries to be certain. In some ways, being this close to the downtown area is a detriment because they'll be able to see everything we do. In other ways, that might benefit us. Most creatures won't want to attack when we're this exposed."

"We'll figure it out. We always do." He brushed his lips against my forehead. "I'll serve as one of the sentries while you guys erect the dreamcatcher. I'll take Luke, Nellie, Seth and Dolph with me."

I nodded, thoughtful. "We'll work as fast as possible. This space isn't tricky. We should be fine."

"We *will* be fine. You don't need to worry."

That was rich coming from him. He'd done nothing but worry about inadvertently hurting me in his sleep for the past two weeks. "The same goes for you."

He shook his head. "It'll be okay. I probably should've said something earlier."

"You definitely should have," I agreed. "We'll fix it. In fact, I already have the potion we need. You'll sleep well tonight."

He sighed. "I can't wait."

. . .

THE MEN LEFT the fairgrounds under the guise of looking around, which was our cue to erect the dreamcatcher. It was quick work. The fairgrounds were in the shape of a square. There were heavy woods on two sides, but everything else was open.

Nixie, Naida, Raven and I had erected so many dreamcatchers we knew exactly what we were doing. We each picked a direction — I took the side closest to the nearest interlopers — and began chanting under our breath as we weaved the magical tapestry.

The dreamcatcher was a device of my making. I came up with the idea in a dream – nice, eh? It took us four tries to get it to work, and then we spent years perfecting it. Now it was a weapon in and of itself. In fact, the dreamcatcher was one of the most powerful weapons in our arsenal.

I lost myself to the process, forgetting to scan the area around me as the dreamcatcher weave tightened. We were close, almost finished, and I felt the power pulsing through me.

The Latin words escaped in a rush. I no longer had to think about them. Protection. Strength. Power. All those things were channeled into the dreamcatcher. The final ingredient was one most people wouldn't consider. It was love, and that was the thing I channeled hardest.

Then, just as soon as it started, the chanting finished. The dreamcatcher was up and ready to be tested. That's what I did, sending a boost of magic to a nearby thread. The dreamcatcher contracted and held, just as it was designed to.

"That wasn't so bad," I said to myself as I dusted off my hands. "All done."

Slowly, I lifted my eyes and met the steady gaze of the blonde from the newspaper. She was exiting the building — I'd forgotten she was still there — and stopped in front of her car. She didn't look upset or even accusatory. She was obviously curious, but she didn't say a word. She simply stared.

Crap! I had to say something, come up with an excuse. I opened my mouth to make up a story, but she broke eye contact and reached for her door handle. She didn't as much as look over her shoulder as she climbed in and started the engine.

I remained rooted to my spot as I watched her leave, confusion and worry washing over me in continuous waves.

"All done?" Kade asked as he materialized out of the growing darkness.

I nodded woodenly. "All done."

"Are you okay?"

He could read me better than most, so I didn't bother making up a lie. "She saw us putting up the dreamcatcher."

"Who?" Kade glanced around. "Who saw you?"

"The woman at the newspaper. She came out and stared directly at me."

"That doesn't mean she saw you," Kade said pragmatically. "She might've assumed you were simply walking around talking to yourself. She probably thinks you're odd, not magical."

I thought back to the expression on the woman's face. "Maybe. I guess." I didn't believe it, but there was nothing I could do. "Come on." I linked my fingers with his and led him toward our trailer. "I have your potion and then we can get some sleep."

"I can't wait."

I smiled. "You should've told me you weren't sleeping."

"I didn't say I wasn't sleeping."

"No, but I can tell. You're stretched. You need to give in to this potion and get as much sleep as possible. It's important that you're healthy."

"I'm healthy." He thumped his chest with his free hand and grinned. "I'm like an ox."

"You're starting to sound like Luke."

"Okay, there's no reason to get nasty."

"I wasn't trying to be nasty."

"That's what's really nasty about it."

I smiled. "Come on, Sleeping Beauty. It's time for some rest."

. . .

I WOKE BEFORE KADE the next morning, grinning into his shoulder for the first time in weeks. Now that I knew it was fear driving him rather than the irrational need to distance himself from other magical beings I could relax and get a solid night of sleep myself.

I gave him the potion upon entering the trailer. We went through our usual evening ritual, brushing our teeth and checking the doors, and then he downed the vial of purple liquid before climbing into bed. He snuggled close, which is how we used to sleep before he unleashed his powers for the first time. He was out within seconds.

I followed soon after.

The fact that he was still asleep when I woke to the dawn told me he'd slept hard, which was exactly what he needed.

"I hear your mind working," he murmured, kissing my forehead before slowly opening his eyes. They were clear and full of light, which is exactly how I liked them. "What's wrong? Are you still thinking about the woman who saw you working last night?"

I'd almost forgotten about her. "If she saw something, there's nothing I can do. This is a town full of fake witches anyway. She probably thinks it was part of the show. If she thought we were really doing something she would've called out to me."

"You're probably right." His hand was warm on my back as he rubbed it up and down. "I feel like a million bucks."

I lifted my eyebrows and smirked. "Because of me?"

"Always because of you. But this time it's because I slept. I didn't wake once. I don't think people realize what a miracle that is."

"I'm glad you're well rested." I meant it.

"It's all thanks to you."

The simple declaration made me want to squirm. "I think you had a part in it, too."

"Yes. I slept. You gave me the potion so I could sleep. You saved the day."

His earnest nature made me uncomfortable. "Kade ... ."

"Don't." He silenced me with a kiss. "I hate it when you don't want to take your props. You did an amazing thing for me last night. I expect you to do it again tonight. I don't want to argue over it."

That made two of us. "Fine. What do you want to do?"

As if on cue, his stomach growled. "I'm thinking breakfast is in order. There's something about a good night's sleep that makes me hungry."

"I believe I can help you there."

MOST OF THE CAMP was already stirring when I finished showering and made my way to the grill at the center of the kitchen area, my hair damp. Kade left to check the perimeter, whistling as he went, and I started in on the eggs, hash browns, bacon and toast with Nixie, Naida and Raven.

"He's in a good mood," Raven noted as she watched him go. "I take it you guys played a rousing game of farmer in the dell last night. It's about time. He was looking a little waxy there for a bit."

I scowled. "That's none of your business."

"Since you walked in without knocking and interrupted Percival and me in the middle of our business, I think I'm entitled."

In addition to being Raven's boyfriend, Percival Prentiss was one of our clowns. He had a fake British accent that he refused to explain and apparently liked dressing in chaps and full-on clown makeup when playing private games with Raven. I was still scarred from witnessing one of those games.

"Whatever." I focused on whisking eggs. "Was everything quiet around the camp last night? I mean ... I'm not expecting things to get loud, but you never know."

"To my knowledge, everything was quiet," Raven replied. "The pixie twins took off in the middle of the night when they thought no one was watching and didn't return until shortly before dawn, but that's hardly news."

Naida, the stronger of the two fairies, openly glared. "Why can't you ever mind your own business?"

"What fun would that be?" Raven replied, blasé.

"We weren't doing anything," Nixie offered. She was the peppier of the sisters. "We found a lake that was deserted and some slow-running creek that was completely shrouded by trees for swimming. You know how Naida gets if she can't get in the water."

She essentially turned into a mermaid when wet, so I was well aware of Naida's water antics. "I'm glad you found a place to swim."

"It's not big, but it will do," Naida said. "I prefer the lake even though it's more open. The other place — it's called Hollow Creek — has the remnants of magic hanging over it."

I jerked my head in her direction, surprised. "What kind of magic?"

Naida shrugged. "I'm not sure. I'm guessing witch — a powerful witch at that — but there are multiple shards hanging from the stars in that area."

Occasionally Naida slipped into talk from her dimension and it didn't make much sense. This was one of those times. "Can you give me a little something extra to go on?"

Naida merely tilted her head. "Someone brought a tempest down on a man out there and killed him. But it's okay; he was evil."

"And you can feel that?"

"I can."

"How long ago?"

"At least a year. He's gone. That's all that matters."

"And the witch who cast the spell?"

"She remains. I don't know what to tell you."

Oh, well, great. The witches in the area were constantly casting spells, so many that one little creek was inundated with memory sparkles. That couldn't be good. "We'll have to be careful," I said after a beat. "Make sure you don't let anyone see you doing your thing in that lake."

"I've got it under control."

I didn't want to play mother hen, but I was about to do just that when a sharp cry from the far side of the fairgrounds caught my attention. I exchanged a quick look with Raven, and it was obvious she'd heard the same shout.

"What do you think that is?" I asked.

"I think it's best we find out."

We left breakfast preparations with Naida and Nixie and hurried toward the sound of voices. I was practically running when I caught sight of Luke and Kade. They were staring at something on the ground, something beyond the dreamcatcher, and I was worried a fight was about to break out.

"What is it?"

Kade caught me by the waist before I could blow past him. "Careful, Poet," he said, tugging me to his chest so I couldn't trample the grotesque tableau taking shape. I recognized right away that the body on the ground had already lost some sort of fight. "You don't want to contaminate the scene."

I narrowed my eyes as I stared at the body. A man, probably in his forties, if I had to guess. His features were difficult to make out because of the blood coating his face. "What's that on his forehead?" I asked, squinting.

"It's a symbol of some sort," Kade replied, grim. "I don't recognize it."

"I don't either."

"I'm taking a photo," Luke offered. "We can look at it later if necessary."

That was smart. Still ... . I glanced around. "Why are we just standing here? Why haven't we done something with the body?"

"We're not doing anything with the body." Kade was firm. "I sent Dolph to the police station. He should be back with help in a few minutes."

"You purposely called the police?" I wasn't sure how I felt about that. "What if this is some sort of ritual and we have to fight witches? The police will get in the way of that."

"I'm well aware. We have no choice. We can't cover this up."

"Why?" Raven asked, dubious. "We've covered up deaths before."

"Yes, but we have no idea who this guy is." Kade kept his voice even. "He could be a local. Someone could be missing him."

"And he could be some evil freak who deserved to die," Raven shot back.

"If that's the case, the cops will sort it out." He showed no signs of backing down. "I don't want to start our stay here by hiding a body. We're going by the book on this one."

Even though part of me wanted to argue, I knew it would be wasted effort. It was too late. The police were on the way, and we were in the middle of a very uncomfortable situation.

4
FOUR

The chief of police was a tall man, barrel-chested and seemingly annoyed at being dragged to the fairgrounds before his first cup of coffee. He glanced between faces, and to my utter surprise, ultimately landed on me to answer questions.

"What's going on?" he asked without introducing himself.

I pointed toward the body. "We found that when we got up this morning."

"Oh, well, great," he muttered as he caught sight of the body and moved closer. "This is just ... crap!"

I took the noises he was making to mean he knew the victim. "Is he a local?" I asked.

He nodded. "Yup. Darren Rappaport. He owns the cauldron shop."

I glanced over my shoulder to focus on Main Street. I'd seen the cauldron shop Brewed to Perfection the previous day and made a mental note to visit. I loved the kitschy name, even if I had no need for a cauldron.

"What is your name?" The man's eyes were clear as they met mine.

"Poet Parker," I automatically answered.

"I'm Terry Davenport."

"It's nice to meet you ... I guess."

He grinned. "The circumstances suck," he agreed. "This is not normal, and you're the newbies. It might not be fair to question you, but if I don't ... ."

I filled in the rest of it. "Your residents will have meltdowns."

"Some of my residents are going to have meltdowns regardless," he admitted. "The thing is, there's a symbol carved in this man's head. It looks to have been done with a knife. I'll need the medical examiner to confirm that, but it seems like a safe assumption."

For a small-town police officer – correction, the word "chief" was embroidered on his shirt – he was remarkably calm when faced with a ritual death ... and that's exactly what we were dealing with.

"We'll answer whatever questions you have."

"Great." He flashed a smile. "You're in charge, right?"

"How did you know that?" I was legitimately curious.

"I know a few things about bossy women. You have the look."

"And what's the look?"

He shrugged. "You're the boss and the others look to you for answers. It's fine. If you could all go over by those picnic tables, I'll be over as soon as I can."

I shared a quick look with Kade, who had remained quiet for the duration of the conversation. "Is it okay if we cook breakfast?" I asked finally.

Terry bobbed his head. "I think that's a good idea. It might take me thirty minutes to get over there. I have a local FBI agent on tap I'll have to call. We'll question you together."

Kade spoke for the first time since Terry took over the scene. "You have a local FBI agent in a town this small?"

If Terry was surprised by the question, he didn't show it. "It's a long story. We'll be over there in thirty minutes. Go about your day as you normally would, other than wandering around town, that is."

"I guess we'll see you in thirty minutes," I said.

Terry nodded. "You will."

. . .

KADE WAITED UNTIL WE were a safe distance from the body and on our way back to the kitchen area to speak.

"Why would they have a dedicated FBI agent in a town this small?"

He seemed to be fixated on that tidbit, though I had no idea why. "I'm not sure why that matters."

He put his hand to the small of my back as he prodded me forward. "This is a tiny town. It has one stoplight. FBI agents get paid well. How could one be stationed here and stay busy?"

I hadn't considered that. "Maybe he handles the entire area."

"Maybe." Kade didn't look convinced. "He recognized you were in charge. Terry, I mean. He looked at everyone and focused on you."

"I noticed that, too," I acknowledged. "Most places we stop people assume you're in charge. He went straight for me. I find that ... impressive."

Kade snorted. "You just like being the boss."

"I think he's intuitive."

"And I think he was really calm," Kade countered. "That Darren Rappaport guy was killed ritually. You saw that mark on his head. There was enough blood on his chest to make me think that's a mess, too."

"There was no weapon left behind," Raven noted from behind us. "That means the killer took it with him or her."

"I'm more interested in the fact that the murder happened right outside the dreamcatcher lines," I said. "We're talking five feet from the barrier. I have trouble believing that's a coincidence."

"That's suspect," Kade agreed, rubbing his hand over my back as he heaved a sigh. "The whole thing is weird, but we can't really talk about it until after the police leave."

"Do you think he'll assume one of us is the culprit?" Raven asked. "He didn't seem overly suspicious, but we all know circus folk make easy targets."

"They do," Kade agreed. "He was somehow ... different. I'm not sure what he'll do. We need to play it by ear."

"I'll tell the others." Raven picked up her pace. "Let's hope they've got a kill-happy local who likes to carve symbols into people's faces to focus on. Otherwise, I think we're going to be under the microscope on this one."

I had a feeling she was right. "What else is new?"

WE MANAGED TO FINISH breakfast and were in the middle of cleaning the dishes when Terry appeared again. This time he was accompanied by a younger man, and they had their heads bent together as they crossed the field.

The other man, who I assumed was the FBI agent, boasted black hair that brushed the tops of his shoulders (since when is that okay in the FBI?) and piercing blue eyes. He seemed interested as he glanced around the circus set-up, but he didn't smile in greeting.

"This is Landon Michaels," Terry said as they joined us at the table. "He's with the FBI."

"No offense, but I'm curious how Hemlock Cove managed to snag its own FBI agent given its size," Kade interjected as Nixie and Naida brought the two mugs of coffee.

"I live here," Landon explained simply.

"Yeah, but that's not usually enough."

"My office is in Traverse City." Landon rubbed the back of his neck. "I used to live there. I spent as much time here as possible, though, so my boss allowed me to move here and commute. I have a special arrangement."

There was something he wasn't saying, but I didn't push. It was obviously none of my business. "Well, do you know how Mr. Rappaport died?"

"Badly," Terry said as he sipped his coffee. "Wow!" His eyebrows flew up. "This is good."

Nixie beamed at him. "It's my own personal blend."

Terry returned the smile. He didn't seem put off by her aquamarine hair, which made me like him even more. Most people simply dismissed the pixie twins because they looked different. Terry didn't have that problem.

"We need to ask if any of you spent time with Mr. Rappaport yesterday," Landon started. "Did you meet him? Talk with him? Did anyone have words with him on the street?"

I shook my head and glanced around. "I don't think so. We arrived a little later than normal yesterday. The only person we really talked to was Margaret Little."

"You have my sympathies on that," Landon drawled.

"Why would we need your sympathy?" Raven asked, suspicious. She positioned herself close to Landon, making sure she was at the proper angle to send him flirtatious looks without having to strain herself, but he paid her little interest.

"He just means that Margaret is ... a unique individual," Terry said, clearly choosing his words carefully. I didn't have to read his mind to understand he'd had issues with Margaret over the years. I could guess that she was high maintenance, and for a police chief with limited manpower that probably meant she was a regular pain in his posterior.

"She seemed nice enough, if on edge," I offered. "At first she thought we might be playing a prank on her, which I didn't get. She was agitated until she found out who we were."

Landon and Terry exchanged a weighted glance, and I swear the younger man almost looked as if he was hiding a smile.

"Margaret is paranoid sometimes," Terry said. "But you don't have to worry about her. She's determined that this festival is going to be the greatest thing to ever hit Hemlock Cove. It's getting national news coverage in pagan circles, which she's very excited about."

"I guess I'm not sure what you're talking about," I admitted, wrapping my hands around my coffee mug to keep my fingers warm. "Why is this festival so special?"

"It's going to be huge," Landon replied. "Vendors and witches are coming from every corner of the United States. Heck, if you believe Mrs. Little, they're coming from Europe and Australia, too. They're framing this as the biggest pagan festival in the world.

"I happen to believe that's probably a stretch, but who am I to argue with her?" he continued. "It's a big deal for the town, which is why they took on the added expense of booking your circus. They want this to be an event."

"I wondered," I said. "I wasn't sure what to think when I saw the size of the town. Now I get it ... but I'm still not sure there are enough hotels and inns in the area to house the amount of people we need make this worth the town's effort. It is what it is, though."

"Oh, trust me," Terry nodded. "There are more than enough hotels in the area. Tourism is all we have here. We do it right ... and we have more hotels than you can imagine tucked in on the back roads and highways."

That was good to know. "What about the dead guy?" I asked. "The manner of death seems a bit suspicious given the fact this place is going to be hosting a witch festival in two days."

"Yes, well, we've discussed that ourselves." Terry rubbed his chin, considering. "None of you talked to Darren last night, right?"

I shook my head. "We were busy setting up. In fact, we have more stuff coming in about an hour. Our second load is right behind us. We didn't have time to look around the town. We planned to wander a bit today. No one here met him. I wanted to check out his shop, but that's it."

"I figured you didn't have time," Terry said. "You were the talk of the town when you arrived. I was in the diner for dinner last night and everyone was lamenting the fact that you were eating at the fairgrounds."

"I take it that we're being watched," Kade said, his lips quirking.

Terry nodded. "This town likes its gossip. There's no getting around that. Until the festival hits, you're the new element ... along with the tourists who are steadily trickling in. You might as well get used to that."

"We're used to being stared at," I supplied. "It's not a big deal. What about the body, though? I can't help thinking the placement of it wasn't coincidental."

"Yeah, I've been considering that, too," Terry admitted. "I don't know why anyone would drop a body out there. The medical examiner is taking care of that right now, by the way. He should be finished before lunch. Please steer clear of the area until he packs up and leaves."

"I'm sure we can manage that," Kade said. "I'm chief of security. I'll make sure our people don't bother your people."

"It should be fine." Terry waved off the offer. "I don't suppose you folks saw anyone hanging around here yesterday? I mean ... you didn't notice anyone watching you from the woods or anything, did you?"

"No," I automatically answered.

"Wait a second." Kade held up a finger. "What about that woman you said you talked to yesterday? The one who stumbled out of the woods."

Terry looked keen as he leaned forward. "Did you talk to a local?"

I'd almost forgotten about Tillie, which seemed impossible in hindsight. "Oh, well, there was one person. I very much doubt she's a killer."

"More like a goddess," Nellie offered, taking on a dreamy expression as he sipped his coffee.

"Did this goddess have a name?" Landon asked.

"Who are you talking about?" Raven demanded before I could answer. "Wait ... are you talking about that old lady? The one wearing the combat boots and carrying a whistle and a shotgun? That is a fantastic ensemble, by the way."

The looks on Landon's and Terry's faces were almost comical.

"A shotgun and a whistle, huh?" Landon asked, shaking his head as he dug into his pocket. "I'm going to kill her."

"You know her?" I couldn't hide my surprise.

"You have no idea," Landon muttered. "I just ... hold on." He hit a button on his phone and lifted it to his ear as he waited for someone to answer. When whoever he was calling picked up, he started talking without issuing a greeting. "I need you to come to the fairgrounds. It's about Aunt Tillie. We're by the picnic tables." He disconnected without waiting for a response. "That old lady will be the death of me," he groused.

"If she hasn't killed me yet, I'm guessing you're safe," Terry said, finishing his coffee. "Seriously, this is the best I've ever had."

Nixie hurried over to pour more. "Stop by whenever you want while we're here. I always have some ready for those who appreciate my greatness."

I WAS SURPRISED when I realized who Landon had ordered to the fairgrounds. It was the blonde from the newspaper office, and she looked to be in a hurry — and obviously worried — when she joined us.

"What's going on? Is Aunt Tillie okay?" She flicked her eyes to the rear of the property, to where the medical examiner's team toiled. "She's not ... ."

"No," Landon said hurriedly, grabbing her arm. "I'm sorry. I should've given you more information. That wasn't fair." He lightly tugged until she sat on the picnic table bench next to him. "Try this." He shoved his coffee toward her mouth.

Because she had little choice, she sipped the coffee and smiled. "Very good."

"You need to learn their secret so we can have this at home," Landon said, causing things to slip into place for me. She was the reason he lived in Hemlock Cove. Whoever she was, she was everything to him. She'd been calling for Tillie the previous day, causing the older woman to disappear when she realized people were on the hunt, so I figured there were some rather interesting family ties about to be revealed.

"This is Bay Winchester," Terry said by way of introduction. "She owns The Whistler, the newspaper. She's also the great-niece of the woman you met yesterday."

"Oh." I studied Bay for a long beat. "Um ... it's nice to meet you."

Bay met my gaze, steady and even. "You, too. You met my aunt?"

"She kind of popped out of the woods," I explained. "She was ... hunting. At least that's what I think she was doing."

"She had her whistle and shotgun," Landon said. "She also had on her combat helmet."

"And some very intriguing leggings," Kade added, snickering at the memory.

Bay narrowed her sea-blue eyes. "Leggings? Are we talking zombies or mummies?"

"Dragons," I replied.

Bay's mouth dropped open. "Oh, no! She promised she was going to get rid of those. My mother will have vampire bats flying out of her mouth when she finds out those dragons are still plundering for treasure."

I pressed my lips together to keep from laughing. She'd obviously fallen victim to the dragon leggings on more than one occasion. "She wears them well," I offered lamely.

"Oh, they're horrifying. You don't have to lie." Bay slapped her hand to her forehead. "What was she doing out here? Did she say?"

"I think she was messing with Margaret Little," I answered honestly. "I can't be sure, but that's the feeling I got."

"Of course she was messing with Mrs. Little." Bay scowled. "I told her to stay away from Mrs. Little until after the festival. I was firm, put my foot down. So, of course, what's the first thing she does?"

"Goes after Mrs. Little," Nellie answered automatically, grinning. "I knew I liked this woman. She's awesome ... and I want to adopt her."

Bay shot him an odd look. "What?"

"Ignore him," I said hurriedly. "I believe he's developed a crush on your great-aunt."

"Crush smush," Nellie countered. "I only have one question for you, little girl: Is your aunt single? Oh, and is she open to mingle?"

Luke, who had just joined the party after securing the animal tent to make sure nobody could enter unattended, heard the last part and turned accusatory. "Hey! You can't steal my shtick. I'm the one who is supposed to say stuff like that."

"Oh, stuff it," Raven muttered. "It's not as if either of you says witty things."

I shifted an apologetic look toward our guests. "We're a little cranky in the morning."

"Don't worry about it." Bay forced a smile, although it didn't make it to her eyes. "You guys are family. Trust me. I know about dealing with ridiculous family."

Something told me that was only the tip of the truth iceberg.

5

FIVE

Bay hung around with Landon and Terry for a full hour. She seemed comfortable with both of them, even smiling when Terry called her "sweetheart" and offered up teasing words. She jotted down a few notes, which seemed odd until I remembered she owned the newspaper. She skirted the scene, watching the medical examiner pack up the body, then offered me a half wave before disappearing.

"You don't think this Tillie woman is the culprit?" Kade asked Landon as the two police representatives stood from the picnic table and prepared to leave.

"Tillie is a unique individual," Terry replied, echoing the exact statement he'd uttered more than an hour ago. "I very much doubt she killed Darren, but I can guarantee we'll be talking to her about the shotgun." He cast a derisive look toward Landon. "I was under the impression the shotgun had been confiscated."

"Hey, don't look at me," Landon complained. "You try telling that woman what she can and can't do. You know she doesn't listen."

"Well ... *I'm* going to talk to her this time." Terry sounded sure of himself. "As for you guys, just go about your normal day. I might be back with more questions, but I have to follow the investigative line and talk to Darren's friends and family first. I'm sure I'll be back, for the coffee if nothing else."

"You're welcome back whenever you want," I offered. "If we can provide information, we're glad to help. Though I really don't know what we can tell you." In truth, I was bothered by the death, especially because the body was so close to the dreamcatcher. I couldn't help but wonder if whoever took out the victim recognized the boundary for what it was. That might offer a unique problem, one only we were equipped to deal with. "I hope you find the answers you're looking for."

Terry's smile was wan. "That makes two of us."

ONCE THE TWO LAW enforcement representatives disappeared, we set about our normal day. The second delivery arrived on time, which meant we had hours to fill with actual work. The medical examiner had vacated the spot where the body was found, so that allowed me the opportunity to check out the scene.

I wasn't surprised when Kade joined me.

"There's not much blood," he noted as he studied the ground. "I mean ... I guess it's possible the dirt and leaves absorbed it, but I'm guessing he was killed elsewhere and moved here."

I nodded as I paced a circle. "I don't think he was killed here. Someone would've heard something. Sure, this spot is right behind the clowns and most of them aren't paranormal, but still ... you would think someone would've heard something."

"Everyone was exhausted after the long trip," Kade pointed out. "Maybe they simply slept hard, like me. Of course, I had help."

I pressed the heel of my hand to my forehead. "He wouldn't have gone quietly. I'm pretty sure he was stabbed."

"Which leads me back to my earlier supposition. He died somewhere else and was dragged here."

"And dumped just outside the dreamcatcher," I muttered.

His eyes tracked to me, curious. "Do you think that's important?"

I held out my hands and shrugged. "I have no idea. It bothers me, though. I would be lying if I said otherwise."

"Well, I guess we'll have to be more careful going forward." Kade put on his security persona as he regarded the area. "We'll do regular spins around the fairgrounds, just to be on the safe side."

"I'm not sure that's a good idea. What if it draws attention from the locals? We're in a precarious position here. We need to be extra careful because we're smack dab in the middle of town."

"Yeah, but you were convinced the blonde from the newspaper saw what you were doing last night," Kade argued. "She seemed fine when she visited this morning."

"Maybe because we had an audience." I rolled my neck. "I kept catching her staring at me. I think she knows something."

"Maybe she's staring at you because you're so pretty."

I rolled my eyes. "That was ... ."

"Charming?"

"I was going to say weak."

"I happen to think I'm charming." He slipped his arm around my waist and pulled me close. "I also think you're worrying too much. This is hardly the first time we've garnered police attention since I started this gig. We'll get through it just the same as we've gotten through everything else."

"I'm not sure this is like the other instances."

"Why?"

"Because ... ." How could I explain the power surge I felt when close to Tillie? How could I make him understand that I was positive there was something odd about Bay even though we'd barely spoken?

"You have a feeling," Kade surmised, his lips curving. "You think something big is going to happen here, don't you?"

"I think we should keep our eyes open," I clarified. "I want everyone to be on their best behavior."

"I'm always on my best behavior."

"I was thinking more about Nellie and Naida. They tend to ... do whatever they want."

"Then we'll talk to them." He gave me a soft kiss and then pulled me in for a lingering hug. "It'll be okay. You're a worrier. Sometimes I think that's good. Other times, I fear you'll drive yourself crazy with this nonsense."

He wasn't the only one.

AFTER LUNCH, WE DECIDED TO take a walk around town. Kade clearly had high hopes it would just be the two of us, but he didn't put up an argument when Luke invited himself on the trek.

"I think this place is neat," Luke said as he stared in the window of a bookstore. "I mean ... seriously. They have all sorts of spell and charm books in there. I want to buy the love potion one. I think I would benefit from love potions."

"You don't need love potions," I argued, shaking my head. "You do fine on your own."

"I don't think I'm going to do fine in this town," he said dryly.

He had a point. The town was too small for him to pick up a date. Still, in my experience, love potions were never a good idea. They backfired regularly.

"Yes, well, you'll survive," I said. "We're heading to Detroit after this. The pickings won't be so slim there."

"Good point." He brightened considerably. "Hey, check this place out." He moved down the sidewalk and stared at the beautifully painted window of a store named Hypnotic. The design on the window was ornate, and it was obvious someone spent a lot of time designing it. "Let's check it out."

"Sure." I was as intrigued as he was.

Kade, who kept his fingers linked with mine, was clearly only along for the ride because he let Luke and me decide on the stops. He seemed more interested in studying the town from a tourist's perspective. It was part of his security training, although he didn't often comment on it.

Wind chimes clanged as we walked through the door, and the smell of anise and cloves was enough to put me at ease. There was something homey about the space, and that was before I noticed the couch and chairs placed in the middle of the store, as if it were a small living room.

"Wow!" Luke was immediately entranced by a display of candles and headed in its direction. I was curious enough to follow.

"These are really cool," I said as I took one shaped like a skull from the shelf. "They're also homemade." I flipped over the candle and studied the workmanship. "Whoever did these put a lot of time in them."

"Thank you," a woman said from behind me, causing me to jolt.

When I turned, I found a dainty woman with long dark hair watching me with brown eyes. She had a smattering of light freckles across the bridge of her ski-slope nose and an open and inviting smile overtaking her face. "Your work?" I asked, lifting the candle.

She bobbed her head. "All the candles are homemade. We take pride in our work."

"*We?*" Another voice joined the fray, and when I turned my attention to the counter I found the green-haired woman I'd seen crossing the road the previous day openly glaring. Thankfully, her annoyance wasn't aimed at us. Instead, it was directed at the brunette.

"Yes, *we*," the first woman said.

"I made the candles, Clove," the green-haired woman snapped. "You've never helped me with the candles. I do all the work ... and own the pride associated with the work."

Clove — and the name fit her — wrinkled her adorable nose. "I'm the one who put the display together, Thistle. I'm the one who dusts the shelves and makes everything look pretty."

"You wouldn't have anything to make look pretty if it weren't for me," Thistle shot back. Oddly enough, her name fit her, too. "Stop taking credit for my work."

I pressed my lips together to keep from laughing as I returned the candle to the shelf. "We can come back if you have other things going on," I offered lamely.

"Oh, don't worry about her," Clove said, waving dismissively. "She's in a mood. That's pretty much normal where she's concerned, but she's *really* in a mood today."

"I am not in a mood," Thistle barked.

Clove, apparently used to the other woman's foul temperament, merely shook her head. "She made a statue that she wants to display at the festival, but it's not allowed because the woman depicted is naked. You can't have a naked woman statue in the middle of town. Apparently it's in the rules or something. I don't know why she didn't realize that would be a problem."

"First, I didn't carve the sculpture for the festival," Thistle argued. She had a personality like a rabid bear, as far as I could tell. She hadn't as much as smiled once since we'd entered. "I made it for the stables. But Marcus says it will offend parents and scare kids. I thought the festival would be the perfect place to unveil it."

"You mean unload it," Clove corrected. "Just admit you're trying to get someone to take that sculpture off your hands."

"No." Thistle folded her arms across her chest, adamant. "That sculpture is awesome."

"Whatever." Clove rolled her eyes until they landed on me. "Are you looking for something particular? You're with the circus, right? We saw you guys arrive yesterday."

"We're just looking around," I replied. "Your shop is wonderful. We've never seen a town like this during our travels."

"That's because Hemlock Cove is one big out-patient mental facility," Thistle supplied. "Everyone is off their meds, so be careful."

It took everything I had not to laugh. In some ways she reminded me of Nellie ... which was a frightening thought. "We like the town," I offered. "It's quieter than our usual venues."

"Except for old ladies running around with shotguns and combat helmets," Luke offered.

I didn't miss the look Clove and Thistle shared. "Is something wrong?"

"Nothing is wrong," Thistle said hurriedly. "It's just ... you might want to stay away from the crazy woman with the shotgun. She's the most mentally unbalanced of them all."

That sounded ominous. "She seemed okay to me," I hedged. "Er, well, the leggings were a bit weird."

"Uh-oh." Clove made a distressed sound deep in her throat. "What leggings?"

"I'm going with clowns," Thistle said. "She'd probably wear those freaky clown leggings in honor of the circus coming to town."

"They were dragons," Luke supplied.

"Oh, man." Thistle slapped her hand to her forehead. "I thought Mom burned those. She's going to be in so much trouble."

Something occurred to me. "You're related to the woman at the newspaper office, right? She knew about the dragon leggings, too."

"Bay?" Thistle nodded. "We're cousins. All of us." She gestured toward Clove, too. "Our mothers are sisters. Aunt Tillie raised them when our grandmother died. We're one big happy family."

"Aunt Tillie is ... eccentric," Clove explained. "She's perfectly harmless, though. You don't have to worry about her."

"She's evil incarnate," Thistle groused. "If you see her, run in the other direction and hide. She's completely mental."

I spared a glance for Kade and found him fighting off laughter. He clearly enjoyed the banter.

"I'll keep an eye out for her," I said finally. "She was perfectly pleasant, and one of our performers has developed a crush on her."

"Really?" Officially intrigued, Thistle rested her elbows on the counter and leaned forward. "Which performer? Please tell me it was a clown. Landon has a thing about clowns and if we invite one to dinner he'll melt down."

It was clear the Winchester family had a wicked way of interacting with one another. "Actually, he's our bearded lady. Only ... he's more of a cross-dressing dwarf ... I mean, little man. It's hard to explain."

Thistle's eyes lit with amusement. "Oh, I totally want to meet him. He sounds right up Aunt Tillie's alley."

"I kind of want to meet him, too," Clove admitted. "It sounds like your bearded lady and our great-aunt have a lot in common, especially on the fashion front."

I hadn't yet put that together, but she wasn't wrong. "Well, I'm sure we can work something out. In fact ... ." Whatever I was going to say died on my lips when the door burst open to allow the woman in question entrance. Today she was dressed in the clown leggings mentioned earlier, but sans shotgun and combat helmet. She did, however, boast a very odd gardening hat that featured a pair of scissors poking out the top.

"And here is the woman of the hour right now," Thistle drawled, her eyes narrowing as she focused on her great-aunt. "We were just talking about you."

"I'm great to talk about," Tillie said breezily as she stepped into the store. "I love talking about me. But I don't have time today. I'm here for a reason. I need some Blue Flag. I'm out."

"Blue Flag?" Thistle knit her eyebrows. "The only thing you need Blue Flag for is money spells. You're not allowed to cast money spells after that incident where you accidentally turned Mrs. Little into a prostitute while you acted as her pimp."

Tillie's expression was withering. "Who said that was an accident?"

"We don't have Blue Flag," Clove volunteered. "There was no reason to keep any around because the only spells you can cast with it are negative."

"Oh, you guys suck." Tillie made a face before focusing on me. "I remember you. You're with the circus."

"And we want her to take you with her when she leaves," Thistle called out. "We think you'll fit right in at the circus."

"You'd miss me too much if I left, Thistle," Tillie barked. "I could never leave you."

"You could try."

"Do you want to be on my list?"

I had no idea what that meant, but I was amused. "The police and an FBI agent were around this morning," I offered. "I believe they're going to talk to you because we found a dead body on the outskirts of the fairgrounds this morning. They wanted to know who had been hanging around."

Thistle jolted. "You found a dead body?"

"Who was it?" Clove asked. "Was it someone local?"

"Um ... I believe they said it was Darren Rappaport."

"The cauldron curmudgeon," Thistle murmured. "He was a crabby old thing. I can't believe he's dead."

"He was a pervert," Tillie volunteered.

"He was definitely a pervert," Clove agreed. "Once he used one of those shark grabber things, you know with the teeth, to grab the front of my shirt and try to look down it. I was sixteen."

Tillie scowled. "You should've told me about that. I would've made sure those teeth grabbed something else ... permanently."

"That's exactly why I didn't tell you."

"How was he killed?" Thistle asked. "I mean ... did he fall and hit his head while trying to spy on your women or did someone shoot him? Either is a possibility."

"I believe someone stabbed him, although there was so little blood it was hard to tell. He also had a symbol carved into his forehead."

Kade cast me a curious look. It practically screamed, "Why are you telling them all this information?" I didn't have an answer. It was almost as if I was compelled to share with them, if only to read their reactions. There was something rather interesting about this little group, and that included the reporter cousin who made me nervous.

"Huh. I wonder what Bay knows," Thistle mused. She was clearly talking to Clove and Tillie, but she didn't exclude us from the conversation.

"Landon will tell her what's going on," Clove said. "I'm sure she'll fill us in over dinner."

"That must be why Terry called wanting to talk to me," Tillie mused. "He said it was important and not to pretend that I didn't receive the call."

"Are you going to talk to him?" Clove asked.

Tillie snorted. "Did you just meet me? I'm going to pretend I didn't receive the call. He'll find me when he finds me. I'm not difficult to track down."

Something told me that was true only when she wanted to be found. There was something wily about her ... and powerful. She was an interesting woman, to say the least.

"Well, we should probably get going," I said finally, uncomfortable at intruding on their private family meeting. "We have more work to do."

"I'll be by to visit later," Tillie said. "I want to talk to you about a few things."

That was unexpected. "Um ... okay."

"We look forward to seeing you." Luke's expression was fond as he stared at Tillie. "You remind me of my grandmother. You're just so ... fun."

Tillie beamed at him. "I am fun ... but I'm nobody's grandmother. I'm in my prime. Ask anyone."

"She is," Thistle acknowledged. "She's a prime pain in the butt."

"That's it!" Tillie's eyes flashed. "You're definitely on my list."

Thistle didn't look bothered. "What else is new?"

6

SIX

It was time for lunch, so we opted to head to the diner rather than cook. Our groceries were running precariously low, and until we stocked up we didn't have many options.

The diner was exactly what I'd expected. It had a lot of homey charm, and the guests clearly knew one another. I pulled up short when I entered, my eyes traveling to the center table. There, holding court, was Margaret. She seemed to be having a good time telling those gathered around her about the dead body, even as she made tsking sounds about how awful it was. She mentioned how quickly the medical examiner cleaned up the mess.

She wasn't the source of my surprise. That happened to be Max Anderson, the man sitting next to her. Not only was he the owner of Mystic Caravan, he also was Kade's father. They'd recently put the past behind them in an effort to forge a real relationship, but it was tenuous right now. That's what made Max's appearance all the more interesting.

"Hello." Max greeted his workers with a bright smile. "I was hoping to track you down. Raven said you went for a tour of the town. I checked here first ... and have been entertained ever since."

I could read between the lines of that statement. Max came

looking for us, ran into Margaret, and then was forced to sit with her at the diner so she could act like a big shot. The more I learned about the woman, the more I disliked her.

"We were at the magic store," Luke said as he slid into one of the open seats at the large table. "It's really cool. They have homemade candles, and the two women who work there are cousins who constantly fight."

"Yes. Thistle and Clove." Margaret's expression darkened to the point I felt uncomfortable.

"They seemed nice enough," I offered awkwardly as Kade pulled out a chair so I could sit between Max and him. "They were friendly." Mostly, I added silently. I wasn't sure Thistle could ever be considered truly friendly. "They seem to know a lot about the herb business."

"That's because they're witches," an older woman positioned on the other side of Margaret whispered rather loudly. If she thought she was being quiet, she was sadly mistaken.

"I thought everyone in Hemlock Cove was a witch," I said. "Isn't that what it says on all the brochures?"

"Yeah, but they're real witches." The woman was ominous. "They curse people ... and create thunderstorms ... and sometimes people disappear around them and never come back."

She sounded deathly serious, which sent a chill down my spine.

"Don't give them more power than they deserve, Agnes," Margaret barked. "We've talked about this. Tillie gets her power from fear. That's why we can't be afraid of her."

"Speak for yourself," Agnes shot back. "I've always found a healthy dose of fear is good. That's why I don't have that recurring boil-on-the-butt problem you have."

It took everything I had not to burst out laughing when I slid my eyes to Max. He was watching the scene, amusement positively oozing off him, and he seemed content to listen to the stories. He'd positioned himself in such a way that he could observe, absorb the gossip, and learn about potential murderers in our midst.

"And Tillie is the town's resident witch?" Max asked, giving the impression he was genuinely interested in the conversation.

I mouthed "thank you" to the waitress as she delivered a menu and pointed toward Max's iced tea to indicate that's what I wanted. Luke and Kade did the same, both fascinated by the ongoing conversation and unwilling to break the spell hanging over the table.

"Oh, there's a whole clan of them," Margaret said, her eyes sparkling. If I had to guess, she was excited to have a new audience for her tales. "Tillie is the one in charge. She's definitely a nut. She's been after me since we were in high school together."

Polite as always, Max merely gave her an encouraging smile. "And how does that work? You'll have to forgive my curiosity, but I'm fascinated by the idea of witches."

"Well, you should get over that," Margaret admonished. "Witches are terrifying creatures, and Tillie is the scariest thing imaginable."

I pictured the clown leggings and couldn't help but agree. They were truly frightening.

"What did she do to you?" Max asked.

"Well, for starters, she enchanted a man." Margaret lowered her voice to a conspiratorial whisper. "His name was Calvin and he was the sweetest thing ever. He was helpful, always volunteering his time when someone was in need, and he once held an umbrella over my head so I wouldn't get wet during a storm."

"He sounds like a true gentleman," Max noted. "However, I'm curious how he plays into the story."

"Tillie cast a love spell on him," Margaret explained. "He was going to ask me to the senior prom. I'd heard from more than one friend that it was going to happen. Instead, he asked her out. He started carrying her books and following her around like a lost puppy dog. It was sickening."

"I see. It sounds horrible," Max intoned.

I had to bite the inside of my cheek to keep from chuckling at his reaction. I could tell he thought Margaret was full of herself, but he was still curious enough to keep the conversation going.

"And then what happened?" Luke asked the obvious question. "Did he accidentally walk in front of a truck and die because of this spell or something?"

Margaret shook her head. "No. He married her."

"And then what?"

"Isn't that enough?" Margaret's agitation came out to play. "She stole that man from the life he was rightfully supposed to live."

"A life with you?" I asked.

"Of course."

"Huh." I slid a sidelong look to Kade and found him watching the exchange with unreadable eyes. "I guess it would suck to lose the person you're destined to be with."

He squeezed my knee under the table and flashed a full-wattage smile. He didn't speak, though, instead letting Margaret keep to her rhythm.

"I tried to talk to Calvin over the years, break the curse, but the spell was too strong," Margaret explained. "Then he died ... and there was nothing left to fight for."

"That's kind of sad," Luke lamented. "When did he die?"

Margaret made an obnoxious face. "Does it matter? He was gone, and all that was left was Tillie. She'd already raised those girls by that point. There are times I wonder if Calvin realized he was bamboozled after the fact but chose to stay because they had those girls to take care of."

"And what girls are you referring to?" Max asked.

"Winnie, Marnie and Twila. They were Tillie's sister's girls. She died and left them when they were still teenagers. Tillie took them in ... and made them witches, too. They weren't as bad as Tillie. I had hope."

Margaret's expression was so dour it made me think something truly terrible had happened. "Did the hope not last?"

"Winnie, Marnie and Twila all married not long after graduating from high school," Margaret explained. "They each had a daughter. Bay was first. The other two followed quickly. They were cute kids and I thought there was a chance they would grow up normal.

"Instead, all three women got divorced around the same time and they took those girls and moved in with Tillie," she continued. "They were all lost causes after that. And, let me tell you something, the most recent generation of Winchesters is just as bad as Tillie. You wouldn't believe the things they've done."

I was officially intrigued. "What have they done?"

"Well, for starters, Bay used the same curse Tillie did to snag Calvin and got herself an FBI agent. I heard they met in a corn maze of all places, if you can imagine that, and she was a suspect in a murder at the time. The next thing you know, they're in love and all over each other. He's never far when she gets in trouble. I find it mighty convenient."

I pictured the FBI agent in question and the way he interacted with Bay at the scene. If he was under a spell, it didn't show. He was clearly fond of the woman. That was obvious by the way he looked at her, but he didn't show signs of being muddled or glazed.

"Why would she want an FBI agent?" Luke asked. "I would think, if you're a witch, the last thing you'd want to do is get on the FBI's radar."

The look Margaret shot Luke was pitying. "She makes him cover up her crimes."

"What crimes?" I asked. "I mean ... do you have knowledge that they've committed crimes?"

"Of course I do." Margaret looked insulted that I would dare question her. "I wouldn't make the accusations without proof."

I waited for her to expound, which she seemed more than happy to do.

"It started with yellow snow."

That wasn't the sentence I was expecting. "Excuse me?"

"She said it started with yellow snow," Luke replied. "I think we're all going to love this story. I, for one, know I'm looking forward to hearing it. Don't ask unnecessary questions until I know exactly where the yellow snow talk is going. Please continue, Mrs. Little."

Kade coughed to cover a laugh and then moved his arm around my back. He was clearly enjoying himself.

"Tillie has a snowplow," Margaret explained, obviously missing the way my boyfriend and best friend kept fidgeting in their chairs. "She's had it for years. She used to make extra money with it during rough winters, towing people out of snow drifts and such. This is on top of the illegal wine she makes and the pot field every teenager in this town knows is up on that bluff. That's a whole other issue, though.

"Anyway, she used to wait until my regular guy plowed my drive after every snow and then she would plow me back in," she continued. "Every single time."

"I don't see how that requires magic," I pointed out.

"I'm getting to it."

"Yes, let her get to the yellow snow," Luke chided. "I *have* to hear the story about yellow snow. If I don't, I'll never get over it."

"Oh, geez," I muttered under my breath.

"For once, I'm with Luke," Kade admonished. "I need to hear the story about yellow snow, too. You need to shush." He lifted his finger to his lips for emphasis.

"This went on for a good two or three years," Margaret supplied. "Every snowstorm I would end up trapped in my house for days. She would even bring those little girls with her when she did it. I'd see them in the truck. She put football helmets on them because they were ramming into the snow so hard their heads sometimes bounced off the dashboard."

I tried to picture the scene and smiled. Tillie Winchester very well might have been a witch — and I had no doubt she was — but she also sounded like a fun great-aunt. She clearly spent a lot of time with her family.

"Tillie got bored just plowing me in," Margaret said. "It wasn't enough of a challenge. Then, magically, the snow at the end of the driveway started turning yellow. Like ... huge rivers of yellow. People thought that I was somehow doing it because Tillie told them I had bladder issues."

I choked on my iced tea as I tried not to laugh. Luke and Kade weren't strong enough to contain themselves. Even Max looked amused.

"It's not funny," Margaret snapped. "I was traumatized by the whole thing."

"You're leaving out the best part of the story," Agnes complained.

"You forgot to tell them about the time she turned the snow brown and put up a sign near the road that said you were full of s— ."

"Thank you, Agnes," Margaret barked. "It's my story. I'll tell it."

Agnes sat back in defeat, but she looked rather pleased with herself. "Whatever."

"You see, that whole Winchester brood is evil," Margaret said. "They do terrible things and cast spells to get their way. Bay has enchanted an FBI agent — and she's had Terry wrapped around her finger since she was a child — and now they get away with whatever they want."

Margaret had a dramatic flair about her, and she delivered the last line with real zest at the same moment the diner door opened to allow Terry and Landon entrance. It was obvious they'd heard what she said, because the look on Landon's face was downright murderous.

"What did we miss this time?" Terry asked dryly.

"Mrs. Little was explaining about how real witches have taken over the town and how they put yellow snow in her driveway every winter," Luke offered helpfully.

The corners of Terry's mouth tipped up. "Yes, well, I don't think there's anything witchy about the yellow snow. I think that's simply sixty-five years of animosity and food coloring."

He said the words, but there was something evasive about them. It was clear he had a long history with Margaret, one that wasn't exactly pleasant, but he was also covering for the Winchesters. That was definitely interesting. He knew as well as anyone that the yellow snow was more than simply an industrious senior citizen burning time.

"She also said that Bay bewitched an FBI agent ... and maybe you when she was a little girl," Luke added, steadfastly ignoring the way Margaret glared at him.

"We've heard those stories before," Landon said as he sat at a nearby table and perused the specials menu. "The only thing she's bewitched me with is bedhead and tickles."

Terry rolled his eyes. "How many times have I told you not to say perverted things about my little sweetheart in front of me? She still has pigtails as far as I'm concerned."

"You should take it up with her," Landon countered. "She's the one who starts the tickling. Perhaps you should simply accept the fact that she's the pervert."

"And I'm done talking to you." Terry raised his hand to block out Landon's face and slid his eyes to me. "Have you been enjoying your tour through town? I saw you went into Hypnotic."

Did he want me to think he was watching us? Or was he more interested in seeing if I would say anything about Clove and Thistle? It was hard to decide. "It's a fun town," I said, tracing the ring of condensation my glass left on the table. "I like all the kitschy stores. I also saw someone I believe you're looking for in the magic shop."

Terry's expression turned dark. "Was she armed?"

"That depends on if you believe clown leggings are a weapon."

Landon shuddered. "Ugh. She bought those to torture me. I couldn't believe it when she trotted them out the first time. They'll haunt me the rest of my life."

"Not a fan of clowns, huh?" Kade asked.

Landon shook his head. "Is anyone?"

"I know one person who is," Luke said. "Hey, that's a fun story. How do you feel about leather chaps?"

"Like I don't want to hear that story," Landon replied. "As for Aunt Tillie, did she say where she was heading when she left?"

I shook my head. "No. She didn't say much of anything. Er, well, she put the girl with the green hair on her list. I don't know what that entails, but I'm curious enough that I might want to see this list."

"You don't," Terry countered. "As for Thistle, she's used to being at the top of the list. I wouldn't worry about her. Regarding Darren, we're still investigating, but have no leads. We might swing back around to question more of your workers this afternoon, if you're okay with that."

He was testing me. He wanted to see if I would balk at being interrogated. He clearly didn't know me well enough to realize that there was nothing he could say or do to frighten me. "That's fine." I looked to Max for confirmation and he nodded. "You don't need to ask before visiting. We're open for questions any time. Just don't enter the animal tents without an escort. We have liability issues. You're more than welcome to visit; you just need to be accompanied by a certified animal trainer."

"I don't think we need to interview the animals, but we'll probably want more coffee," Terry said. "For now, we have more people to interview around town. We also need to get some insight into that symbol. You didn't recognize it, did you?"

The question caught me off guard. It felt like another trap, and yet his mind was open enough that I could read his surface thoughts. He wasn't trying to trap me. He was legitimately curious.

"I didn't recognize it," I said. "I can ask around, though. I could look on the internet, too."

"We can handle that," Landon said. "Thank you for your time. We really appreciate it. I can guarantee that my bewitching girlfriend will not be attacking you with yellow snow due to your efforts."

"It's not funny!" Margaret exploded when everyone at the table started laughing. "Those Winchesters will be the death of us all. Just you wait!"

7
SEVEN

I felt compelled to talk to Landon outside the diner after we'd finished lunch. I wasn't sure why, but there was something I wanted to get off my chest.

"We don't believe the stories Margaret was telling, if that's what you're worried about," I offered.

"Speak for yourself," Luke shot back." I happen to believe the yellow snow story and will hold it near and dear to my heart for the rest of the days of my life."

I ignored him. "It's clear that Margaret has a vendetta against Tillie that she's taking out on everybody else."

Landon was calm as he met my gaze. "Margaret Little is ... a righteous pain in my backside," he said. "This is not a new development."

I had no doubt that was true. "I just don't want you to be upset."

"I'm not upset. This is normal behavior from her."

"But ... she was saying things about Bay casting a spell on you," I persisted.

"Bay *did* cast a spell on me." Landon's grin was mischievous. "She used her mother's cooking, bacon, and a really pretty smile as potion ingredients."

I realized quickly that he didn't care what anyone thought. He was fine with his relationship and the whispers. He understood Hemlock Cove's gossip river, and he was seemingly fine with swimming upstream without a flotation device.

"Oh, well, I just wanted to make sure." I felt awkward as Kade moved to join me after trying (and failing) to pay for our lunch. "We were simply curious and asking questions after running into Thistle, Clove and Tillie at Hypnotic."

Landon snorted. "You'll have more questions by the time the week is out. I can guarantee that a circus is going to be too much for Thistle and Aunt Tillie to ignore. They're going to be all up in your business."

He seemed amused at the prospect. "Why does that make you happy?"

"Because that means they won't have their noses in my business and I can sleep in for a change."

"But ... ."

Landon waved me off before I could continue. "I know you're worried that Mrs. Little somehow hurt my feelings. She's not capable of that. Bay is fine. I'm fine. You have no reason to worry."

Well, if he wasn't upset, there was no reason for me to be. "I just wanted to make sure."

"Thank you. We're used to her crap. We'll be fine."

"What will you be fine about?" Terry asked as he exited the restaurant, pocketing his wallet.

"Poet here is worried that I'm upset by what Margaret Little said."

Terry scowled. "That woman ... ."

I found I was amused by the fact that Terry was more agitated than Landon. "She said Bay enchanted you when she was a kid."

"She did," Terry agreed. "She did it with smiles and licorice whips. I've been involved with Bay, Clove and Thistle since they were kids because they got in a lot of trouble. I'm tight with them."

"You're their father," I mused.

"They have fathers ... and they're in town. I'm something else that defies categorization."

I thought back to the story Margaret told before they'd entered. "I thought their fathers were chased out of town after multiple divorces."

"They returned about a year ago," Landon explained. "They own an inn called the Dragonfly. It's fine. Although ... I am curious about everything else Margaret told you before we walked through the door."

"She said that Tillie cast a spell on someone named Calvin so he wouldn't follow his true destiny, and that Tillie is evil."

"Aunt Tillie is definitely evil." Landon made a face as he shook his head. "I never met Calvin, although I've gotten a clear picture of him over the years." Something about the far-off expression Landon adopted caused my stomach to flip. It was as if he was briefly visiting another time. I tried to invade his mind with my magic, nothing too deep, but I was dying to see his surface thoughts. I was rewarded with a brief glimpse of a wind monster with eyes. It moved past Tillie, Bay, Clove and Thistle, and toward what looked to be a threat. I wanted to look harder but the vision dissipated almost as fast as it appeared when Landon shook his head.

"You don't have to worry about Calvin," Landon said. "My understanding is that he loved his nieces. He also loved Aunt Tillie ... and I'm pretty sure it wasn't a spell."

"What about his great-nieces?" Kade asked. "Did he love them?"

"He died before they were on the scene. They know enough about him to cherish his memory, though. They love him and will never forget what he did for their mothers. I'm pretty sure that's enough."

I nodded in agreement, even though my stomach was tied in knots. I waited to speak until we were on our way back to the fairgrounds and clear of potential eavesdroppers.

"You saw something," Max noted as he walked with Luke behind Kade and me. "I felt it the moment you dove into his head. What did you see?"

"I don't know." That was the truth. "Four women holding hands. Landon and Terry standing to the side, watching in abject terror. Some sort of creature that looked to be made of wind with red eyes."

Max arched an eyebrow, surprised. "I've never heard of a creature like that."

"I think they made it."

"Really?" Max's voice was laced with intrigue. "I want to meet these witches. They sound delightful."

I could think of a few other words for them.

WE SPENT THE REST OF THE day working. The circus was almost completely assembled by the time we'd finished. A few things remained, but overall the grounds looked good ... and it was nice to have that weight off our shoulders.

Kade, Luke and I made a trip to the grocery store in Gaylord. Even though we could eat for free in town, that didn't seem feasible over the long haul, so we stocked up on everything we thought we'd need for the rest of the week. It seemed the safest bet.

Upon returning to the fairgrounds, we set about cooking steak and corn for dinner. Nellie and Dolph built a bonfire, and after eating and cleanup, we grouped around it for a necessary discussion.

"I don't think the police are trying to pin this on us by any stretch of the imagination," I offered, keeping my voice low. "Terry seems legitimately interested in finding out the truth. He didn't stop by this afternoon like he intimated, but that doesn't mean he won't tomorrow.

"We have to be careful," I stressed. "We need to make sure that we don't give him cause to ask too many questions. We need to be really diligent about the animal tents. In fact, I think we should strengthen them with double wards ... just to be on the safe side. Tillie seems the type to go hunting through our personal business."

"How can she get past the dreamcatcher?" Kade asked. "Won't it alert if she crosses? She's magical."

"The dreamcatcher is meant to snag *evil* beings," I replied. "Whether or not she would alert is up for debate."

"I don't understand." He leaned back in his canvas chair and grabbed my hand to hold. "Margaret said she was evil in the diner. I didn't realize that was up for debate."

"No offense, but I don't think dumping yellow snow at the end of someone's driveway constitutes evil," Luke argued. "It's darn funny — especially because she seems dedicated to it and does it after every large snowfall — but it's not evil. It's more taunting than anything else."

"Margaret seemed convinced she'd cursed that Calvin dude," Kade persisted.

"Yeah, but Landon seemed equally convinced that Calvin actually loved Tillie. I tend to think Landon and Terry know the Winchesters better than Margaret."

"You've been close to most of them now," Raven interjected. "What do you think?"

I shrugged, noncommittal. "I don't know."

"Oh, don't play that game." Raven wasn't about to back down when she sensed blood in the water. "You know something. What is it?"

Kade slid his eyes to me, curious. "Do you know something?"

"I don't *know* anything." I was firm. "I might have felt something when Tillie was here yesterday," I hedged. "I don't know how to explain it. She's ... powerful. There's no doubt about that. I didn't get a sense of evil from her, though. I think we're fine as long as we don't cross her."

"You think we're fine?" Kade was incredulous. "Does that mean you believe she could hurt us?"

"I don't know what to believe." I opted for honesty. "What I felt when we briefly connected was ... powerful. She knows what she's doing. I didn't sense evil there. Sure, it's clear she likes to torture certain individuals — and I think Margaret is her favorite target — but what I saw in the memory I gleaned from Landon's head is that she was standing with her great-nieces and protecting them. It was the man with the weapon who was threatening them."

I involuntarily shuddered when I thought about the wind monster again. "I don't think that's a family you want to trifle with," I added.

Kade gripped my hand tighter. "What do we know about them? If they're dangerous, maybe we should leave."

He was still getting used to the idea of magic, so that was often

Kade's go-to response. If he didn't understand something he wanted to flee. He needed to learn that we only ran when ... well, in truth, we never ran. That might eventually be our downfall, but we were the sort of fighters who stood our ground.

"I don't think they're dangerous to us," I argued, and the more I thought about it, the more I believed it. "You guys are overlooking something important here. I saw them going after a killer. I'm sure that's what he was. It's entirely possible they're exactly like us."

"Handsome and strong?" Luke asked.

I glared at him. "Out to rid the world of evil," I replied without hesitation. "We're not the only monster hunters out there. We're not the first and we won't be the last. It's possible the Winchesters are hunting monsters in their own way."

"That right there is a thought," Max mused. He rarely joined us for bonfires, but he seemed keen on the idea this evening. "I'm going to place a few calls and see what I can find out. I'm curious what my colleagues have heard about these witches."

"Well, while the rest of you were wandering around gossiping with the townsfolk, I asked several insightful questions of the people I ran across," Raven noted. "I think I might have some information to add to this discussion that's not conjecture."

Her tone rankled, but we were short on information, so I merely nodded.

"First, they're definitely real witches." Raven sounded completely convinced. "A series of interesting incidents has happened around these women for decades, and things seem to be picking up in frequency."

"How do you know that?" I asked.

"Because I invaded the mind of the woman at the bakery. Her name is Ginny Gunderson and she's ... a fountain of information. Apparently she used to be good friends with Tillie, but they had a falling out years ago. This was after Ginny's husband died. She thought Tillie did it, but that turned out to be wrong. That Little woman — the busybody — her husband did it because Margaret Little was sleeping with Floyd Gunderson. It's a whole big thing.

"Anyway, the dude was such a jerk he turned into a poltergeist that was unearthed years later and attacked the Winchesters," she continued, warming to her story. "The blonde witch fought him off and basically shredded what was left of his soul with the help of her great-aunt."

"Bay," I volunteered. "Her name is Bay."

"Well, Bay — and that's a stupid name — is growing pretty strong apparently," Raven said. "Ginny doesn't want to know some of the things she knows, but she witnessed Bay fighting some kid who was trying to kill people while playing a game, and she saw Bay send ghosts after the kid to kill him."

I was dumbfounded. "What?"

"It's true. I saw the memory in her head. Ginny saw the ghosts. They became visible at the last second and looked like angry flashes of light, but she knows what she saw. The killer was going after Bay with obvious intent, and she unleashed a pack of ghosts on him."

I rubbed the back of my neck as I looked to Max. "What do you think that means?"

Max looked equal parts intrigued and confused. "I don't know," he said finally. "My understanding is that seeing and talking to ghosts is a family gift. If Bay has it that probably means others in the family do."

"This sounds like a little more than ghost whispering," I pointed out. "Lots of people can ghost whisper. Technically I can do it if pushed hard enough, although I hate it because I find ghosts creepy."

"Yours is an ability you try to control, though," Max pointed out. "Bay's is an ability that seems to invade her senses. As for sending the ghosts after the killer, I've never heard of that. Perhaps the ghosts wanted to hurt him because he was their killer."

Raven's eyes sparked with interest. "I didn't think of that, but it makes sense. Maybe the ghosts were grouped together like that because he killed them and they wanted revenge. Perhaps Bay simply asked them to intervene."

It was an interesting hunch, but I wasn't sure I believed it. Right now, though, that was the least of our worries. "I did a cursory search this afternoon," I offered. "This area is thick with stories about paranormal beings. At one time it was inundated with shifters. They seem to have moved to the middle of the state, at least for the time being."

"That could mean they ceded the land to the witches," Max pointed out. "Perhaps these witches are even stronger than they imagine. It's possible they ran entire clans off the land, which would be impressive."

"That's not the only creature rumored to live in this area," I pointed out. "There's also something called the Dogman. I guess it could be a shifter, but people here seem to think of it like Bigfoot."

"I think we can take the Dogman," Luke said dryly. "In fact, I volunteer to take on the Dogman if it becomes a thing. I could use a good slap fight to lift my mood since there are no eligible bachelors in this town."

The look I shot him was withering. "Not everything is about you."

"What isn't about me is boring."

"Yes, well ... ." I trailed off when a howl filled the air. I snapped my head to the east to scan the horizon. It was too dark to see anything but treetops, but that didn't stop my heart from doing a somersault.

"What was that?" Kade asked, instantly alert. "Was that the Dogman?"

I shook my head. "I don't think so."

"You don't think so?" Kade's voice ratcheted up a notch. "I don't like it when we can't figure out what sort of monster is stalking us."

Uh-oh. The nerves I thought laid to rest were about to raise their ugly head. "Hey, it's going to be okay." I rested my hand on his arm and searched his eyes. "We don't know that whatever is out there even cares about us. This is a sparsely populated area. Sound carries."

Kade looked momentarily placated. Then Raven opened her mouth and made things worse.

"I think it's a wendigo," Raven announced, causing my stomach to threaten a revolt. "It was a weird cry, but it sounded more like a wendigo than anything else."

We'd taken on a wendigo in California during our last fight. It turned out to be a tortured soul controlled by humans, but Kade was barely back on his feet. Seeing a wendigo — a creature that eats human flesh to prolong its life — so soon after the fact, well, it wasn't going to go over well.

"We don't know it's a wendigo," I said calmly, shooting Raven a warning look. "It's hard to make out the sound in this area because of the way things echo. Let's not get worked up."

"Who cares if it's a wendigo?" Nellie asked. "We've taken them down before. We'll take them down again. The last one was a real disappointment because it wasn't even evil. I could use some good wendigo action after the disappointment of that last one."

I wanted to pull his dress over his head and give him a good punch in the gut. "We don't know it's a wendigo, Nellie," I snapped. "Let it go."

As if sensing my unease, Max glanced between Nellie and me — and then to Kade — before deciding to take control of the situation. "Whatever it is, it's clearly not coming after us tonight. If it does, the dreamcatcher will alert. I suggest everyone go to bed and get a good night's sleep. We'll pick up this discussion in the morning."

His tone was such that no one put up an argument. Even Kade, who stuck close to me as we walked back to our trailer, seemed resigned to sleep rather than argument. "You have more of that potion, right?" He looked desperate.

I nodded, concern rolling through me. "I do. Are you sure you don't want to at least try sleeping without it?"

"Not tonight. I ... just ... not tonight."

The fear rolling through him was palpable. I simply didn't know if it was the possible wendigo that set him off or the idea that his magic would escape during the night and somehow wrap a sparkling fist around my throat. "I have it." I linked my fingers with his and sent him an encouraging smile. "You'll sleep like the dead ... again."

"Good." He looked relieved. "We need to make sure we lock the doors before bed. I plan to sleep hard."

"We will. Everything is fine. There's nothing to worry about."

I said the words, but I didn't believe them. Something was definitely going on here.

8
EIGHT

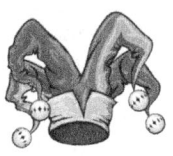

I didn't immediately give Kade the potion. I wasn't keen on the notion because it seemed he was more than ready to use it as a crutch of sorts. Instead I wanted to attempt to calm him through other means.

"Let's go to bed," I suggested as he double-checked the locks.

He nodded without hesitation. "Sure. Where is the potion?"

"I have it if you need it. I thought we might spend a little quality time together first."

His lips spread into a slow smile as realization washed over him. "Oh, really? What kind of quality time are we talking?"

I snickered at his expression. "Come with me and I'll show you." I extended my hand as he switched off the lights and took it. He followed me without complaint.

I directed him toward the bed, and he stripped out of his shirt and pants without prodding. I followed suit, although once we were in bed I forced him to his back and rested my hand on his heart rather than immediately engaging in romance.

"What are you doing?" he asked, curious. "I thought we were ... you know."

I couldn't swallow my chuckle. "We will. I need you to relax for me, though." His heart rate was higher than normal, which worried me. "Close your eyes."

He made a face. "Are you about to get kinky?"

"I might, but I want you to calm yourself first."

He sighed but did as I instructed, one hand coming to rest on top of mine as he took a deep breath and exhaled. "Are you about to tell me I'm being ridiculous?"

"No." That was true. "I'm about to tell you that you can't let the way we live our lives overwhelm you." I kept my voice soft, hoping to soothe him. Maybe even lull him. I was up for romance if that's what it would take, but I was also eager for him to relax, and there were myriad ways for that to happen. "I'm afraid for you," I admitted after a beat. "You're letting what happened overrule everything that you are."

He shifted his head but kept his eyes closed. I could see his profile thanks to the streetlight that offered illumination through the bedroom window. "You're saying that you don't like how I've been acting. I'm doing the best I can."

"I'm not accusing you of anything."

"It feels as if you are."

"Then you're misreading the situation." I drew a symbol with my fingertip over his heart. It was an ancient rune that represented peace. "I care about you a great deal and I want this to work." We still weren't saying the L-word. It was on the tip of my tongue, but I wasn't brave enough to utter it ... yet.

His eyes popped open. "And you think it won't?"

"I didn't say that." His nerves were so intense I was starting to feel them invade my skin. "I can't lie about being worried, though. What you did in California was ... impressive."

"It didn't feel impressive. It felt ... scary, as if something clawed its way free from inside of me. I don't know how to describe it."

"Close your eyes," I repeated.

He groaned but acquiesced. "I don't want to become a monster."

"You can't become a monster," I said. "It's not in you. Look at Gillian Dodd. She was forced to become a wendigo. Everything we know about wendigos says that they should become soulless beings upon transformation. She didn't because she didn't want to be a monster."

"She was still forced to kill."

"But she held true to herself," I reminded him, tracing the rune again. "She managed to remember who she was, hold to the beliefs that she grew up with, and remain strong. She made friends when she shouldn't have been able to do it. She protected those she loved when it should've been impossible."

"I get what you're saying." His voice became softer as I continued to trace the rune. "I don't want to become a monster who strives to be human, though. I want to be me, the man here with you who would never purposely hurt an innocent."

"You *are* that."

"Am I? I don't feel as if I had control of what happened in California. I killed, and I didn't feel guilty about it at the time."

"You killed a threat," I reminded him, my finger moving steadily across his muscled chest. The power I was emitting was slowly being absorbed. I could tell by the way his breathing deepened. He was going to sleep on his own, and it would be peaceful, without fear. I was determined to make it happen. "The threat was real, and we could've died during that fight. You know that."

He sighed. "I would kill a hundred times over to protect you. That's what scares me most."

"And I would do the same for you." I felt that to my bones. "We won't be forced into that situation at every turn. The key is to work together to overcome our obstacles, not constantly kill to protect each other. I won't say that's never going to happen, but you'll come to see that's the exception rather than the rule."

"I don't know that I can keep up with all the rules," he said, his breath deepening as sleep began stalking him. "How do you tell the difference between good witches and bad ones?"

"The bad ones try to kill you."

He chuckled, the sound low and throaty. "How else?"

"You have the tools inside to recognize friend and foe," I pointed out. "You're a mage. Your father is a strong mage, the strongest I've ever come across, in fact. They say there are stronger mages, but I've never met one.

"The thing is, you have someone here who can teach you about control," I continued. "I know you're still struggling with the fact that Max never told you he was your father. You mourned a man who never existed, and your mother and Max perpetrated a hoax on you for your entire life.

"Max is a good man," I said. "He loves you. He was trying to give you a normal life. Your mother died before you could question her, and that's a big rip that's likely not to be mended. You'll eventually move past it.

"I don't want you living in fear. It's not good for you, for us. I can't force you to let it go. That's something you have to decide yourself. Max is here, and he's not going anywhere. You're here, and you're not going anywhere. Perhaps you should work together."

He was quiet for so long I assumed he'd fallen asleep, which was a bit disappointing. I wanted him to have a peaceful night, but I also wanted to get this conversation out of the way. It looked like only one of those things would happen.

When he finally spoke, I almost jolted. Instead, I managed to hold it together and keep drawing the rune.

"You think I should let Max teach me."

"I think you should let him try," I agreed. "It can't hurt, and if you let go of some of the fear ruling you, it can only help. You made a choice to stay in this life. Sometimes I worry you made the choice for me rather than yourself, but you're in it now. I think you should try to live the best life possible."

Another sigh. "I really do adore you."

I smiled, warmth enveloping me. "I adore you, too." The words had their own magic, and it was a soothing balm as it washed over both of us.

"I'll talk to Max tomorrow, at least mention it to him," Kade said, moving his hand so it was around my waist. "Now I need sleep. I ... need you. Put your head on my chest."

I smiled to myself as I stretched out beside him and rested my ear above his heart. "Thank you."

"I'm doing it for us. I think we both need it."

"I think you're right."

We were asleep within seconds. We needed that, too.

I WOKE IN THE MIDDLE of the night, something ripping me from a pleasant dream that involved Kade, a picnic and stars that showered us with glitter.

I took a moment to absorb my surroundings. Kade slept deeply beside me, his chest rhythmically rising and falling. He didn't stir, which meant he hadn't heard anything.

So what woke me?

I flicked my eyes to the window and stared at the darkness. My inner clock told me it was after midnight, the dead zone of the night, and Hemlock Cove was completely quiet and devoid of movement.

There was nothing out there. I'd almost convinced myself of that and was going to return to slumber when a shadow flitted past the window.

I rolled to a sitting position and peered hard, looking for a figure I was convinced I'd seen. There was no additional movement, but my inner danger alarm was emitting a low hum. That meant something was out there, watching. I had to figure out what that something was.

I briefly rested my fingers on Kade's forehead and whispered a suggestion that sleep was his friend. If he truly wanted to wake, he would. I felt it was important for him to sleep through the night on his own without fear, so I left him behind as I slipped from beneath the covers.

I found flip-flops by the front door and slid them on, being careful to make as little noise as possible as I let myself out of the trailer. I expected to be alone when I hit trailer row, but I could see something – someone, really – walking toward me.

"Raven?" My voice was barely a whisper.

She nodded as she tightened her robe sash. "There's something out here," she said, matching my tone.

"I know. It woke me from a dead sleep."

She looked over my outfit, which I'd forgotten to cover. Thankfully I tended to sleep in boxer shorts and a T-shirt, so I wasn't revealing too much. "I take it you didn't get any loving tonight. Is Kade still messed up over what happened in Eureka?"

I nodded. There was no sense in lying. Raven was intuitive, and she had a specific skill set. She would know regardless. "He's afraid he'll turn into a monster."

She rolled her eyes. "He needs to get over that. The power he wielded that night we were attacked was impressive. I think we would've been fine without him, but he stepped in at the exact right time and saved us from bloodshed. I don't know why he's not proud of his actions."

"Because he didn't know paranormal beings were real until he met us," I said, moving past my trailer and standing in the open as I studied the area where I was convinced I'd seen something stirring minutes before. "He had barely wrapped his mind around that when he found out Max was his father, but magical, too. It was a hard blow."

"I remember. He didn't speak to you for weeks. I thought I had a chance with him."

I cast her a derisive look. "Can we please not go back to that time? I was miserable and considered murdering you in your sleep."

Instead of being offended, Raven grinned. "I know. That was a great time for me. I enjoyed watching you suffer."

"I thought you were happy with Percival."

"I am. Chill out." Raven narrowed her eyes. "This way." She pointed west.

"Are you sure?" It wasn't that I doubted her. Sometimes her senses were more in tune than mine and I accepted that. But I didn't want to risk losing whatever was stalking us from behind the dreamcatcher line. "I thought I saw something over there when I first woke."

"I'm sure. There's nothing there now."

"Okay." I fell into step with her as we moved toward the midway workers' trailers. "What do you think it is?"

"I have no idea, and that's what bothers me," Raven replied. "I can usually get a sense of interlopers, even if it's a random evil human. Whatever is out there is different."

"It senses the dreamcatcher line," I said. "I ... ." I trailed off when I saw another dark flutter. It was accompanied by a flash at the far end of the fairgrounds. "That's where the body was found."

"Come on." Raven broke into a run and we raced toward the light, prepared to do battle. All thoughts of fighting fled when we came upon four figures standing in the dark. They were all whispering, and none of them looked happy.

"This is a bad idea," one of them hissed. "You know I don't like wandering around in the dark. That only makes it easier for Bigfoot to get us."

"Oh, shut up, Clove," another voice demanded. "I hate it when you turn whiny."

Raven and I exchanged amused looks as we stepped closer. The movement was enough to cause four heads to snap in our direction.

Tillie, Bay, Clove and Thistle stood in the spot where Darren's body was discovered. If they were surprised at being caught, they didn't show it. Okay, Clove showed it a little. She looked unbelievably nervous. The rest merely met our curious gazes with challenging ones of their own.

"Can we help you?" Tillie asked.

I folded my arms over my chest. "We heard noises, people creeping about."

"I don't creep, so you must be looking for someone else."

Raven snorted. "We also saw sparks, like perhaps someone was conducting magic. Do you want to explain that?"

Tillie was defiant as she met Raven's gaze. "Do you want to explain this net thing you guys have cast to cover the ground? Yeah, we sensed that. It's a rather intricate form of magic. I'm impressed."

"We're impressed by the yellow snow stories," I offered, smirking when Thistle rolled her eyes.

"I told you those stories were going to come back and haunt us, old lady," Thistle complained. "You just had to mess with Mrs. Little."

Tillie's expression was withering. "Oh, don't even. You enjoy dumping yellow snow on her driveway just as much as I do. You suggest it half the time."

"I was a child," Thistle sputtered.

"You suggested it four times this past winter. Were you a child then?"

"No. It was a long and boring winter."

I chuckled. "What is it you're doing?" I asked finally, stepping beyond the safety of the dreamcatcher and joining them. If they were dangerous, I was convinced I would sense it. Now I was simply curious.

"We're trying to figure out what killed Darren," Tillie answered. "We think it was a ritual killing."

"It was definitely a ritual killing," Raven offered, joining me. "Somebody carved a symbol into his head."

"Did you recognize the symbol?"

"No." Raven shook her head. "We could research it."

"I was going to research but we went shopping instead," I said. "I thought the police were handling the investigation."

"I'm smarter than 'The Man,'" Tillie countered. "I think this one might be above their pay grade."

"So ... you help the police?" I asked, genuinely curious.

"We're independent contractors of sorts."

Bay made a disgusted sound in the back of her throat. "We are not. They don't want our help. We snuck out to take a look, and we're going to be in trouble if we're caught."

"That's what I said," Clove complained. "You didn't listen when I said it, though. You said, 'Oh, Clove is being a baby again.' Well, I'm not being a baby. Bay thinks the same thing, but you don't call her a baby."

"Bay is a different sort of baby," Tillie said. "You're still the big baby, Clove. You've had that title wrapped up since you were six."

"I don't know why I go on these adventures with you people," Clove muttered, jutting out her lower lip. "I get absolutely no respect."

"There's a reason for that," Thistle said dryly, her eyes locking with mine. "What are you? I know you're something. Aunt Tillie said she got a power reading off you that was ... off the charts. Those were her words."

"I'm a fortune teller."

"You're more than that," Thistle pressed.

"I'm ... different. Like you," I said finally. "I'm not a witch, but I have a few abilities."

"And what about you?" Thistle fixed her full attention on Raven. "I have a feeling that the two of you are out here because you're the most powerful."

"I wouldn't underestimate anyone in our group," Raven countered. "We're all powerful."

"Except for the clowns," I added. "They're just clowns."

"Which means they're evil," Bay muttered.

I couldn't exactly argue with that, so I merely shrugged. "I think we should have a talk. There are things to discuss."

"There are," Tillie agreed. "But not tonight. We thought we could cast a spell to track how the body got here since Darren was killed elsewhere, but we had to substitute some ingredients because my nieces are morons." She gave Thistle a disgusted look. "You need to do better when ordering herbs."

Thistle rolled her eyes. "Yeah, yeah, yeah."

"We have to get back," Bay offered. "People will miss us if we're gone too long."

I knew exactly who would miss her. "Does that mean Landon will get angry if he knows you're sticking your nose into his murder investigation?"

"He'll be ... difficult to deal with," she hedged.

"Don't worry about that." Tillie offered a dismissive wave of her hand. "He can be bribed with bacon and Bay's giggles. He's a total softie."

I smiled. "Well, we still need to talk."

"We'll swing around tomorrow morning," Thistle offered. "We'll be early, so we expect some of that magical coffee you have. Be ready, because we'll have questions."

"I was about to say the same to you."

Thistle smirked. "I'm always ready."

Something told me that wasn't an exaggeration.

9

NINE

Kade woke well rested, and the smile he gave me when shifting to stare down at my face was almost miraculous.

"Hey, baby." His voice was low and throaty.

"Hi." I returned the smile and tested his heart rate. It was back to the reliable beat of before. "How are you feeling?"

"Good. I slept well."

"And without the potion."

"Yeah, well ... ." He broke off, sheepish.

"It's okay." I pressed a kiss to his cheek. "You didn't really have the potion the first night either." It was time to be truthful. "I mean, you drank something from a bottle, but it wasn't magical. I simply told you it was."

His smile slipped. "What?"

"You didn't need the potion." I refused to back down. "You're fine. You're strong. You'll never hurt me. I knew you needed sleep, though, so I told you the potion would ensure you got it. You believed ... so you slept."

"You lied?"

Lies were something of a touchy subject between us. I lied to him after finding out Max was his father, and that caused our estrangement. I promised I wouldn't lie again. I'd meant it. But in this particular case, I wasn't sorry.

"I didn't lie," I lied. "I told you the potion would help you sleep, and it did. You needed the sleep. I would've done it sooner if I realized how little you were sleeping."

"But ... ."

"No." I shook my head, firm. I wasn't in the mood to argue. We had other things to worry about. "You needed it. I'm always going to do what I believe is right for you. If you don't like that, well, we'll have to talk about it later. We have guests coming for breakfast."

Kade was flabbergasted. "That's it? And what guests?"

"That's it," I confirmed. "As for the guests ... well ... ." I told him about the Winchesters' late-night antics, and when I'd finished I couldn't decide if he was furious or curious. "If you're going to yell, you need to do it in the shower. We should get ready for our guests."

"I don't even know what to say." Kade ran his hand through his hair. It was a little longer than when he first joined us. He preferred to keep it neat. I figured that was part of his military background. He was handsome either way.

"I'm sorry I gave you the potion and made you think it was something it wasn't."

"What was it?"

"Tea with valerian."

He scowled. "I think I should be angry about this, but I slept so well last night I can't quite muster the energy to start another fight."

"Does that mean you'll let it go?"

"For now. I might get a second wind later in the day, though."

"That's fair."

He stared at me for a long beat. "As for the witches, why didn't you wake me?"

"You know why."

"Yeah, but ... I'm head of security. You should've called me to go with you. That's my job."

"I wasn't sure if something was really out there," I admitted. "I thought I could've been imagining it. Once I saw Raven, I knew that wasn't the case. We decided to investigate."

"And it was the Winchesters."

"They were conducting some sort of spell, but they said they didn't have the right ingredients. It was late and they couldn't stay. They said they would swing around again this morning."

"And you just let them go?" Kade's temper ratcheted up a notch. "They could've been lying. They might very well be dangerous. I don't think simply letting them go was the smart thing to do."

"I understand that." I really did. "I don't think they're dangerous. Well, check that. I don't think they're dangerous to us. In fact, I think they're a lot like us. They were searching for their own answers. I think if we join forces we might be able to figure this out faster."

"But ... you heard Margaret Little. She says the great-aunt is evil."

"I have a feeling Margaret is the evil one," I admitted. "She has issues with Tillie for a variety of reasons. I'm not saying I believe Tillie is innocent in this — the woman has pot-stirrer written all over her — but I don't think a petty fight that carried over from childhood makes her evil."

Kade pursed his lips. "Fine. I'll follow your lead on this because you have a sixth sense about this stuff."

"Thank you."

"I'm reserving the right to be angry about the potion thing later, though. I need to think about it."

"Fine." I gave him another kiss. "Do you want to make up right now and log it for the future fight? We have a bit of time before we're expected for breakfast. It's not much, but it might be just enough to ... ." I left the suggestion hanging.

Kade's lips curved. "I don't know why I even try staying angry with you. It never works."

"That's my philosophy, but you're your own person."

He sighed. "Fine. Let's make up. I can't wait to hear what these witches have to say for themselves."

. . .

I HAD AN EXTRA SPRING in my step when I joined Raven, Nixie and Naida in the kitchen area. I couldn't stop myself from humming, which wasn't a regular occurrence, and when Raven slid her eyes to me there was a hint of devilish delight lurking there.

"I take it your night improved upon returning to your trailer," she drawled.

"It improved this morning," I corrected, glancing over my shoulder. "Have you seen them yet?"

"No, but I have no doubt they're coming. I wouldn't worry about it. Besides, it's not as if we don't know where to find them."

"Good point." I rolled my neck. "What do you think about them?"

"I think that old witch is powerful."

"Tillie," I corrected. "I don't think you should go around calling her the 'old witch' if you want to remain curse-free for our stay here."

"Whatever. It's clear she boasts a lot of power. But the blonde is the true threat."

I was intrigued. "I kind of thought that myself. Why do you think that?"

"She's ... something different ... from the others," Raven replied. "I can't put my finger on it yet, but there's something about her that is truly terrifying. She was quieter than the others last night, but I don't think that's normal. She was focused on you, as if she sensed something from you that made her curious."

"She saw us laying the dreamcatcher that first night," I admitted. "She was leaving the newspaper office. She didn't say anything, but I got the distinct impression that she was aware of what we were doing."

"That's because she recognizes magic in others. She's definitely got something under the hood that's above and beyond the others. The two loud ones have magic, but they're not as powerful as she is."

"I think they often work together," I offered. "My guess is their power is four-fold because they combine their resources. That's normal coven work, but they're more powerful than normal witches."

"That's because they're born witches. They didn't seek out power after the fact. They were born with it."

"How is that different?"

Raven shrugged. "They're simply stronger. I don't know why, although I have a few theories that revolve around blood magic. Tillie understands blood magic. You can tell. The others, I think they were probably dabblers their whole lives, even though the blonde is extremely powerful. I'm curious to hear what they have to say."

"I am, too. Do you think they'll tell us the truth?"

"As much as we'll tell them the truth," Raven replied. "We don't plan to hide anything. That doesn't mean we'll tell them everything. I think the same holds true for them. They're loyal to a fault, despite the squabbling. They'll share, but they won't expose themselves."

"And we'll do the same," I mused. "We really are a lot alike."

"We definitely are."

BAY ARRIVED FIRST, Clove and Thistle not far behind. As for Tillie, she didn't appear to be coming.

"She's in trouble," Bay explained. "My mother grounded her."

I wasn't sure what to make of that. "Excuse me?"

"She's, like, ninety," Raven complained. "How can she be grounded?"

"Oh, please let me be there when you tell her she looks ninety," Thistle pleaded. "I don't want to miss that lovely ... explosion."

I pursed my lips. "I thought she was going to discuss things with us," I said. "Wasn't that the deal?"

"We're here," Thistle pointed out. "We can discuss things with you."

"It's probably best that Aunt Tillie isn't here," Clove offered. "She makes things ... uncomfortable ... at times."

I could see that. I supplied the women with coffee and then gestured for them to follow me away from the prying eyes of my fellow circus workers. You would think people often put on display for physical abnormalities would understand that it's not polite to stare. When it came to Mystic Caravan workers, you'd be wrong.

"How long have you known you're witches?" I asked as I led them through the circus aisles.

"We were born knowing," Bay replied, her eyes on Dolph as he singlehandedly raised a tent. "Is he magical?"

I followed her gaze. "He's our strongman."

"That wasn't really an answer."

"No, it wasn't," I agreed, absently scratching a nonexistent itch on the side of my nose. "I'm not sure how much I want to tell you. You're probably feeling the same way about us. The yellow snow story was entertaining, but I hardly think it's the limit of your powers."

"I could say the same about you," Bay said, her expression thoughtful. "In fact, I saw you the other night. That was an impressive showing of power. The net thing you built is ... interesting."

"We call it a dreamcatcher."

Realization washed over Bay's face. "That actually makes sense. I saw the weave bounce when you tested it."

"You shouldn't have been able to see it at all," I pointed out. "We're careful about what we do, who we show our true natures. I made a mistake the other night. I didn't realize you were still in the newspaper building. Despite that, a normal human would've had no idea what we were doing."

"I'm not normal, although compared to Aunt Tillie I'm a regular Mary Sue," Bay said. "I saw what you were doing, recognized it as magic, and was fascinated by the process. I still don't know what it does."

"It detects magic. When someone with power crosses the threshold, it alerts. It's basically a home-security system for us because we're always on the road."

Bay looked impressed. Thistle, not so much.

"We crossed it," Thistle pointed out. "It didn't alert when we moved over the barrier."

"I guess I phrased that wrong," I said. "When evil beings — human or magical — cross the threshold it alerts. The good news is, you're not evil."

"I'll be able to sleep better at night knowing that," Thistle said dryly, causing Clove to smirk.

"I think it's faulty," Clove argued. "Thistle is definitely evil."

"Zip it," Bay ordered, shaking her head. "Did you create the dreamcatcher?"

I nodded. "I had the idea for it years ago. It took us a bit of time to perfect it. It failed several times until we got things exactly right."

"And is it always the same four women who build it?"

I found that an invasive question. "Do you need four witches for all your spells?"

Bay shook her head. "I suggested coming out to the scene to cast the spell last night," she admitted. "I thought maybe if we could track Darren's movements that we would have an easier time figuring out who killed him.

"Thistle and Clove love adventures," she continued, ignoring the ridiculous look Clove made in response to the statement. "We've always done stuff like this together. Occasionally Aunt Tillie invites herself along for the ride. That's what happened last night."

"And why she got grounded?" I asked.

"Oh, no, she didn't get grounded for sneaking out of the house," Bay answered. "She got grounded for the leggings. My mother has confiscated them at least fifteen times. They keep showing up. Mom doesn't want her wearing them in public because they're indecent."

"Yeah, and the second Aunt Tillie realized they bothered Winnie, well, that was simply incentive to wear them every stinking day," Thistle added. "She likes poking people with her shotgun."

I smirked. I couldn't help myself. They were a family. Unlike my family, it was simply inherited rather than made. "It sounds like growing up in your house was a lot of fun," I said.

"Then we're telling it wrong," Thistle groused. "That old lady is a menace."

"Ignore her," Bay said, waving a dismissive hand at Thistle. "She's a grouch most days. She's especially annoyed at the influx of fake witches arriving in town. She finds it tacky and annoying."

"Because they're not real?"

"Because they're pretenders and we hate fake people," Thistle answered.

"I get that." I honestly did. "I prefer that those I keep close to me are real."

"Like that hot security guard?" Clove asked, shrinking back when Thistle gave her a dirty look. "What? I have eyes. I can see how hot he is. I can also see he's hopelessly devoted to Poet."

"You're getting married," Thistle noted. "You're not allowed to stare at guys when you're getting married."

"Since when is that the rule?" Clove protested. "I didn't agree to never look at a guy again. I simply agreed not to touch. Besides, even if I wanted to touch that guy she would kill me. She's clearly more powerful than I am."

That was true. I was definitely more powerful than Clove and Thistle. I was still debating whether that statement applied to Bay and Tillie. "It's fine. Kade is very attractive. I understand staring at him."

"See." Clove stuck out her tongue.

"What's your next step?" I asked Bay. "Are you going to keep looking into the situation?"

Bay nodded without hesitation. "I am. This is my town. A ritual death on our soil is ... troubling."

"Because you keep the unseemly element at bay?"

"Aunt Tillie *is* the unseemly element," Thistle countered. "We like to know who is operating in our sandbox, though. We were nervous when you guys came to town. But other than a few oddities, you seem fairly normal."

My eyebrows migrated up my forehead. "And what oddities are you referring to?"

"Well, for starters, you don't have any animals in the tents," Thistle fired back despite the hand Bay kept slashing across her throat to silence her blunt cousin.

"I'm sorry," Bay said hurriedly. "We don't mean to intrude ... or trespass when we're not invited. We were merely curious and looked really quickly."

"Clove has always wanted a pet lion," Thistle offered.

"It's true." Clove nodded solemnly. "I would name him Leo and put a collar on him. It would have pink sparkles."

"I would send him after Mrs. Little," Thistle said. "And Maybe Aunt Tillie."

"Our animals are ... in transit," I lied uncomfortably.

"Your animals are working for you," Bay corrected, extending a finger toward Seth as he worked at one of the game booths. "He's a shifter."

"How do you know that?"

"It's a feeling. We don't care, and we're not going to share your secret," she promised. "Aunt Tillie keyed us in that you didn't have animals."

I racked my memory. "She was nowhere near the animal tents the day she stopped by."

"That you know of," Thistle countered. "She's slyer than a Kardashian seeking television time. You don't know when she's sneaking around. Trust me. We've dealt with this for almost thirty years."

"She's not wrong," Bay agreed. "Aunt Tillie can get anywhere she sets her mind to. She was probably inside your animal tents."

That was a sobering thought. "Well ... ." I had no idea what to say.

"What I want to know is how Aunt Tillie crossed your dreamcatcher without alerting," Thistle said. "I mean ... she is definitely evil."

"We didn't have the dreamcatcher up when she first stopped by," I offered. "But ... I don't think she would alert regardless. Your idea of evil is probably far different from our idea of evil."

"It might not be that different," Bay countered. "I'm not going to lie. I am curious about your operation here."

"I can give you a general tour," I offered. "Keep in mind, though, I have no intention of sharing our secrets with you."

"I can live with that, as long as you respect the fact that we won't be sharing secrets either."

"That seems a fair compromise. No lies, but if we don't feel we can tell the truth, we're given a pass."

"That definitely seems fair," Bay agreed, her eyes moving toward the midway. "By the way, our mothers want us to invite some of you for dinner at the inn."

I was confused. "What inn?"

"The Overlook. It's the inn on the bluff. Our mothers own it."

"The Overlook?" I made a face. "Like in *The Shining*?"

Thistle made a disgusted sound in the back of her throat. "Don't even get us started. We tried to tell them. They wouldn't listen."

"The inn is actually nice," Clove said. "You should stop by."

"Our mothers really are the best cooks in the county," Bay added. "They want to meet you. You won't regret it for the food alone."

"Well, I'm sure I can get a few people together for a meal."

"Great." Bay brightened considerably. "Now, give us a tour and tell us everything you can. I used to dream of running away and joining the circus."

I barked out a laugh. "I didn't think that was a dream for most people."

"You didn't grow up with Aunt Tillie," Thistle supplied. "The circus would be a dream come true compared to her."

"I wouldn't be so sure about that."

10
TEN

The tour with the Winchesters went as well as could be expected. After spending a full hour with them — time that was closely monitored by Kade and Luke from afar — they reiterated their invitation to dinner and then said their goodbyes. Tour buses full of witches were due to start arriving today, and they had work to complete before that happened.

"How was it?" Kade asked, catching up to me as I slipped into our trailer to look for a hoodie. The morning was cooler than it should've been — a byproduct of Michigan's wild weather patterns — and I'd taken on a bit of a chill.

"It was fine," I replied, pinning him with a curious look as he followed me to the closet. "Is something wrong? Are you okay?"

"I'm fine." He watched me select a simple black hoodie. "I watched them to make sure they didn't touch you or anything, but they seemed sort of ... normal."

I bit back a laugh. "How did you expect them to act?"

"The last witches we crossed paths with were evil," he replied darkly. "They did things, purposely tried to hurt people just so they could be in charge. I thought maybe they would be like those witches."

"I don't think they're like that." I opted for honesty. "They're not telling us everything, but we're not telling them everything either. Raven pointed that out, and I really hate that she was right. They're not lying to cover for nefarious deeds. They're just trying to protect their family."

Kade nodded as he rubbed his strong chin. "Okay. What did you learn from them?"

"Their mothers are mostly kitchen witches, which means they pour their magic into food. We've been invited for dinner, by the way, and supposedly they're the best cooks in all the land. I think we should take them up on it."

The shift threw Kade for a loop. "Seriously? You want to eat dinner with them."

I shrugged. "They invited, and it seems important to them. It's not important to us, so I don't see the problem."

He sighed. "Fine. We'll eat dinner with them. They'd better not try to poison us, though."

"I think you're missing the point." I tugged on my limited patience. "They don't care about us. They're mildly curious about what we can do, but they're looking for a killer. They're no different than we are."

"They have a great-aunt who wears borderline pornographic leggings and carries a shotgun."

"And we have a cross-dressing dwarf masquerading as the bearded lady. He carries an ax and beheads creatures great and small. We have a pixie who carries around shrinking dust so she can turn evil humans into voodoo dolls, which she then sells. We have another pixie who can control the weather when she has PMS. We have a lamia running around with a clown who wears leather chaps. Who are we to point fingers?"

Kade inadvertently cringed. "Well, when you put it like that ... ."

I smiled. "They're a family. That's the one thing I took away from our conversation. They love each other. They also irritate each other. I have no doubt they would die for each other. They're very much like us."

His lips curved as he carefully ordered my hair and leaned forward to give me a soft kiss. "Okay. I get it. I'm being ridiculous. I'm sorry."

"You're not being ridiculous," I countered without hesitation. "You're being protective, which is your job. They won't hurt us."

Kade appeared marginally placated. "You read people well, so I'll take your word for it."

"That's probably best."

He grinned as he tugged on the waistband of my shorts and pulled me to him. "If you're cold, I can warm you up."

Now it was my turn to arch an eyebrow. "I thought you already warmed me up this morning."

"I did, but ... I don't feel done."

"Ah, well, I do prefer a job be finished right."

"We're on the same page there."

IT WAS WELL BEFORE lunch when we emerged from our trailer, and I didn't miss the wolf whistles Luke lobbed in our direction from the kitchen area as everyone gathered around the table.

"What's going on?" I asked, instantly alert as I zipped my hoodie. It was warmer, but not so warm that I wanted to embrace the weather without backup. "Has something happened?"

Raven's expression was derisive. "Why do you assume something is wrong?"

"Because ... well, because you're all grouped together and it's not lunchtime yet."

Raven snorted. "Perhaps you were inside playing reindeer games with your boyfriend for longer than you imagined."

I refused to let her get to me. "It's still two hours until lunch."

"If she can remember the time you're not doing it right, stud," Raven said to Kade, who merely rolled his eyes and poured some iced tea from the pitcher on the table. "We're not gathering for lunch or because something is wrong. We're gathering to watch."

"Watch what?" I was beyond confused. "What are we supposed to be watching?"

Raven's finger straightened as she pointed toward the downtown area. There, in the middle of Main Street, a bus waited as a steady line of passengers disembarked.

"Oh, well, huh." I straightened as I watched, oddly fascinated by the parade of women flooding the downtown streets. "I knew they were coming today. They look interesting."

The women were in every shape and size imaginable. Some wore street clothes, others cloaks. Some even boasted conical hats as they tugged their suitcases off the bus.

Kade chuckled as he moved behind me and rested his hands on my shoulders, giving them a light rub as he watched. "That's an understatement. Look at how they're dressed. Some of them are actually wearing witch hats, although they look more fashionable than the ones you can get at the Halloween store."

"I think that's a deliberate choice," I noted.

Kade tugged me back against him and pressed a kiss to the top of my head. "Funnily enough, I'm not as nervous about facing off with witches again so soon after the last time after seeing them."

"These are not the witches you have to worry about," Raven offered. "These are ... wannabes." She lifted her nose to the air, making me wonder if she was scenting the tourists from afar. "I don't sense any real power emanating from them."

I was dubious. "You can't scent power from that far away."

"I can do anything I set my mind to," Raven challenged.

"You can't do that." I was almost certain that was true. "They're too far away."

"I have a sense about these things," Raven persisted.

"You just don't want to deal with them, so you're assuming they're not magical. We don't know either way what they are."

Raven wasn't the type to concede, even if she was wrong. "I'm telling you that they're completely boring and ordinary. We don't have to worry about them. The only ones we have to worry about are the Winchesters."

"And the murderer, right?" I challenged.

Raven let loose a long-suffering sigh. "Well, of course we have to worry about the murderer. That's the head of security's job, though.

Of course, he'll need to stop taking hour-long mid-morning *naps* if he expects to solve that particular case."

Kade didn't look ashamed in the least to be called out by Raven. "Why don't you go back to spanking your yipping clown and not worry about the rest of us?" he suggested, causing me to bite the inside of my cheek.

"Send in the clowns!" Luke sang in a deep voice. "Then send them away again because they're weird."

"Oh, your wit astounds me," Raven drawled, her gaze withering as it landed on Luke. They had something of a tempestuous relationship. Luke was naturally drawn to the people he could irritate most, and Raven didn't have much of a sense of humor. "You'd better start running now, dog."

"I'm a wolf," Luke shot back. "Get it right."

"What's the difference?"

"How would you like it if people got you confused with an eel? Although ... you're slippery enough to actually be an eel. Perhaps you would like that."

"Listen here ... ."

I stepped between them and held up my hands to urge silence. "Hey, we can't do this here." I was deathly serious. "We're right on the edge of the downtown area," I reminded them. "People can see what we're doing, monitor how we're interacting. There are witches around — *real* witches — who recognize magic. You can't fly off the handle here like you usually do."

"Then you should tell your buddy to take a step back," Raven suggested.

"Luke, leave Raven alone." I was serious. "If you want to torture her, wait until our next stop."

Luke looked put out. "Oh, you're absolutely no fun."

"It's a total bummer, I know, but we need to be careful," I stressed. "This isn't a normal job."

"Poet is right," Kade said. "Everyone needs to be on their best behavior."

"Oh, that's easy for you to say," Luke shot back. "You have Poet to entertain you. What do I have?"

"A tour bus full of people," I replied, pointing toward town. "Come on. I'll go down there with you so we can check out the tourists up close and personal. That will entertain you for a bit." And allow me time to think about our situation, I silently added. My discussion with the Winchesters left me believing one thing with absolute certainty: A killer was on the loose, and there was every chance he or she was nowhere near done.

KADE DECIDED TO STAY behind and monitor things at the fairgrounds, which left me to talk Luke from the ledge. I figured it was a purposeful choice on Kade's part. Luke often rubbed him the wrong way, and it was best if I handled Luke during these instances.

"Your boyfriend is a putz," Luke announced as we selected a spot on a bench and watched the tourists giddily make their way through town. "Like a complete and total putz."

"I happen to like him."

"You only like him because he's hot," Luke argued, a pout in full effect. "That'll wear off eventually."

I very much doubted it would. "I like him for more than his looks."

"Sex stuff doesn't count. That will wear off, too."

I slid him a sidelong look. "What's really bugging you?" I could read Luke better than most, and it was obvious he was struggling. "Is there something you're not telling me?"

"No. I ... ." He snapped his mouth shut when two girls strolled past. They were young — in their teens — and they seemed giddy as they whispered excitedly and gestured toward store windows.

"Look at that," one of them squealed. "It's an actual magic shop."

"And it's called Hypnotic," the other girl giggled. "We should totally go inside."

I focused my full attention on Luke. He looked morose. It made me wonder if I'd been neglecting him, which was something I desperately tried not to do. Still, Kade had garnered the lion's share of my attention the past few weeks — for obvious reasons, of course. That didn't mean Luke deserved to be neglected.

"Kaley Burrows and Lizzy Dobbs," I announced, causing Luke to snap his head in my direction. "They're sixteen ... at least I think." I cocked my head to the side as I tried to pick up on their surface thoughts. It was a game Luke and I used to play when we were not much older than them.

Luke was already with Mystic Caravan when I'd joined. Max picked me up on the streets of Detroit — which was weird, because we were about to return to that area for the first time since that trip — and he was calm and collected, never raising his voice, even though I tried to pick his pocket. He knew right away I was magical, and he offered me a place with the circus.

I didn't have to say yes. He made that clear. I could've gone on my way and continued living on the streets. There was something about him, though, that gave me pause. I was a street-smart kid with nothing to hold on to, and he offered me everything. I never looked back.

My first few weeks with the circus were uncomfortable. I worried I would never make friends. Luke immediately took me under his wing, and we bonded, and the psychic game was one of the first we ever played.

Remembering that, Luke's lips curved as he watched the teens. "Are they thinking about boys?"

I wrinkled my nose and frowned. "I don't know. I think they're so excited to be here that all they can think about is the witch stuff. They're very scattered."

"Hey, there's nothing wrong with having fun."

"No," I agreed, linking my fingers and resting them on my stomach as another group of women moved past us. This group was made up of three women, and they looked to be in their early twenties. They also looked to be bored and blasé about everything they saw. They were unhappy with their current environment, which I found interesting.

"What do you have?" Luke asked eagerly, lighting up at my expression.

"Madison Connor, Emily Wilde and Jamie Blake," I replied, extending my magic as the women walked away from us. "They're ... not happy with their lot in life."

Luke rolled his eyes. "Even I could read that, and I don't have a psychic bone in my body."

I chuckled, genuinely amused. "They're true witches," I explained. "They think they're the only ones here serious about their craft, and they're annoyed that they're not being taken seriously because of their ages."

"They look as if they've smelled something awful," Luke noted. "I mean ... have you ever seen people that unhappy before?"

I had, but for entirely different reasons. "They're educated. They've read a lot." The trio was moving too far away for me to continue picking up stray thoughts. "They think the police officer standing in front of the station is really hot."

Luke cocked an eyebrow. "Terry?"

I shook my head. I picked up a stray vision from Emily's head and it was obvious who she'd caught sight of. "Landon. He's standing there, looking very GQ, and now they want to get arrested so he'll cuff them."

Luke chuckled. "Do it again. We haven't played this game in ages."

My heart rolled at the serious expression on his face. "I'm sorry I haven't been spending enough time with you. I didn't mean for it to happen. The cross-country trip came at the absolute worst time and ... and ... ." I wasn't sure how to finish without agitating him.

"And you're worried about Kade," Luke finished, matter-of-fact. "I see it written all over your face when you look at him. But whatever happened between you last night appears to have eased the tension a bit."

"He's afraid," I explained. "The magic frightens him, and he's terrified he's going to somehow lose control and hurt me in his sleep. I'm trying to help him through it. I don't mean to neglect you in the process."

"I'm a big boy," he reminded me. "I know how to take care of myself."

"That doesn't mean we don't still take care of each other when it's necessary. If you need me ... ."

"I'm always going to need you." Luke flashed a wan smile. "I just feel ... lonely."

I understood. It was hard on him. He often had trouble connecting with people, and if we were in a rural area there were usually few opportunities for him to meet someone because people were forced to go underground with their homosexuality more often.

"We'll go out in Detroit," I promised. "We'll find someone good for you."

His smile was fleeting. "We'll see if you have time."

I grabbed his wrist and squeezed. "I'll have time. I promise."

He heaved a sigh and nodded. "Okay. Let's go back to the game. I like it."

I nodded and smiled as two older women – they had to be in their late-sixties or early-seventies – strolled past.

"Shirley Peters and Adele Wood," I whispered as the women cackled amongst themselves. "They're just excited to be on an adventure." I rested my head on Luke's shoulder and grinned. "They're wondering if there's a senior center nearby to find dates."

"Shut up." Luke was clearly tickled as he slid his arm around my shoulders. "They're here to get some loving?"

"Apparently so."

"I think that's awesome. We should help them."

I gave in to his whims without complaint. "I don't see why that can't be arranged."

11
ELEVEN

The hour with Luke was well spent, and I'd felt better when we returned to the fairgrounds. Once there, I decided to point my assistant Melissa toward my tent to take over prep work — she was a fortune teller, too, but we were working on designing a booth just for her — and she didn't complain when I dumped the task on her diminutive shoulders. She was still recovering from a rather terrifying incident on the West Coast, one in which she was possessed and used as a weapon, so she remained leery about spending too much time out in the open.

Kade and Luke were busy with their own tasks, so I decided now was the perfect time to take a walk in the woods. To my surprise, Raven fell into step with me as I left the safety of the dreamcatcher.

"What are you doing?" I asked, confused.

"The same thing you are."

"And what am I doing?"

"Making sure there's nothing dangerous in the woods."

While I wouldn't have been so simplistic in my response, she wasn't wrong. "I just want to make sure," I said after a moment. "The woods are thick ... and Tillie surprised us that first day by getting close without us sensing her presence."

"She's a witch," Raven reminded me, her eyes keen as they scanned the trees. "She got close without detection because she wanted to."

"Yes, but it's our job to make sure that doesn't happen," I argued. "We're supposed to be able to protect ourselves — and those we work with. We would've failed if Tillie had decided she wanted to attack."

"I think you're in a mood," Raven countered, her eyes busy as we picked our way through the woods. It was early in the season, but I was guessing Michigan had a warmer spring than normal given how lush things looked.

"I don't see how telling the truth equates to me being in a mood," I grumbled, scuffing my shoe against the ground as we continued.

"What truth are you talking about?" Raven's tone told me she was in the mood for a fight.

"We're supposed to protect the others."

"From what? An old lady in a combat helmet and leggings? She wasn't a threat."

"She could've been."

"But she wasn't." Raven stared at me for a long beat before exhaling heavily and resuming her pace. "If she'd been evil we would've felt it."

"I think you're giving us more credit than we deserve."

"And I think you're looking for a reason to feel sorry for yourself," Raven shot back. "It's not your fault that Kade is feeling off his game. Given what happened in Eureka, it's going to take him some time to find his footing. Don't you remember the first time you realized you possessed magic?"

"Honestly? No. It's just something I always had but was never allowed to talk about."

Raven's expression was thoughtful. "I don't know if that's better or worse than what I had. My family knew the odds of me manifesting were good, but they sat back and waited for it to happen. They thought it was funny the first time I set something on fire without realizing I was doing it. They laughed the entire night."

"Your family sounds like a bunch of jerks."

"Yeah, well, they're long gone now." She adopted a far-off expression. "I never thought I would miss them until they were nothing but memories and it was too late to change things."

"At least you had a family. I did, too, although mine wasn't especially helpful."

"They wanted you to hide who you were, didn't they?" Raven tilted her head to the side as she studied a nearby tree. "This way." She pointed west and I didn't question her instincts. While I was drawn into the woods for a specific reason, it was obvious Raven was being enticed by something as well. I was fine figuring out what that something was on her timetable.

"They were afraid that someone would notice what I could do," I replied, choosing my words carefully. "They wanted to make sure I never gave the neighbors reason to talk."

"Did you?"

I shrugged. "I think I probably caused a bit of gossip here and there. Ultimately, it didn't matter. My parents didn't live long enough to see the true breadth of my power."

"You manifested early but didn't really grow into your abilities until after puberty," Raven muttered, talking more to herself than me. "That's not unheard of, but I find it interesting."

"I've never really thought about it," I admitted. "Once my parents died, I had other things to worry about."

"You were in the system for a time, right?"

I nodded. "I was too old for anyone to want to adopt, which was fine with me because I didn't want another family. I was traumatized a bit, feeling sorry for myself. A few of the homes I stayed in were okay, but they were transitional. It was when they attempted to put me in a permanent home that things fell apart."

A sliver of a memory flashed in my mind, unbidden. An image of an abusive foster father who wanted to exert control. I'd learned over the years that the foster system was full of people who cared, who wanted to do the right thing. They made up ninety-five percent of the ranks. It was the other five percent who got the most attention, and that was unfair. Still, that was the memory that always haunted me.

I didn't blame the system for what had happened. Even when I fled to the streets, I didn't tell anyone what almost occurred in that house. Instead, I forged a new life as a grifter and thief, which is how I met Max. I wasn't sorry I'd run, but there were times I was angry with myself for not reporting that man and having him removed from the system.

Raven's expression was thoughtful as she watched me, clearly picking up on a few of my stray thoughts. "We'll be back in Detroit in a week," she pointed out after a beat. "You could make sure he's been removed from the system then. I mean ... if you're that worried about it."

I pinned her with a dark look. "Stay out of my head."

"Stop making it so easy to see inside your head," she countered. "Usually you're good at shuttering. You've been all over the place for the last couple of days."

"That's because I've had a lot on my mind."

"Yes, well ... you need to chill out." She was matter-of-fact as she rounded a tree. "Things will work out as they're supposed to. I'm a big proponent of destiny."

In a roundabout way, so was I. That didn't mean I could fight the urge to help things along now and then. "I have every intention of making sure things turn out as they're supposed to," I said. "You don't have to worry about me."

"That's good." Raven's expression was hard to read as she focused on the huge tree in front of her. "We don't have time to worry about you."

"What are you talking about?" I shifted my eyes to the right and frowned when I realized what I was really looking at. "What the ... ?"

"Runes," Raven breathed, her eyes going wide as she traced a set of ornate carvings. Someone had been out here — and fairly recently if I had to guess — carving a series of ancient symbols into the tree. Given the woods' proximity to the fairgrounds, I had a hard time believing it was coincidental.

"Do you see any blood?" I asked, swiveling quickly to search the ground.

"Why would there be blood?"

"Because Darren Rappaport wasn't killed in the same spot his body was found," I replied without hesitation. "I thought maybe he was killed here."

"Oh. Good idea."

We spent a few minutes walking around the small clearing, and then I took photographs of the runes for later perusal. After that, there was only one thing to do.

"I can't believe you're willingly calling the cops," Raven complained as I tugged my phone out of my pocket. "That seems counterintuitive."

"We have to cover all our bases. So far, we're not suspects."

"So they say. We don't know that they mean it."

I searched my memory of the interactions I'd shared with Landon and Terry. "I believe them, at least for now. We have to go by the book on this one. If we don't call them and they find this spot, we're going to have a hard time explaining our footprints around the scene."

"We could modify their memories."

"To what end?"

She shrugged. "I don't know. It just seems weird to willingly work with cops."

"We've done it before. I think it's the right move here. I'm going to call them and we'll go from there."

"Okay, but if they're jerks and turn suspicious, don't say I didn't warn you."

"Somehow I think I'll refrain."

NOT ONLY DID LANDON and Terry not turn suspicious, they thanked us for calling them. They took photos — just like us — and then called Bay to join them. She was out of breath when she finally found us, her face flushed with color, and Landon looked alarmed when he took in her sweaty face.

"Where have you been?" he demanded. "You look like you've gone ten rounds with Bigfoot."

Bay rolled her blue eyes. "Don't mention Bigfoot in front of Clove. Early summer is Bigfoot's busy season in this area and you know how she gets."

Landon smirked. "I do. That's why I'm surprised you and Thistle haven't tortured her with your usual shtick this year."

"We haven't had the time ... what with all the other stuff going on."

There was something pointed about Bay's statement and I cast her a sidelong look. "What stuff?"

She pretended she didn't hear the question and turned her full attention to the tree. "Well, this is interesting," she mused, moving forward. She reached out a hand to touch one of the carvings, but Landon grabbed her wrist before she could.

"Are you sure it's a good idea to touch that?" he asked, his eyes wide. "What if it's cursed or something?"

Raven and I exchanged amused looks.

"We touched it," Raven offered. "We're fine."

"I hear you're dating a clown," Landon shot back around a grimace. "That's pretty far from fine in my book."

I was amused enough that I snorted out a laugh. "He has a point."

"Oh, don't you start," Raven sneered. "I'll have you know, Percival is a beast in the sack. You should try a clown some time. You might find more than you imagine."

My cheeks burned as several sets of eyes shifted in our direction. "Thank you for that lovely ... sentiment."

"And not a beast like Bigfoot," Raven added. "It's more like he's a beast like Ron Jeremy."

Sadly, I knew who she was talking about. "I so want to be out of this conversation," I muttered, shaking my head.

Bay barked out a laugh. "Oh, you guys are funny. It's like hanging out with another version of Thistle." She inclined her chin toward Raven. "Of course, not even Thistle would date a clown."

"And rightfully so," Landon said, shuddering.

"What is it with all the clown hate?" Raven challenged. "There's nothing wrong with dressing like a clown."

"I think you're preaching to the wrong demographic here," Landon said dryly, his hand clasped around Bay's fingers. "But that's not the point of the conversation. I don't think you should touch those carvings, sweetie. What if you get cursed or something?"

"I'm related to Aunt Tillie," she reminded him. "I think I'm already cursed."

"You know what I mean."

"I do, but they're not cursed." Bay sounded certain of herself. "Besides, you heard them. They've already touched the carvings and are fine. If there was a curse, they would've triggered it."

Landon looked to me for confirmation and I nodded. "Fine." He released her hand. "But if you get cursed, we're going to have a really big fight."

"I'll keep that in mind." Bay was thoughtful as she cocked her head to the side and ran her fingers over the runes, muttering to herself as she absorbed whatever message she found there.

"It's going to be bigger than the fight we had this morning when I found out you snuck out last night," Landon added, causing my eyebrows to fly up.

"You snuck out last night?" Terry was incensed, his attention completely on Bay. It was almost as if he'd forgotten he had an audience. "Why would you sneak out when there's a killer on the loose?"

Bay was calm as she shrugged. "We wanted to check out the scene where the body was found, see if we could figure out where Darren was killed."

"We?" Terry arched a dubious eyebrow. "Oh, let me guess, you had Clove and Thistle with you. The terrifying trio strikes again."

"They were a foursome last night," Landon volunteered.

"Ugh." Terry smacked his hand to his head. "That makes things even worse."

"You're quite the tattletale, aren't you?" Raven noted as she graced Landon with a squinty-eyed look. "I bet you were popular in grade school."

Landon didn't bother to hide his glare. "I'm not tattling. I'm merely relating a set of facts to my partner."

"If that's what you need to tell yourself." Raven was clearly bored with the situation and had decided to make her own source of amusement. "The truth is, you just tattled on your girlfriend to her father figure. You want him to do the yelling so you don't have to, because that makes him the bad guy."

Landon balked. "That is so not true."

Raven wasn't in the mood to be trifled with. "I'm very good at reading people. That's my job."

"Wait ... are you trying to make me the bad guy?" Terry was incredulous. "Is that why you tattle on her to me so often? It is, isn't it? You want me to do the yelling so you can get all the kisses. You're a sick, sick man."

"I could've told you that," Bay said, her fingers busy as they moved over the runes. "I don't know what these are." She flicked her eyes to me. "Do you?"

I shook my head. "No, but I'm considering doing some research."

"I think that's probably a good idea." Bay shifted her eyes over the clearing. "I don't see any blood. If Darren was killed here, they did a really neat job of it."

"The blood could've seeped into the ground," Terry pointed out. "We need to get some Luminol out here just to be on the safe side."

I could think of another way to check for blood — we had some very sensitive shifters in our employ after all — but now didn't seem the time to broach that subject.

"Go ahead and check, but I don't think you'll find any blood," Bay said. "In fact ... ." She trailed off and jerked her head to the south, her eyes focused on the trees littering that side of the clearing. I followed her gaze, sensing nothing until the exact moment a waifish figure burst through the foliage line.

Thistle, her chest heaving, rested her hands on her knees as she collected herself. "Your secretary told me you were out here, Chief Terry," she huffed.

"What's wrong?" Terry was instantly alert. Bay may have been his favorite — and she obviously was — but he was clearly dedicated to Thistle, too. "Did something happen?"

"I guess that depends on how you look at things," Thistle replied.

Terry growled, his patience on life support. "Tell me!"

"Two girls came into the shop," she volunteered. "Teenagers. They were young. They wanted Borage, Camphor, Comfrey, Devil's Shoestring and Henbane."

Terry and Landon didn't react, but the way Raven shifted told me she understood what Thistle was getting at.

"Why is that an issue?" Landon asked finally.

"Those ingredients should never be mixed," Bay replied, thoughtful. "The Henbane alone is poisonous. The Camphor is dangerous ... as is the Comfrey."

"They were insistent," Thistle said. "They demanded we provide them the ingredients. Instead of arguing and tipping them off that we were suspicious, we gave them what they wanted."

"Even though it was dangerous?" Terry exploded.

Thistle's lips quirked into a mischievous smile. "Well, we might've shifted out a few — or pretty much all — of the ingredients when they weren't looking. We made sure they left with something harmless. That doesn't change the fact that they wanted something dangerous."

"No," Terry agreed, "but I'm not sure that's my problem. I'm looking for a murderer, not two little girls trying to cast a spell they probably don't have the magic to conjure."

Thistle glanced at Bay. "He doesn't get it. I'm betting you do."

"We need to figure out what they're up to," Bay said without hesitation. "There's absolutely no spell they could make with those ingredients that ends well. They're clearly up to something."

"Great," Landon blurted. "I think you should go after the junior witches and rein them in, and we'll focus on the murderer. That seems like a great compromise ... and a way for you to stay in the house in the middle of the night."

Bay rolled her eyes. "Oh, geez! You're not going to let this go, are you?"

"Not anytime soon."

"Well, then we're definitely going after the junior witches." Bay was firm. "I don't need another lecture."

"I can wait until tonight," Landon warned.
"Yes, but then there will be chocolate cake to distract you."
The look in his eyes turned from worried to covetous.

12
TWELVE

Questioning teenagers over herbs seemed like a job for paranormals. Once Thistle started describing some of the spells they could cast – things that turned Landon and Terry ashen – they decided to handle things themselves.

The second Thistle explained about causing heads to explode – literally, mind you – Landon started wagging fingers in Bay's face and shaking his head.

"No, we're going to question them about the herbs," Landon said firmly.

"You don't even know what herbs they bought," Bay shot back. "You said not ten minutes ago that you were fine with us finding them."

"I did, but I've thought better of it. As for the herbs, I do so know what they are."

She folded her arms over her chest and narrowed her eyes. "What were they?"

"Basil, garlic salt and paprika," he shot back, refusing to back down. "Make me a list of the herbs and we will question them."

"You don't know their names," Thistle argued.

"I ... ." Landon broke off, working his jaw. "Fine. What are their names?"

"I don't know," Thistle replied, snark rolling off her tongue. "They paid in cash, so I have no idea what their names are."

I searched my memory of my afternoon with Luke. "Kaley Burrows and Lizzy Dobbs," I answered automatically, earning a surprised look from Landon.

"And just how do you know that?" he asked, suspicious.

"Yeah, how do you know that?" Bay echoed. She was more curious than suspicious.

"I was downtown with Luke," I replied. "We were playing a game."

"That includes getting names out of tourists?" Terry asked, instinctively moving closer to Bay. I wasn't sure he realized it, but he was essentially putting himself between her and me, as if I were a danger to his favorite newspaper reporter. It made me want to laugh.

"I didn't talk to them to get their names," I hedged, wondering exactly how much I should share.

"Oh." Realization washed over Bay's face as she stared me down. "You're psychic."

I wasn't a fan of the word. "I'm a fortune teller," I corrected quickly. "I can see fortunes."

Landon opened his mouth to argue, but Bay shook her head and rested her hand on his arm. "It's okay," she said quietly. "She's not trying to sucker the tourists out of money or anything. You don't need to go all FBI crazy."

"That would be a nice change of pace," Thistle muttered. "'The Man' acts like a normal man. News footage at eleven."

Landon ignored the dig and remained focused on me. "How can you be sure those are their names if you didn't talk to them?"

"The same way you know that Tillie isn't using food coloring to create the yellow snow."

Landon sighed and rolled his neck. "Fine. I don't want to know any more." He lifted his hands for emphasis. "We'll find these girls. It can't be that hard to track them down. My guess is that they read about this spell in a book and wanted to act older than their years."

"That's my guess, too," Thistle confirmed. "I thought it was wise to warn you all the same."

"It was definitely wise." Landon stroked his hand down the back of Bay's hair to get her attention. It was a simple and sweet gesture that almost made me smile. He gave her a quick kiss when she turned to him, and then lowered his voice. He thought he was speaking so quietly I couldn't hear him, but I had other ways to listen.

"I want you to be careful, Bay," he whispered. "I know you trust these people, but we don't know enough about them for me to risk your life, so ... I think you should come back with me."

Bay's lips quirked as she met my gaze. She knew I could hear him, which was mildly fascinating. "I think I'm going to stay with Raven and Poet for a bit. You said you needed to know what the original symbol means. Now we have more symbols. I'm going to make that my primary focus for the day."

He sighed, his hand remaining firm on the back of her head. "Bay ... ."

"They're not going to hurt me." She didn't bother to whisper. "They think you're funny, though. I'm sure we'll have a great time talking about you behind your back once you leave."

"Definitely," I agreed, bobbing my head when Landon slid his gaze to me. He looked tortured at the prospect of being separated from Bay. "I'm dying to hear about the bacon costume you want her to wear."

Raven barked out a laugh. "I'm more interested in having her describe what you look like naked," she drawled, amusement rolling off her in waves. "Either way, we'll find something to entertain ourselves."

Landon didn't look thrilled at the prospect. "Thistle, maybe you should stay with Bay."

"Who's going to show you the girls when we get back in town if I stay here?" Thistle challenged. "Besides ... Bay is perfectly fine. They don't want to hurt her. They are, however, having a grand time messing with you."

"I figured that out myself," Landon said dryly, rolling his eyes.

"Fine." He exhaled heavily, resigned. "We're heading back to town. I expect answers on these runes, Bay." He directed the statement to his girlfriend, but kept his eyes on me. "If something happens to her ... ," he trailed off.

"Nothing is going to happen to her." I considered messing with him further but I could read the worry in his head and recognized that wasn't fair. It would be no different if someone messed with Kade regarding me, and that wouldn't exactly be a happy affair. "I promise."

Landon sighed before tapping Bay's chin to get her to look up. He gave her a quick kiss before stepping away from the trees. "I'm not going to pretend this situation isn't weird," he said after a beat. "I don't fully understand what's going on here, and I'm pretty sure that's by design. It won't matter if something happens to her."

"Nothing will happen to her." I meant it. "We're going to work together to figure out the meaning of the runes. That's all that's happening here."

"And we'll probably talk about your butt," Raven added, earning a scowl for her efforts.

"Call me when you get back to the office, Bay," Landon instructed.

"I will."

Thistle lingered for a few seconds after Landon and Terry disappeared into the trees, sharing a weighted glance with Bay before disappearing with the others. She was needed in town. That left Bay outnumbered by Raven and me, but she didn't look worried about the shifting power structure.

"Have you ever seen runes like this?" she asked, pointing toward what most people would assume was chicken scratch.

"No." I moved closer to her and hunkered down to stare at the rune. "It's interesting. I feel as if I should recognize it, but I don't." I cast a glance over my shoulder and found Raven staring at a different tree. "You're old," I reminded her. "Do you recognize the runes?"

"Not offhand, but that doesn't mean I've never seen them," Raven replied, tilting her head to the side so her silver hair spilled over her shoulder in soft waves. "Look at the top of the trees. There are eyes carved into them."

"Eyes?" I made a face as I lifted my chin to stare in the direction she indicated. Sure enough, higher up, there was a huge eye carved into the tree. It seemed to be staring directly at me, and was surrounded by a triangle. "I've never seen that symbol before."

"Me either," Bay said, her expression grim. "It kind of reminds me of the symbol of rebirth."

That was an interesting observation. "It does," I agreed. "Usually there's another triangle inside of the triangle for rebirth, though."

"Yeah." Bay appeared lost in thought as she circled. "There's another one up there." She pointed. "And up there."

"There's a fourth over here," Raven noted.

We circled the clearing three more times to make sure we caught them all.

"Four," I noted, my mind busy. "There are four eyes at regular intervals. I doubt that's a coincidence."

"It's the four corners," Bay announced as she thoughtfully tapped her chin. "Earth. Air. Fire. Water. North. South. East. West. Witchcraft is often practiced in fours."

"I thought it was threes," Raven challenged.

"It can be done in threes. We do it in multitudes of threes sometimes. We're more powerful when calling to the four corners."

Intrigued, I leaned forward. "How does it work?"

"North is earth," Bay replied. "It's always earth. The others shift. East can be air or fire. South can be fire or air. West is always water. It's the middle two that can shift. If you practice your craft often, you tend to pick one route and stick with it."

"What's your route?"

"East is air, south is fire," Bay answered automatically, her eyes going back to the runes on the trees. "I feel as if I should recognize these."

She wasn't the only one. "Do you use runes a lot?"

She shook her blond head. "Rarely. We're more into charms, curses, potions and spells. Runes are more archaic."

"You look worried," Raven pointed out.

"I'm worried that someone is determined to make Darren's death seem ritual in origin," Bay said. "I don't think that's ever a good thing."

I could agree with her there. "So ... what do you suggest we do?"

"Find out the meanings of the other runes," she answered simply. "There's meaning to the drawings themselves, and meaning to the order. I'm sure of it."

I tugged my phone from my pocket and started snapping photographs. "I'm guessing we'll need these for our research."

Bay smiled. "Does that mean we're researching together?"

"Even though your boyfriend will probably hate it, I think we'll move faster if we share knowledge."

"I agree." Bay was relaxed when she fell into step with me for the walk back to the fairgrounds. "You don't have to worry about Landon," she offered after a moment, calm. "He's mostly talk. He's a worrier by nature, and he doesn't fully understand our world."

That was something we had in common. "Kade is the same way, but he's keen to learn." That was mostly true ... other than the fear he was constantly living with, of course. "How did you and Landon hook up?"

"It was on a case," she replied, her lips curving at the memory. "He was undercover with a bunch of meth-selling bikers. I thought he was a jerk. He thought there was a chance I was a murderer because he kept catching me sneaking into a corn maze so I could investigate after a dead body was found strung up in the center of things."

"It sounds like a match made in heaven," I teased.

"We worked things out." She was serene as we picked our way through the dense foliage. "We have a bit of a problem," she said after a moment. "By 'we,' I mean your group and my group as a whole. You don't fully trust us, and we don't fully trust you. It's going to make for strange bedfellows."

"Yeah, well, I don't see a way around that, do you?"

She shook her head. "Aunt Tillie senses your power."

"I sensed her power, too."

"She's ... the suspicious sort." Bay snickered to herself, clearly enjoying whatever thought flitted through her mind. "She's not a bad person, mind you. She's merely set in her ways."

"Anyone worth their salt is set in their ways," Raven said as we escaped the trees. "I have work to do at the House of Mirrors. I'm assuming you can do your rune research without me."

I nodded. "Thanks for serving as backup earlier."

"We served as backup for each other," Raven said, her eyes sliding to Bay. "You're not going to attack Poet, are you?"

Bay snickered. "I'm not. You don't have to worry about your friend."

"Oh, she's not my friend." Raven was calm. "She drives me crazy. I simply don't want her to die. She's part of our foursome."

Bay pursed her lips, suddenly intrigued. "That's right. There were four of you erecting the dreamcatcher. You don't call to the four corners, but you do use magic designed to be issued in fours."

I'd never really considered that. "Do you think it's important?"

Bay shrugged. "I honestly don't know," she said after a beat. "There were four eyes, and I find that interesting. You work magic in fours.."

"You mostly work in threes, though," I argued. "It's you, Clove and Thistle."

"Not for the big spells. For the big spells, we add Aunt Tillie into the mix."

"So, you work in fours, too."

"We do," she agreed. "I don't know that it's important. I do find it interesting."

We lapsed into amiable silence for a beat, both of us considering our options. Finally, I was the first to break it. "So ... what do we do?"

"Find the meaning of the runes. It's the only thing we can do."

"I don't suppose you have any rune books?"

"Not really," she admitted. "Thistle and Clove might."

"Before we head over there, I have a few books we might be able to check in my trailer." I pointed toward the home I shared with Kade. "Come on. We might be able to find something in there."

. . .

INSTEAD OF COMMENTING ON our limited space, Bay let loose a low whistle as we entered the trailer.

"This is kind of nice, huh?"

I smiled at her reaction. "It's probably not as nice as your house, but it's home to us. We like it."

"I live in the guesthouse on my mother's property," Bay explained. "Clove, Thistle and I used to live together, but we've been changing up living arrangements of late."

That sounded intriguing. "Why?"

"Clove is getting married and moved in with her fiancé. They live in a lighthouse."

I'd seen glimpses of the lighthouse through the trees when we'd arrived. "I've always thought it would be cool to live in a lighthouse."

Bay chuckled. "Me, too. Clove has worked hard to fix up the Dandridge with Sam — he's her fiancé — and it's a lovely space."

"And she's not far from you," I pointed out. "You're still in the same town."

"We are," she nodded.

"What about Thistle?" I found I was curious about their family dynamics. I couldn't help myself. They seemed extremely attached to one another, something I wasn't used to when it came to a genetically linked family. I loved the family of my choosing, but she loved the family she was born into. They were different worlds, and yet seemingly similar.

"Thistle lives with her boyfriend Marcus. He converted one of the downtown barns into a house. It's ... great. I wouldn't have thought a barn could be that great. It's perfect, and Thistle is a nonconformist, so she works well with the odd space."

I thought back to the first day we landed in town, to when we saw Thistle crossing the street and entering the stables. Now it made sense. "So ... you live by yourself now," I mused. "Is that considered a weakening of your power base?"

"I live with Landon," she corrected. "He moved in with me when the others left. It's been a learning experience."

"How is it that he can be stationed in such a small town? I would think the FBI wouldn't allow that."

"They didn't at the beginning," Bay agreed as she accepted the book I handed her and started flipping through it. "He commuted for more than a year, and then earned a promotion that allowed him to make demands on where we lived. I would've moved to Traverse City if it came to it, but he didn't want that."

"Because he loves your family as much as you do," I surmised, thoughtful. "You live in a family that's made up of people you were born to and others who you chose. I don't like to think about the family I was born into because it's painful. I love the family I chose, though."

"I guess I never really thought about it," Bay mused. "You're constantly on the road. I'm guessing that means most of the people in your unit don't have a home base."

"No," I agreed. "We've made our home together. You were born into your family, and yet you add on to it. Landon ... Terry. They are your family."

"They are." Bay smiled. "I would miss them more than some of my actual blood relatives."

I couldn't help but smile. "Yes, well, Tillie is clearly an acquired taste."

"That's putting it mildly." Bay's eyes moved to the next page in the book before stilling. "Huh. Look at this."

Conversation of family fell by the wayside as I leaned over to stare at the symbols. "Those were on the trees," I said excitedly.

"I know." Bay read the block of text beneath the symbols. "Gnomes. Sylphs. Salamanders. Undines."

I ran the words through my head. "Sylphs are butterflies."

She nodded. "You know your stuff."

"You'd be surprised the weird things I have to know in this world. How else would I know what undines are?"

"They're water nymphs," Bay said. "I know it, too. I've never seen one in person or anything, but I know what they are."

My eyes automatically traveled to the window, which faced the food area. There, Nixie and Naida chatted to themselves, seemingly without a care in the world. "Do you think water nymphs are important to what we're facing?"

Bay shrugged. "I don't know. I'm more interested in the fact that we have another foursome attached to the corners."

I jerked up my head, surprised. "What do you mean?"

"Gnomes are for earth. Sylphs for air. Salamanders for fire."

"Undines for water," I finished, realization washing over me. "I'm starting to think you're right about this four corners business."

"In the immortal words of Aunt Tillie, I'm always right."

"What does it mean? Why is it important?"

"That, I can't answer." Bay dragged a hand through her flaxen hair. "I don't know why it's happening now, or why. I don't know who is doing it. All I can say with absolute certainty is that we're dealing with someone — or multiple someones — who plan on utilizing the four corners. That's all I know."

"That is ... not a lot to go on."

Her smile was rueful. "You're telling me."

13

THIRTEEN

Bay stayed through lunch, and she seemed to enjoy herself. Nellie was in full "I'm going to make you laugh or else" mode, and he was keen to ask her questions about Tillie.

"Is she single?"

If Bay found the question odd she didn't show it. "She has a beau of sorts, although he's extremely intermittent. She only goes to him when she has a particularly annoying task she's about to embark on and knows the rest of us will shoot her down if she tries to include us."

Never one to be dissuaded, Nellie kept peppering her with questions.

"I heard she was married," he pressed. "She didn't have any children of her own?"

Bay shook her head. "She helped raise my mother and aunts. I think she was fine with that. In the end, she had to take them full time ... although Marnie and Mom were mostly grown. She likes to boss people around and was fine being the favorite aunt."

"You spent a lot of time with her as kids, right?" I popped a fresh blueberry in my mouth as Kade settled next to me. He seemed intrigued by Bay's presence, but he was the protective sort and wanted to make sure he served as a barrier should she try to attack. I didn't foresee that happening, but Kade wasn't the type to lower his guard until he was absolutely sure.

"We did." Bay smiled as she forked a chunk of watermelon. "She enjoyed making us her sidekicks. I used to think my mother was nuts letting that woman be in charge, but now I see there was a method to her madness."

"And what was the method?" Raven asked.

"We didn't always play well with others," Bay explained. "We were unusually close to one another, but that turned off many kids our age. We were ... targets, I guess would be the right word. Aunt Tillie taught us how to deal with our enemies and stand up for ourselves."

"She sounds awesome," Luke noted, adopting a far-off expression. "My grandmother was a mean old biddy who threatened me with silver bullets whenever I got into her knitting stuff. It sounds much more fun to have an Aunt Tillie."

Bay made an odd face at the mention of "silver bullets" but didn't comment. She was clearly figuring out the dynamics of our group — and quickly — but she wasn't interested in forcing us to reveal our secrets. I liked that about her.

"Aunt Tillie was ... a force to be reckoned with," Bay said. "It's hard to explain. For a time, I believed she didn't like us all that much because she was always complaining about having us with her. Now I realize that was simply her way. She likes to talk tough, but she's got a heart in there, buried deep down inside."

"You love her," I noted, smiling. "She's a pain in your backside, but you love her."

"I love her," Bay agreed. "That doesn't mean I'm not looking for the occasional circus to adopt her."

Nellie bobbed his head. "We're totally on board for that. Send her our way."

"I think you should ask Max about that," I supplied. "He might have something to say about bringing a powerful and bossy witch into our midst."

"Who is Max?" Bay asked.

"He's our ... leader," I replied after a beat. "He owns the circus."

"And he clearly knows that you do more than perform," Bay mused, thoughtful. "I kind of like your setup. I always thought I wanted to travel when I was younger. Then I moved down to Detroit for a few years and realized I really wanted to be here."

"I can see wanting to be here." I meant it. "Your family is here, it's quiet. You get to be witches in public."

"Oh, don't kid yourself about that." She made a tsking sound with her tongue and I didn't miss the dark look she shot toward the unicorn store. "Even in a town full of witches we're not allowed to be ourselves. It's okay. There are whispers. Everyone talks about us. Very few people know the truth."

"And you're okay with that?" Melissa asked, speaking for the first time. She'd spent the entire lunch period watching Bay with a curious expression I couldn't quite identify. "I mean ... it doesn't bother you to have to hide who you are?"

Bay smiled at the young woman, perhaps sensing her angst. "I'm happy with who I am ... for the most part. Life is never easy. It doesn't matter if you think you have everything you could possibly need, you'll still have problems.

"What matters is what you believe about yourself," she continued. "I happen to think I've got it pretty good. I have cousins who I think of as sisters, a mother and aunts who cook for me all the time, my real father and the surrogate father who has never once let me down, and a boyfriend who — yes, may have a bit of a thing about bacon — but otherwise is pretty darned appealing.

"You can't craft the perfect life," she added. "You can live life to the best of your ability. That's what I'm doing. It's not easy ... or perfect. It's never going to be easy or perfect, but it's the life I want."

"Oh, that was profound," Raven drawled.

Instead of being offended by her tone, Bay chuckled. "I think you should spend time with Thistle. One of you might die in the process due to acute snark intoxication, but I bet it would be a funny interaction."

"I think I'll pass."

. . .

BAY LEFT AFTER LUNCH. She had work of her own to do and said she wanted to run the runes by her family members. She promised to be in touch.

We weren't yet open, so I had a gap in my schedule. I spent it with Luke and Melissa outside the ice cream shop.

"This is called Candy Cauldron Calamity," Luke noted as he licked his cone. "It's freaking awesome." The ice cream was green, and so was his tongue. He didn't seem to care, so I didn't comment. Melissa was lost in thought.

"What's up with you?" I asked, flicking her ear as I licked my cone. I opted for the Peachy Keen Potion flavor and wasn't disappointed. "You've been quiet all afternoon." In truth, she'd been quiet for weeks. I thought she would snap out of her funk on her own, but I was starting to wonder if she wouldn't need a bit of a push. I was already dealing with Kade and his issues, so I wasn't sure I had time to force Melissa to move forward instead of continuously looking back.

"I was just thinking about what Bay said," Melissa admitted, her tongue a funny shade of lavender thanks to her Wicked Blue Brew cone. "Do you think people are happier on the road or settled?"

I wasn't expecting the question, but in hindsight, I should've been. "I don't know. I think I am settled. It's simply in a home we move on a weekly basis."

"That's how I look at it," Luke added. "I like moving around, seeing different things."

"I thought that's what I wanted," Melissa offered. "Now I'm not so sure."

The revelation caused my heart to ping. I'd grown attached to the girl rather quickly — which was often a mistake in this business because only certain personality types could adjust to the circus life — and if she opted to leave I would genuinely miss her. If that's what she needed, though, I would willingly let her go.

"Don't make any rash decisions," I cautioned, choosing my words carefully. "Just a few months ago you were keen for the life we're living."

"Yes, but that was before ... well, before."

"Before you were turned into a human Chucky doll and forced to attack us?" Luke asked.

I scorched him with a dark look. "Luke!"

He ignored me. "That wasn't your fault, Melissa," he continued. "Sure, you made some bad decisions, but we all do. I think your problem is that you're embarrassed. You need to get past it. You don't see me wallowing about that pesky little gambling problem I had, do you?"

Melissa slowly shook her head. "I don't think it's the same."

"No? I brought danger to my friends. Poet could've been hurt multiple times during the course of our stay there. She saved me ... and put herself at risk to do it. She did the same for you."

"You all did the same for me," Melissa corrected. "You all could've died."

"And there will be times we'll be able to say the same for you when it comes to other members of this team." Luke was rarely pragmatic, which made his tone all the more noticeable. "Don't shut us out. That won't help anyone. Tell us what you're feeling and we'll try to help. That's how a family operates. Even Bay, who clearly has a crazy family, pretty much said the same thing."

"I don't know how I feel. That's the problem."

"So wait until you do know." Luke finished his ice cream cone and dumped the wrapper before wiping off his hands and pointing toward the bus. "Come on. They're going on a tour and I want to see what this town has to offer."

I was surprised by the conversational shift. "We're going on a bus tour?"

"That's the only way to see everything."

"I ... ." Hmm. Why not? He was right about seeing everything. We could've driven around on our own, but Margaret was on the bus and she would be able to point out important landmarks. "That sounds like a good idea." I patted Melissa's shoulder. "Come on. You're still part of this group. It might do you some good to focus on something other than yourself."

Melissa heaved out a sigh. "Fine. I never thought I'd be excited for a bus tour, though."

That made two of us.

THE BUS WAS PACKED, but there was room for us to join the tour without upending anyone's seating arrangements. Margaret seemed thrilled with the notion that we wanted to drink from her Hemlock Cove fountain. We picked seats toward the middle of the bus so we could hear her, but not so close that we'd make enticing conversation targets.

I recognized several faces on the bus, including the teenagers Landon and Terry had been looking for earlier in the day. They had sour expressions on their faces as they shared a seat and bent their heads together. I wondered if Landon found them, but it didn't take long for me to suss out an answer.

"I think it's complete and total crap," Lizzy complained, looking out the window. "It's none of their business the spells we want to do."

"They're just doing their jobs," Kaley argued. "They probably guessed we're strong witches and didn't want to risk us doing something that could blow up the entire town."

"We weren't going to blow up the town. We knew what we were doing."

"Yes, but they didn't know that."

"It was still stupid." Lizzy folded her arms over her chest and stared out the window. "I thought this trip was going to be so much more fun. It's like we're surrounded by fifty parents. Who wants that? Now we're going to have to start all over again."

Luke, who had opted to sit in the seat across from me so Melissa wouldn't be alone, shot me an amused look as he watched the foliage stream by. At the front of the bus, Margaret kept up a running commentary.

"This right here is The Overlook," she announced, wrinkling her nose.

I recognized the name and moved closer to the window, smiling at the beautiful inn as we slowed to allow everyone a better look. The property was littered with trees — and a rather impressive bluff as a backdrop — and part of me ached to get out and visit that bluff. There was power there, I could feel it, and it called to me. Now wasn't the time for an unscheduled stop, though.

"I hear they have the best food in the area," a voice piped up from behind us. When I shifted to glance over my shoulder, I recognized one of the women from the game Luke and I played. It took me a moment to put a name with the face. Emily Wilde. That was her name. She didn't seem happy to be on the tour, although mention of food perked her up.

"I've never eaten at The Overlook," Margaret said stiffly. It was obviously difficult for her to hold her tongue. Her dislike of the Winchesters was obvious. As a festival bigwig, though, talking smack about business owners would be frowned upon. She was clearly struggling between her natural instincts and duty.

"But ... I heard they have dinner theater every night," another woman offered, her attention rapt on the inn. "Supposedly they have a great witch who lives there and puts on a nightly show."

I could just imagine the nightly show that Tillie put on. She probably got a charge out of messing with the guests. It made me wonder if I should take Bay up on her offer to have dinner with the family one evening. It might be worth it for the laughs alone.

"Yes, well, if you are the type who likes dinner theater then The Overlook is probably the place for you to visit," Margaret said stiffly. "Personally, I prefer polite conversation rather than arguments. It's better for digestion."

"I like arguments," the woman said, clearly missing Margaret's annoyance. "We tried to stay at The Overlook, but it was already booked. I was so bummed out. That place is legendary."

"I heard they have a pot field right on the grounds," one woman offered.

"I heard they dance naked under the solstice moons," another said.

"I heard the great-aunt curses everyone in the family to keep them in line," yet another voice added.

I couldn't stop myself from smiling as my gaze fell on the pretty greenhouse at the back of the property. It really was a lovely place. I never considered myself the sort to settle down, but I could see why Bay yearned to return after leaving home. She was rooted here, even though she didn't initially realize it. Everything she needed was in one place, and that included companionship and love.

I couldn't accept the quiet of Hemlock Cove forever, but it was certainly a nice place to visit.

"I don't want to spend the entire tour talking about The Overlook," Margaret complained, her eyes flashing. "The town is full of beautiful inns and wonderful people. I ... ." Whatever she was about to say died on her lips because there was a scuffle at the front of the bus as people jumped to their feet to better see out the window.

Curious despite myself, I slowly stood. Melissa, who had the seat next to me, was also on her feet.

"What's going on?" she asked, her eyes widening as a ripple of power flicked over the bus. "What is that?"

I had a feeling I already knew, and when I tilted my head to the side for a better look over the shoulder of the woman standing in front of me I wasn't disappointed.

There, in the center of the road, stood Tillie. She wore a different pair of leggings today. I was too far away to see the pattern, but I had a feeling they were selected to provide maximum outrage. Her combat helmet was firmly in place, although she was sans whistle. She also — wisely — opted to visit unarmed today.

"What is she doing?" Luke asked, squinting as Tillie extended her arm toward the bus and started making slashing motions with her fingers.

"She's casting a spell on us," someone screeched from the front of the bus. "Oh, man, she's totally going to curse us. This is awesome!"

"She most certainly is not going to curse us," Margaret snapped. "Just ignore her. She's out here looking for attention."

Her voice was largely drowned out by the excited tourists.

"Go," Margaret shouted, slapping the driver on the shoulder. "Get out of here. We can't stay behind and encourage Tillie's ... madness."

"I'm going," the bus driver groused, turning the wheel as far as he could to avoid hitting the elderly woman in the street. "Don't crowd me," he barked at Margaret. "This is a hairy turn."

I pressed my lips together to keep from laughing as the bus slowly eased past Tillie, who was still drawing symbols in the air. Because I was magical, I could see the trail of power she left behind, and it took everything I had not to dissolve into giggles.

Because she also was magical, Melissa recognized the bright power trails, too. "She's drawing emoticons."

I nodded. "Yes. Smiley faces ... weepy faces ... even a turd with a face."

"Oh, I love a turd with a face," Luke commented, grinning. He kept his hands on the front and back of the seat as he stared out the side window and winked at Tillie as we passed. Even though it was quick, I was certain she returned the wink. "I'm starting to see Nellie's infatuation with her. She's all kinds of awesome. I want to adopt her."

I opened my mouth to comment about how fond of her I was becoming when I noticed Margaret had sidled down the center aisle and was standing close to us. The look on her face was murderous.

"I'm really enjoying the tour," I said finally. I had no idea what else to say. "Where are we going next?"

Margaret scowled. "You have no idea how much I hate that woman."

Oh, I had an idea. I also didn't doubt that the feeling was mutual, which was why Tillie remained in the middle of the road drawing emoticons with her finger.

"Well ... at least she's entertaining," I offered.

"I'll make her pay."

Something told me that it would be the other way around, but I kept my mouth shut.

14

FOURTEEN

I walked through the fairgrounds before dinner. As Max's second in command, it was my job to make sure everything was up and running. Our workers — even the irregular ones who dressed as clowns and ran the midway — knew what they were doing.

Things looked good, which was one less thing to worry about.

Despite the invitation to The Overlook, we opted to eat dinner as we normally would. There were several things I wanted to discuss with everyone, and that would be impossible in front of an audience.

"I hear you went on a tour this afternoon," Max said as he joined us. It was rare for him to eat dinner with us during the week — he preferred dining alone in his trailer — so my antenna was up.

"We did," I confirmed, handing the platter of corn ears to Kade before settling in the spot between Luke and him. "It was ... interesting."

"I think you mean hilarious," Luke corrected. He was still wound up from the afternoon tour, and he was talking the ears off anyone who would listen about the things we saw. "I want to adopt that old Winchester witch."

"Hey!" Nellie extended a warning finger. "Who are you calling old?

She's in her prime. If she was a dwarf she'd still be cranking out babies."

That was a frightening thought. "She's not a dwarf," I reminded him. "She is, however, massively entertaining."

Luke didn't give me a chance to continue, instead launching into a reenactment of what we'd seen on the road in front of The Overlook. Even though she was present for the event, Melissa giggled like a schoolgirl, which was nice to see.

"And you're sure she was drawing emoticons?" Raven asked, knitting her eyebrows. "That's ... weird."

"I'm sure," I confirmed. "She left a small trail of magic behind as she did it. Only paranormals would've seen what she was doing. She was clearly having a good time."

"What's an emoticon?" Max asked, confused.

I elbowed Kade. "You're on."

He made a face. "Why me?"

"Because he's your father and I don't know how to explain it."

Kade moved his mouth, but no sound came out. Thankfully, Nixie swooped in — phone in hand — and demonstrated. When she was done, Max roared with laughter.

"Okay, that's some funny stuff," he said as he swiped the tears from his cheeks. "I kind of want to adopt her, too."

Nellie brightened considerably. "I'll ask her."

I shot him a look. "She has a family here. She won't want to leave them."

"She has a boring family here," he stressed. "They're nowhere near as much fun as we are."

I wasn't so sure that was true. "She's not going to leave them." I was firm. "I don't see why she can't hang out with us a bit during the festival, though. She's probably a lot of fun when there's a crowd to mess with."

"I can't wait to meet her." Max's grin was easy, but I didn't miss the furtive look he shot Kade, as if gauging his mood. Something was definitely up. "What else did you see?"

"Well, it was mostly a tour of various inns," I replied, spearing a steak from the platter at the center of the table and transferring it to my plate. "I have a feeling they envisioned it as free advertising, but I did learn a few things.

"First, they have a place called Hollow Creek," I continued. "I think it's where Naida went the other night."

"It is." Naida nodded, solemn. "There's magic fragments flying everywhere."

"There is," I agreed. "We were allowed out at the creek. It's beautiful ... and peaceful ... and some very dark things have gone on there. I walked through at least three memory echoes while I was there, and all of them featured the Winchesters."

"That's interesting." Max was sober as he considered the statement. "Do you think they conduct rituals there?"

That was an interesting question. "No," I said finally. "I think they've been down there several times when things went wrong, but I don't think they're conducting rituals in that particular location. That's what they're doing on the bluff behind their inn."

"How do you know that?" Raven asked, intrigued. "Did you see them doing something?"

I shook my head. "The bluff is toward the back of their property. It's beautiful, but I could feel the power emanating from the space. The whole plot is magical, don't get me wrong, and there are memory echoes flying over it left and right. The bluff, though, is the source of their real power."

"Or it's simply the place where they've anchored their power," Max suggested. "From what you've told me, I tend to think they're born witches, so the magic is tied to their blood. If it's gone on for generations, they would need a place to serve as the heart of their realm. I'm guessing that's the bluff."

"Me, too. I want to head out there later and take a look."

"Really?" Max's eyebrows hopped. "Were you invited?"

"Not technically," I hedged, uncomfortable. I stared at my plate so I wouldn't have to meet Max's steady gaze.

"What did they 'technically' say?"

"They want us to come for dinner."

Nellie was incensed. "Then why are we eating here? We should be out there with them."

I shot him a quelling look. "We didn't set up an official time. I'm sure we'll manage it before we leave."

Nellie grumbled something under his breath that I couldn't make out.

"I don't understand why you want to go out there," Max persisted. "That seems invasive."

I couldn't deny that. I was big on people deserving their personal space. I was also drawn to the plot of land, and that natural curiosity was stronger than my ethical boundaries. "It's a full moon tonight."

"So?"

"So ... people on the bus said they dance naked under the full moon."

Nellie's mouth dropped open. "Are kidding me? I'm going with you!"

The fact that he was mostly interested because people were going to be naked made me leery, but I opted to tell myself that he was genuinely interested in the magic, too. It made me feel better to embrace the lie.

"Are you saying you want to watch the witches dance naked?" Raven asked. "If so, you're a lot more interesting than I thought. That's a little perv-y. I didn't know you rolled that way."

"Hey, I'm gay and I want to see it, too," Luke admitted. "I can't help it. I find them fascinating. That old one is the funniest thing I've ever seen. If you look up the word 'eccentric' in the dictionary, I'm convinced you'll find her photo."

"And I was convinced her photo was by the word 'nuts,'" Raven drawled.

"Honestly, I think she's fine with either description," I admitted. "She seems to embrace being odd. Also, she knew we were on the bus, even though I'm not convinced she could see us through the windows."

"How did she know?" Max asked.

I shrugged. "Maybe she senses me like I sense her ... and like I sense Bay."

"Yeah, well, Bay is another matter entirely," Raven said. "While we were with her in the woods today I tried to climb into her head. Do you know what I found?"

I knew exactly what she found. "A wall of bacon."

Max choked on his bite of steak. "I'm sorry, ... what?"

"That's how she shields," I explained. "I managed to see a thing or two, mostly surface thoughts, but there came a time when I was certain she knew I was poking around in her head. The next thing I knew, all I could think about is bacon. It was ridiculous."

"Landon is obsessed with bacon," Raven noted. "That's all that was in his head. Well, little tidbits about the case and a bunch of fuzzy feelings for Bay. Bacon is his go-to image. Have we considered that he's magical? If he can shield that well, it's a possibility."

I gave it some serious thought. "No," I said finally, shaking my head. "He understands about magic, at least to a certain degree. But he's not magical. He's just a man ... who happens to love his witch very much."

"Then Bay has taught him how to shield," Raven said. "I've never met a human with such strong defenses who wasn't trained."

"She may have, but I don't think they deal with mind readers very often," I countered. "I think he's simply a guy who thinks about three things at any given time. His work, Bay and bacon. Those are the most important things to him."

Max chuckled. "I've never met anyone that obsessed with bacon."

Kade raised his hand. "Hey, if you dug in my head you'd probably find bacon there, too."

"Who doesn't love bacon?" Nellie agreed. "It's like ... the best thing ever."

I loved breakfast foods as much as the next person, but that sounded odd. "That must be a guy thing," I said after a beat. "It's not normal."

"I'm a man and I don't think about bacon constantly," Max argued.

"No, but you think about pickled okra more than anyone I've ever met."

He smirked. "Have you been poking around in my head?"

"You project it half the time."

"Fair enough." Max stroked his chin, thoughtful. "We've weaved off course a bit. What do you think you're going to find at this bluff tonight? What do you hope to accomplish?"

"I don't know." That was true. "I just have an overwhelming urge to head out there. I can't explain it."

"Maybe the old witch planted the suggestion," Raven said.

"Maybe. I want to see what they're doing, and I think it has to be tonight."

Max let loose a resigned sigh. "Okay. It's up to you. I'm not sure it's a good idea, but this is your thing and I've learned that ignoring your instincts is a bad idea. Have at it."

"Great." I beamed before sawing into my steak. Something occurred to me that ultimately soured some of my expectations. "You don't think they'll be, like, totally naked, do you?"

"I hope so." Nellie's eyes gleamed. "It'll be the best night ever if they are."

I wasn't sure I agreed with that particular sentiment.

KADE WAS QUIET THROUGH dinner, and when he caught me outside of our trailer there was trouble in his eyes.

"I don't think this is a good idea," he said. "What if they catch us and don't take kindly to being spied on?"

That was a fair worry. "I guess we'll find out what sort of power they really have."

"And that doesn't bother you?"

"No." I opted for honesty. "I think they're good witches. I know that's hard for you to wrap your head around because we've only had dealings with bad witches for the most part, but if there was something evil afoot I would feel it."

"People have bamboozled you before," he persisted. "You have great instincts, but you're not infallible."

It stung to hear, but he wasn't wrong. "You don't have to go. In fact, I think you'll be more comfortable staying behind."

A flash of something — maybe hurt, maybe annoyance — flitted across his handsome features. "You don't want me to go?"

"I don't want you to go if you're not into it," I clarified. "I love hanging out with you, going on adventures and stakeouts, but ... you don't always have to agree to do something simply because I'm going to do it. That doesn't seem healthy."

"What if you get in trouble?"

"Well ... then there will be a fight. I don't think it will be a big deal, though. They're powerful. There's no getting around that. We're powerful, too."

"I guess." He made an annoyed sound in the back of his throat as he stroked his chin. "I'm uncomfortable spying on them, especially if they're going to be naked."

I patted his arm, amused. "I can't tell you how relieved I am that you don't want to see other women naked."

"I don't mind the thought of the younger three, but the older one? Um ... no."

My smile slipped. "I see."

Now it was his turn to flash a mischievous smile. "I'm mostly interested in seeing you naked. Why not stay and spend some quality time with me?"

He was so earnest he had me considering the offer. Then Max swooped in to interrupt us, and things took a surprising turn.

"You'll be spending quality time with me tonight, Kade," Max volunteered, his expression unreadable. "Poet can't be part of that — at least not yet — so it's probably best that she's going to lead the charge to spy on the witches."

"I can't be a part of what?" I asked, instantly alert. He was finally making his reason for attending dinner known, and I was willing to chuck all previous urges in an attempt to stand with Kade. "What do you have planned?"

Max's sigh was long and drawn out as he regarded me. "There's no reason to get upset, Poet." He was calm. "Kade and I need to talk about a few things, and then we're going to practice his magic."

I was surprised by the turn of events. "You're going to practice his magic?" The way Kade's body stiffened next to mine told me that's the last thing he wanted to do. "Are you sure this is the right time?"

"I'm sure that we'll have a quiet night to practice and the privacy of the woods to do it," Max clarified.

"But ... ."

He shook his head to cut me off and focused on his son. "You've been quiet since Eureka. I've allowed it because I knew you had to think about things. You get that from your mother. You're a ponderer.

"It's time, though," he continued. "You can't hope to master your magic, use it as a weapon, unless you learn about your abilities. What happened in Eureka was born of necessity. You care deeply for Poet and want to keep her safe. Now you need to learn to use your powers for reasons other than terror."

Kade immediately started shaking his head. "I don't even know if I want to use my magic. I haven't decided yet."

"You don't have a choice." Max was firm. "You need to explore your birthright. I wasn't sure you had magic until the moment you let it loose. Now it's a reality. We have to deal with it."

"But ... ." Kade looked to me for help.

"Maybe he's not ready to deal with it yet," I said gently. "Maybe he needs more time."

Max slid me a sympathetic look. "You want to be with him when he goes through this, and you will be later. Kade won't truly try if you're around. His fear that he'll hurt you is too great. He needs to get past that."

"I would feel better if Poet was with me," Kade argued. "She's my ... anchor. That's what you called it, right? You said the Winchesters anchored their magic in a place. Well, she's my anchor."

"She's your heart," Max corrected, refusing to let the sentiment sway him. "You feel a great deal for her — I do, too — but you can't make her your excuse. You need to practice, and to do that, you have to be willing to let go. As long as Poet is close, you won't do that."

Kade ran his tongue over his teeth as he glanced around. It was only then that I realized how torn he truly was. I made up my mind on the spot.

"You need to do this," I said gently, grabbing his hand and giving it a good squeeze. "We both know it. You didn't sleep for the better part of two weeks because you were terrified you'd hurt me. Max is the best person to teach you how to use your powers."

"Why can't you teach me?" Kade was plaintive.

"I don't have the same type of magic ... and we're too emotionally linked." I ran my finger down his cheek. "It's going to be okay. He's your father. He wants the best for you. Besides, you're not going to want to perform on demand in front of an audience.

"Max is right," I continued. "I wondered why he was okay with us spying on the witches, but it makes sense. He'll be able to spend quality time with you while we're gone."

Kade didn't look convinced. "You're going to be stuck with a cross-dressing dwarf who is hot for an octogenarian."

I merely smiled. "Think of the stories we'll have to tell each other when we're reunited."

He still wasn't placated. "What if you're attacked and I'm not there?"

"We're not going to be attacked." I was sure of that. "We're supposed to see something out there. I know it. We'll both be okay. I promise you that."

Resigned, Kade merely pulled me close for a hug and focused on his father. "Fine. If something happens to her, though, I'm going to be really ticked off."

"I would expect nothing less," Max said.

"The same goes for me," I offered as Kade kissed my forehead.

Max chuckled. "You really are an adorable couple."

I agreed wholeheartedly.

15

FIFTEEN

Leaving Kade to practice magic with Max was difficult, but necessary. I waited until the two of them changed clothes and then met in front of the trailer a second time before departing.

"It's going to be okay," I reassured him, squeezing his hand. "Don't let this mess up your head. It's a good thing."

He cast me a sidelong look. "You're just eager to get me out of here so you can spy on the naked witches."

He wasn't wrong. Well, he was wrong about the naked part. I wasn't particularly looking forward to that. But I couldn't deny there was a shimmy of excitement running up my spine about the other stuff.

"I'll take video if I can, come back with a full report."

He absently ran his hand down the back of my head and pressed a kiss to my mouth before focusing his full attention on Max. "This isn't going to hurt, is it?"

Max's smile was benign. "No. It won't hurt. You'll be better for it."

Kade didn't look convinced, but he nodded and heaved a sigh. "Let's do it." He stepped in front of Max, leaving me to share a long look with my boss.

"Take care of him," I ordered.

"I will. You take care of the rest of them. Make sure Nellie doesn't run off with the elderly witch. That could be hard to explain."

"I think she can take care of herself."

"That's what I'm afraid of."

I smiled. "I don't know how long we'll be gone. It will probably be a few hours."

"Have fun ... and don't get arrested. I'm not sure I have enough cash on hand to lay bail for all of you."

"Then make sure you bail me out first."

"I don't think Kade would allow anything else."

OUR RAGTAG GROUP OF busybodies turned out to be smaller than I initially envisioned. Naida and Nixie were curious, but the water beckoned, and they ultimately headed off in their own direction.

Dolph and a few others remained to watch camp. It wasn't wise to empty of it every magical figure, so he opted to stay behind with a few shifters to watch our boundaries, for which I was thankful.

That left Luke, Raven, Nellie and Melissa to travel with me to the Winchester stronghold. Thanks to the smaller group, we could take one vehicle. Luke opted to drive, and he parked almost half a mile away from the driveway, which meant we had to hike through the woods. I would've preferred the getaway vehicle to be closer, but his approach was smart, so I wordlessly agreed.

We set off from the road, all of us dressed in dark clothes, carefully picking our way through the trees.

"There are no magical traps that I can see," Raven mused, her eyes impossible to read in the darkness.

"Did you expect death and destruction at every turn?" I asked.

She shrugged, noncommittal. "I don't know what I expected. You can feel magic ... and yet it's unobtrusive. It's ... interesting."

I couldn't argue with that, so I didn't.

We were in the woods almost fifteen minutes before we stumbled across what looked to be a small house. There was a side road we didn't notice upon our earlier visit – two vehicles parked in the driveway – but the windows were dark and it appeared empty.

"What's this?" Melissa asked, moving to my right.

"Let's go inside and see if my witch is in there," Nellie suggested, excited.

I immediately started shaking my head. "No way. That's someone's house." Something occurred to me. "That's Bay's house." I knew it without hesitation. "She mentioned she lived in the guesthouse on the property. This must be it."

"It's cute," Melissa said. "Not too big. Does she live out here alone?"

"She used to live with her cousins. Now she lives with Landon."

"Who is hot as Hecate," Melissa said. "Seriously, I'm not sure I've ever seen a guy that hot in real life."

I balked on Kade's behalf. "Um ... I think our chief of security is pretty hot."

"Yeah, but he's like a big brother to me. I can't look at him in that manner."

I could see that. "Well ... ."

Luke cleared his throat in such an obnoxious way there was no choice but to look in his direction. "I think you've forgotten about me," he said dryly.

Melissa giggled at his put-upon expression. "I think of you like a brother, too."

"A big, gay brother," Raven added.

I bristled. "It doesn't matter that he's gay. He's still hot."

"Thank you, Poet." Luke preened. "I *am* hot."

"You're also gay, and there's no chance of a romance coming to fruition," Raven pointed out. "I don't care that you're gay. I care that you're annoying, but that's another argument entirely. Melissa can't crush on you because there's no chance of you ever crushing back.

"She could crush on Kade because we all know he's going to get tired of Poet's crap before it's all said and done," she continued. "He might look at her ... after he's done drooling over me. But you're a lost cause."

Wait a second. "Kade isn't going to get tired of my crap. I mean ... I don't have any crap."

"Calm down, tiger." Luke's lips quirked, amusement evident. "Of course Kade isn't going to get tired of your crap. That would've happened long ago if it was going to be an issue."

"I don't have any crap," I repeated.

He snorted. "Right. You're perfectly normal and not at all obsessive or bossy."

I was fairly certain I'd just been insulted. "I'm done talking to you."

"Yeah, yeah, yeah." He made a dismissive hand motion. "Let's go back to talking about me."

"Let's not talk about any of you," Nellie shot back. "You're not important here. I want to find the lead witch. She's why we're here."

His obsession with Tillie was starting to get out of hand. "What is it with you and her?" I asked. "You know there's no hope of a romance, right?"

"I don't know that." Nellie wore a simple cotton skirt that fell to his ankles and a flannel shirt this evening. It was an odd combination ... even for him. "She might take one look at me and fall head over heels."

"Right," Raven drawled. "She's going to instantly fall in love with you and abandon her family. That makes perfect sense."

Nellie extended a warning finger. "I've had about enough of you."

"Oh, I'm shaking with fear," she taunted.

"Okay, we need to stop this." I stepped between them and held up my hands. "We're close, which means we can't be loud if we hope to escape discovery. You two need to call a truce, perhaps agree to disagree."

"Or we can simply make a date to argue when we get back to the fairgrounds," Raven suggested.

Nellie bobbed his head. "Sounds good to me, sister. I've got my ax back there anyway."

"Ugh." I tossed derisive looks in both their directions before pointing toward a well-worn pathway on the other side of the guesthouse. "I'm betting that leads to where we need to go."

Raven glared a bit longer at Nellie before nodding. "Let's get this over with. I'm warning you right now, though, if those witches aren't doing anything entertaining I'm totally blaming you."

WE STUCK TO THE PATH for the rest of the trip, ceasing all conversation. This was hardly the first covert mission we'd been on together. We knew what we were doing.

We didn't have to wait long. The sound of voices assailed our ears before we saw a hint of movement. Sure enough, there were multiple bodies on the bluff, and I pressed a finger to my lips as a form of warning as I crouched behind a patch of bushes.

"Oh, do you think we should be quiet?" Raven hissed, her eyes flashing.

I ignored the sarcasm and focused on the scene in front of us.

A large bonfire crackled in the center of a circle, illuminating a set of huge rocks. I saw runes carved into the rocks, but I was too far away to make out the symbols.

The bluff was filled with bodies, three middle-aged witches sitting on a blanket and drinking wine as they cackled about something they found entertaining. Closest to us, I recognized Bay's blond head as she sat on another blanket. I wasn't surprised to see her. The man who sat next to her, though, absolutely stunned me.

Landon was dressed in simple cargo shorts and a T-shirt. He reclined on his elbows as he watched Tillie skip around the circle. He seemed relaxed, his smile easy and always accessible for Bay as she kept up a steady stream of conversation. At first, I thought she was admonishing him. It became obvious relatively quickly, however, that she was merely telling him about her day.

"I think the runes are important," she finished. "I don't know how to track who made them. I need time to think."

Landon absently nodded as he watched Tillie (who was thankfully dressed). I saw sparks darting off her fingertips, but I wasn't sure he could. He was a normal human, after all. Magic should've been a mystery to him.

"You'll figure it out, sweetie," he said, grinning when Tillie almost tripped over an exposed tree root and had to struggle to maintain her footing. "Don't trip, Aunt Tillie," he admonished. "It will make the dancing harder if you have a head injury affecting your balance."

The look Tillie shot him was withering. "Why are you even here? You've never celebrated the full moon with us."

"That's not true. I love celebrating the full moon."

"You just like looking at your future mother-in-law naked," Tillie shot back.

Landon blanched but held strong. "I don't care what you say, you're not getting rid of me. I'm here to spend time with Bay. You can keep doing whatever it is that you're doing. I won't interfere."

"You always interfere," Tillie snapped.

"Aunt Tillie, focus on your circle," Bay ordered, weariness weaving through her voice. "If you spend all your time worrying about Landon, your tribute to the four corners will be weak."

"You could always help instead of telling me what I'm doing wrong," Tillie suggested.

Instead of answering, Bay rolled so she could rest her head on Landon's shoulder. "This was your cockamamie idea. I'm here to serve as babysitter for the evening to make sure the four of you don't get out of control. The last time we did this, Twila got lost in the woods and we didn't find her for two days."

One of the middle-aged witches, the one with flame-red hair and an indignant expression, lifted her chin and glared. "I was not lost. I was communing with nature."

"You were naked and grinding against a tree," Bay muttered, causing Landon's chest to shake with silent laughter. "You called the tree Sid and said you were going to marry it. You wanted to know if you would have trouble securing a marriage license."

"I still maintain that was a good idea," Twila argued. "A tree can't leave the toilet seat up or refuse to stop shaking you until you supply bacon for a midnight snack."

"I did that once," Landon complained. "I'd just finished saving

Bay's life from a murderous poltergeist, if I remember correctly. I earned that bacon."

Bay rolled her eyes. "Who saved whose life?"

Landon grinned as he kissed her cheek. "I think we saved each other. That's the way I remember it anyway."

"You're lucky you're cute," she muttered, shaking her head.

"That's what I say about you at least once a month."

"Yeah, yeah, yeah."

They sank into a kiss, completely wrapped up in each other. It was so sweet it nudged a sigh from my right. When I looked, I thought I would find Melissa making the noise. Instead, I realized it was Raven.

"What?" she whispered, annoyed at being caught. "They're straight out of a Disney cartoon. What do you want from me?"

I bit the inside of my cheek to keep from laughing as I turned back to Tillie. The magic sparking from her fingertips was interesting. She sang out the occasional spell as she uncorked her powers, and it became clear relatively quickly that she was warding the area. It wasn't completely different from the ceremony we participated in whenever we erected the dreamcatcher, but it wasn't the same either.

"That's an interesting protection ward," I murmured as a green arc lit the sky. "I didn't even know it was possible to conjure something like that."

"She's good," Raven agreed, pursing her lips. "She's giving me ideas for things we can do with the dreamcatcher."

We watched for a good ten minutes, absorbing the atmosphere and trying to get a feel for the players. In short order, we managed to identify Winnie and Marnie on the blanket. They seemed to be happy for the time being with their wine – which I assumed would help contribute to the naked dancing at some point – and they laughed as they told stories.

Across the way, Bay and Landon focused on each other. They seemed to be present in a supervisory capacity, but they had their own bottle of wine as they stared into each other's eyes and murmured.

Only Tillie was in constant motion. She was almost a blur at times, despite her age. Her fingers danced, the magic fired, and her bare feet deftly hopped a circle around the bonfire. Her movements were mesmerizing, until they suddenly stopped and she turned her eyes in our direction.

I froze when I realized she was staring directly at us, the hair on the back of my neck standing on end.

"Uh-oh," Luke muttered under his breath.

"There really is no reason to keep hiding over there," Tillie called out. "I've known you were visiting for quite some time."

Apparently she was the only one, because Landon and Bay scrambled to their feet and stared into the darkness. They didn't look directly at us, but it was clear they believed Tillie's assertion. They were ready for a fight if it became necessary.

"Where?" Landon asked, his hand automatically moving toward Bay so he could shove her behind him. I found the move interesting, because she clearly had power to call on should it become necessary.

"Don't get your panties in a twist," Tillie admonished, her eyes narrowing as she stared directly at me. It was something of a dare.

I risked a glance at Raven. She looked amused more than worried and held her hands palms out. "I don't see the harm," she said, keeping her voice low. "I think we'll be okay."

"It would be rude not to show ourselves," Nellie added.

I knew what he was suggesting … and why. I didn't want to encourage him, but I didn't see where we had much choice. "Ah, well." I slowly stood, taking the time to dust off the knees of my capris as I forced a wan smile. "So … we were just looking around the property and didn't want to bother you."

Tillie snorted. "Please. I knew you would come this afternoon. I sensed you on the bus."

"I wondered about that." I opted for honesty. "We were curious."

"And that's why I invited you."

"I don't really remember getting an invitation," I said. "I simply invited myself … and a few friends."

Tillie tilted her head to the side. "What do you think the wink was?"

"I told you she knew we were on the bus," Luke said as he stood. "They want us here."

Landon's expression said otherwise. "May I ask why you're skulking around?"

"They're curious," Bay answered for me, her stance relaxing as she rested her hand on Landon's forearm. "They're mostly curious about Aunt Tillie, but they're willing to hang with all of us."

Landon arched an eyebrow as he slid her a sidelong look. "And you're okay with this?"

She nodded. "I think it might be fun."

"Fine." Landon held up his hands in defeat. "Don't do anything weird. That will make it easier for me to pretend I didn't see anything if you decide to strip down and dance later."

It wasn't the friendliest of invitations, but I laughed all the same. "I don't think you have to worry about us getting naked."

"Speak for yourself." Nellie pushed past me, his gaze eager as it locked with Tillie's amused orbs. "What kind of wine is that?"

Tillie held up a bottle. "I make it myself. It has some kick."

"It definitely does," Landon agreed, leading Bay back to their blanket. "I don't want to see any men naked," he warned. "I'll get out the cuffs if I do."

Nellie made a face. "That's sexist."

"I don't care. Keep your underwear on. It's not that difficult."

Nellie rolled his eyes. "What if I don't wear underwear?"

"You're wearing a skirt," Landon reminded him.

"Because I like to feel the breeze on my bits."

"Oh, geez." Landon slapped his hand to his forehead as Bay laughed. "I don't want to see you naked. You'd better wait until I'm drunk enough to see double to unveil any of your ... bits."

"Sure." Nellie flashed him a saucy salute. "I'll make sure you're completely tanked before stripping. You have my promise on that."

"Ugh. Why can't anything ever be normal around here?"

16
SIXTEEN

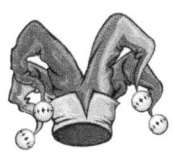

*T*illie's wine did indeed have some kick, so much so that we were all drunk within an hour. Those used to the kick managed to pace themselves, but the rest of us were goners from the start. Only Melissa didn't imbibe, because she was underage. I didn't think that would stop Tillie from offering, but Melissa wasn't keen on losing control after her previous experience, so she happily watched the rest of us engage in what turned out to be a regular occurrence for the Winchesters.

"You're so cute," Luke chortled as he poked Landon's side. "Have you ever considered playing for the other team?"

Landon, who surprisingly didn't seem freaked out by the question, merely smiled. "I *am* playing for the other team. The witch team."

Luke laughed so hard I thought he might throw up. "Witch team. Do they throw curves or curses?"

"Both." Landon idly played with the ends of Bay's hair, making sure to keep his eyes from the circle around the fire. Naked dancing was indeed part of the festivities, and Landon clearly knew better than to look. He was a master at keeping his focus elsewhere.

Me? I was having more trouble.

"Is it difficult for you to participate in stuff like this?" I asked him, genuinely curious. "I mean ... your girlfriend's mother is drunk ... and naked ... and dancing with our bearded lady, who is also drunk ... and occasionally doing lewd somersaults."

Landon's lips curved as Bay began to giggle. "It was difficult when I first realized what was going on," he replied, rubbing his cheek against Bay's and making me wonder if he was drunker than I initially realized. He had a plan to finish out his evening, and it was obvious by the way he kept cuddling closer with his girlfriend. The shuttering he seemed so adept at before was completely eradicated, and I saw glimpses of his plans on his surface thoughts. "I'm kind of used to it now."

"What about you?" I asked Bay. "Was it hard for you to show him this?"

"I didn't technically show him," she replied. "He stumbled upon us ... like you did."

"Technically we spied," Luke pointed out, rolling to his back when he heard Nellie chanting with Tillie. "Are they casting real curses?"

Bay followed his gaze. "I believe Aunt Tillie is calling for yellow rain to fall on Mrs. Little's house. Nellie thinks it's a great idea."

Melissa blinked several times in rapid succession. "Do you think it will happen?"

Bay shrugged, unbothered either way. "It wouldn't be the first time Aunt Tillie has controlled the weather."

Naida could also control the weather – which meant she mostly caused tornados and thunderstorms when she was in a bad mood – so I understood the look of consternation that briefly flitted across Bay's face.

"I know she's probably a pain, but I bet she was fun when you were growing up," I offered. "I mean ... she's dancing with a dwarf."

"I thought it was politically incorrect to use that word," Bay noted.

"Except he really is a dwarf from another dimension."

Her eyes widened. "What?"

"I mean ... ." Crap! I realized my mistake too late. "I ... um ... ."

"I can't deal with whatever you just said," Landon said, shaking his head as he slipped his arm around Bay's back. "Sweetie, we need to go to bed. We both have full days tomorrow, and if we have even one more drink we'll regret it."

Bay's eyes stayed on me for a long time before she finally smiled at him and nodded. "I'm with you. I set water and aspirin on the counter before I left, just to be on the safe side."

"That's my girl. Always thinking." He gave her a long kiss that was hot enough to cause Melissa to break out in a sweat. She clearly had a crush on the FBI agent, which he was thankfully oblivious to. "Come on." He pulled her to her feet, taking a moment to make sure his footing was sound before slinging an arm over her shoulders.

"I'm glad you guys decided to stop by," Bay offered, her arm around Landon's waist. "Be careful going home. If you've had too much to drink you might want to sleep it off out here. We've done it before. It's not so bad."

"Melissa hasn't had anything to drink." I pointed toward her. "We'll be fine."

Bay nodded, momentarily sobering. "We need to put our heads together on the runes."

"Because of the festival set-up, we're not opening until the day after tomorrow. It's different from our usual gig, but that gives us a full day to help. Stop by when you're up and about."

"I have a feeling that's going to happen before you're up and about."

I snickered. "I'll be fine. I can hold my liquor."

"Yes, she's a world-class drinker," Luke agreed, his head coming to rest on my shoulder. "I am, too. Although ... I think I might throw up."

I scowled. "We should probably finish up, too. Even though the circus isn't open tomorrow there's plenty for us to do."

"I'm definitely going to throw up," Luke complained. "Ugh ... how much do you want to bet this wine is worse coming up than going down?"

There was no way I would throw money at that wager. "You can ride in the flatbed of the truck."

"Good idea."

. . .

I'D SOBERED UP A BIT by the time we returned to the fairgrounds, but I almost tripped hopping out of the truck. I was hopeful I would be able to stave off a hangover, but nothing was certain given the potency of Tillie's wine.

Kade exited the door to our trailer when he heard us, worry etched across his face. His grimace dissolved into a smile when he saw me. "I take it things went okay."

I instinctively threw my arms around his neck as Luke tumbled from the bed of the truck and immediately started throwing up. "We might've drunk some wine," I admitted.

Kade ran his hands over my back as he chuckled. "Other than that, I don't see any bruises. No magical fights or anything?"

I shook my head and swayed. "Nope. Just homemade wine. Oh, and Nellie danced naked with the witches."

Kade stiffened. "There was actual naked dancing?"

"Only with the older witches, so don't let your mind run away with you. Landon and Bay did not get naked. Although ... they're probably naked now."

"Oh, you think?" Raven drank as much as I did, but she seemed steadier on her feet. "Those two were about to mount each other in the middle of the clearing. They're definitely naked."

"Definitely," Luke echoed, rubbing the sides of his mouth. "I wish Landon would've danced naked."

"Me, too," Melissa said as she handed Luke his keys. "I'm going to bed to dream about it."

Luke beamed at her. "Me, too."

I merely shook my head. "How did your night go?"

Kade took the bulk of my weight and dragged me toward the steps. "We'll talk about it in the morning."

I searched his face for a hint of discontent, but he looked fine. "You're okay, right?"

He nodded. "Yup. You're the one who needs looking after tonight."

"I'm fine."

"You're going to have a hangover unless we get some aspirin and water into you."

"I'm fine," I repeated. "I can hold my liquor."

"You're still drinking a bottle of water and taking aspirin."

"Okay." I wasn't in the mood to argue, especially since my head was on the verge of spinning. "Have I told you lately that I love you?"

"Yes." He kissed my forehead when we reached the top of the stairs. "It's always nice to hear."

"Yeah. You know what?"

"Hmm." He was distracted as he opened the door.

"I think I might be drunk."

He laughed as he pulled me inside. "I think you might be, too."

MY HEAD ACHED WHEN I woke the next morning and tugged the covers over my face. I violently cursed the sun – and my own stupidity – as I tried to force my stomach to cease rolling. I could've been on a rollercoaster with all the ups and downs.

"Hey, Sunshine." Kade appeared in the doorway, already showered and dressed. His smile was wide when I peeked from beneath the covers and scowled. "How is my favorite mind reader?"

That had to be a trick question. "How about you read my mind?" I suggested, annoyance rolling through me in waves. "What am I thinking?"

He winced as he moved closer to the bed. "Is that any way to treat your knight in shining armor?" He held up a bottle of water. "Last time I checked, you were telling me how much you loved me while trying to get me naked."

I vaguely remembered that. "I seem to recall you refusing to get naked."

"Yes, well, I might adore you to distraction, but that won't last if I let you puke on me."

"I was in no danger of puking," I argued as I forced myself to a sitting position. "In fact … ugh." I felt lightheaded as my stomach threatened revolt.

"Not good, huh?" He tsked in sympathy as he slid onto the bed next to me and surrendered the water. "Drink that." He held up his other hand and shoved another bottle in my direction, this one pink and promising stomach relief. "And take a few shots of that."

I glowered at the amused expression on his handsome face. "You're enjoying this way too much."

He grinned. "I'm not enjoying this as much as ... how much did you drink last night?" He changed course quickly when he realized I wasn't going to believe the denial no matter what.

"I honestly don't think I drank that much," I said, frowning when I couldn't untwist the bottle cap. "Oh, why is nothing going my way?"

Kade attempted to smother a laugh ... and failed. "Hand it over." He took back the bottle and opened it. "You're very cranky when you're hungover. You rarely drink too much, so I guess I forgot. The last time you were like this was when you thought I didn't want anything to do with you."

"You didn't want anything to do with me," I reminded him, taking the bottle and sucking down half the contents before speaking again. "We were on a timeout."

"I was upset because of the Max situation."

"Yeah." I leaned against the pillows and took a moment to look him up and down. "Are you okay? I didn't get a chance to ask how your thing went last night. I'm guessing that means I got a big red mark in the girlfriend column last night, huh?"

"If this were a regular occurrence, I might agree with that. I was so happy to see you alive, so I opted to look at it as a good thing. You broke bread and drank wine with your enemies."

"They're not our enemies." I meant that. "I don't know that they're our friends – they have secrets they want to keep, the same as us – but they're definitely not our enemies."

"I'm glad for that." Kade's fingers were gentle as they brushed the hair from my face. "It would be nice if we didn't have to wage a magical war before leaving town."

"It would be," I agreed, resting my head against his shoulder. "Tell me about your night with Max."

"You don't have to listen before you feel better."

"I want to listen."

"I ... don't know how to describe it." An emotion I couldn't quite identify washed over his features. "I was afraid when I first went out there with him, afraid that he might make me so angry I might explode."

"You're still not over the fact that he lied about being your father," I mused. "I get it."

"I don't feel angry. I mean ... I'm disappointed. I think about all the things I lost out on as a kid, and it makes me sad."

"You're angry at your mother," I noted quietly. "Part of you wishes she was still around so you could yell at her for keeping him from you."

"Do you think that's wrong?"

I shook my head. "No. You thought he was a family friend, an uncle of sorts who stepped in and spent time with you because you didn't have a father. He was giving with his time. In truth, he was a father who didn't spend enough time with you.

"When you add to that the fact that he passed on some of his magic to you, it's a lot to swallow," I continued. "You've had to absorb a lot over the past few months. First you found out magic was real, and that was a blow. Then you found out Max was your father and that I hid it from you. That was a knife to the chest. Then you found out you were magical, and that was kind of like being run over by a truck.

"I think you've handled it better than most people would've been able to do," I said. "You're the strongest person I know, simply because you didn't shut down when all this was thrown at you. I think you're pretty remarkable."

He was quiet so long I had to turn my eyes to him to make sure I hadn't somehow made him angry. He was smiling.

"I think that's the nicest thing anyone has ever said to me." He leaned over and pressed a kiss to the tip of my nose. "You might think I'm strong, but I *know* you're the strongest person I've ever met. For you to say that ... it means a lot."

My heart went out to him. "I couldn't not say it, because it's true."

"It still means a lot."

"Yeah, well ... ." I was embarrassed. "I like you a great deal."

His grin widened. "I like you a great deal more."

"Is this a competition?"

He shrugged. "I have no idea. I'm just enjoying the moment. I have a feeling you're going to turn crabby again the second you get out of bed."

The statement was like a heavy wet blanket thrown over my head. "I have no idea why I allowed this to happen. I thought I was fine until ... well ... now."

"That's the way it goes with homemade hooch. My mother had a friend who made wine in her garage. It would knock you on your ass."

"I definitely feel as if I've been knocked on my ass."

"Well, we'll get some breakfast into you, and a lot of fluids, and that should help. You need to shower before that happens, though. You smell like stale grapes."

I shot him a look. "I smell like a field full of daisies."

"If that's what you need to tell yourself."

"I want to hear about your night first," I pressed. "You started to tell me about it and then conveniently tried to distract me. I want to know how it went."

He sighed. "It was ... good. I was afraid at first, and for more than one reason. I thought I might hurt him – and he was right about not having you there because that would've paralyzed me – but I got over it. Once I was over it, he started to test my abilities. He seemed ... impressed."

Kade's cheeks colored under my steady scrutiny.

"You're impressive," I said finally. "What did you manage to do?"

"Not much. He asked me to set a tree on fire, which I was terrified to do. He promised to douse it right away so there was no danger of a forest fire."

"And you did it?"

He nodded. "I did it a few times. Then I doused it myself. That was harder, but I managed it. I think he wanted me to know that I was capable of multiple things, and that burning down the world wasn't my true purpose."

My heart grew at his smile. "Of course that's not your true

purpose. Those who burn the world down only have hate to fuel them. You're the best person I know. You have too much love to allow that to be your destiny."

His smile was heartfelt. "How do you know the exact right thing to say?"

I shrugged. "I thought that was your superpower."

"Maybe we share it."

"That would be nice, huh?" I snuggled closer and sipped my water. "I kind of wish you'd been with me last night. I would like to get your take on the Winchesters, to make sure I don't like them simply because I want to like them. It sounds as if you got exactly what you needed last night."

"I did. Next time, I want you with me. Max agrees it's probably good for you to be there so I can get over the fear of hurting you."

"You won't hurt me. I wish you wouldn't think things like that."

"That's why I want you there next time. I ... like having you close. You're kind of like a cool breeze on a really hot day."

"Oh, that's sweet." I leaned in for a kiss but he pulled away, causing my stomach to threaten a riot. "What's wrong?"

"You know you're my favorite person in the world, right?"

His tone set my teeth on edge. "I guess."

"You know," he corrected. "You're my favorite person in the world ... but your breath is horrible thanks to the stale wine. I need you to brush your teeth before we get mushy."

I frowned. "I thought our adoration was eternal ... and without limits."

"Oh, it is. Kisses are another story."

I rolled my eyes and pulled away. "You're no longer my favorite person."

"Oh, don't be like that," he called to my back, although I heard the laughter in his voice.

"No, no, no." I stomped my feet against the trailer floor. "Luke is going to be so happy to have his crown back."

"You'll feel differently once you have breakfast in you."

"You're on my list," I barked.

"What is that supposed to mean?"

"Oh, you'll find out. I know all about lists now." That was true. Tillie told me about her list and how it worked. I was enamored with the idea. "Oh, boy, you're not going to like being on the list."

"I'll take your word for it."

17
SEVENTEEN

I wasn't above using a little magic to cure my hangover. I didn't possess the appropriate skills, though, so I had to slip away from Kade and track down Nixie. She appeared to be ready for me, because she held out a packet of herbs the second she took in my wan complexion.

"You were one of the bad ones last night, too, huh?"

I pursed my lips. "What makes you think I was bad?"

She grinned, the expression lighting her perky features. "Luke was here before sunup asking for a cure. Nellie just helped himself to what he needed."

"And Raven?" I asked, suspicious.

Nixie merely shrugged. "Raven doesn't get hangovers."

"Is that a lamia thing?" It didn't seem fair.

"She's too mean to be hungover," Nixie replied. "Take the herbs with a glass of water and you'll be fine."

I nodded in thanks and pocketed the offering. There was something I wanted to say, but I wasn't sure how to broach it. As if reading my mind, Nixie's smile grew broader.

"I'll keep it between us and pretend you didn't need the help," she volunteered, which was enough to have some of the tension weighing down my shoulders dissipate.

"Thanks." I was rueful. "This morning reminded me of exactly why I don't drink myself to oblivion very often. I feel like the stuff you scrape from your tongue after a three-day bender."

Nixie made a face. "Lovely."

"Well, that's how I feel."

"Take the herbs. You'll feel better as soon as you do."

I GRABBED A BOTTLE OF water from the kitchen area before disappearing into my tent. I hadn't been inside for more than a cursory glance since we'd arrived, but everything was arranged exactly as I liked it. That meant Melissa had been busy. I had to remember to thank her later ... for more than one thing.

I upended the packet of herbs into my water and secured the cap before giving it a good shake. The water turned a disgusting green, but I ignored it. The color meant nothing. The magic in the herbs was what I wanted.

I steeled myself for the awful taste – it truly was gross – and downed the entire bottle, closing my eyes as I swallowed. I was already feeling markedly better when I finished, and I wiped the corners of my mouth as I sucked in a steadying breath.

That's when I felt Kade's presence in the tent. When I opened my eyes, I expected to find him laughing at me. My intention was to let him think I'd overcome the hangover on my own so I didn't have to be embarrassed. Now that he knew otherwise I would simply have to let the laughter roll off me.

To my surprise, Kade wasn't laughing.

"What is it?" I asked, hopping to my feet. The look on his face told me something had gone very wrong. "Are you okay?"

He nodded as he stepped forward, a muscle working in his jaw. "We have a situation."

Those weren't words I wanted to hear. "What situation?"

"Come with me."

"Why?"

"Just ... come on." He held out his hand.

I trusted him implicitly, so I took it. "I'm going to hate this, aren't I?"

There was no hesitation in his answer. "We're all going to hate this."

I DEFINITELY HATED WHAT he had to show me. In fact, I was so agitated my right eye began twitching.

"Son of a ... !" I rubbed my eye and shifted from one foot to the other. "I don't understand how this happened."

Kade looked as uncomfortable as I felt as he pressed the heel of his hand to his forehead. "I don't know either. I didn't walk the perimeter when I returned last night." He dropped to one knee so he could get a better look at the body on the ground because, yes, there was most definitely a body. "I have no idea when this happened, but it's on me."

Fury bubbled up in my chest. "This is not your fault."

"No?" Kade didn't look convinced. "He's one of ours, Poet."

He most certainly was. Boney Billy, the midway worker who ran the ring toss booth, was spread eagle on the ground between the House of Mirrors and the midway. The area where his body had been discovered was empty – it would be filled with people milling about the following day – but there was no attraction in the locale.

Billy, who earned his name because he was ridiculously thin – and enjoyed dropping his pants at the drop of a hat – looked to have died screaming. His mouth was frozen in a silent "O" and his eyes were wide. Someone had carved a rune into his forehead, but the blood made it difficult to ascertain the design.

"I can't believe this," I muttered, rubbing my cheeks to get the blood flowing and ward off the shock. "I don't understand. I ... ."

"He's dead," Raven offered helpfully as she moved from the House of Mirrors to the body. "I'm guessing someone killed him while we were out playing Whack-A-Witch last night."

Her smug attitude made me want to throttle her. "Oh, really?" I drawled, disdain dripping from my tongue. "Is that what happened?"

Raven didn't appear bothered by my tone. "In my expert opinion, that's exactly what happened."

In an effort to keep me from attacking, Kade slipped his arm around my waist and anchored me to his side. "Not now," he whispered as I fought the constraint. "Did anyone see anything?" He took his job as security chief seriously, and the sadness etched on his face told me he blamed himself for what happened. That was enough to still my temper.

"No one heard anything," Seth replied, stepping out from the group of gathering workers. "We were here last night. We didn't hear a thing."

"What were you doing?" I asked, thankful when Kade tentatively eased his grip on me. He seemed to sense I was no longer in the mood to attack Raven.

"We sat by the fire," Seth replied. "We told stories, walked the perimeter three times. Didn't see a thing."

"Were you drunk?" I recognized the hypocrisy of the accusation even as the words were escaping my mouth. That didn't stop me. "Is there a chance you missed what happened?"

Seth didn't as much as flinch. "No. We had a few beers. Not many. We would've heard. Besides, you can see his body for yourself. That was a ritual death. The dreamcatcher should've sounded."

Guilt pooled in my stomach all the same. "I'm sorry," I offered lamely, briefly pressing my eyes shut. "I shouldn't have attacked you that way. It wasn't fair."

He shrugged. "It's fine. We're all shaken by this."

"It's not fine," I pressed, firm. "I shouldn't have said that. I just ... didn't expect this." I pinched the bridge of my nose. "I don't understand how this happened."

"Well, I'm sure we're going to get plenty of time to dwell on it," Raven said, inclining her head toward the other side of the fairgrounds and causing me to swivel quickly. Sure enough, Landon and Terry were heading in our direction, and they didn't look happy.

"You called the police?" I turned toward Kade, dumbfounded. "What were you thinking?"

"That we have a dead man and the scene looks a lot like the one we found outside the dreamcatcher the morning after we arrived," he replied calmly, refusing to back down. "We're going to have to answer questions about this. Keeping it secret helps nobody."

That was true. Still, we weren't the type to spread our business far and wide. When one of ours was killed, we handled it ourselves ... and pain was almost always involved. "We're going to need to talk about this later," I muttered.

"I'm fine with that." Kade didn't back down as he took a step away from me and toward the approaching cops. "I stand by this. If you have a problem with what I've done ... well ... you're going to have to suck it up."

I didn't like his tone, but I understood his attitude. It seemed I was stepping on toes in every direction this morning. "I'm sorry," I said, shaking my head. "This is why I shouldn't drink. I don't do well with hangovers."

He flashed me a small smile. "It's good to know you're not perfect one-hundred percent of the time. They had to be called, so that's what I did."

"And now we have to deal with them." I braced myself as they closed the distance. "This is a big mess."

"What was your first clue?" Raven drawled.

She was officially on my last nerve.

LANDON AND TERRY DIDN'T LOOK happy about the new development. In fact, the grim look they shared told me they were extremely bothered by another body dropping so quickly.

"What can you tell me about him?" Landon asked as he crouched by our fallen comrade.

"Boney Billy," I replied dully. "He worked the midway for us."

"How long has he been with you?"

"Five years."

"Does he have a real name?" Terry asked.

"What?" I yanked myself out of my fuzziness. "Yeah. William Caputo. He's twenty-seven, at least I think. I'll have to check his personnel file."

"Did he have any enemies?"

"Here?" My eyebrows hopped. "We're a family. No one here did this. It's the same person who killed your cauldron maker. Did we do that, too?"

Landon held his hands up in mock surrender. "It was a simple question. There's no need to get worked up."

"No reason to get worked up?" The fact that he seemed perfectly fine after a night of drinking increased my irritation. "How can you say that? He's been with us for five years. Sure, the last thing he said to me was two weeks ago when he mentioned my butt looked ready for a spanking, but that doesn't change the fact that he was one of us."

Landon's expression remained flat. "I'm sorry for your loss."

"Is that all you have to say?"

He shrugged. "What do you want me to say? It's a terrible thing. We have a monster in our midst. We're going to figure out who did this. I don't know what else to offer you."

"I know a few things about monsters," I offered. "We're dealing with something else here."

"What's that?" Landon was intrigued. "What's worse than a monster?"

"A monster doesn't always realize that it's the bad guy," I answered. "Whatever we're dealing with knows and doesn't care."

He pursed his lips. "I take it you get philosophical when you have a hangover. If you're worried we think you're a suspect, we don't. We can clear five of you right off the bat. You were too drunk to commit murder."

"And the others?"

Landon held his hands palms out. "It's an ongoing investigation. We don't even have a time of death. I think the manner of death is pretty obvious."

"Oh, you think?" Raven's disdain was palpable. "That big wound in his chest is kind of an obvious tip, isn't it? You've got a happy stabber in this town. I think the question is which Hemlock Cove resident likes jabbing people with pointy things?"

Several of the men snickered, causing Raven to scowl.

"Why do you always have to go the perverted route?" Raven complained to Luke, who must have appeared when I was busy talking to Landon.

Luke shrugged. "We are standing over Boney Billy's body. He got that name for more than one reason. It's an homage, of sorts."

"Whatever." Raven rolled her eyes to the street, her body tensing when she caught sight of something she wasn't expecting. I caught a barrage of images from her mind. She wanted me to see, because otherwise she would've shuttered. I internally cringed when I realized what was about to happen.

"Margaret Little is coming," I announced.

Landon and Terry jerked their chins toward the street in unison, and the sound the FBI agent made was something between a groan and a growl.

"Oh, this is the last thing we need," Terry said, wiping his hands on his jeans. "She is going to be all up in our faces."

"I'm guessing you're used to that," I supplied. "Is there anything that woman doesn't complain about?"

"No, but I can guarantee this will be worse than anything you've seen from her yet." Terry pasted a bright smile on his face that seemed unnatural given the body on the ground. "Good morning, Margaret," he called out. "Top of the morning to you."

Luke mouthed "top of the morning" to me and saluted, which was surreal enough that I choked on a laugh. It was wrong given Boney Billy's death, but I couldn't stop myself.

"What is going on here?" Margaret bellowed, the sound of her stomping feet preceding her. "Is it true we have another body?"

There was obviously no reason to lie, so Terry merely extended his hand toward the body. "What do you think?"

Margaret's face twisted into something unpleasant, which was saying something because the woman never gave me a warm and fuzzy feeling. "What are you going to do about it?"

"Well, we thought we might throw a party," Landon deadpanned. "Everyone is going to take a turn dancing with the body. And we thought we would invite the tourists to make it extra special."

If looks could kill, Landon would be long since deceased. Margaret's glare was ice cold. "You've been spending too much time with the Winchesters. When you first arrived in town, you were charming. People flocked to you, wanted to help. Now you're just an extension of that old bat ruling the roost out there."

"I'll take that as a compliment," Landon said dryly. "What are you doing here, by the way? Is there something specific you want?"

"I want to know what you're going to do about this," Margaret barked.

"Well, we're going to do what we normally do," Terry said. "We're going to call the county's crime scene team to process this. Then we're going to question people. Then we're going to follow the clues. Then we're going to arrest the guilty party."

"So ... nothing as usual?" Margaret challenged.

"That seems unfair," I interjected, speaking before I realized I would've been better off keeping my mouth shut. I managed to hold it together despite the hateful glare Margaret shot in my direction. "I just meant ... this barely happened. They haven't had time to figure it out yet."

"Thank you for standing up for us," Landon said, "but it's okay. This is normal."

"He means it's normal for them not to solve the crime," Margaret countered. "I mean ... they've dropped so many crimes in the last year and a half that I can't even keep them all straight. Suspects disappear. Others are caught so fast that I have trouble believing they got the right person. It's almost magical how they solve some cases."

Ah, that explained it. Magic. The Winchesters were obviously involved in several of these takedowns, which meant Terry and Landon were constantly covering for them. It was an interesting set-up ... and I had a million questions. Those would obviously have to wait for later.

"Margaret, we're really busy here," Terry said. "Unless you have something to add to this conversation, we've got a long day ahead of us."

"Oh, I've got something to add to this conversation," Margaret intoned. "I've got a big something."

"Aunt Tillie would probably say the only big thing you have is your butt," Landon offered, avoiding the dirty look Terry lobbed in his direction. "Oh, like you weren't thinking it."

Margaret planted her hands on her hips. "I don't have time for games. The festival kicks off tonight, which means that the rest of the tourists arrive today. The last thing we need is for tourists to learn we have a killer on the loose."

"We had a killer on the loose yesterday and you were fine with it," Landon pointed out.

"I wasn't fine with it, but one death can be explained away and adds a little mystery to the event," Margaret snapped. "Two deaths – unacceptable!"

"So ... you want us to keep it quiet?" Terry asked.

Margaret nodded. "I most certainly do. If this gets out, I'll find a way to make sure you lose your job."

"I don't think that's going to be as easy as you think," Terry argued.

"I guess we'll find out, won't we?" Margaret's tone was frigid. "I don't want this getting out. If it does, it's on you. That includes spreading information to your girlfriend, Landon. You're not allowed to talk to her about this."

Landon was having none of it. "You can't stop me from talking to Bay."

"I can call your boss and explain my concerns, if that's what you want."

Landon didn't back down. "If you feel that's necessary, go for it."

"You'll be sorry."

"I think you'll be sorry, but that's neither here nor there," Landon said. "We have a job to do. You need to keep your nose out of it. Do you understand?"

Margaret's face flushed red. "I think we're at an impasse."

Landon was calm as he crossed his arms over his chest. "I can live with that."

18

EIGHTEEN

Margaret's insistence on watching the fairgrounds was an annoyance I wasn't prepared to deal with.

"You need to stop glaring at her," Kade insisted an hour later as he moved up behind me, his hands automatically going to my neck to rub at the tension pooling there. "It won't do any good."

"Maybe it makes me feel better. Have you ever considered that?"

Kade moved closer, pressing his chest to my back, and stared hard at my profile as I squirmed. "How much of this is real anger and how much is your hangover?" he asked after a beat.

I scowled. "I don't have a hangover. I can handle my liquor."

He waited.

"Fine." I blew out a sigh. "I no longer have a hangover because Nixie gave me some of her famous herbs to chase it off. I'm fine ... other than that crazy woman watching us as if we're the murderers."

Kade grinned. "So ... you cheated."

"I don't cheat." I was offended by the assertion. "I simply took advantage of the options afforded me." That sounded good, right? "Our playing field isn't level. We have special privileges given who we are, and I took advantage of that. Sue me."

Instead of arguing, he chuckled. "You are a crabby little thing this morning." He pressed a kiss to my cheek before releasing me. "I like it when you're feisty. It gives me ideas."

I shook my head. "We don't have time for those ideas. We need to focus on the fact that one of our own has fallen."

Kade instantly sobered. "I know. How well did you know him? I think I probably said two words to him the entire time I was here."

"I really didn't know him all that well either," I admitted, the truth of the words causing a pang in my heart. "We're cliquey, in case you haven't noticed. We stick to our group and the midway workers stick to their group."

"And the clowns stick to theirs," Kade added.

"I don't know why you always have to bring up the clowns."

"You know why."

I couldn't stop myself from smiling despite the pall hanging over the fairgrounds. "We're going to have to explore your clown fear later. For now ... we need to question the other midway workers so we can get a timeline."

"You don't think one of them killed Billy, do you?"

I shook my head. "I think the odds are against it. Still, it wouldn't be the first time we had a monster hiding in our midst."

He kissed my cheek again. "Where do you want to go first?"

There was only one answer to that question, and it was one neither of us was going to like. "Where do you think?"

"Ugh." He made a face. "That guy is so slimy."

MARK LANE WAS FORTY-NINE YEARS old and oily enough to make a bodybuilder jealous. His black hair, which was shot through with gray, was messy from sleep when he opened his trailer door.

At first, he grinned when he saw me. I had no idea what he was thinking — but if I had to guess it was something perverted — and the way his eyes lit set my teeth on edge. Very slowly he realized I wasn't alone. The look he shot Kade was positively hateful.

"I don't roll that way," Mark said finally.

Kade's forehead puckered. "What way?"

Mark winked at me, clearly amused. "Poet knows."

I did. I also knew Kade wasn't in the mood for Mark to say something disgusting and derail the conversation. I had to take control before things flew off the rails.

"We need to talk, Mark." I kept my tone even. "It's important. Something has happened."

Mark narrowed his eyes. "Am I going to like this?"

"Not even a little."

"Well ... then I guess you should come in." He held open the trailer door to allow us entrance, gesturing toward a small living room set that featured a recliner and loveseat. Kade headed straight for the loveseat, tugging me with him to make sure Mark didn't try to put the moves on me and ease him out of the seating arrangements. Even though we were about to deliver bad news to Mark, that didn't mean he was above being a disgusting pervert.

"You two are adorable," Mark drawled as he lowered himself into the recliner. "Has anyone ever told you that?"

"I tell myself that when I stare in the mirror every morning," I said, taking a moment to indulge in my rampant dislike for the man before sobering. We had official business today, and it couldn't wait. "Boney Billy is dead."

I could've tried to couch the news, take a moment to build Mark up and gracefully delivered the tidbit. But I didn't like Mark enough to put in the effort, and he worked better when dealing with facts.

"What?" Mark blanched, his face going white. "Is this some sort of joke?"

"Yes, we pick a random person to wake every morning to prank with a fake death," I deadpanned.

Mark glared. "This isn't funny. In fact ... !"

Kade held up a hand to quiet him. "This most definitely isn't funny," he agreed, refusing to back down. "There's nothing funny about it in the least. That doesn't change the fact that it's true ... and we have to deal with it."

I gestured toward the window. "There is an FBI agent standing near the midway right now. The chief of police is with him. They're waiting for the county medical examiner. This isn't a joke."

Mark swiveled in his chair and stared out the window. "I don't understand how this happened."

Kade was serious as he rubbed his hands over his knees. "When was the last time you saw Billy?"

"I ... you ... um ... ." Mark trailed off, lost in thought. Finally, he pulled himself together and seriously pondered the question. "I guess it was last night. We all went to the diner for dinner, which is allowed because that was negotiated in our package with the Hemlock Cove officials."

"I have no issue with you eating dinner downtown," I said. "Did you all go together?"

Mark nodded. "We had a good time. We ate a lot of food. We listened to the locals. A few of them are nutty, by the way. Did you know that there's supposedly a witch who lives nearby who has enchanted a pot field so law enforcement gets the trots if they try to find it?"

That was news to me. I had a sneaking suspicion I knew exactly what witch he was referring to. "No, but that sounds mildly interesting."

"Apparently it's really good pot."

I shot him a warning look. "Don't try tracking down some random person's pot field. That is just ... tacky."

"I didn't say I was going to." Mark held up his hands to ward off my fury. "It was a normal dinner. Billy was there. He made his usual comments about a few of the women he saw. The town is full of people who are here for the festival. They all fancy themselves witches ... although most are pretty far from it."

Mark wasn't supernatural in origin — unless you considered grifting magical — but he was well aware of our extracurricular activities. He merely chose to ignore them because making money was his primary endeavor.

"Did anything out of the ordinary happen?" Kade asked. "I mean ...

did you guys talk to anyone in particular? Did Billy show an interest in anyone? Did he split from the group?"

Mark rubbed his chin as he searched his memory. "Nope," he said finally, exhaling heavily. "I would've noticed that. We went to dinner as a group, had a good time and came back together."

"Did you do anything after you returned?" I asked. "You usually have a bonfire every night. Did you do that?"

Mark nodded. "Yeah. We were up until a little after eleven. I'm pretty sure Billy was there until we doused the fire and called it a night."

"Where did he go after that?" Kade queried.

Mark shrugged. "I wasn't watching. I assume he went back to his trailer."

Kade slid me a sidelong look. "What do you think?"

That was the problem. I had no idea what to think. "I don't know. Someone managed to do evil smack dab in our center last night. Even if everyone was asleep, someone should've heard what was happening."

"And the dreamcatcher should've alerted," Kade finished, understanding. "How did this happen without a single sound?"

That was a very good question.

I LEFT KADE TO SEARCH Billy's trailer and headed for downtown. I needed air, room to breathe. My mind was a jumbled mess and I had no idea how to handle any of this.

I grabbed a coffee from the cute shop at the corner closest to the police station. The woman inside introduced herself as Ginny Gunderson – a woman I recognized from one of Raven's stories – and she seemed keen to talk about life in the circus.

"How do you live so close to clowns?" she asked, completely serious.

I smiled. "I carry a big knife."

"I can understand that." She patted my shoulder as she delivered a doughnut and sat in the open chair next to me. The shop was almost empty, and those who remained were focused on their phones. "I heard you had some trouble this morning."

I widened my eyes. Margaret wasn't going to like it when she realized news was already spreading. "How did you hear that?"

"Landon and Terry stopped in for coffee and doughnuts. They usually do. This morning they were talking."

I knew exactly what they were talking about. "It's difficult," I admitted. "He worked for us, but he was with the midway crew and we weren't really close. I'm upset about his death and all, but ... it's not as if I'm grieving. I don't know how to explain it."

"You don't have to explain it. I get it." Ginny leaned back in her chair and regarded me with curious eyes. "What's it like to travel with the circus? There was a time — decades ago, really — when I thought about running away from my life. The circus was one of the options I entertained."

"You wanted to join the circus?" I was amused enough to scan her surface thoughts. Then I caught a glimpse of a screaming man, red-faced, with spittle forming in the corners of his mouth. It was clear he was about to dole out violence, and Ginny (who was much younger in the vision) was on the receiving end. Then, a woman who looked oddly familiar appeared and stopped the man – Floyd, his name was Floyd – from hurting his wife further.

I'm coming for you, Floyd!

It all flashed through my head in an instant, causing sympathy to roll through me as I regarded the friendly bakery owner. "You probably would've liked the circus. Obviously things worked out well for you here, though."

"They worked out." Ginny's smile was soft. "I'm sorry about your co-worker. He might not have been a friend, but that doesn't mean you don't have a right to be upset about his death."

"Yeah, well ... ." I shook my head. "We can't figure out how anyone got on the fairgrounds without us noticing. It shouldn't have been possible." I didn't mention the dreamcatcher. There was no need. Ginny seemed to understand.

"It must be disconcerting to know it happened so close," she said.

"Darren's body was found right behind where you're staying, too. That can't be a coincidence."

"It's definitely not a coincidence," I agreed.

"What are Terry and Landon saying? Believe it or not, even though this is a small town, they're good at their jobs. I'm sure they will find answers before you leave."

"How well do you know them?"

She shrugged, noncommittal. "I've known Terry for a long time, since he was a kid. He grew up to be a good man, the sort who takes on other people's children to make sure they get all the attention they need."

Another flash. This time, I saw a small blond girl with Terry as he explained why yellow snow wasn't always funny. She walked into the coffee shop with him, her small hand engulfed in his, and she was rapt as he explained why her great-aunt Tillie wasn't always the smartest woman in the room, no matter what she said.

"He sounds like a good man." I smiled at the flash. "What about Landon? Do you like having an FBI agent around so often?"

Ginny shrugged. "He's a good man, too. I don't know him as well. He's dedicated to Bay, which makes me like him. He's rushed to her rescue more than once. Of course, I think the reverse is also true."

"You think she's run to his rescue?"

She nodded without hesitation. "I try to stay out of their business because ... ." She trailed off and I heard something echoing through her mind. *I'm coming for you, Floyd!* "Landon is a good man, too," she said finally. "They'll figure this out. They always do."

Given her chattiness, I decided to take advantage of Mrs. Gunderson's knowledge of the town. "This place used to be called Walkerville, right?"

She nodded. "Yes. We rebranded years ago because we saw the writing on the wall. We had no industrial base to speak of, and if we wanted to do more than survive we had to come up with a plan.

"Without an industrial base, it's difficult to draw the right people in," she continued. "We needed people who paid their taxes and contributed to the community. No one is going to do that without a good job."

"So you shifted the town's focus and decided that tourism was the way to go," I mused, wrapping my fingers around my cup and tilting my head as I considered the miraculous feat they'd managed to pull off. "It's ingenious really," I offered after a beat. "You managed to rebrand the entire town, fully commit. I understand this festival has sold out accommodations in several towns."

Ginny bobbed her head. "It worked for us. I wasn't sure it would, but when we decided to do it everyone agreed that we would put everything we had into it. That was the only way to save the town.

"I mean, sure, it would probably still technically be alive today if we hadn't rebranded, but it certainly wouldn't be thriving," she continued. "We got lucky that things worked out so well. Apparently, people really love witches."

Something occurred to me. "Who suggested you focus on witches?"

"Margaret. She claimed for years that Tillie Winchester was a witch." Mrs. Gunderson smiled. "I think she actually tossed out the idea at one of the planning meetings because she thought it would get a rise out of Tillie.

"We talked about numerous things at those early meetings," she continued. "We considered focusing on hunting for a bit. Golf courses, ski resorts and snowmobiling trails were tossed around, too. We realized that focus was too narrow. When Margaret suggested witches ... it kind of clicked.

"Before we knew it, people were throwing out suggestions left and right, and Hemlock Cove was taking shape," she said. "You wouldn't believe how fast things came together after that. We found we had a knack for festivals ... and people loved the kitschy shops. It didn't take much money to repaint everything. It happened fast."

"Well, it seems to have worked out well," I noted. "You're one of the few towns in the area who aren't in survival mode. You did a great job."

"The key is not to sit on your laurels," Ginny explained. "We're constantly expanding. Marcus is finishing up expanding the stables and adding a petting zoo. And Sam finished renovations on the Dandridge and bought a tanker to add a haunted attraction out at the lighthouse."

"Really? I kind of want to see that before I go."

"I don't believe they're done with it yet. They've been working hard, especially Clove and Thistle."

"Winchester? Are you talking about Clove and Thistle Winchester?"

"Do you know anyone else named Clove and Thistle?"

That was a fair point. "Well, thank you for your time and information." I dug in my pocket for a tip and left it on the table as I collected my coffee and doughnut. "I have to get going. I'm assuming Landon and Terry will have more questions as the day progresses."

"I hope you find answers fast." Ginny's smile was heartfelt. "I'm sorry this happened to you. It's supposed to be a fun weekend. I'm not sure how things will go now."

"Yeah, well, ... thank you for your time." Before she walked away, I decided to say one more thing to her. "I'm glad you weren't forced into the circus," I said quietly. "I'm sure he got what was coming to him."

Mrs. Gunderson didn't seem surprised by the statement. "You don't have to worry about that. The circus life was ruled out for me decades ago."

I'm coming for you, Floyd!

I kept hearing the words on a roar but wasn't sure who was delivering them.

I nodded. "The circus would've been better for having you. These doughnuts are amazing, by the way."

"Stop back before you leave and I'll make sure you get to try my famous pumpkin muffins."

"I don't want to miss that."

"No, definitely not."

19
NINETEEN

Margaret was on the street giving a tour when I left the coffee shop. The look she shot me was straight out of a *Gossip Girl* rerun (I know because Luke was the biggest Chuck and Blair fan ever), and I had no doubt we would exchange words before the day was out.

Because she fancied herself the most important woman in town, Margaret was keen to be professional. I heard her droning on as she pointed at various business, spinning yarns that couldn't possibly be true.

"Just right over there Magdalena Bowman Cranwell Hawkins was burned at the stake in front of the townsfolk for witchcraft in 1691, one year before the witch trials began in Salem."

I narrowed my eyes. "She was burned at the stake?" The question was out of my mouth before I could think better of it.

Margaret's eyes narrowed to dangerous slits. "Do you have a problem with the story?"

I shook my head. "It's just ... that's a myth. No witches were burned at the stake in Salem. Fire was used commonly in Europe, but over here we hanged people."

I swear my rear end was smoking thanks to the fiery glare Margaret lobbed in my direction.

"Do you need something?" she asked, her voice deceptively mild.

"I'm simply interested in your tour," I replied. "I love hearing about local history."

"Yes, well ... this tour is full." She snapped her fingers to get everyone's attention. "This way, please. I want to show you the lake where witches were thrown to see if they could float." She led the tourists toward a waiting bus as I folded my arms across my chest and watched the show.

"She's a real pain, huh?"

I jolted at the new voice, shifting my eyes to my left as I prepared for attack. Instead of finding an enemy, I found Tillie ... and she wasn't alone. Nellie was with her.

"What are you doing here?" I exploded, taken aback. "Where did you come from?"

"I live here," Tillie reminded me.

"I was talking to Nellie."

"He's my new sidekick," Tillie replied, matter-of-fact. "We've decided we make a fearsome twosome. I have a list of people he's going to help me terrorize before leaving town."

I slid my eyes to Nellie, dumbfounded. "You're going to help her terrorize people?"

He shrugged. "I'm not doing anything else. I like being helpful."

That was news to me. "I don't ... ." I stopped myself before launching into a full-on diatribe. "It doesn't matter." I held my hands up to silence whatever snarky comment was about to escape Nellie's lips. "If you want to be Tillie's sidekick, that's totally up to you."

"I'm not her sidekick. She's my sidekick."

Tillie snorted. "I most certainly am not. I'm the head witch." She thumped her chest for emphasis. "That makes you the sidekick. Besides, everyone knows that dwarves are sidekicks."

Nellie made an exaggerated face. "Where did you hear something stupid like that?"

"Um ... *Snow White and the Seven Dwarves*. She was obviously the lead."

"Are you're Snow White in this scenario?"

She shrugged. "I'm most certainly not a dwarf."

"You kind of look like a hobbit," I offered as I watched the last few participants in Margaret's tour board the bus. Two of them were Shirley and Adele, the elderly witches who couldn't stop laughing whenever they were together. They were slower than the rest due to their age, but I couldn't deny they were having a good time. "You should be having elevensies about now, right?"

"Hobbits aren't real, but I would totally be a hobbit if I could," Tillie said. "If you'll remember, though, dwarves were the sidekicks in all those movies, too. The hobbits were the leads."

"I preferred Aragorn," I admitted.

"He was hot," she agreed, "but it doesn't matter. Dwarves are destined to be sidekicks."

"I can't even." Nellie held up a hand, offended. "Do you really think so little of me?"

Tillie shrugged. "I think you're going to make a fantastic sidekick."

"No, you're my sidekick." His voice raised a notch. "Poet, will you tell her that she's obviously my sidekick?"

This was not a conversation I wanted to be involved in, especially because I vaguely remembered having a similar argument with Luke back in the day when he informed me I was his sidekick. If I remembered correctly, the conversation went over equally as well.

"I don't care who the sidekick is," I admitted. "I care about them." I gestured toward the last two people to get on the bus, the ones helping Shirley and Adele navigate the steps. They seemed fine with helping, but the furtive glances they shared after the elderly women disappeared set my teeth on edge.

Something was going on.

The younger girls looked as if they were trying to slink away, but Margaret was paying close attention to their actions and she tugged the girls onto the bus even though they were clearly hoping to escape on a different sort of adventure. "What do you think is up with them?"

Kaley and Lizzy cast desperate looks in my direction, as if they thought I might be able to help them.

"They're teenagers," Tillie said dryly. "Teenagers should be shipped off to an island to live until they stop being annoying."

"So ... send them away for five years?"

"Bay, Clove and Thistle are still annoying. It should be a sliding scale."

"Good to know. I ... ." I lost my train of thought when the bus finally moved away, revealing a lone blonde standing on the opposite side of the road watching it. Bay. She was clearly as interested in the bus as I was. That was interesting.

"What do you think she's looking at?" I asked Tillie.

The elderly witch followed my gaze and shrugged. "Why would you care?"

"I don't know." It was a fair question, but I didn't have an answer. "I sense something about her." I meant to say the second part in my head, but my Foot-In-Mouth Disease wouldn't allow it.

Tillie merely shook her head. "You and Bay are a lot alike."

"Is that a compliment?"

"Take it however you want." Tillie gestured for Bay to cross the street, which her great-niece reluctantly did.

"I don't think it was a compliment," Nellie offered.

He wasn't the only one.

Bay seemed agitated at being summoned. "What are you doing down here?" I didn't think the question was for me because her eyes were fixed firmly on Tillie. "I seem to remember a conversation this morning in which you were forbidden to leave the inn until you removed the charm on the basement door."

"How do you know I didn't remove the charm?" Tillie asked.

"Because you have three cases of wine down there you don't want anyone to know about."

"How do you know about the wine? You'd better not have nipped any. I counted those bottles, and if one is missing ... well ... you know what will happen."

"What will happen?" Nellie whispered with reverence. "Will you shoot her?"

"Worse." Tillie held Bay's gaze for an extended period. "Do you understand what I'm saying?"

Bay nodded without hesitation. "Oh, I understand. You snuck out of the inn and I'm going to be the one in trouble when you get caught. Mom is going to call and ask if I've seen you at some point, and I'm not going to lie to her."

"Of course you're going to lie to her," Tillie countered. "I taught you how to lie for a reason."

Bay sighed and pinched the bridge of her nose as she collected herself. "Okay, well ... I'm done talking to you." She waved a hand in Tillie's direction and focused on me. "I heard you found a body on the fairgrounds this morning. My understanding is that it's a member of your group."

I held her gaze for a long moment. "He worked the midway for us."

"I'm sorry."

"I didn't know him all that well," I admitted.

"His name was Boney Billy and not just because he was skinny," Nellie offered.

"He means that Billy had a lot of boners," Tillie offered.

"Thank you, Aunt Tillie," Bay snapped, causing me to have to bite back a snicker.

"Did Landon tell you what happened?" I was honestly curious. "Margaret didn't seem keen on word spreading."

"Yes, well, Mrs. Little isn't keen on anything that she didn't think of herself," Bay muttered. "I saw the medical examiner at the fairgrounds and headed over to take a look. When I realized you weren't there, I decided to look for you."

I was surprised. "You decided to look for me? Why?"

"We've had two ritual deaths in a short amount of time. Both bodies were discovered close to your camping spot. I don't think that's a coincidence, do you?"

I shook my head. "No, but ... I'm not sure what you expect me to do about it. We don't have anything to go on."

"That's not entirely true. We have a pattern of behavior. We also have a town full of witches. I think it's entirely possible that someone came to town with a plan, perhaps to engage in a ritual or something. This would be an ideal place to do it."

"And why is that?" I asked.

"Because ... there's magic here." Her answer was simple. "And, more importantly, people believe there's magic here. If you believe something hard enough, often times you create a self-fulfilling prophecy of sorts."

She had a point. "So ... what do you think we should do about it?"

"I think we should follow the tour bus."

"Why?"

"Because the young witches who wanted to purchase the destructive potion ingredients are on it."

"And you think they had something to do with this?" I was incredulous. "They're kids."

"They're kids who want power." Bay refused to back down. "Besides, we don't have anywhere else to look. It couldn't hurt to look at them."

"I guess." I rolled my neck and shrugged. "Okay. We'll follow the tour bus. I don't suppose you know where they're going, do you?"

She nodded as a slow smile spread across her features. "As a matter of fact, I do."

THE DANDRIDGE LIGHTHOUSE WAS like something straight out of a movie. I didn't know how to describe it, other than to say it was simply breathtaking.

The tall spire cut a fine figure as it reached into the sky, and it was clear that those who refurbished the property had poured a lot of blood, sweat and tears into the project.

"This is amazing," I breathed, my heart sighing at the splendor of the vision. "I can't imagine getting to live out here."

Bay's amusement was obvious as we walked from the parking area toward the structure. "It's pretty. Clove loves the water."

"She did all this?" I was officially impressed.

"Sam did a lot of it before they hooked up," Bay replied. "Actually, Sam did a lot of it while they were hooking up. They kept their relationship a secret at the start and things were well on their way — with the building and the relationship — before we found out about it."

"Why did they keep it secret?"

Bay shrugged. "It was just something they wanted to do."

"Oh, stop pussyfooting around," Tillie barked from behind us. She and Nellie insisted on being included in the adventure — which was tedious for Bay and me — so we were a foursome rather than a twosome. I was convinced I would live to regret it.

"Sam came to town looking for witches," Tillie explained. "His mother was a witch and he had questions. He immediately started hanging around us and went so far as to spy on Bay. We weren't sure if we liked Sam at the start, and that's why Clove hid him."

Bay glared at her elderly aunt. "Way to open your big mouth."

"What?" Tillie adopted an air of innocence. "What did I say?"

"I'm pretty sure that Sam doesn't want you spilling his private business."

"And I'm pretty sure that you're being a kvetch." Tillie wasn't in the mood to kowtow to anyone, especially her great-niece. "Now, where are the evil teenage witches? I want to smite them and get home in time for *General Hospital*. Jason is supposed to take his shirt off today and it feels like years since it last happened."

Bay rolled her eyes. "Oh, geez!"

"You can't smite them," I argued, genuinely worried for the first time. "They're kids."

"I can do whatever I want," Tillie argued. "I'm queen of the world."

That didn't sound good. "But ... ."

"Ignore her." Bay offered up a small half-wave. "There are times she simply likes hearing herself talk. She's a complete and total pain in the cauldron that way."

"You're on my list, smart mouth," Tillie warned.

Bay ignored her. "I think the tour winds through the gardens Clove planted at the back of the property," she offered. "The thing is, I don't think teenagers would be interested in that. Given how Lizzy and Kaley were acting, I'm guessing they went in the opposite direction."

"Which is where?" I asked, glancing around.

Bay pointed toward a spot to the west. "There. The dock is that way ... and so is the cove."

"What's in the cove?"

"It's hidden," Bay replied. "It's a quiet place. If they're looking for a spot to disappear, that's the one."

"Well, then let's head that way."

"You read my mind."

"I SHOULD'VE BROUGHT MY AX."

We'd been walking only three minutes when Nellie decided to take the conversation into a tangent.

"You don't need your ax," I argued. "They're teenagers. They most certainly don't need to be beheaded."

Tillie perked up and her eyes shifted to Nellie. "You behead things? That is so awesome. I've only ever shot things. Winnie won't let me have an ax."

"There's a reason for that," Bay called out. "You're not supposed to have the shotgun either. You'd better hide that thing well if you don't want Mom and the aunts to confiscate it."

Tillie rolled her eyes so hard I was surprised she didn't topple over. "Thank you, Little Miss Bossy. I'm so glad I have you around to explain the wrath of Winnie to me. I don't know what I would do without you spoiling my fun."

"I hear that," Nellie intoned. "Poet is our Little Miss Bossy."

"That's because I really am the boss," I reminded him. "I sign your paychecks."

"I get direct deposit," Nellie said. "You don't sign squat."

"Oh, geez." I rubbed my temples as I followed Bay through the foliage. She seemed to know where she was going so I let her lead the way. "We should've left you guys back in town."

"You could've tried," Tillie countered. "I have a truck. We simply would've followed you."

"And they would've been armed if left to their own devices," Bay said. "It's fine. Just tune them out. I like to pretend I have earplugs in whenever Aunt Tillie decides to put on a show."

"That sounds annoying."

"You have no idea. I ... ." Bay slowed her pace and held up her hand. Her body language said she meant business, so I pressed my finger to my lips to quiet Nellie and Tillie before moving closer to her.

"What are they doing?" Nellie asked, pushing his way past Bay for a better look, his eyes narrowing when he caught a hint of movement toward the water's edge. "Is that ... ?"

"Lizzy and Kaley," Bay replied, her voice barely a whisper.

"What are they doing?" I couldn't see very well from my vantage point, but something told me Bay could ... and she wasn't happy.

"They're spreading herbs," Bay replied, grim. "It's the same herbs Thistle and Clove gathered for them. They think the herbs are for one thing, but they're for another."

"I thought Terry and Landon were going to talk to them," I pressed. "Isn't that what they said?"

"The girls claimed they were only interested in the herbs for keepsakes," Bay explained. "They said they were going to throw them away."

"Obviously they didn't do that," Tillie said, all traces of mirth fleeing from her features. "I think it's time we had a talk with the little witchlings."

Bay was resigned as she nodded. "Yeah. We should approach from two sides just in case."

"Just in case of what?" I asked.

"In case they're something other than what they pretend," Tillie replied. "Not everything is as it appears. You're with the circus. You should know that."

I was offended. "Of course I know that."

"Then you go with Bay," Tillie ordered. "I'll take Nellie. We'll take those witches down and make them wish they'd never been born."

Bay snagged the back of Tillie's shirt before she could wander too far. "We're talking to them, not cursing. No spells unless they're necessary. Do you understand?"

"You're not the boss of me."

"I'll tell Mom about the still you're building in your greenhouse."

Tillie balked. "You little narc. I mean ... I'm not building a still. I promised your mother to take down the old one, and I always keep my promises."

"Yes, but you didn't promise not to build a new one. Perhaps one that's bigger and better than the last."

Tillie's eyes narrowed until they were nothing more than glittery slits. "What do you want?"

"Behave. We don't know these girls are up to anything evil. Until we do, no curses."

"You're such a kvetch."

"I can live with that."

20
TWENTY

On one hand, I thought allowing Nellie and Tillie to be a team was a terrible idea. On the other, in this particular instance, having Bay by my side seemed my best option. She was less likely to freak out ... or threaten someone with beheading.

We waited for Tillie and Nellie to disappear into a stand of nearby trees before making our move. I assumed that Lizzy and Kaley would either run or take up fighting stances when they saw us. Instead, their eyes merely went wide.

"You're not going to kill us, are you?" Lizzy blurted out.

I spared a glance for Bay and saw she looked as confused as I felt. "Probably not," I said finally. "It depends what you're doing."

"We're ... calling to the goddesses," Kaley volunteered, her eyes darting between faces. "We're not doing anything wrong."

"If you're not doing anything wrong, why did you run into the woods to cast your spell?" Bay demanded as she stepped closer, narrowing her eyes as she studied the herbal packs piled on the ground. Most of them bore tags from Hypnotic, but a few were unadorned. "What's in the baggies without names?"

"I ... it's nothing." Lizzy straightened her shoulders. "It's none of your business, so you should shoo."

I arched an eyebrow. "Shoo?"

Lizzy nodded her blond head. "Shoo." She made little motions with her hands meant to drive us away. "Shoo, shoo, shoo."

Bay rubbed her cheek as she regarded them. "I need to know what's in the baggies."

"It's none of your business," Kaley hissed, her eyes flashing. "Why can't you just mind your own business, you witch? Oh, that's right. I called you a witch. I know what you are."

"Both of you," Lizzy added. "You're both witches ... and we're strong witches, too. In fact, we're way stronger than you, so ... shoo."

They both made hand motions now.

"Uh-huh." I rubbed my forehead to ward off a building headache. This was not going as planned. "I think we should have a talk."

"And I think you need to take a step back," Kaley snapped, lunging forward to grab one of the baggies from the ground and raise it over her head. "If you don't leave, I'll curse you into oblivion."

I slid a curious look toward Bay. "Can she do that?"

Bay shrugged. "I'm guessing no. I can't really see what's in the bag. In fact ... ." Whatever she was going to say died on her lips when two figures jumped out of the bushes behind the girls.

Nellie went straight for Kaley, tackling her from behind and causing her to pitch forward. She hit the ground with a loud thud. Tillie, who had older joints, opted to be more practical and simply kicked the back of Lizzy's knees to get her to drop.

"Don't move or I'll blow your heads off!" Tillie bellowed.

Lizzy clamped her hands over the back of her head as if she were trapped in a prison movie and kept her face pressed to the ground. "Please don't kill me! I don't want to die. I have so much life left to live."

A few feet away, Nellie continued to grapple with Kaley, who fought the only way she knew how, with slaps and bites.

"Ow!" Nellie brayed as if he was dying and flapped his hand. "She bit me!"

"Knock it off," I ordered, striding forward. "You're going to hurt her."

Nellie didn't stop fighting, instead sliding his arm around Kaley's neck in an attempt to put her in a chokehold.

"Knock it off," I repeated, surging enough magic through my fingers to burn Nellie's arm without alerting the girl something odd was happening. He grunted as he released her, which she took as a sign that she'd won. When she attempted to regain her footing, I took a page from Tillie's book and kicked her knee. In the confusion, she released the bag, which I grabbed before taking a step back.

"That's mine!" Kaley screeched when she realized what I had in my hand. "I'm calling to the dark goddess so she'll do my bidding. You have no idea the wrath you've wrought!"

"Who is the dark goddess?" Bay asked, ignoring the rest of the overly emotional statement as she plucked the bag from my hand without asking. She pulled it open and inhaled. "Leek," she said after a beat. "Are you trying to conduct an exorcism?"

My mouth dropped open. "Is that a thing?"

"There aren't many magical uses for leek," she replied. "Aunt Tillie once bought some because she swore my mother was possessed."

"I haven't been proved wrong on that," Tillie noted. She'd given up standing watch over Lizzy and was busily rooting through the rest of the herbs. "Juniper berries. Goats Rue. Dandelion." She made a face as she scented another bag. "Ugh. Ginseng. You know how I feel about ginseng, Bay."

Bay nodded, blasé. "Yes. You think it's a useless herb that's been co-opted by fake witches the world over. It does nothing for weight loss and is one of the most useless herbs."

"Exactly." Tillie upended the bag and dumped the contents on the ground. "None of this stuff can conjure anything."

"That's not true," Lizzy protested, turning her head enough to see Tillie. "Hey. You don't have a gun."

"I don't," Tillie agreed. "I have this." She held up her fingers, which she'd positioned in the shape of a gun, and pointed them at the girl. "Don't make me use this. I would rather not have a murder on my conscience."

"Knock it off," Bay warned, hunkering down to look into Lizzy's eyes. "Get up, please."

Lizzy looked as if she would rather find a hole to crawl into. "I'm fine here."

"She's not going to hurt you."

"But ... people in town say she's a powerful witch," she argued. "Supposedly she can kill people with a wink of her eye."

"A blow of her whistle," Kaley countered, her glare reserved solely for Nellie as she sat on the ground and rested her palms on her knees. "She kills people with her whistle. That's what that crazy lady running the tour said."

"She said I kill people with my whistle?" Tillie was obviously offended. "Why would I need a gun if I could kill people with a whistle?"

"I don't know." Kaley rolled her neck. "Can we have our herbs back? We have a ritual to perform."

"To call to the dark goddess?" Bay pressed.

Kaley nodded. "We have a few tasks we want her to complete."

"There is no dark goddess." Bay was firm. "None of this stuff you've acquired will call anything. It's just ... herbs. Why are you out here playing around?"

"We're not *playing* around," Lizzy said as she slowly pushed herself to a sitting position, her eyes constantly darting to Tillie's finger gun. "We're powerful witches. We're going to rule the world."

"Is that all?" Tillie made a face as she dropped her hand. "Listen, as someone who regularly rules the world, it's nowhere near as much fun as it sounds. Trust me. It's better to rule your own corner of the world."

"But ... we're sick of being told what to do," Lizzy persisted. "We just want to have fun. Is that so much to ask?"

"No." Tillie was solemn. "But you're still kids. In fact ... where are your parents?" She looked around, as if expecting people to hop out of the trees and claim the youngsters. "I've seen you several times since you arrived. I've never seen an adult other than Margaret with you, and she hardly counts."

Now that she mentioned it ... . I cleared my throat to get everyone's attention. "Where are your parents?"

Lizzy and Kaley exchanged wary looks.

"Your parents aren't here, are they?" I pushed. "How did you get here without parents? How old are you guys?"

"We're eighteen," Lizzy replied quickly.

"Do you believe that, Bay?" I asked.

Bay shook her head. "How old are you really?"

"Sixteen," Kaley replied. "We're old enough to take care of ourselves."

"Do your parents know where you are?" Bay asked.

Kaley nodded. "We left a note."

I almost didn't want to hear the answer, but I asked the question all the same. "Where do you live?"

"Ohio. We left a note. We were responsible. I'm sure my mother is ready to have kittens, but she'll get over it. She always does."

Well, crap. "I'm betting someone is looking for these two," I supplied. "We should probably get your boyfriend on it."

Bay looked resigned. "Yeah. This isn't going to make him happy."

"Who cares about him?" Lizzy challenged. "You're ruining our fun."

"Get used to that," Tillie commiserated. "She ruins my fun all the time. She's good at it."

Well, that answered that question. Lizzy and Kaley weren't dangerous; they were simply young and adventurous. We were right back where we started.

"SO ... THEY'RE ON THEIR way back to Ohio?"

Kade listened to me recount my day in the shade of a large maple tree on the edge of the fairgrounds several hours later. He read the weariness weighing on my shoulders the minute he saw me, and he was all too happy to drag me away for a private talk. That included positioning me so I was cushioned between his legs as he rested against the tree. When I told him the story, instead of being upset, he couldn't stop laughing.

"They are," I confirmed, rubbing the back of my neck. "It's not funny."

"It's a little funny." He nudged my hands so he could massage away the tension. "I was starting to get worried when you were gone so long. If I'd known you were busy babysitting, I wouldn't have bothered."

"You're having way too much fun with this story." I groaned when he hit a particularly sensitive spot. "Ugh. Right there."

"If you hold still I'll massage you until my fingers fall off."

"Don't make promises you can't keep."

"That's not my style." He kissed the back of my head and kept rubbing. "Did you learn anything else?"

That was a loaded question. "I learned that sixteen is the new thirty, at least according to Lizzy and Kaley. They're totally mature, man."

Kade chuckled. "I'm sorry I missed Tillie and Nellie wrestling with teenagers. That sounds fun."

"Then the story is missing something in the telling."

"Oh, don't be a spoilsport." Another kiss brushed against my hair as he worked overtime to relax me. "How did the girls take it when you called Landon?"

I pictured their faces when we handed them over to the handsome FBI agent. "Well, it wasn't as bad as I thought. They whined a bit. There was some foot-stomping. They were so wowed by his good looks they forgot what they were crying about pretty quickly."

"He's not that good looking."

I grinned, even though he couldn't see it. "He's pretty good looking. I can see why Bay is head-over-heels for him."

Kade gripped my muscles a little tighter than necessary. "Whoops. Sorry. I got a little overzealous."

I snorted. "You're handsome, too."

He squeezed again. "I'm way more handsome than him. What kind of FBI agent is allowed to have hair like that?"

"I asked Bay during the ride back to town. She said he grew his hair for undercover work."

"I don't get the feeling he's undercover very often these days."

"No. She says he likes it, primps in the bathroom longer than her in the morning."

Kade's fingers were back to being gentle. "You like her." It was a statement, not a question.

"I do, but she's still hiding something"

"What do you think that is?"

"I don't know." I'd been asking myself that question for most of the afternoon. "I think it has something to do with her abilities. I think she's stronger than the rest."

"Even stronger than Tillie? I thought you said she was really strong."

"She is. The power is ... different. I don't know how to explain it. Bay is more contained. She's not flashy like her great-aunt. They're both powerful, and they share some attributes. Bay has something extra."

"Have you considered asking her what that extra is?"

"Yeah, but it seems invasive." I leaned back to rest against his chest. He stopped rubbing and wrapped his arms around me, placing his chin on my shoulder as we relaxed in the shade. "It might not be important. Luke says I'm a busybody. Maybe that's all this is."

"Luke is the busybody."

"I can't pretend I'm innocent when it comes to that. Remember when you first joined Mystic Caravan and I spent all my time trying to find information about you? That wasn't technically my place."

Kade's lips curved against my cheek. "I like to think you did that because you were hot for me and didn't want to admit it."

"Hot for you, huh?"

"Yup. I was hot for you, too. It all worked out in the end."

"Yeah." I pressed my eyes shut, absorbing his strength and warmth. "It worked out better than I imagined." I wasn't planning on saying the words, but they slipped out. "I love you."

He froze almost instantaneously, making me realize what I said far too late to cover.

"I mean ... ." I tripped over my tongue as my brain spun out of control. "I shouldn't have said that. I ... um ... ."

"Shh." Kade's breath was a gentle breeze on the ridge of my ear. "Don't take it back."

I couldn't take it back if I wanted to, which I didn't. Still, I felt exposed. "This probably wasn't the right time to say that."

"There is no right or wrong time to say it."

"That's easy for you to say," I muttered, shifting so I could escape his arms. "I should probably head back. We need to make dinner."

"No, no, no." He tightened his hold on me. I could've fought the effort, utilized my magic to force him to release me. That would've made things worse.

"I really think I should get back," I persisted.

"Why?"

"What do you mean? I feel like an idiot." That was an understatement. "Don't look at me." Tears, unbidden, threatened to spill. "I have to go."

"Don't cry." He was firm as he kissed my cheek. "You're making this more difficult than it has to be."

"I'm making it difficult?" I wanted to pinch him. "How am I making it difficult?"

"Because you're uncomfortable and you always make things difficult when you're uncomfortable. Stop squirming." He rubbed his cheek against mine. "I have something I want to say to you."

I wasn't sure I wanted to hear it. "I think we've said enough for one day."

"Not even close. Shh. No, shh." He linked his fingers with mine and exhaled heavily. "I love you, too."

The words were like a salve. I didn't say "I love you" because I expected him to say it back. It was something that happened in the moment, something I felt from my soul. I had a feeling he felt that way — I certainly knew I did — but I thought exchanging the words would come a bit down the line. We always balked when it came up before, even in jest.

"I love you," he said again, trying the words on for size. "Don't be embarrassed or turn away."

"I'm not embarrassed." I was mortified to my very bones. "I just didn't think you were going to say it, too."

"You didn't give me a chance to say it."

"I gave you plenty of chances."

"Shh." He kissed my ear and shifted me so I faced him. The look of naked emotion on his face was enough to cause my heart to stutter. "I wanted to tell you first. I had a big plan."

"You had a plan?"

His smile was sheepish. "Candles. Romance. Schmaltzy stuff."

"Why didn't that happen?" I was legitimately curious.

"Because my hands caught fire and I've spent the last two weeks feeling sorry for myself."

Well, at least he was honest. "I wish you would've talked to me about that. I have hands that can make fire, too. It's not exactly the same, but I could've helped."

"I know. I wasn't ready."

"Are you ready now?"

He nodded. "Yeah, but I'm still kind of annoyed you said it first."

He could have no idea how that simple statement made me feel like the luckiest woman alive. "Well, you weren't all that far behind."

"I guess."

"I was still first, though."

He poked my side. "I love you." His words were simple and to the point. "Now I've said it three times to your one."

I barked out a laugh. "Are we keeping score?"

He shrugged. "It's a relief to be able to say it."

He wasn't wrong. "How about we skip dinner tonight, go to bed early, and see who can say it the most times before dawn?"

His lips slid into a sly grin. "That's the best offer I've had all day." He leaned forward and kissed me. "I bet I'll win."

"I bet *I'll* win."

"I guess we'd better get to competing, huh?"

"You're on."

21
TWENTY-ONE

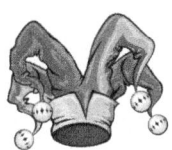

No one questioned why we retired early. Even Luke didn't knock on the door to rouse us ... or to complain pathetically outside our window. Everything was blissfully silent for our bonding exercise. It was early when we fell asleep, but neither of us cared. It was the perfect evening.

Until it wasn't.

I bolted awake just after midnight, something causing my brain to switch on as I rolled to a sitting position and stared into the darkness. There was nothing to see in our bedroom. When I looked through the window, which was mostly covered by the blinds, I didn't see anything – or anyone, for that matter.

That didn't mean we were safe.

"What is it, Poet?" Kade murmured, his hand finding my back.

"I don't know." That was the truth. I had no idea how to answer him. Instead, I cocked my head and listened with my ears and senses. "I think someone is outside."

Before, Kade had sounded sleepy when he asked what was wrong. Now, all traces of weariness were gone from his voice. "Where?"

"I don't know." I got out of bed and felt along the floor until I found my shirt. I pulled it on without thinking (or bothering with a bra) and grabbed a pair of yoga pants from the dresser at the far end of the room. When I turned, Kade was already dressed in gym shorts and a T-shirt. His eyes were trained on me instead of the door.

"What?" I asked, suddenly self-conscious.

"The fact that you're not wearing underwear gives me ideas," he admitted.

The look I shot him was withering. "Is now really the time for that?"

"No, but I'll remember it for later."

"Yeah, yeah, yeah."

Kade's hands were deft when we reached the front door. He opened it without a sound. He wasn't armed, which I found interesting. When he first arrived at Mystic Caravan he thought weapons were necessary. It appeared he finally realized he was a weapon, which was an intriguing – and perhaps frightening – development.

The fairgrounds were quiet when we landed in front of our trailer. I took a long time to look to my left and right, hoping I'd spy a hint of movement.

There was nothing.

"What do you think?" Kade's mouth was directly next to my ear when he spoke. "Are we in danger?"

I wasn't sure how to answer. Finally, I shrugged. I honestly didn't know.

He met my gaze for what felt like forever, and I was convinced he was going to start yelling ... or at least make a snarky comment. Instead, he merely nodded and pointed toward the left.

I understood what he was saying. He wanted us to take the main aisle through the circus. If someone else was present, we would have a better chance of discovering him or her from that vantage point. I nodded, allowing him to squeeze my hand before we started moving through the silent attractions.

Most people would find a dark and empty circus freaky. The mere idea of creepy clowns hiding behind tents would be enough to cause "normal" individuals to run screaming into the night. I wasn't most people, and I knew the circus layout better than anyone.

I was sure-footed as I moved through the gloom. Fog had settled over the area sometime while we slumbered, which only served to remind me of the ordeal in Eureka. Fog haunted us as much as the witches and ghosts during that stay, and it wasn't something I wanted to revisit.

Kade obviously felt the same way.

"Ugh. I hate this stuff," he grumbled under his breath. "It reminds me of every bad horror movie I've ever seen."

I shot him a sympathetic look before continuing. The closer I got to the heart of the circus, the more my inner alarms screamed to be noticed. The thing was, they weren't exactly pinging "danger" as much as "intruder." It was an interesting feeling.

I opened my mouth to explain just that to Kade when I caught a hint of movement out of the corner of my eye. I jerked my head in that direction, my muscles going tense, and I felt Kade's body press against mine from behind.

"I don't see anything," he whispered.

"There's something over there." I felt it more than saw it. "Prepare yourself."

"For what?"

That was the question, wasn't it? I didn't answer. I couldn't. Instead I turned down the nearest cross aisle and headed toward the movement, my hands ready to call for magic in an instant as they flexed at my sides.

We didn't have to go far. The sound of voices told me we'd found our quarry before I managed to make out movement again. I recognized the voices.

"Knock it off, Clove."

"You knock it off, Thistle."

"You're being stupid. Stop shifting like that. You're going to draw attention."

Three figures stood in the spot where Boney Billy's body was found. I recognized them right away, even though I'd had limited contact with them.

"Shut up," Bay snapped, her eyes expectant as she stared at something near the entrance to the midway. "I need to concentrate."

"Is he here?" Clove asked.

Bay nodded. "He is."

"Was he always here or did you make him appear?" Thistle countered. "What? Don't look at me that way. It's an honest question."

I was confused. Who was the "he" they were referring to? I saw only three figures, and they were alone. Kade was pressed to my back as he watched over my shoulder. His expression was hard to read when I slid him a glance, but he didn't look happy.

"Just make him answer your questions and then let's get out of here," Clove whined. "You know I don't like sneaking into places where clowns could attack. That's my least favorite thing to do."

Thistle made an exaggerated face, which was only visible because of the large moon. "When have we ever snuck into a place where attacking clowns were a legitimate worry?"

"Exactly." Clove bobbed her dark head. "That's something we don't want to happen. I mean .... why would we want it to happen? That's the stupidest thing I've ever heard."

Despite the surreal situation, I relaxed a bit. The witches obviously weren't here to hurt us, although what they were doing remained a mystery.

"I'm going over there," I whispered to Kade.

He shook his head and grabbed my wrist. "They could hurt you."

"They're not here to hurt me." I wasn't sure what they were here to do, but I had a feeling it had more to do with investigating than maiming. "Trust me."

He shot me a dark look but moved to follow. I was barely out of the shadow of the nearest tent — which belonged to Nellie — when Thistle's head snapped up and she stared directly at me.

"Bay, there's someone over there," she said urgently, her hand shooting out and grabbing Clove's arm. "We need to get out of here right now."

Bay, who had been intent on a point of interest behind the other two, turned her head to the left. I thought she might run, try to save face. Instead, all hell broke loose.

I'm still not sure the order of events. I know that Clove screamed, but I'm pretty sure it was in reaction to seeing Nellie and Dolph rush out of the nearby tent. Nellie had his ax and looked to be out for blood, but he didn't swing.

Thistle instinctively shoved Clove out of the way as she barked a small curse and sent a wall of energy flowing in Dolph's direction. It wasn't a strong spell, but it caused him to rock backward as he tried to maintain his footing.

For her part, Bay's eyes went wide as the area surrounding her illuminated with ethereal spirits. I recognized Billy as one of them, and I was fairly certain the face floating behind her belonged to Darren Rappaport. I did not recognize the woman on her left, but she was obviously a ghost, too.

"Protect," Bay intoned, her voice going deep. The ghosts instantly hopped to attention and raced toward Dolph and Nellie, their intentions obvious.

"Wait!" I almost tripped when I raced out to join the fray, waving my hand to get everyone's attention.

Bay looked in my direction a split second before Billy broke off from the rest of the ghosts and careened toward me. He didn't look as if he recognized me, and it was obvious he was ready to dole out pain.

"No!" My fingers sparked as I threw up a protection charm, which was basically a wall that cut Kade and me off from the ghosts.

Kade's hands were in the air, fire floating around his fingertips, but he looked terrified to risk unleashing it. I didn't blame him. It was utter bedlam, which was about to get worse.

The sky above us lit up, almost as if fireworks were igniting in every direction, and Max appeared out of the shadows. His expression was terrible, as if he was ready to raze the world, and I could sense the pooling magic as he geared up to release it.

"Don't!" I gasped, jerking in his direction.

Kade stopped me with a hand around my waist. "Don't get involved," he ordered. "Max has this." He sounded relieved.

"He doesn't have anything." I squirmed to escape from Kade's iron grip. "I think this is a misunderstanding."

"It doesn't look like a misunderstanding to me," Raven said as she moved to my left and watched the unfolding scene. "Max is going to massacre them. This looks like fun."

That was hardly the word I would've used. "No!"

My scream was drowned out by the appearance of another figure, this one cutting in from the west. It was Tillie, and she was dressed for war. She boasted leggings that looked as if they had spider webs on them, and her combat helmet was firmly in place. She was unarmed, but the gun was obviously unnecessary.

"*Tempestas*!" She screeched the word as she raised her hands above her head.

In an instant, the previously clear sky turned cloudy and thunder roared in conjunction with the approaching storm.

"Is that Naida?" Kade asked, confused.

I shook my head. "It's Tillie. She can control the weather."

"And who is controlling the ghosts?" Raven asked, confused.

"Bay."

"Huh. That's interesting. I ... ." Whatever she was going to say died on her lips as one of the ghosts started barreling in our direction.

"Poet!" Kade held tight as he tried to move me out of the way, but I knew I only had one chance to stop this. If I didn't, someone would most certainly die.

"I can't." I shoved away from him and raced toward the spot between Tillie and Max. They eyed each other with great interest ... and murderous intent. "Don't!" I screeched as I skidded to a stop between them, holding up my hands. "Don't do anything!"

Max was calm as he met my gaze. "I believe we're under attack."

I shook my head. "They were here looking for Billy's ghost because they wanted answers. I don't think they meant to wake us ... or hurt us." I looked for Bay's face in the darkness, and when she finally appeared under the limited moonlight her cheek was streaked with dirt. "That's why you're here, right?"

She nodded, licking her lips as she glanced around. "We thought we could sneak onto the property without you knowing."

Raven snorted. "Good job."

Thistle straightened her frame and glared. "No one needs your lip, snake girl."

"How do you know what she is?" I asked, legitimately curious.

"We know more than we might've let on," Bay admitted, sheepish.

"I was just about to tell you the same thing."

She pursed her lips, considering. "I guess we should talk."

"That would probably be best," I agreed.

"Wait ... so there's no fight?" Dolph looked disappointed as he dropped his fists. "Well, this just bites."

Nellie patted his arm. "I know, big guy. If it's any consolation, that's the witch I was telling you about." He winked at Tillie. "She's the peanut to my M&M, man. I'm not kidding."

Ugh. If things weren't bad enough to give me a headache, that statement alone would've sent me over the edge.

"Well, this was fun," Kade said brightly.

I could think of other ways to describe it.

WE SETTLED AT the picnic tables, Nellie delivering bottles of water to everyone. Max took his spot at the head of the table. Tillie conjured a chair from somewhere and placed herself at the other end, essentially giving herself equal power.

It was mildly amusing.

"How did you get across the dreamcatcher without it alerting?" Max asked right off the bat.

"The dreamcatcher is for evil beings," Tillie replied, unbothered. "We're not evil."

"But ... you obviously had evil intent tonight," Max pressed.

"I don't think they did," I argued, my eyes landing on Bay's weary features. "You're a necromancer, aren't you?"

She didn't deny the charge, instead rubbing her forehead. "Kind of. I'm still figuring it out."

"Well, you'd better put some work into it," Tillie groused. "That was a poor showing. They would've beaten us if this one hadn't stepped in to end things." She jerked her thumb in my direction. "Those ghosts were not strong enough to serve as an attacking force. Do you want to know why? Because you didn't put your heart into it. That needs to change."

"Speaking of the ghosts ... ." I broke off, looking over my shoulder. "How did you know they were here?"

"I've always been able to see and talk to ghosts," Bay explained. "It started when I was a kid and I've never been able to shake it. It's only recently that I've been able to control them. It's a ... long story."

"We appear to have time," Max hedged.

Bay opened her mouth and then shook her head. "It doesn't matter. I really don't know how it works. In a nutshell, one day a killer was after me and I could use ghosts to protect myself. That's basically it."

"You're forgetting about the part where you were the reason the ghosts stayed behind in the first place," Thistle offered, earning a dark look for her contribution. "I was just saying." She steadfastly avoided her cousin's murderous gaze. "Lovely night, huh? Is there anything better than fog?"

"We're not exactly fans of fog after witches hid in the last batch and tried to kill us," Nellie volunteered.

"I can see where that would put you off witches," Clove said. "We're not here to do that. We simply wanted to talk to the ghosts to see if they knew who killed them."

"Anything?" I asked Bay hopefully.

She shook her head. "They're both confused. With a little time I might be able to get through to them. Not right now, though. Right now we're ... still at a loss. We don't have answers, and you don't have answers, which means there are no answers."

"Oh, that was profound, Bay," Thistle drawled.

"Shut up, mouth," Tillie warned, extending a finger. "I can take only so much from you in one day, and you're officially at your limit."

"Yeah, yeah, yeah." Thistle waved off her great-aunt's admonishment and focused on Max. "So ... what are you?"

Max merely cocked an eyebrow. "What do you think I am?"

"I don't know. That's why I asked. You're definitely powerful."

"I definitely am," Max agreed, slowly pushing himself to his feet. He seemed to have made up his mind about the witches, and he was no longer at red alert with murder on his mind. "Next time, announce yourselves. You can wander wherever you want on the grounds. We're working on this one together, are we not?"

Tillie shrugged. "That's not generally how we operate. We're used to having to break rules."

"Well, in this particular case it was unnecessary. Things could've gone very badly had Poet not intervened. I was ready to end you."

Tillie snorted. "You could've tried."

"I would've succeeded."

"So typically male," Tillie huffed. "You assume you're stronger because you're a man."

"Are you accusing me of being sexist?" Max's anger was on full display.

"Knock it off," I snapped, frustrated. I ignored the surprised look Max shot me. I rarely raised my voice with him. "We need to work together on this. No more sneaking around and hiding things."

Bay's expression was thoughtful, but she nodded. "I thought I saw one of the women from the tour group earlier this evening. She was at the edge of the fairgrounds watching all of you."

"When was this?" I stiffened, surprised. "I didn't see anyone."

"That's probably because you and Kade had dinner in bed this evening," Raven shot back. "You guys were MIA the entire night. I didn't see anyone watching us, for the record."

"She was over there." Bay pointed toward the line of trees. "I saw her when I was leaving the newspaper office. I thought it was weird, because the second she saw me watching her she ducked back and I didn't see her again."

That was definitely interesting. "Do you think you would recognize her if you saw her again?" I asked.

She nodded. "Yes."

"Then that's where we'll start tomorrow." I rubbed my neck as I stood. "Everyone should go home and get some sleep. We'll talk about strategy and our next step tomorrow morning over breakfast. How does that sound?"

"Sounds good to me," Nellie replied, sending Tillie an air kiss that turned my stomach.

"I'll be here," Bay said as she gestured for Tillie to cede her chair. "Come on. We need to get home before Landon wakes up. He's going to be angry."

"That's what you get for falling in love with 'The Man,'" Tillie said. "I don't feel sorry for you."

"I'm not asking you to feel sorry."

"Yeah, well ... hey!" Tillie brightened as she fell into step with her great-nieces. "Who wants to head over to Gaylord and go through the drive-through? I could totally eat tacos right now."

I smirked as I watched them go, my stomach rumbling at the idea of tacos. What? I skipped dinner.

"Well, that was fun," Kade said as he moved up beside me. "Can we trust them?"

I nodded without hesitation. "If they wanted to hurt us they would've already done it. They're looking for answers, same as us."

"Well, hopefully tomorrow we will start getting those answers." He slid his arm around my shoulders. "Let's go back to bed."

"Okay." We turned in that direction, lost in thought and each other.

"Oh, just one other thing," he added when we hit the stairs that led to the trailer. "I love you."

My lips curved, unbidden. "Thank you. I love you, too."

"Doesn't that feel nice?"

"It's the best feeling in the world."

22
TWENTY-TWO

Bay and Tillie were at the picnic table eating breakfast with our crew when Kade and I exited our trailer the next morning. We were still basking in the love because ... well, we're schmaltzy, but there was no accusation in Bay's eyes when they locked with mine. In fact, she seemed to be in a relatively good mood.

"I take it you managed to get into your house without anyone noticing last night," I said as I sipped my coffee and settled in a spot across the table from her.

"Oh, no, Landon was waiting for me when I got back. He noticed the dirt." Bay didn't look particularly bothered by the admission.

"Did you argue?"

She nodded. "Then we made up. It was fine."

"Yes, Landon is like a dog," Tillie noted. "He wags his tail as long as you scratch his favorite spot and bribe him with bacon."

Bay didn't argue with the assertion, so I decided to let it go. "I'm assuming we're focusing on the individual you saw loitering in the woods yesterday," I said, smiling in thanks as Naida delivered a plate of eggs and hash browns to me. "We need to figure out who she is."

"I've already done that," Bay said, smirking when I forked a huge mouthful of eggs into my mouth. "Are you feeling peckish after last night?"

"I'm simply hungry."

Kade's plate was even bigger than mine. He didn't say a word as he steadily shoveled food into his mouth.

"Yeah, well, I know how that goes." Bay's smile was small but heartfelt. "I managed to get a look at the registrations for the festival first thing this morning. I know who we're looking for because Landon ran a few of the registered visitors while looking for background hints. He had the files at the guesthouse."

Hmm. "And he just let you look at them?"

"I noticed them on the table when we were arguing," she replied. "They were sitting out. He needed something to do while stewing about me sneaking away in the middle of the night."

"The good news is, she does it quite often," Tillie offered. "Most people think she has a second job as a prostitute. We let them think that so they don't uncover our real secret."

Kade choked on his eggs, which meant Luke took the opportunity to thump his back as hard as possible. "Thank you, Luke."

"Don't mention it." Luke winked at me, clearly amused. "So, who are we dealing with?"

"Her name is Emily Wilde," Bay replied. "She's staying at the Dragonfly."

I was impressed. "How do you know that?"

"The manifest lists lodging locations."

"Do you know where the Dragonfly is?"

She nodded. "Yeah. In fact ... we're very familiar with the Dragonfly." She cast a warning look in Tillie's direction before the older woman could say something derisive. "My father owns it ... along with Thistle's and Clove's fathers."

That was ... odd. "Okay. Um ... can we go out there to talk to them?"

"That shouldn't be a problem. Although ... I thought you were opening today." Bay looked uncomfortable as she shifted on the bench. "I could head out to the Dragonfly alone and question them."

That didn't sound safe. "We open at noon. I have time to go out there with you. Unless, well, you don't want me to accompany you."

"It's not you I'm worried about." Bay slid her eyes to Tillie, who was busy drinking coffee and shooting small finger waves in Nellie's direction. "Aunt Tillie and my father don't exactly get along."

"Ah." That made sense. "We can leave her here with the others if you want."

I thought Tillie had mostly tuned us out. I was wrong.

"No way." Tillie vehemently shook her head. "If those witches are dangerous, you'll need me."

"I think Bay and I are more than capable of handling ourselves," I argued.

"And I think ... ." She broke off and blew a loud raspberry at me, which caused Nellie, Dolph and Luke to break into riotous guffaws.

"We need to keep her," Luke said, swiping at his eyes. "I mean ... she's awesome."

"Did you hear that, Bay?" Tillie sneered. "I'm awesome."

"I can think of a few other ways to describe you," Bay said calmly. "The fact remains that we don't have much time. I can drive us out to the Dragonfly. We don't actually know this woman has anything to do with what happened. I simply found it odd that she was hiding in the trees and spying on your group."

"We have no other place to look," I agreed. "I have to be back here by noon, but we should definitely check them out. It's better to be safe than sorry."

"It's better to be drunk than sorry," Tillie countered. "I think the odds of this woman being a threat are slim, but I never pass up a chance to bother Jack."

I was confused. "Who is Jack?"

Bay rubbed her forehead and grunted. "My father."

I always thought that I was missing out once I lost my family. Being an orphan sucked. There were times I was on the street and I imagined things would be perfect if my family had only lived.

Watching the Winchesters in action disavowed me of that notion.

"Let me finish my breakfast and we'll head out," I said, hiding a smirk behind my coffee mug when Tillie let loose a mischievous grin. She was obviously looking forward to the trip.

"Do you want me to go with you?" Kade asked, finally coming up for air.

"No." I shook my head. "We have no proof Emily is involved in this. In fact, odds are she was just curious and didn't want to be seen staring at us. It will be fine. Besides, you're needed to keep an eye on the perimeter here."

"All the area inns are full," Bay explained. "The tourists will be bussed downtown starting at eleven. It's going to be a madhouse ... and I fully expect things to grow tense for different reasons when that happens."

"Okay." Kade met her gaze evenly. "If something happens to Poet, I will come after you."

Tillie snorted. "Oh, geez. We have another alpha man making threats. Someone give him some bacon to shut him up."

Kade shifted his eyes to her. "I'm not afraid of you. I know that you derive strength from terrorizing others, but that's not going to work with me."

"I guess we'll just have to wait and see whether that's true or not, huh, Sparky?"

Kade's lips curved down. "What do you mean by that?"

"Nothing. Drink your coffee."

"No, you meant something."

Tillie heaved out a long-suffering sigh. "This is why men should be seen and not heard." She looked to Bay for support. "Didn't I tell you that men were only good for mowing the lawn and caulking tubs?"

Bay snorted. "I believe you may have mentioned something along those lines. You're all talk, though. I know you loved Uncle Calvin beyond reason and you wouldn't be saying those things if he was still around."

"Your uncle was the lone exception. That man was a saint."

"He put up with you. He was definitely a saint."

"Oh, I know what you're trying to do." Tillie narrowed her eyes and wagged a finger. "You're trying to irritate me so I don't go with you to the Dragonfly. That won't work. I haven't seen your father in weeks. We're due for a reunion."

Bay made a disgusted face. "That's exactly what I'm afraid of."

IT WAS A GOOD THING Bay drove, because I had no idea what to make of the ridiculous two-lane highway that led to the Dragonfly. Tillie sat in the passenger seat, leaving me in the backseat alone. I was much more interested in the scenery than anything else, even as I bounced around thanks to the rutted roadway.

"This place is really beautiful," I noted as Bay pulled into a winding driveway. "I bet you had fun running around the woods when you were a kid."

"Not out here," Bay countered. "They only bought this inn about a year ago."

"Margaret mentioned something about that." I was uncomfortable admitting I'd listened to gossip about the Winchester family. "She said your fathers all left around the same time."

"Yes."

"That must have been difficult."

"It was ... what it was." Bay briefly slid her eyes to Tillie as the Dragonfly rolled into view. "It wasn't so bad. I got to live in a big house with Clove and Thistle, we always had fresh cookies, and Aunt Tillie took us on adventures."

"I did," Tillie agreed, unfastening her seatbelt. "Come on. I'm sure Jack is dying to see me."

I had my doubts, but I couldn't stop myself from smiling as I climbed out and met Bay in front of her car. "I'm not as effusive as the rest of my co-workers, but I kind of love your aunt," I admitted, sheepish.

"You've only known her for a few days," Bay pointed out. "She's not nearly as much fun when you've spent twenty-nine years with her."

"I don't know ... I bet you have stories that you'll be able to tell to your grandchildren. She'll never really die because she'll be alive in the stories."

Bay cocked her head, intrigued. "I never asked, which feels stupid now, but I kind of want to know. How did you end up in the circus?"

This was hardly the first time I'd been asked the question. Bay was so sincerely curious, though, that I was caught off guard.

"Well ... my parents died when I was a kid and I was put into foster care. It didn't go well. I ended up on the street, where I learned to do lifts and live in parks. And then I ran into Max and tried to pick his pocket. The rest is ... a rather long tale."

Bay widened her eyes. "You were on the street?"

"It's not as bad as it sounds."

"I don't think I could've survived that." She was earnest. "I'm glad you did. Thank the goddess for Max, huh?"

I'd thought that so many times over the years I'd lost count. "He saved me."

"No." Bay shook her head, firm. "You saved yourself. I've watched you, and I'm in awe. You made yourself. He might have helped, given you a nudge, but you're a self-made woman."

"So are you."

"No. I'm a product of my environment. All the women in my family had a hand in molding me."

"I think you're being too hard on yourself." I opted for honesty. "If you were simply a product of your environment, you would have your own whistle."

She snorted. "I guess."

"We're all the sums and parts of our environment," I pointed out. "Your environment was vastly different from mine, yet we ended up in much the same place. Sure, your boyfriend has pretty hair that I'm fairly certain isn't allowed in the FBI no matter what he says, and mine looks like he's fresh out of the military, but they're both good men.

"I have a loud best friend who says whatever comes to his mind ... and you have Thistle," I continued. "You have a father, but you're obviously close to your father figure. That's how I am with Max. Sure, it complicates things that he's Kade's father, but not so much that it matters.

"We have a cross-dressing dwarf and you have a great-aunt who likes to carry around a gun," I said. "I haven't yet met your mother and aunts, but I'm willing to bet they're unique, too. We have very different parts making up the whole, yet we live in the midst of powerful families that are largely interchangeable.

"I don't think that's a coincidence."

Bay's features lightened as she smiled. "That was almost poetic."

"How do you think I got my name?"

She chuckled. "I ... ." She trailed off when something occurred to her, swiveling quickly. It was too late. Tillie was already inside the inn. She'd disappeared from view while we were talking. "Oh, geez. This won't end well."

I was mildly curious to see if that were true. "We should find her, right?"

"Definitely. She'll give my father an aneurysm if we don't head her off."

THE DRAGONFLY WAS BEAUTIFUL.

Whoever decorated the inn took a lot of time and great care in selecting every item. The lobby was cute and inviting, and the parlor looked like a place to spend a lot of time thanks to the comfy couch, endless bookshelves and quaint fireplace.

The only thing the inn didn't appear to have was Tillie, which I found odd.

"Where would she go?" I asked, glancing around.

"Wherever she thinks she can cause the most mayhem," Bay replied, grim. "Come on." She motioned with her hand. "I've got twenty bucks that says she's in the kitchen."

"Why would she be there?"

"Because she's a busybody who likes to poke, and breakfast probably wrapped up ten minutes ago."

"Ah. You know best."

"If that were true I would've left her at The Overlook this morning."

Bay practically stomped through the inn, not stopping until she let herself through the swinging door that led to the kitchen. There, three men worked cleaning the counters and dishes while Tillie waxed poetic about ... well, actually, I had no idea what she was talking about.

"You really should spend more time joining in community events, Jack," Tillie said as she leaned against the counter and smiled as an annoyed-looking man tried to slide around her. "If you did, you wouldn't be so surprised when we stop in for visits because you would recognize when the schedule warrants it."

The man, who I assumed was Jack because of the way he glowered at Bay, merely shook his head. "Oh, so you are here."

Bay plastered a smile on her face. "I am," she agreed. "How are you, Dad?"

Jack remained grim for a long beat, and then he dissolved in a smile as he moved in front of her to exchange a hug. "I was in a great mood until your aunt showed up to explain we were doing dishes wrong."

"You need to scrub the dishes before you put them in the dishwasher," Tillie explained. "Everybody knows that's important."

Bay pressed her lips together, annoyance obvious. "I'm sorry. I was talking to Poet in the driveway and Aunt Tillie got away from me. I shouldn't have let it happen, but ... you know how she is."

"Oh, we know." One of the other men patted Tillie on the head as he passed. "We're just waiting for news that you've finally put her in a home."

"I heard that, Warren!" Tillie snapped. "You'll be in a home long before me."

"Not that I'm not happy to see you — and I'm always happy to see you, so don't go getting weird or anything — but what are you doing here, Bay?" Jack asked. "I was under the impression you were slammed for the entire week because of the festival. We scheduled dinner for next week, right?"

"We did." Bay nodded. "It's just ... are you aware of what's going on in town?"

"Yeah. Thousands of witches are descending to cast curses in the square and revere Tillie for being the head witch."

"There is no such thing as a head witch," Tillie countered. "But ... that's not a bad idea. Maybe I should suggest making someone the head witch. That might be fun."

"Oh, geez." Jack rubbed his forehead. "Why are you here again? And, more importantly, why did you bring Tillie?"

"She insisted on coming," Bay replied. "We have a bit of a situation."

"There's always a bit of a situation where you're concerned," Jack said. "What situation are we dealing with today?"

"Two people have been murdered downtown. One was a local. One was with the circus that's here for the festival."

"I suggest looking at the circus troupe," Jack supplied. "Those people are always strange."

I managed to keep from shouting at him, but just barely. This was technically Bay's show.

"Poet is with the circus," Bay said tightly. "She's perfectly normal."

"Oh." Jack had the grace to be abashed. "Sorry about the circus crack."

"I'm used to it." I waved off his apology. "That's hardly the worst thing I've heard since joining Mystic Caravan."

"If it's any consolation, I would much prefer you to Tillie. In fact, can you take her with you when you leave?"

"I heard that!" Tillie glared at Jack. "Do you want to be on my list? It's pretty full these days thanks to Thistle and Margaret, but I can always make room for you."

"I think I'll pass," Jack said dryly. "You still haven't told me what you're doing here."

"We need to speak with one of your guests," Bay said. "Emily Wilde. My understanding is that she checked in early Sunday, before anyone else showed up."

Jack's expression turned thoughtful as he nodded. "I know who you're talking about. She came with two other women."

"Jamie Blake and Madison Connor," I volunteered.

He nodded again. "Yeah. They split two rooms. They didn't seem thrilled to be here. It was almost as if they were on a business trip instead of vacation."

"Maybe that's because they had plans of a different sort," Bay mused. "I don't suppose you could tell us what room they're in?" She adopted a wheedling tone as she batted her eyes at her father.

He sighed. "I shouldn't tell you that because of privacy rules, but it doesn't matter. They checked out first thing this morning. They're gone."

I stilled. "Gone? The festival doesn't start until today."

"That's why I was surprised when they came downstairs with their suitcases packed. They said an emergency came up and they understood their credit cards would be charged for the entire stay even though they were leaving early. They seemed eager to get out of here."

"I wonder why," Bay muttered, shaking her head. "Crap. We missed them."

"And now they look even more suspicious than before," I added. "Why would they run like that?"

"I have no idea." Bay held her hands palms out. "But I intend to find out."

23
TWENTY-THREE

We had a problem.

The disappearance of Madison, Jamie and Emily left us with a host of questions, and absolutely no answers.

Did they leave because they really had a crisis that necessitated returning home?

Did they leave because they worried we were on to them and thought it best to flee?

Did they leave because they'd finished what they started, whatever that was, and had no reason to stay?

Or, and this was the most worrisome scenario of all, did they only pretend to leave?

Tillie, of course, assumed they were still around and in need of smiting. She thought that word a lot. *Smiting*. She seemed keen to smite someone. I had no idea if she'd ever really done it, but the dark look on Bay's face whenever Tillie mentioned it made me think there was a real possibility she was capable of carrying it off.

The other problem was a bit more urgent. The circus was opening today, and no matter how badly I wanted to track potentially evil witches I had a job to do. That meant returning to the fairgrounds, changing into my performance outfit and focusing on actual work.

That didn't sit well with Tillie, who was determined to smite someone before the day was out. Bay was more gracious. She understood ... and she had a plan.

"So, basically you're saying that Tillie and Bay are going to be running around the circus the entire time we're trying to work today," Kade drawled as he watched me tie a scarf over my dark hair. It seemed ridiculous to wear a costume when telling fortunes, but the guests appreciated it and I learned long ago not to mess with expectations when it came to making money.

"Not just Tillie and Bay," I responded, patting away some of the shine on my face with pressed powder. "Thistle and Clove will be in and out, too. They have their shop to run — and someone has to be there the entire time because this will be a big day for them — but they're going to try to schedule some time to act as lookouts, too."

"Well, great."

I cast him a sidelong look. His tone said he was feeling something other than great. "If you don't want them here I guess I can track down Bay before the gates open and tell her to abort the plan."

"You're obviously not keen with that suggestion."

"I'm not," I agreed. "We're going to be busy today. They have extra eyes and understand the potential stakes."

"And what are the stakes?" Kade wasn't ready to back down. "We don't know these women have anything to do with what happened. They could be innocent."

"They disappeared."

"Maybe they really did have an emergency. They could be halfway to Pittsburgh right now for all you know."

He wasn't wrong. "Bay saw one of them watching us from the trees."

"I hate to break it to you, but circus folk have been the subject of fascination for hundreds of years. Maybe she was just curious. Maybe she decided she was hot for me and was trying to spy to see if I was single."

I narrowed my eyes. "I'm guessing you'd like that."

His lips curved, amusement obvious. "Actually, I have a girlfriend.

You might know her. She's a sexy Romani with a laugh that makes me go warm all over and a smile that makes my stomach do somersaults."

Ugh. That was disgustingly sweet, and he knew it. "Behold the king of schmaltz," I teased, gesturing toward him.

He nodded without hesitation. "You make me schmaltzy. There's no getting around that. If you're uncomfortable about the possibility of her watching me, then we'll change it up. Maybe she was watching Luke and they left because they realized he didn't play for the right team."

I tilted my head to the side, considering. Finally, I shook it. "No. That doesn't fit. There's something wrong with the way they bolted out of town with so little notice. People with a legitimate emergency would try to get their money back on the room. These women simply ceded thousands of dollars."

"Thousands of dollars?" Kade knit his eyebrows. "How do you figure that?"

"The festival," I replied simply. "The closest rooms are going at a premium. Bay said the rooms at her mother's inn are going for a grand a night because of the demand."

"You have got to be kidding me." He was dumbfounded. I didn't blame him. "Wow! Maybe we're in the wrong line of work. Have you ever considered opening an inn in a witch town? We might be good at it."

I chuckled. "I don't know that you and Luke could run a business together."

"I didn't invite Luke to play house with us."

My expression softened. "Is that what you want? To play house, I mean."

"I want you. I'm fine playing house in the trailer right now. Where we'll end up, I have no idea. I do know we'll be together for all of it, though."

The words were comforting. "I love you."

He grinned. "I'm still ahead in that competition."

"Yeah, well ... I've been distracted. That will change once we figure out who's killing people."

"I guess we'll have to wait to see." He strolled closer and tapped my chin to get me to lift it. "I want you to be careful today regardless. I know you trust Bay — and I see no reason not to trust her — but if she's as powerful as you say ... ." He left it hanging because the idea of finishing the statement was too much for him to bear.

"She's definitely powerful." I knew that without a doubt. "She's not a threat. She wants to solve this as much as we do."

"You put a lot of faith in her, especially since you just met."

"Perhaps I think we're kindred souls."

He sighed. "And because I love your soul, I should be comfortable with her. That's what you're saying, right?"

I shook my head. "You need to feel what you feel. That's only fair. It would be helpful if you didn't attack her, though. You're just getting the hang of your powers, and she can order ghosts to attack. She'd kick your ass."

He smirked. "Fair enough. I'll keep my eyes open for the witches and try not to get in their way while making my rounds. Does that make you happy?"

I nodded. "Also, I guess her mother and aunts are coming. I'm not sure what they look like, but according to Bay, they're likely to act oddly, too."

"Well, great. A whole circus full of witches. What could possibly go wrong?"

"I'M READY FOR MY FORTUNE."

Margaret was the first person to enter my tent. I couldn't decide if I was surprised or should've expected her. She was dressed in an expensive suit — seriously, she must've spent a thousand dollars on the pink monstrosity — and the hat she wore was straight out of a Kentucky Derby fashion faux pas show.

"Um ... hi." I plastered a fake smile on my face. "I didn't realize you would be here so early."

"But you were expecting me?" Margaret was prim and proper as she sat in the chair across the table.

"I definitely expected you." I reached for my tarot cards. "What kind of reading do you want?"

"Well ...," she licked her lips. "I'm not sure. What are my options?"

"I can tell you about your future or help you with a problem from the past. It merely helps with the outcome to focus on what I'm trying to ascertain."

"Oh, well ... ." Margaret's smile was tight. "Surprise me."

The answer was off-putting, but I merely smiled. "Sure. I'll surprise you." I dropped the cards on the table and extended my hands. "Give me the hand you were born with."

"I believe I was born with both of them."

"Your right."

She acquiesced. "What's the difference?"

I merely smiled. "Your non-dominant hand signifies your potential. Your dominant hand will tell me what you're doing with that potential."

"Oh." She preened. "I'm doing a lot with my potential."

I had my doubts. "Well ... let's see about that, shall we?"

I wrapped both my hands over Margaret's and closed my eyes. Almost instantly, I was transported to another time. I recognized the players right away.

"What's the problem?"

Tillie might have been younger, but she had the same challenging tone. "They're kids. They've lost their home right before Christmas. Why wouldn't we want to help?"

"They're not kids," Margaret shot back. "They're ... hoodlums!"

I noticed they were standing in a room full of people. A few of the women sitting close to the front nodded as they bent their heads together, a low murmur going through the crowd.

"I still don't understand," Tillie pressed. "They're kids."

"They're kids who have been arrested."

"Not for violent crimes, though, right?" Tillie looked to Terry for confirmation.

Terry nodded. "The kids who are in that facility are there because most of them come from troubled homes," he said. "They've gotten into general mischief and the like – some vandalism and maybe a stolen car here or there – but that's not the reason they're in the home. They're in the home because their parents either couldn't or wouldn't take care of them. I don't think calling them 'hoodlums' is exactly fair."

"And what do you know about the situation?" Margaret challenged.

"Just what I've heard through my position as a police officer – you know, where I investigate crimes," Terry replied dryly. "I'm not saying that the kids won't cause a spot of trouble, but I think holding things that are out of their control against them is unfair."

"Yes, well, nobody asked you." Margaret's tone was dismissive. "While I respect Terry's position and opinion, I think he's overlooking something very important: This is a family-oriented town. We care about our families. Keeping them safe and not exposing them to dangers that could be avoided is our primary concern."

"So why are you even bringing this up?" Terry barked.

"Because it's a town matter and it should be a town decision," Margaret huffed. "I'm not queen. I can't decide for everyone. I thought everyone should be aware of the issue so they can decide for themselves."

Tillie shifted from one foot to the other. "Come on, girls." She prodded three little girls who looked suspiciously like Clove, Thistle and Bay to stand. "This is absolutely ridiculous."

"Did you say something, Tillie?" Margaret narrowed her eyes.

"I said this is ridiculous," Tillie repeated, unruffled. "You just said this was a family-oriented town in one breath and then tried to dissuade people from helping at-risk kids with another. That's not what a family-oriented town would do."

"They're dangerous."

"No, you're dangerous. You're a terrible person. If you can't see those kids need help – that this is the time of year when we should all want to help – then I feel sorry for you."

"I don't feel sorry for you," Tillie continued. "I think you're a petty and foul individual. I'm not going to let you sway my decision. If I can help those kids – and I will be making calls as soon as I get out of here to find out – I'm going to offer my help.

"It's the Christmas season, after all," she continued. "We're supposed to give of ourselves for others. That's what I'm going to do."

"Then you'll be the only one," Margaret snapped.

Tillie looked to the other residents. "I guess we'll have to see about that, won't we?"

Margaret folded her arms over her chest, determined. "I guess we will."

Clove whispered something to Tillie that I could barely make out. "Now can I say something mean about her?" the petite girl asked.

Tillie nodded.

Thistle stilled Clove with a hand on her arm. "I've got it. You might not be mean enough, and we've only got one shot at this." She turned to face Margaret, her hands clenched into fists at her sides. "You look like a plucked chicken when you dance naked in front of your mirror every morning."

Everyone in the room looked as if they were about to start laughing.

"How do you know I dance naked in front of my mirror?" Margaret was incensed, spittle forming at the corners of her mouth. "How could you possibly know that? I mean ... I don't do that. Why would you think I do that? Don't tell people I do that. I'll sue if you ever say anything of the sort again."

"I'm not backing down from this, Margaret," Tillie called out. "I'll help save Christmas for those kids. Shame on anyone else who won't help."

And with that, she swept out of the room like a superhero.

I was surprised by the emotions that barreled through me. The strongest was dislike. I greatly disliked Margaret ... and the way she looked at people as if they were less than her. I also felt like laughing, because Tillie was clearly the best great-aunt ever.

I cleared my throat. "It seems you've had some trying times," I said.

She nodded. "I have. You wouldn't believe the way I've suffered."

"Your husband?"

"He died way too early."

"Yes, well ... ."

Another image danced in my head, this one featuring Margaret and her husband screaming at each other due to the affair with Floyd Gunderson. More images followed, including an argument with Ginny.

Then there were the myriad memories with Tillie, and all of them cascaded together in one big potential slap fight. One in particular stood out.

"Shut up!" a man I didn't recognize screeched, spittle appearing at the corners of his mouth. "That's not what happened. I was used and abused by these ... whores."

"Mrs. Little and Aunt Tillie treated you badly," Bay volunteered. "They know it. Aunt Tillie admits it. Mrs. Little will never admit it because she's sad and pathetic. She's only happy when others are miserable. I think she's going to be the miserable one going forward because she's out of friends."

"Hey!" Margaret was beside herself. "How did this become my fault?"

"Shut up, Margaret," Tillie ordered. "Let Bay talk." She was focused on the man.

"Victor, what you did was worse," Bay said. "Patty really loved you. You used and abused her just like Mrs. Little and Aunt Tillie used and abused you. You abandoned a child in the process. Then you stalked someone who didn't care about you. You're pathetic."

"Stop it!" he howled, his right hand crossing his chest as he rubbed his left arm.

"What's going on?" Another man asked. This one looked like a Fed, but it wasn't Landon.

"Get ready," Tillie ordered. "Hey, Victor!"

The man in question shifted his eyes to Tillie, sweat beading on his forehead. "What?"

"No one really wanted to win you," Tillie said. "We only wanted to beat each other. That's why we picked a loser like you. We figured you would be grateful we let you play at all. I guess we were wrong."

"That's it!" he reached for yet another man's gun (I was having trouble keeping track of the faces because they flitted by so fast). He gasped as he

missed and pitched forward. "Oh, God!" *He grabbed his chest as he writhed on the ground.*

"Grandpa?" *A third man jolted, confused.* "What's going on?"

Bay was on her feet, ready to fight, but she didn't have to. Landon barreled through the trees and tackled the man with the gun, forcing it to discharge as he fired wildly into the sky. Terry was close behind.

"Is everyone okay?" *Terry, out of breath, huffed.*

"Victor is having a heart attack," *Tillie offered.* "Also, Margaret should be locked up for being the worst person ever."

Margaret's outrage was palpable.

"I'll consider it," *Terry wheezed, his attention on Landon as the other man delivered a punch before scrambling toward Bay.*

I managed to hold it together even though I wanted to gasp at the end. It seemed the past Margaret shared with Bay and Tillie was even more dramatic than I'd imagined.

"You've definitely lived a busy life," I said dryly.

"I have," she agreed. "I have a lot of life left in me. I ... wait. You said you could see the future. Do you think I'll ever beat Tillie? Please tell me I'll outlive her ... and make her cry before it's all said and done."

The fact that she actually wanted that troubled me. "I think you're going to have a busy life twilight," I said finally.

"What's a life twilight?"

"The last years of your life."

She balked. "Excuse me, but I'm nowhere near the end of my life. I have plenty of time left to live."

She was in no danger of dying ... at least right now. The quality of the life left before her was up for debate.

In general I tended to tell the truth when it came to certain clients. Mostly clients I didn't like. Margaret was definitely one of those. Still, I learned a long time ago that most people wanted to hear something good, so I searched for that in the din. Occasionally, however, there were people who were so far gone on the wrong path I had no choice but to try to help them. Margaret was one of those, but it was obvious that she was beyond help.

"You're going to have a good life," I said finally, swallowing hard. "In fact, you're going to have a great life. I think you're going to get everything you deserve."

"Really?" She squealed as she shifted on her seat. "Can you tell me how I'm going to take Tillie down?"

She was going to need a bazooka to take Tillie down. That wasn't what she wanted to hear. "I can't tell you," I hedged. "You might change something if I do. Let me just say ... what's to come will be magnificent."

That wasn't exactly a lie. I caught a glimpse of Margaret's future and it was going to be magnificent. But it was Tillie who was going to come out victorious.

"Oh, yay!" Margaret clapped her hands. "This is so much fun. I can't believe how much I'm enjoying this."

That made one of us.

AN HOUR LATER, I DECIDED TO take a ten-minute break. My head hurt from the busy brains I had to delve into since opening. Each and every one belonged to one of Margaret's friends.

Kade found me in my tent, my head resting on the table, and for a brief moment he looked concerned. "What's wrong, baby?" He knelt next to me and placed his hand on my forehead. "Are you sick? Do I need to get you to the hospital?"

I offered a wry smile. "I love you."

He stilled. "Are you saying that to win the competition or because you're dying?"

"I'm not dying. I have a headache. Margaret Little and her merry band of senior citizen cohorts gave me a headache. She insisted I see them all in a row."

Relief washed over his features before he chuckled. "Well ... you're alive."

"Am I?"

"Yeah. You scared me there for a second." He pressed a kiss to my forehead before lowering his voice. "By the way, it would be great if you could never get sick or die. It freaks me out when you look weak."

"Does that happen often?"

"Very rarely. That's why it freaks me out."

I sighed. "I'll do my best, but only if you do the same for me."

"Deal." He pressed his lips to mine. "It's going to be a long day, huh?"

"You have no idea."

24
TWENTY-FOUR

I didn't initially recognize the woman who came into my tent after the break. She was blond, and I felt I should know her but I couldn't figure from where, so I pushed the notion out of my mind.

"What do you want to see?"

"The future ... and maybe a little of the past," she hedged, holding out her left hand first, giving me the impression she knew exactly what she was doing. That was interesting. She wanted to see her potential.

"The past first?" I asked.

She nodded.

"Okay." I held her hand and closed my eyes. "Is there something specific in the past you want to see?"

"Kind of. I ... well, you'll see."

"I will?" I chuckled as my mind started fogging at the edges. "Oh, well ... I guess you do know what you're doing."

"Yeah. I need to see it again and Bay says you're good at your job. I figured you could help."

"Bay said?" Things slipped into place. "You're Winnie."

"I am. I want to see Terry."

I pursed my lips. Apparently love was in the air all around. "Okay. Let's visit Terry."

I saw things from Winnie's point of view this go-around. She was watching a young Bay – twelve, maybe thirteen – from afar.

"I shouldn't have yelled at you," Terry said to the little girl at his side. "It wasn't fair, and it wasn't nice."

Bay was morose. "It's fine."

"It's not fine," Terry said. "You're not a monster. None of you are monsters."

"What about Lila?"

"Lila is a small monster," he conceded. "She's going to grow up to be a big monster. You're going to grow up to be an angel."

"You always say that." Bay giggled. "I'm not an angel."

"You are to me. Sometimes I can even see your halo. It almost never needs to be shined."

"You're only saying that because you feel bad about me taking off into the woods. I didn't do that because of you."

"Why did you do it?"

"Because Donna came to me in the cabin," Bay said. "She needed me to find her, and she knew she was running out of time."

"Why didn't you tell your mom?"

"I don't know."

"You don't know?"

"She has trouble with the ghosts," Bay said. "She doesn't like it that I see them. I can see that when I talk about them. She's embarrassed."

"Like you were embarrassed to have her run the camp this weekend?"

Bay nodded.

"Your mom isn't embarrassed by you seeing the ghosts," Terry said. "She thinks everything you do is magic. Well, most things. That sneaking around stuff you and your cousins like to do isn't fun, but most kids do that, so I think she'll probably let it slide.

"She's proud you want to help the ghosts, Bay," he continued. "She's proud of you. She's also afraid that if anyone else finds out what you can do things will become ... difficult. She doesn't care whether things are difficult for her, but she wants your life to be great."

"I think she's embarrassed."

"I think you want to think that," Terry said. "I think, in your heart, you know that's not the case."

"If I promise to tell her next time, will you stop with the deep talk?"

Terry grinned. "No. We're not done yet."

"I knew you were going to say that," Bay grumbled.

"You can't wander off in the woods by yourself, Bay. You could get lost. You could fall. Something could happen to you. You have to promise me that you won't do that again."

"I promise."

"Don't just say the words," Terry said. "Mean them."

"I can't promise I'll always go and get my mom. I promise to at least take Clove and Thistle with me next time."

Terry sighed. "I guess that's better than nothing."

"Can I ask you something?"

Terry nodded.

"Why did you come back to our camp this morning? I would have thought you'd stay away ... at least until lunch ... because of what happened."

"I really don't know why I came here," Terry said. "I only know that I had a feeling I needed to be here. I had a feeling you needed me to be here."

"What do you feel now?"

"I feel we should probably take a kayak ride and enjoy the lake one last time before we go," Terry said. "I think Donna would like that."

"You do?"

"I do."

Bay jumped to her feet and leaned over, giving him a quick hug. "Can I tip you over?"

"No."

"Please?"

Terry sighed. "I don't even know why you're asking," he said. "You know I can't say 'no' to you."

"I know. I'll get Clove and Thistle."

Bay skipped off in her cousins' direction, leaving Terry to stare at me ... er, Winnie. "I may spoil her a little," he said.

Even though it was a somber memory, I smiled. The image of Terry with Bay helped me better understand their relationship. It also helped me understand her mother.

"You're afraid that something bad might happen to Bay's father figure if you screw up your relationship with Terry," I said finally, my lips curving. "You're afraid that you'll hurt Bay."

"She needs Terry." Winnie's response was simple. "He's important to her."

"He's important to you," I stressed. "He always has been. You put your needs on the back burner for Bay, though, because you were afraid for her. Ghosts. She saw so many ghosts."

My heart pinged at the naked emotion on Winnie's face.

"You don't have to worry about the ghosts any longer," I said finally. "They're never going away, but they're not the issue you believe them to be."

Hope flitted across her face. "So ... Bay will be okay no matter what happens."

I knew what was going to happen, and there was no doubt Bay would be perfectly fine. "I think you're good." I grinned at her. "Have fun. That's what Bay wants most of all. She loves Terry, but she loves you, too. Besides, she's hopeful that you'll stop poking your nose into her life if you're focused on Terry. That's what she really wants."

Winnie's smile slipped. "Well, I'll show her."

I had no doubt about that.

THROUGHOUT THE DAY I played host to various visitors. Most I didn't recognize, but others ... well, others were familiar faces. Twila and Marnie stopped by. Whether it was to introduce themselves on the sly or get a real reading, I couldn't be sure. Still, they giggled their way through glimpses of their past and I was amused enough to pay attention.

The Winchester family was hard to define. They were loyal to a fault, but no strangers to strife and struggle. They messed with one another, divided into groups for wars, and yet remained devoted.

It was hard to imagine.

"Um ... are you busy?"

I was about to take a break when Terry showed up. I knew he would be hanging around the fairgrounds — it only made sense given the investigation — but I never believed he would stick his head in my tent.

"I have time for you." I flashed a smile as he darted inside, discomfort rolling off him in waves. He was nervous, which I found interesting. "Is something wrong?"

"Well ... ."

I thought back to Winnie's visit. "You're worried about Bay."

His eyes went wide. "How could you possibly know that?"

I snickered. "I could lie and say it's part of my job, but Winnie was in here earlier and she was worried about Bay. I saw a bit of her future, and past, so I think I know what you're worried about."

"Do you think I'm being stupid?"

I held up my hands. "I think that's a loaded question. No one goes through life without being stupid about something. It seems you're mostly worried about somehow upsetting Bay because she's used to having you in her life."

"That's true." He absently sat in the chair across from me. "I love her."

"You love all of them."

"How can you know that?"

It was a complicated question. "I can do things."

"Like Bay and the others?"

"Different things," I clarified. "Although, in your mind, they're probably similar."

"Yeah, well ... ." He exhaled a shaky breath. "What did Winnie say? I mean ... did she leave happy?"

"I'm not supposed to tell you that."

"But you're going to." He was matter-of-fact. "You like Bay and you want to help, so you're going to tell me the truth."

"I'm going to tell you what you need to know," I corrected. "First I need your left hand."

He narrowed his eyes. "Why? You're not going to do some hocus-pocus and make me squawk like a chicken, are you?"

"That's not on the agenda for the day, but I can make it happen if you're so inclined."

He sighed and did as I asked. "What are you looking for?"

"I just want to see." I closed my eyes and slipped into his brain, smiling when I found a memory that suited me. I recognized teenage Bay right away, and the way she looked at Terry was almost heartbreaking.

"Thank you for keeping them safe and ... doing whatever you did out there," Terry said to Tillie, who looked weary and beaten down.

"I didn't do anything," Tillie countered. "You saved them. You put your life on the line to take out the man with the gun."

"And you made it storm."

"I have no idea what you're talking about." Tillie winked. "Get a good night's sleep. Winnie, Twila and Marnie woke up long enough to see what all the fuss was about and then went back to bed. They plan to cook up a storm for their hero tomorrow."

Terry's cheeks flushed. "I'm nobody's hero."

"Oh, no?" Tillie cocked a challenging eyebrow. "Look around, Terry. You have three fans who say otherwise."

He shifted his eyes to Bay, who was already asleep with her head on his shoulder, and then to Thistle and Clove, who slept on the other side of him.

"Take care of our girls," Tillie said, climbing the stairs. "They're going to be unbelievably obnoxious tomorrow."

"Why is that?"

"They were right about someone evil staying at the inn. We're never going to hear the end of it."

"Yes, but they were wrong about who was evil," he pointed out.

"They won't remember that part," Tillie said. "All they'll remember is the way their blood pumped and how happy they were to curl up with their hero on the couch for the night."

I was choked up when I opened my eyes. "You are a good man."

He met my gaze without flinching. "I know what I want. The thing is, I need it not to hurt Bay."

"You've always known what you want," I insisted. "Before, you put Bay first because you worried she was too young to understand. Then you put your needs on standby because you didn't know how she would react as an adult.

"What's funny is that you think of those girls as your daughters," I continued. "You never thought of it as missing out on having your own family, because they were your family."

He rubbed his forehead with his free hand. "I just want to know that I'm not going to screw this up. I don't want to lose any of them."

"But especially Bay," I surmised, grinning at his discomfort. "You'll be fine. She loves you no matter what. Besides, she has her own love match to worry about. What makes you think she's going to worry about your relationship with her mother?"

His expression turned withering. "Oh, please. You've met them. You've seen how they are. They're all up in each other's business. That's not going to change."

I barely managed to swallow a chuckle. "So, what you're really worried about is the teasing."

"No." He was solemn. "I need to make sure this isn't going to screw up things."

"And if it will screw up things?"

"Then ... ." He was at a loss for words.

I couldn't take his misery. "You'll be fine," I repeated. "Nothing in life is ever perfect, but you're already a member of this family. The Winchesters take family very seriously. You'll never be allowed to leave."

The relief washing over Terry was palpable. "Thank you."

"You're welcome."

KADE SLID INTO THE TENT mere seconds after Terry left. He looked as tired as I felt.

"I don't suppose you're due for a break?"

I smiled. "I think I can swing one. Why? Do you want to sneak back to the trailer and compete for an hour or so?"

It took him a moment to comprehend what I was suggesting. "No, but now that you brought it up ... ."

My smile slipped. "Oh. If you're not here for that, what are you here for?"

"Now I kind of want to do that."

I poked his side as I stood. "You're making me nervous."

He chuckled as he leaned over and nipped at my bottom lip. "I want you to see something. I'm a little disappointed in myself that I didn't come an hour ago so we could enjoy your idea."

"Well, we have a long life ahead of us," I said pragmatically. "It seems to me we'll have plenty of time to do that going forward."

"Good point. I ... ." He sensed movement behind us and swiveled quickly, his hands going up in a protective stance. I was mildly impressed. Even though he didn't immediately call to his magic, he looked ready to wield it if forced.

Bay and Landon pulled up short in front of us, their eyes bouncing from face to face as they absorbed the scene.

"Are we fighting or talking?" Bay asked finally.

"Talking," I replied, resting my hand on Kade's arm. "He's just a little nervous. He's had a busy few weeks."

Bay nodded, seemingly unbothered by the fact that I didn't expound. "We've all had busy weeks," she agreed. "I know how that goes."

"Try living on the same property with Aunt Tillie," Landon drawled, tossing his arm over Bay's shoulder and grinning. "So ... how are you guys today?" His eyes remained on Kade as my boyfriend carefully unclenched his hands. "Doing okay?"

"I'm fine," Kade said finally. "I ... well, I'm fine."

"Good." Landon ran his tongue over his teeth before focusing on me. "You good, too?"

"Why wouldn't I be?" I challenged, part of me wondering if he was digging for specific information I couldn't quite identify.

"I was simply asking." Landon was calm. "I understand you went to the Dragonfly with Bay and Aunt Tillie this morning. That couldn't possibly have been comfortable."

"Oh." I relaxed a bit. He was simply worried that I was emotionally overwhelmed. It was almost sweet how concerned he was. "It's fine. I'm used to people bickering. Everyone at the circus isn't biologically related, but you'd be surprised at the way we all fight."

"So much fighting," Kade wagged his head. "I blame Luke for most of it ... and Nellie."

"That's funny." Bay's expression was bright. "I blame Thistle and Aunt Tillie."

"Well, there you go." I grinned. "What's going on with you two? Have you seen our witches?"

"No, but that's part of the reason we're here." Bay turned solemn. "Landon checked their credit cards and they haven't been used at any gas stations in the state. That's both north and south."

I pursed my lips. "They could be using cash."

"They could," she agreed.

"But who carries that much cash in this day and age?" I finished, sighing. "You think they're still in the area."

"I think it's likely," she conceded. "Whether they're dangerous or not, though, is anybody's guess. I simply don't know."

"Well ... I guess the only thing we can do is keep on the lookout for them." I rubbed the back of my neck, thoughtful. "Odds are, they won't make a move until after dark. Although ... we have no idea who they want to make a move on."

"Yes, well, you've been invited for dinner," Bay said. "I ran into my mother, and she couldn't stop blathering about how you're the real deal. Like ... the biggest deal ever. I think she wants to adopt you."

My cheeks burned under her intense scrutiny. "Oh, well ... she just stopped by for a little fun."

"Don't bother." Bay was resigned. "I know Chief Terry was here, too. They're both freaking out a little bit now that they're gearing up to start dating, aren't they?"

It was a difficult question to answer. "I can't tell you what I talked about with them. It's against the rules."

"Uh-huh." She rolled her eyes and sighed. "This is going to be a nightmare. They're acting like children."

Instead of commiserating with his girlfriend, Landon looked amused. "I think this is going to benefit me."

Bay was dubious. "How?"

"He's going to need advice on how to woo a Winchester. Who better than me to give him information?"

"Marcus," Bay answered without hesitation. "He's dating the most difficult Winchester and he's the easiest man in the world to get along with."

Landon made a face. "No. I'm essentially his partner. He's going to come to me ... which means I can lord it over him."

"Yes, you're a real paragon of virtue." Bay patted his stomach. "You need to come out with a group for dinner tonight. Otherwise my mother is going to melt down and it won't be pretty."

"I guess we can come for dinner." I felt put on the spot. I had no idea why she was so worked up about dinner. "Should we bring anything?"

"Just your appetites. Oh, and Nellie. Make sure he's in the crew. If he's not, Aunt Tillie will make us all pay."

"Speaking of Nellie, I haven't seen him all day," I noted. "He usually stops by to chat. He's not getting into trouble, is he?"

Landon snickered. "I think it depends on what you mean by trouble."

"Well ... ." I turned suspicious. "Why?"

"Come over here." Bay motioned for me to follow her, so I did.

When I got to the tent flap, she scanned the crowd for a long beat and then pointed. "There they are."

"They?" My stomach did a little somersault when I realized exactly who "they" were. Sure enough, my gaze fell on Tillie first. She wore leggings with what looked to be huge sharks on them, their maws open in a variety of different places. Around her waist she had cinched a utility belt that held a walkie-talkie and a variety of other items, including a canteen. The combat helmet was back, a small flask tucked into the band at the top. I couldn't see the whistle, but I was convinced she was wearing it because the ensemble wouldn't be complete without it.

"What is she doing?" I asked finally.

"Watching for evil witches," Bay replied, her lips quirking. "Your buddy is helping her."

"My buddy. I ... ." I groaned as I shifted my eyes across the aisle and found Nellie. He was dressed in a bubbly pink dress with a full skirt and a low bodice to show off his hairy chest. His muscular arms were on full display as he made a series of complicated hand gestures. "Is he doing the whole military movie covert operation hand thing?" I asked, already resigned to the answer.

Bay nodded. "Yeah. They've been over the entire circus as far as I can tell."

"I can't even. What will people think?"

Bay shrugged. "People who don't know them will think they're crazy and give them a wide berth. People who know them will know that they're crazy and give them a wide berth. Either way, no one is going near those two idiots."

I blew out a sigh. She was right. "Well ... at least we know we're safe now that they're on guard."

"They're calling themselves Team Nettle."

"Team Nettle?" I was confused. "Why?"

"That's what they came up with. It's supposed to be their names together, but both of them wanted to be first so they couldn't come up with a proper mash-up. Instead, they went with nettle because it has serrated leaves and stinging hairs. They thought that fit their partnership."

I didn't want to laugh. It would only encourage them if they found out. I couldn't stop myself. "Oh, geez!"

Bay's grin widened. "There are all different kinds of families, huh?"

"Yeah. There really are."

"I'm kind of glad for mine ... at least today."

She wasn't the only one.

25
TWENTY-FIVE

Despite seeing snippets of their past, I was nervous when we parked in front of The Overlook. The circus was still open, so only a few of us could escape for dinner. I left Melissa in charge of my tent, collected Luke, Kade, Max and Nellie, and then headed for what I was sure would be a loud meal.

The parking lot was only half full, so we didn't have trouble finding a space. Most of the women (and a few men) visiting the area arrived via bus, which made things easier when worrying about people disappearing. They didn't have convenient transportation at their fingertips.

On the front porch, I raised my hand to knock but the look Luke shot me stilled my motion.

"What?"

"It's not a house," Luke pointed out. "It's a business. You don't have to knock."

"Yeah, but ... they live here."

"Fine. Be a weirdo."

I considered following through for form's sake, but the more I thought about it, the odder it seemed. Instead, I pushed open the door

... and stepped right into Wonderland. That is if Wonderland included screeching witches.

"I've had it with you, old lady!" Thistle bellowed from somewhere inside the house, but I couldn't see her.

"Oh, you've had it with me?" Tillie called back. She sounded as if she was in an entirely different room. "Perhaps I've had it with you. Have you ever considered that?"

"I've had it with both of you," Landon barked, his voice growing louder as he strolled into the room. He pulled up short when he saw us. "Welcome to the zoo."

I pressed my lips together to keep from laughing at his weary expression. "Is this a bad time?" I finally asked.

He shook his head. "No. It's always like this."

As if to prove the statement, Bay hurriedly slid into the spot next to him. She didn't look surprised to see us. "Oh, hey. Just one second." She held up a finger and fixed her full attention on Landon. "You promised me a favor. You can't back out now."

"I thought you meant a private favor," Landon countered. "You didn't mention arresting Aunt Tillie. Besides, you've snuck out of the house twice this week without telling me. I'm not sure you deserve a favor."

She rolled her eyes. "Come on. Don't be a spoilsport. You promised me weeks ago that you would do whatever I wanted if ... well, you know."

"I don't know."

"You *know*." Bay was serious. "You definitely know what I'm talking about. If you deny it, you're full of crap."

I rubbed my hand over my chin, my mind going to a dirty place. Given the way Kade and Luke averted their gazes I had no doubt they were thinking the same thing.

"It wasn't *that*," Landon snapped, his eyes on us. "Get your minds out of the gutter. The favor I asked of her was extremely tame."

"It was," Bay agreed. "There was nothing dirty about it. Weird, definitely. Dirty, no."

"It was not weird." Landon made a face. "Lots of people have pots and pans in their home to cook with. I didn't think it was a big request."

"We eat here every night ... and morning."

"Yes, but with pots and pans we could occasionally sleep in."

Bay narrowed her blue eyes to glittery slits. "Is this an elaborate way to fill our refrigerator with bacon?"

"Hey, when the zombie apocalypse comes you'll be glad I stockpiled bacon."

"Oh, whatever." Bay shook her head. "You promised you would allow me to cash in my favor whenever I wanted. I need it now. She's out of control ... and a total menace."

"You act like that's a new thing," Landon said. "She's always out of control. It doesn't matter, though, because I'm not arresting her. I have more important things to worry about than Aunt Tillie running off the rails."

Even though it felt as if we were intruding, I found the interaction fascinating ... especially given the fact that I could still make out the occasional curse as Thistle and Tillie screeched at each other in the other room.

"This really is a zoo," Luke noted, causing me to laugh. "I thought nothing could be louder than a drunken bonfire before a busy work day. Apparently I was wrong."

He was definitely wrong.

"Maybe we should go," I suggested to Bay. "You seem busy. We don't want to intrude."

"Don't be ridiculous." She made a face. "This is normal. Besides, if you leave before eating, my mother and aunts will melt down. That's a lot more terrifying than what's going on out here."

Envisioning that was difficult.

Ever gallant, Max stepped forward. "We're looking forward to the meal. We wouldn't miss it for anything."

Well, that settled that. Max was in charge and we were staying.

. . .

FREAKY WITCHES

THE TABLE WAS PACKED WITH people, so we had to crowd together at the end. Between guests and family, there wasn't an open seat.

Tillie sat at the head of the table, but instead of looking regal it was obvious she was making plans to terrorize Thistle the second she got a free moment. By luck or happenstance, I couldn't be sure, Max sat at the other end of the table. He made sure to keep Nellie to his left. I didn't think it was a coincidence that he kept Nellie close.

"That smells lovely," Max said as Winnie, Marnie and Twila delivered three huge platters of food to the table. "What is that?"

"It's basically a fancy taco bar," Thistle explained. "One platter has meat — looks like chicken, pork, beef, steak and eggplant."

"Ugh." Nellie made a disgusted face. "Who puts eggplant on a taco?"

"Vegetarians," Thistle replied without hesitation. "There are vegetables on another platter. Warm tortillas over there. Sour cream. All the fixings." She rubbed her hands together, happy. "I love taco bar night."

It took everything I had not to laugh at her enthusiasm. "Who doesn't love tacos?" I agreed. I shifted my gaze to the far end of the table, where Landon sat between Tillie and Bay. It was obvious he served as some sort of babysitter for the eldest Winchester, which made me think of Max, who was doing everything he could to warn Nellie to stop fidgeting.

"This is a great place," Kade offered, unfolding his napkin and smiling at the two elderly women to his right. I recognized them from downtown the day I was playing parlor games with Luke. Shirley Peters and Adele Wood, I reminded myself. They were so thrilled to be in Hemlock Cove they could barely see straight.

"Thank you." Winnie beamed at Kade before winking at Terry, who sat next to Bay. That seemed a weird configuration, but the table was so full I figured they might've had to shuffle things around to accommodate everyone. "We're proud of it."

"Did you design it yourselves?" Max, always adept at comfortable conversation, glanced around the room. "The moldings are gorgeous."

"We did design it ourselves," Winnie confirmed. "The area behind the kitchen is the old homestead. That's the family living quarters now, only accessible through the kitchen and a back stairwell that we lock. We originally built a bed and breakfast before expanding several years ago."

"It's a lovely space." Max leaned back in his chair and focused on Tillie. "I assume this is your property."

"I own half of it," Tillie replied, making a stark throat-cutting sign in Thistle's direction. They seemed to be performing a mime act only they could see. The blond man sitting next to Thistle grabbed her arm before she could return what I assumed was a ruder gesture.

"Aunt Tillie owns half the property and we own the other half together," Winnie explained, gesturing toward her, Marnie and Twila for emphasis.

"And you'll obviously pass the property on to the younger three when it's time," Max prodded. "That's quite the legacy."

"We're not giving anything to Thistle," Tillie countered, plugging her fingers in her mouth as she stuck out her tongue at Thistle. "We only reward nice girls."

Clove brightened. "Does that mean I'll inherit by myself?"

"No, you little suck-up," Tillie replied, dropping her hands from her mouth. "I'm considering leaving the property to Marcus because he's the only one who doesn't annoy me."

"Oh, you say the sweetest things," Landon said, grinning as he grabbed tortillas from the warmer. He placed some on Bay's plate and his own before handing the container to Tillie. "I think you really want to leave it to me."

"Yes, because I want to reward 'The Man' for poking his nose in my business," she drawled. "That sounds just like me."

I pressed the heel of my hand to my forehead to ward off an oncoming headache. This family put our makeshift tribe to shame ... and that was saying something.

"I could still arrest you like Bay wants," Landon warned. "I might be tired, but if you push me ... ."

"I just love the dinner theater here," Adele enthused, leaning closer to Luke as she smiled at me. "Isn't it amazing? I think they deserve Oscars."

Is that what this was? Dinner theater? It seemed somehow worse. Like *Dynasty* meets the Kardashians worse.

"They're very ... spirited," Max said, causing Kade to cough into his hand to cover his laughter.

"Very spirited," Luke agreed. "They're so spirited I think they might be possessed."

"I think I'm in love," Nellie supplied, resting his chin on his hand as he stared at Tillie. "She is a magnificent creature!"

"Oh, good grief," I muttered. "You need to stop mooning like that. Have you no pride? I mean ... come on. I've never seen you like this."

"Hey, you and your security stud muffin have been taking afternoon 'naps' for three days straight," Nellie shot back. "Do you think we don't know what that's about?"

"Oh, give them a break," Luke said. "They just said the L-word to each other. They're floating on clouds and crap. It'll pass."

My eyes went wide as I turned to Kade. "I swear I didn't tell him. I mean ... I was going to. I wanted to. But we needed time to do it right. A best friends night with chocolate. I don't know how it got out this fast."

"I do." Kade was calm. "I told him."

My mouth dropped open. "You told him?"

He nodded, blasé. "Hey, I want someone to gush to occasionally, too. It was either him or Max ... and I wasn't sure I was ready to bond that way with Max."

Instead of being offended, Max smiled. "I think it's cute. It's like my kids are dating."

I made a face. "That's kind of gross."

"Yes, but I think of you as a daughter," Max said. "He's my son. It's as if my kids are dating."

I shook my head to dislodge the thought. "Yes, well ... ." Whatever I was going to say died on my lips as the inn suddenly started flashing an eerie red color and an alarm dinged from the inner bowels of the house.

"What the heck is that?" Thistle screeched, hopping to her feet, a fork clutched in her hand. "Did you guys get a security system?"

"We most certainly did not," Winnie snapped, glancing around. "Who did that?"

The annoyed look on Bay's face when she slid her eyes to Tillie told me everything I needed to know. It was obvious who did it, because the alarm was magical in origin.

"Ha!" Tillie slammed her hands on the table and stood, her eyes wide as she locked gazes with Nellie. "I set a trap and someone sprang it. You know what that means."

Nellie pumped his fist. "Yahoo! But ... I wish I'd brought my ax."

I could do nothing but stare as they scrambled toward the swinging door that led to the kitchen. Then I realized what was about to happen.

"Wait." I lurched at the same time as Bay. "We can't just let them do whatever they want with whoever they catch."

Terry sighed. "There go my tacos."

IN RETROSPECT, IT WAS PROBABLY a mistake to race outside in a big crowd as we did. We essentially looked like complete morons from afar, but that didn't stop us.

Tillie was through the back door first, Nellie and Landon close behind. Thistle, Terry and Bay went through together, and the rest of our group filed outside at a slower pace. Clove was behind us, but I was convinced that was because she really didn't want to see what was happening outside and only came because she didn't want to be left out.

There was no time to study the family living quarters as we raced through them, but the homey vibe made me smile. That didn't last when we reached the back patio, because agitation was the name of the game when Tillie stopped to take a breath.

"Where?" Luke asked, scanning the backyard.

Tillie narrowed her eyes and pointed. "They're on my bluff! Cheeky little buggers."

Those in better shape – Kade, Landon, Terry and Luke – reached the clearing first. Nellie tried to keep up, but his short legs wouldn't allow it. The rest of us arrived a few seconds later, and the sight in front of us was almost impossible to explain.

There, in the center of the bluff, the three women we were looking for stood with their arms stretched toward the sky. They'd started a bonfire big enough to illuminate the entire area, so visibility wasn't an issue. They wore white dresses that were practically transparent in nature, so it was possible to see everything underneath ... and apparently panties and bras weren't invited to the big dance. They appeared to be in their own little world.

"Don't look." Luke slapped his hand over Kade's eyes.

"Knock that off." Kade grappled with Luke. "I don't want to look at them, but I need to in case they attack."

"I don't think they're attacking with anything other than bad dancing," Thistle noted, cocking her head to the side as she regarded the women. "What are their names again?"

"Madison, Emily and Jamie," I supplied. "I saw them in town a few days ago."

"Join us," Madison invited as she skipped around the circle, her hair bouncing. "We're about to start the ritual."

That didn't sound good. "What ritual?"

"Wait." Max extended his hand to keep me from rushing headlong into danger. "Don't go over there in case ... ." He left it hanging.

"I agree." Kade was firm. "You stay right here with us. This is a job for the super witches."

The look Tillie shot him was withering. "Thank you, Captain Wussypants," she drawled. "You're right, though. I will take it from here." She strolled forward, planting herself less than a foot away from the circle the invading witches had drawn with what looked to be colored chalk. "Are you friend or foe?"

I pressed my lips together in an effort to refrain from laughing at the surreal situation.

"We're friends, Mother Winchester," Jamie replied. "How could you think otherwise?"

"Did she just call me 'mother'?" Tillie looked to Bay for confirmation.

"Is there something you want to tell us, Aunt Tillie?" Thistle chortled, clearly enjoying herself. "Do you have a bunch of illegitimate witches running around out there?"

"Shut up, mouth!" Tillie extended a warning finger in Thistle's direction. "There's only so much I'm willing to take right now." She focused on Jamie. "What's your damage?"

"We want to join your coven," Jamie replied simply. "We feel you're in a position to teach us everything we need to know."

I lifted my nose to the air, not to scent like Raven, but to feel for power. There was absolutely nothing of substance there.

"I don't think they're witches," I whispered to no one in particular.

Tillie glanced over her shoulder and glared. "Of course they're not witches. They're wannabes. I mean ... look at that. They started a fire with gasoline and newspapers."

"Hey!" Bay's eyes widened. "They stole those newspapers from the recycling bin at The Whistler. They should be arrested."

"Yes, sweetie, that's what we should worry about," Landon drawled. "Recycled newspaper theft is a blight on this community."

"I'll show you a blight later," Bay muttered.

Landon grinned as he moved closer to the three women. "Ladies, you're trespassing. I have to ask you to leave."

Emily glared at him, furious. "You can't make us leave. We belong here. We're one of them."

"If you claim that, and believe it, I might have you locked up in a psych hospital," Terry said.

"Take Aunt Tillie, too," Thistle suggested.

"Can it, Thistle!" Tillie snapped. Her eyes were steady on the women. "I don't understand what you're doing here. Why would you possibly think we have a coven?"

"There's talk of you online," Emily replied simply. "You've been mentioned several times on the Watcher on the Witchtower website. We want to be members of your coven because we feel we're being ignored by those in our own."

"Yeah, we don't want to light candles and chant," Jamie added. "We want to curse people and put boils on their butts."

Thistle pointed at Tillie. "She's your woman. There's little more she loves than a good butt boil."

"Thank you, Thistle," Tillie groused. "I love it when you say things like that."

"Then don't put boils on people's butts."

"I did that like once."

Thistle folded her arms over her chest.

"Fine. Ten times," Tillie corrected. "I haven't done it in years, though. Not since it went out of style."

Max grinned as he slid his eyes to Nellie. "I think I'm starting to fall in love, too."

Nellie was having none of it. "I'll fight you to the death if you're not careful."

The longer the conversation continued, the more I realized that we were at a virtual standstill. "So ... these probably aren't the women we're looking for," I said finally.

Bay, apparently, had come to the same conclusion. "No. I'm sure they'll have to be questioned, but they're nutty, not homicidal."

Landon rubbed his hand over Bay's back as he watched the women continue to dance while trying to rhyme "toil and trouble" with "on the double."

"I say we lock them up and let them sweat it out overnight," Landon said.

"You just don't want to miss out on time with Bay," Terry muttered.

"There's chocolate cake inside," Landon argued. "They also made turtle cheesecake. Do you want to miss that?"

Terry straightened. "Good point. Ladies, we're going to have to arrest you. I'm sure we can figure out exactly what's going on tomorrow morning, so it shouldn't be a terribly long stay. We need to make sure you're not dangerous."

Kade slid his eyes to me. "I'm kind of glad we didn't miss out on dinner. It makes our meals look downright relaxing."

26
TWENTY-SIX

The rest of the evening went pretty much as I expected. Terry and Landon removed the three overzealous witches from the property. The women kept threatening to curse them, but the rhymes they unfurled were right out of a Poetry for Dummies book.

The food was good, the conversation continued to zing, and the elderly tourists kept cackling with glee thanks to the dinner theater.

I was exhausted when we returned to the fairgrounds and gratefully fell into bed, my mind a bit sluggish. When I woke, I found myself staring directly into Kade's expressive eyes.

"Is something wrong?" I asked, worry coursing through me.

"No. Stay there." He tightened his arm around my back and pressed a kiss to my forehead. "There's nothing wrong."

He was calm, serene even. He also looked as if he was about to burst into laughter.

"What's so funny?" I asked, making a face. "You look as if you're having a good time, which is interesting, because we've been asleep for nine hours."

"I've been up for an hour watching you sleep," he countered.

"That's kind of creepy."

"I find it romantic."

"If some random dude were to watch me sleep, I don't think you'd find it romantic."

"True, but I'm not some random dude."

"Definitely not." I snuggled closer, pressing my cheek to his chest. "Did you sleep okay?"

He nodded as he smoothed my out-of-control bedhead. "I did. It seems that your potion trick worked."

"I only did that once. You did it yourself the other nights."

"Yeah, well, I'm still debating if I should be angry about that."

"I vote no."

He chuckled. "Is it any wonder I love you?"

Instead of offering him a smile and basking in the words, I scowled. "Oh, man, you're already ahead of me for the day."

"I know. Isn't life grand?"

Actually, life was pretty grand right now ... other than the fact that there was a murderer on the loose and every avenue we checked seemed to be a dead end. "What did you think of dinner last night?"

He shrugged. "It was loud. It reminded me of some of our dinners."

"I thought they were louder than us."

"Which is frightening, huh?"

"Maybe a little."

We lapsed into silence, the only sound coming from the overhead fan. I was the first to break it because my busy mind wouldn't allow for tranquility when there was so much going on.

"It was nice that Max joined us."

He cast me a sidelong look. "Are you fishing for information on my relationship with my father?"

"Maybe."

"Well, other than the fact that he called you his kid last night — which kind of grossed me out — things are okay with us. I think it's going to take some time to get back to where we were, but it will probably happen."

It wasn't exactly a ringing endorsement, but it was a much better response than he'd offered up weeks before. When he first found out about Max's duplicity, he vowed to cut him out of his life forever. I knew he didn't mean it, because if he had he would've left the circus. That would've ended with a broken heart for me, but it might've been the best thing for Kade.

Now that option really was out of his reach. He was magical, and he was right where he belonged.

"I'm glad you decided to stay." I burrowed closer. "I thought you might run after ... maybe that you would be happy to get away from me because I lied. I would've been crushed if you'd left."

It was hard for me to admit because I always wanted to appear strong, but it was the truth.

"Hey." Kade cupped my chin and stared into my eyes. "I was never going to leave. I was angry when I found out, but the thought of leaving never entered my mind."

I was dubious. "Never?"

"Okay, maybe briefly, but it wasn't ever a real consideration."

"Because of me?"

He smiled. "Mostly because of you," he replied after a moment's consideration. "I think I knew you were the one for me from that very first meeting."

I remembered things differently. "You hated me. You thought I was a mouthy female telling you how to do your job."

He held up a finger. "Correction. I thought you were a beautiful mouthy female who I wanted to kiss senseless. You were a bossy little thing, I would never deny that. You were also confident and smart, two things I find very attractive."

"Did you think you would make this your home?" I asked, genuinely curious. "Be honest. When you first arrived, did you think this was anything other than a way station?"

"I don't know." He shrugged, uncertainty washing over his features. "I was kind of lost at the time. I didn't know what I wanted. I thought Max was a family friend, one of the few people I knew and respected, and I wanted something new.

"I knew Max worked for the circus when I was a kid, and there were times I grew angry at my mother when I was younger and threatened to run away and join him," he continued. "She would always get a sad expression when I said that. I know, in hindsight, that she always worried I would find this world alluring. She probably figured she would lose me to Max's odd lifestyle. I didn't recognize her worry then. I do now."

"Do you think she wanted to keep you from Max forever?" I was honestly curious. I'd never met Kade's mother. All I knew about her was that she broke up with Max when she was pregnant because she was determined to give Kade a normal life. I respected her devotion to her son, but I often questioned if she made the right decision. If Kade were allowed to explore his magical roots at a younger age, there's no telling how much power he'd now be able to wield.

"I don't know." He rested his cheek against my forehead. "I just don't know. She didn't leave a letter. Wouldn't you leave a letter if you wanted your son to know the truth after you passed? I mean ... she knew she was sick. She knew she didn't have much time. Why not tell me the truth herself?"

I'd considered that question. "I think she was afraid."

"Of what? That I wouldn't love her? No matter how angry I was, I wouldn't have left her. I would've stayed."

"Yes, but would things have been different between you?" I asked. "Would your anger have tainted the last hours you spent together? Would the entire conversation have revolved around Max instead of the good times you shared with your mother?"

He sighed, the sound long and drawn out. "I guess you're right. I never really considered that."

"Of course I'm right." I grinned to lighten the mood. Then I sobered, because it was a serious conversation. "She was your mother. She loved you. She didn't want her legacy tainted. I'm sure she felt guilty. That said, everything I've heard about your mother makes me think she believed in destiny. Your destiny was to find this place, to find me. It was going to happen regardless."

"Ugh. You're sweet in the morning. That's why it's my favorite time of day." He scooted lower, so we were face to face, and kissed me. "I love you so much."

I scowled. "You did it again! It's my turn."

He snickered. "Actually, that time I wasn't competing."

"Oh, well ... ." I kissed the corner of his mouth. "You belong here. Before long you'll understand your magic better and fit seamlessly into our group."

"That's some distinguished company. Do you think I'll be positioned next to the clown with his ass hanging out of his chaps or the dwarf wearing an evening gown in our official superhero photo?"

I poked his side. "You'll be right beside me ... and Luke, because if Luke doesn't get to be at the front he'll melt down and we'll never hear the end of it."

"Good point." Another kiss, and then Kade added some wandering hands to the mix. "We have a long day and we should probably talk about a few things over breakfast. But while we're still alone I thought we might spend some quality time together."

"Good idea."

WE WERE LATE TO BREAKFAST, but only by two minutes. I was hoping we could slide by without shade being thrown our way. Alas, that wasn't to be.

"Oh, look at the lovebirds," Raven teased. "I see you've moved your nooner a few hours earlier today. That's probably wise."

I glared at her. "Must you always say whatever comes to your mind?"

Raven nodded without hesitation. "It keeps me young. Besides, it's not as if everyone doesn't know what you guys were doing in there. Kade is loud."

"Hey!" Kade was mortified. "Stop talking right now. I'll lock anyone up who says another word I don't like."

"Does that include me?" Max asked, sliding around his son as he headed toward the table. "It's been years since I've been incarcerated for any reason. It might be fun for nostalgia's sake."

Huh. Max was joining us for another meal. I couldn't remember the last time he ate with us more than twice in the same week.

"How many times have you been arrested?" I asked.

"Enough times to know that jail is no fun." Max shifted his eyes to a glowering Kade. "You need to calm down and realize that we tease because we love. And, yes, everyone knows what you were doing. You might want to stop yelling 'yippee' whenever you're alone with Poet."

Kade was mortified. "I've never yelled that."

"He's teasing you," I said, poking his side. "There's no reason to get worked up. I mean ... come on. You're being a bit of a baby. You thought it was funny when we teased Raven and Percival about playing Ride 'Em Cowboy."

"And thank you so much for that," Raven drawled.

I offered her a mock salute. "You're welcome. Think of it as payback for starting this conversation."

"I've learned my lesson," she said. "I'll never tease you again. Please don't spank me as punishment."

"I'm gay and I think my head just imploded," Luke supplied, smirking at the visual Raven painted.

"I think this conversation is getting away from us," Max noted, clearing his throat to get everyone's attention. Even though he was amused by some of the banter, he was often uncomfortable when conversations degraded ... and this one couldn't sink much further without dropping into an underwater abyss. "I think we should talk about our plans for the day."

"What plans are those?" I asked, moving toward the grill so I could help Nixie, Naida and Raven with breakfast preparations. "My understanding is that we're to proceed as if it's a normal day."

"That is the plan," Max agreed, nodding in thanks when Nellie poured him a mug of coffee. "We have no idea who we're dealing with, or even if the threat remains. Two deaths signify that whoever is doing this is nowhere near done. I have no concrete information either way, though. This area is thick with magical memory shards. That makes detecting a new threat almost impossible."

"Naida mentioned the shards," I mused. "She said they were all over the creek."

"They're everywhere," Max corrected. "Some of them are heavier than others. I accidentally walked into one yesterday that showed me a rather interesting fight between Bay and what looked to be a killer. She was leading an army of ghosts."

I nodded absently. "She's a necromancer."

Kade made a face as he sat at the picnic table. "I thought she was a witch."

"She is. She's also a necromancer."

"I've known necromancers throughout the years," Raven offered. "It's not a very comfortable gift. Most of the ones I've known lost their minds ... and then some. She might not have a happy future."

I shook my head. "I've seen her future — at least flashes of it — and she'll be fine. I think having such a tight-knit family will save her. Still, you're not wrong about the gift. She's not comfortable with it and hasn't put together the fact that many of the things she views as misfortunes in her life are really the result of her powers."

"How so?" Max asked. "I mean ... I'm interested in the necromancer aspect. I've heard tales about necromancers throughout the years. They're extremely prevalent in the South, or at least they were fifty years ago. Perhaps they've fallen out of fashion."

"I don't think most necromancers live long," I added. "Bay will be okay, though. As crazy as her family is, they can absorb some of the risks she will ultimately face, stand with her no matter what. Landon will help save her, too. He gets her ... even if he doesn't understand everything about magic. When it comes to her, he's willing to take it all on to keep her safe."

Max's lips curved as he glanced at Kade. "It's a rare man who can take that on, but they do exist."

I returned his smile. "Bay will be fine. She's not the one we need to worry about. We have a killer on the loose and only two days left of the festival. At the end of those two days, we're out of here. We have another gig in Detroit.

"When that happens, the killer will either leave at the same time or stay behind and become the Winchesters' problem," I continued. "I don't know about anybody else, but I would prefer Billy's killer to be caught and punished before we leave. I don't want to leave that thread hanging."

"We're in agreement there." Max stroked his chin, "But I really don't know what to do. Once we know who the killer is, I can handle it easily enough. Even if it is a powerful witch, that's not an issue."

"Other than the dead bodies, it's been really quiet here," Raven noted. "I know that's weird to say because ... you know, dead bodies ... but it's almost been a vacation other than that. It seems weird that nothing else has happened."

"Yet," I corrected. "Nothing else has happened yet. Perhaps whoever is doing this has plans for tonight or tomorrow night. That would make sense."

"Mercury is in retrograde tonight," Nixie offered. "That's a magical convergence. It might be happening tonight."

While I didn't follow astrology like she did, I wasn't prepared to completely rule out the possibility she was right. "I don't know what to do besides keep our eyes open," I said. "We have no leads and we're running out of time. I'm at a loss."

"Everyone will keep their eyes open," Kade promised. "If anyone sees anything that's even remotely suspicious, I want you to report it to me."

"We don't know what constitutes suspicious," Raven argued. "Sure, if we see someone running around with a knife trying to carve up people, that's definitely suspicious. What other suspicious behavior are we supposed to be watching for?"

And that right there was the problem. "I don't know." I rubbed my forehead. "There has to be something we're missing. We haven't exactly put our full efforts behind this investigation because we've been distracted by the Winchesters."

"Oh, but what a distraction," Nellie said, taking on a moony expression.

"Ugh. You're going to be all kinds of awful when we leave," Luke complained. "You know that witch is old enough to be your mother, right?"

"I'm older than her," Nellie countered. "I would be robbing the cradle if we hooked up."

That was a terrifying thought. "Listen ... ." The rest of my sentence was drowned out when the dreamcatcher started alerting and a wailing filled the air as I snapped my head to the east.

"Someone's here," Max said, hopping to his feet, his expression intense. "Split into groups. Nobody goes alone. We need to find who crossed the barrier. This might be our only chance."

I wasn't afraid as I nodded. We were finally seeing some movement. I only hoped it would lead to answers.

TWENTY-SEVEN

The dreamcatcher had been breached, but we didn't know where. The one thing our group always came together over was safety, and we wordlessly broke apart like waves hitting rocks as we tried to find the entry point.

I wasn't surprised when Kade opted to stick close to me. He was the security guru — and keeping everyone intact was his highest priority — but he always gravitated toward me in situations like this.

"What do you think?" he asked when we reached the outside wall.

I studied the trees on the other side of the barrier, the same trees that led to the clearing in the forest.

"I don't know." I shrugged as I tilted my head to the side and considered our options. "We could head into the woods."

He extended a hand to still me. "I don't think we should do that without backup."

I understood what he was really saying. He was afraid. If I had to guess, he wasn't yet comfortable enough with his magic to serve as backup should I engage in a fight. I understood his worry, but I wasn't in the mood for faltering courage.

"You can stay here." I opted to approach the issue from a different angle. "I can protect myself. You stay here and watch the border because you're not comfortable being my backup. I'll be fine."

Kade's mouth dropped open. "Excuse me?"

I almost laughed at his outrage. "Stay here," I repeated, only barely managing to keep a straight face. "I'll be fine."

"You're not going out there on your own."

"I'm not?"

"No."

"Are you coming with me?"

Frustration, quick as a snake, coiled around him. "Don't think I don't know what you're doing," he hissed, grabbing my hand and dragging me over the dreamcatcher line. It was clear my dare had done its job. "We'll talk about this later."

This time I let my smirk out to play. "I'm looking forward to it."

"Yeah, yeah, yeah."

THE TRIP TO THE CLEARING turned out to be a waste of time. Kade was on full alert for the duration of our trek through the woods, but the clearing was empty ... and the trees were eerily still.

"Nothing?" I asked after he searched the area directly behind one of the rune-carved trees.

He shook his head, frustration evident. "Nothing." He straightened and held my gaze. "I don't think anyone has been out here."

"Is that something you know or something you assume?"

He shrugged, noncommittal. "I don't know. There aren't any obvious signs, and I can't help feeling we would know if someone had been out here."

He had a point. "We should probably head back and check with the others." I absently ran my finger over one of the runes.

"What are you thinking?" he asked after watching me for a beat. "It's obvious something is on your mind."

Something was definitely on my mind. "I'm thinking that it might be wise to go back to Bay's four-corners suggestion."

"I don't know what that is," he replied, his expression blank. "Is that a thing?"

"The four corners," I explained. "It's a Wiccan concept. North. East. South. West." I pointed in each direction as I turned. "It's one of the more common conjuring techniques for witches."

"Why do you think that's important now?" Kade asked.

"I don't know. The runes. Four corners. The dreamcatcher. Four casters. The Winchesters usually work in fours for their bigger spells."

"Did Bay tell you that?"

I nodded. "She said they do circle work in threes but they need Tillie for the bigger spells. I'm wondering if that's because the younger girls have been dabblers instead of true practitioners for most of their lives."

Kade arched an eyebrow. "And she just volunteered that information?"

I was amused. "How many times do I have to tell you that the Winchesters are not our enemies?"

"I know but ... ."

"They're like us." It was the simplest explanation I had. "Okay, they're not exactly like us, but they're mostly like us. We're not bad people. They're not bad people either."

"I get that. No, I really do. It's just ... I don't want to make a mistake where you're concerned. I don't want to trust the wrong people with your safety."

"And who are the wrong people?"

He shrugged, sheepish. "I don't know. Anyone with the power to hurt you."

"Well, I'm not the most powerful person in the world. Even though you're growing ridiculously amazing on pretty much every front, you're not the most powerful person in the world either. Sometimes we're going to run into people more powerful than us."

"That doesn't make me feel better."

Sometimes he was too cute for words. "We'll be fine. The Winchesters aren't going to hurt us. It's okay to trust the right people."

"And you're sure they're the right people?"

I nodded without hesitation. "I feel their goodness. Sure, they're a little crabby and rough around the edges, but they're good people. If it comes to a fight, they'll stand with us."

Kade's smile was wan. "I hope so. I don't want to have to kill your new friends."

"That would definitely suck."

He chuckled and held out his hand for me to take. "It would totally suck. What do we do now?"

"Check with our friends and then prepare for a day at the circus."

"That's it?"

"The show really must go on."

He grumbled. "I hate it when you say things like that."

"You'll get used to it."

"I'm not sure that's good."

I STOPPED IN THE TRAILER long enough to change clothes after checking in with the others. They came up empty during their search as well. The dreamcatcher never gave off false positives, so we were dealing with something else ... although I had no idea what.

For now I had to contend with the everyday operations of the circus. That meant getting into character.

I opted for one of my bohemian beaded skirts – the blue, because Kade said it reminded him of my eyes and we were living a romantic lifestyle these days – and then made my way to my tent. We were still an hour away from opening, but I thought the solitude would do me good.

It was quiet, but I could tell it was going to be a scorcher, especially by Michigan's standards. The humidity was already building, which meant I was going to need a fan if I expected any relief at all in my tent. Thankfully, Dolph had obviously been thinking ahead because one of the box fans we kept at the ready was already waiting for me in front of the tent flap.

I plugged the fan into the strips running between tents and flicked it on, sighing as I pointed it at me and sank into my chair. My mind was busy, a million different thoughts buzzing. I kept circling back to the same place.

"What are you thinking?" Max asked, taking me by surprise when he appeared in the opening.

I shot him a look before shaking my head. "Make a noise next time. You're quieter than Nixie when she's playing with her dolls."

Max snorted. "That's a creepy comparison." He looked serious as he moved deeper into the tent and planted himself in the chair across from me. "How are you?"

I recognized a loaded question when I heard it. "I guess I'm okay. How are you?"

"I'm doing extremely well." Max's smile was warm. "I have everything I ever wanted. Er, well, mostly."

I pursed my lips, amused. "Because you have Kade?"

"I don't *have* him," he stressed. "But he no longer hates me. I'm considering that a win."

"He never hated you," I said. "He was angry … and afraid … and broken-hearted. He didn't understand why you weren't around when he was a kid."

"We talked about that the other night."

"You did?" I was impressed. "I'm proud of you guys. I thought you would hold that conversation in until you both exploded and made a mess of things. That is the male way, after all."

Max snickered. "I like to think I'm more than a normal man."

"Hey, I wasn't man-bashing. I happen to love men. Like … a lot."

"Like my son." Max's grin widened.

"Especially your son."

"I'm glad for it." He turned earnest. "I think you two are a perfect match."

"Did you think that before or after we started sleeping together?"

His lips curved down. "Let's not get crude. You know I don't like it when you're crude."

"You like it when Luke is crude. It seems a little sexist that you don't like it when I'm crude."

"Ha, ha." He wagged his finger, eliciting a grin. "I'm not falling for that. As for liking Luke's crude comments over yours, that's not entirely untrue. The boy has a certain spark. I don't know how to describe it."

"He's uncouth and blunt."

"That's definitely part of his spark."

I snickered. I couldn't help myself. Then, something occurred to me. "Do you remember the first time we talked like this?"

Max's eyes twinkled, but his smile slipped away. "As a matter of fact, I do. Why are you thinking about that?"

"I have been for the past two weeks," I admitted, rubbing my hands over my knees. "We don't spend much time in Michigan. This is the first time we've been back in ... years."

"That's because Michigan's economy was especially hard hit in the crash a decade ago. Most of the municipalities couldn't afford a circus."

"And now we're doing two shows in Michigan back-to-back."

He nodded, calm. "We are."

He was waiting for me to give voice to my concerns. I recognized the move and waited. "The last three times we've been here, it's been to the west side of the state."

Realization dawned on Max's face. "And you're worried because we're returning to your old stomping grounds."

Was that it? Was I worried? I recognized the sense of unease growing in my gut, but I wasn't sure it was fear. "We're going to be really close to the area where you found me."

"Do you think any of your old crew will be hanging around?" Max was calm as he leaned back in his chair and crossed his legs at the ankles. "Are you worried you'll see them and return to a life of crime?"

Oh, geez. What a kidder. "You think that's funny?"

He shook his head. "No, but I think you're worked up about something. I'd like to know what that is. After all, my children are happy right now. Even though his magic is unfurling faster than he envisioned, Kade is happy. I want you to be happy, too."

"I am, for the most part."

"But?" he prodded.

"But ... I can't help thinking about the past now that we're about to be staring it down in a way that I didn't think I ever would again," I admitted. "It's not that I fear the past ... or that I'm ashamed of what I did. Okay, maybe I am a little ashamed. I stole things and stuff. I lied and told people fake fortunes for money. That probably wasn't a good thing."

Max didn't look bothered. "You were trying to survive."

"And yet when you plucked me from the street the first words you said to me were, 'No more stealing.'"

"That's because I love the wallet you tried to lift. Kade got it for me as a gift when he was sixteen."

That was part of the story I'd never heard. "Seriously?"

He nodded. "Despite that, the stealing was probably a poor idea. I'm glad you outgrew that. It might've become annoying if you were trying to rip off our visitors. Can you imagine the Yelp reviews?"

A laugh bubbled up. "Oh, you're in a funny mood today. I love it when you're in a funny mood."

"Yes, well ... I always fancied myself a part-time clown."

My smile slipped. "That is a freaky thing to say. Now I'll have nightmares."

"You'll be fine." He sounded so sure of himself I believed him. "Tell me what you fear about returning to Detroit. By the way, we have been through that specific area before. You were with us, although it was only a year after you left your life on the street. Have you forgotten that?"

I shook my head. "No. I guess I try to pretend that the person living on the street, the smart-mouthed hood rat who tried to lift your wallet, wasn't real. That was someone else, a different person."

"You are a different person. You're allowed to grow and mature. You're one of the loveliest people I know."

"Oh." That was kind of touching. "Are you just saying that because you think of me as one of your kids?"

"No. It's true. As for going back, I don't think the issue is you. I think it's Kade. You don't want Kade to see that side of you."

I hated how well he could read me. "I ... ."

"No, no, no." He shook his finger. "You don't have to hide your fears from me. I already know them."

"Because you invaded my mind?" The notion set me off, even though I'd been known to delve into people's minds on more than one occasion. It was almost a daily occurrence, in fact. When the tables were turned, I found it invasive.

"I have not invaded your mind." Max refused to back down. "I simply know you better than most. In fact, in some ways, I know you better than anyone."

"I think Kade and Luke would offer an argument to that," I said dryly.

"Perhaps." His smile was back. "They know you differently. Luke is your brother, Kade your love."

"And what are you?"

He shrugged. "I like to think I'm your second father. I know I can't replace the one you lost, the one you already love and guard close to your heart. He would want me to watch over you. I knew that the second I laid eyes on you, even though you were all knobby knees and elbows."

"I wasn't eating all that well on the street," I admitted. "You fattened me up pretty quickly."

"You filled out. I was happy to see it. As for letting your fear of Kade finding out about your past take over, you need to let it go. He knows most of it. What's left is merely details."

It felt like more than details and still ... he was right. "I don't know what I did before I met you," I admitted, grinning. "I'm glad things are going well for you."

"I'm glad they're going well for you, too." He flicked his eyes to the tent flap as if he anticipated an arrival. I wasn't surprised when it opened to allow Kade entrance. The woman with him did surprise me.

"Bay?" I straightened in my chair as the blonde slid around Kade. "Is something wrong? Do you need a reading or something?"

She snorted. "Trust me, I don't want to know my future. If I have to see how many times Aunt Tillie gets arrested before it's all said and done, I'll probably cry."

Max chuckled. "Your great-aunt is a gem."

"She's ... something." Bay looked momentarily perplexed and then shook her head to dislodge whatever dark thought she'd latched onto. "So, I come bearing gifts." She held up a large leather tome. It looked old, and I was interested the second she flashed the cover toward me. It featured a compass needle and runes.

"What is that?" I asked, intrigued.

"It's an old book we had in the library at The Overlook," she replied. "It's all about the four corners ... and the runes that go with them. I thought maybe we might be able to find some answers."

We were finally getting somewhere. We had only one problem. "I have to work this afternoon."

"Oh, I know." Her tone was breezy. "I thought I would sit in here and go through the book and we could exchange information if I find anything interesting during your readings. Otherwise I'll keep quiet and out of your business."

I'd had worse offers. "We can probably make that work."

"Definitely," Max agreed, getting to his feet. "Let me know if you find something. We're not here much longer, and I believe we're due for something else to happen before we leave."

He wasn't the only one who believed that. In fact, I felt it in my bones.

28

TWENTY-EIGHT

Having Bay in my tent turned out to be more fun than I thought. She sat in the corner, the book open on the floor, and offered increasingly hilarious tidbits when she recognized anyone coming in for a reading.

"What are you looking for?" I asked a young man who came in with a cute girl attached to his arm. He was young — eighteen or so, if I had to guess — and he had a bland face that bordered on handsome but didn't quite make it.

"We want to know our future," the girl said, adding a giggle for good measure.

"We definitely want to know our future," the boy agreed.

"We think it's going to be good." The girl couldn't stop giggling as she wiggled her hips.

"Very good," the young man said, waggling his eyebrows suggestively. "I'm thinking there's going to be a lot of sex in my future."

I didn't as much as arch an eyebrow. I'd heard much worse than that over my years reading fortunes with Mystic Caravan. Bay, however, seemed to know the young man and woman, and was having none of it.

"When did you two start dating?" Bay asked, causing the boy to jolt when he realized she was in the tent.

He slowly peered around my shoulder, and when he found Bay sitting on the ground he swallowed hard. "Hey, Ms. Winchester."

Bay's expression was hard to read, but I recognized a hint of mischief flitting across her features. "Hello, Nelson. Haven't seen you around in a bit."

"I've been busy." He avoided direct eye contact with Bay.

"This is Nelson Lyons," Bay offered by way of introduction before her eyes landed on the girl. "And Rosie Summers," she said, her lips quirking. "I haven't seen you since ... well, I think it was around Halloween. You were dressed as a nurse ... ."

"A sexy nurse," Nelson corrected.

Bay ignored him. "You were dressed as a nurse and taking Donovan Jackson's temperature with your tongue."

Nelson's smile slowly slipped. "What does that have to do with anything?"

I wondered that myself.

"I'm merely concerned that something is up." Bay didn't rise from her spot or close her book. She did, however, furrow her brow and stare hard at Nelson. "You haven't by any chance been making wishes in wells again, have you, Nelson?"

The young man's face turned so red I thought he might be having a heart attack. "I haven't been near that well since ... well, you know," he sputtered. "Why would you think that?"

"Nelson?"

Hmm. Something was going on here. "Well, sit down," I suggested, gesturing toward the chairs across from me. "How long have you guys been dating?"

"Shouldn't you already know that?" Rosie challenged, attitude on full display. She kept darting odd looks in Bay's direction. I would have to get to the bottom of this little dust-up. I hated being out of the loop.

"I like getting the basics out of the way so they don't cloud the reading," I answered simply.

"Oh." Suddenly placated, Rosie bobbed her blond head. She had masses of flaxen curls that told me she was very interested in her appearance. Half of telling fortunes was reading people, and Rosie was an open book. Nelson, well, he was something else entirely.

"We've been together two weeks," Nelson said, his smile returning. "It's been the best two weeks ever."

Rosie's giggle was back, and this time there was something grating about it. "It certainly has been a great two weeks, pudding."

Pudding? I barely managed to keep a straight face. "Cut the deck." On instinct, I held out the tarot cards to Rosie. Bay clearly knew something about Nelson, and he was uncomfortable around her. He wasn't the one I sensed trouble from. That award went to Rosie.

Rosie dutifully cut the deck and watched as I dealt the cards. Bay, who had been intent on the book for hours, watched as I worked. She didn't say anything, but it was obvious she was curious.

"Let's see what we have." I studied the cards with interest as I reached out and brushed against Rosie's mind. To my surprise, I found it relatively well shuttered, which wasn't normal unless I was dealing with a paranormal or a human who understood about psychic invasion.

The first card was the World, and it was inverted. "You're feeling unfulfilled."

"No, that's not true." Nelson was firm. "I'm very fulfilled."

I risked a glance at Rosie and found her staring at me with intent eyes. She was listening.

The Temperance card was next. It was also inverted. "You're drowning in emotional extremes. One minute you're happy, the next you're sad."

Nelson looked to Rosie curiously. "That doesn't sound like me either. Does it sound like you?"

"Shh." Rosie pressed her finger to her lips. "I want to hear what she says."

The Wheel of Fortune card. "Things will change, and quickly."

The Emperor, inverted. "You're not feeling nearly as warm as you pretend."

Knight of Wands. "Despite that, you're excited about something to come. You're feeling adventurous, reckless."

I flipped another card, my mind focusing as a picture began to take shape.

King of Cups reversed. "You're feeling moody, unappreciated. You're prone to taking and giving bad advice."

"Does any of this make any sense to you?" Nelson whined.

"Shut up," Rosie hissed, intense. She looked ready to bolt. Clearly I was getting close to something.

Nine of Cups reversed. "You're smug, feeling empowered and think there's no stopping you."

King of Swords. "You listen to your head rather than your heart."

Page of Swords. "You're naturally curious, and that's gotten you into trouble."

The images in my mind were slowly starting to meld with the cards and I finally saw faces emerging. Ah, geez. There was more going on with this girl than I realized.

King of Pentacles reversed. "You're willing to use your sexuality to get what you want, which is how you ended up here."

"Hey, I'm all for her using her sexuality," Nelson offered. "I happen to like it."

I ignored him. He wasn't part of this.

Nine of Pentacles. "You've been living beyond your means. You spend when you shouldn't spend."

The Tower. "You're heading toward a reckoning."

And, finally, the Hanged Man. "You're about to sacrifice yourself to the whims of others." Without hesitation, I leaned forward and grabbed her arm before she could pull away and slammed my consciousness into her head, muttering under my breath as I forced the truth from the dark corners of her somersaulting mind.

"What's going on?" Nelson asked, alarmed. "I ... what's happening?" He reached for my hand, the intent to shove me away from Rosie clear, but Bay intervened and stopped him.

"No, Nelson. Let her finish."

"But she's hurting Rosie."

"She's not," Bay argued, her gaze on the young girl now. Instead of balking or running in fear, Rosie stared directly into my eyes. She was practically daring me to continue.

"Where are they?" I asked once I was done ransacking Rosie's mind. "What do they plan to do?"

"What are you talking about?" Nelson whined. "I don't understand what's happening."

"I don't understand either," Bay admitted. "I ... ." Whatever she was about to say died on her lips as Rosie finally mustered the strength to jerk away from me.

The girl took a deliberate step back, heaved out a sigh and glared. "Don't ever touch me again! Do you understand?"

She sounded dark, dangerous and in control. "I understand that you're in over your head," I replied. "You need to escape from this situation before it takes you down."

"You have no idea what you're talking about," Rosie hissed.

"I know exactly what I'm talking about ... and you're in big trouble, little girl."

"What is it?" Bay asked. "What's wrong?"

I didn't answer her. I couldn't. I had to focus on Rosie. If I broke eye contact, she would run, and there was every chance we wouldn't get her back until it was too late.

"You need to stay out of our business," Rosie threatened. "If you involve yourself, you won't like what happens."

"If you leave this tent I may not be able to help you," I warned. "Don't make that mistake."

"Stay away," Rosie repeated as she reached the tent flap. "We're not afraid of you. Don't think we are."

She was gone before I could say another word.

"What was that?" Bay asked, straightening.

"Trouble ... and now I think I know what's going on." My mind raced. "We need to get Max, Kade and Raven in here."

"And Landon and Chief Terry," Bay added. "We can't cut them out."

I slid her a sidelong look. "I don't usually play well with law enforcement."

"You'll have to this time." Bay was firm. "We're all in this together."

I sighed, resigned. "Okay. I'll try things your way. But if I have to make up the rules on the spot, I'm not going to apologize."

Bay simply nodded. "Fair enough. I'll call Landon and Chief Terry."

"And I'll get the others." I started to move toward the opening, but Nelson stopped me with a wail.

"What about me?" he snapped. "You just caused my girlfriend to freak out and run away. What's going to happen to me?"

I took pity on him. "You need to find another girlfriend. That one is defective."

"That's the story of my life," Nelson griped.

Bay sympathetically patted his arm. "You really do have terrible luck with women. Have you considered dating men?"

Nelson scowled. "That's not funny."

"I wasn't trying to be funny. You either need to become a monk or take a break from women altogether. I was trying to be helpful."

"I am done hanging around you." Nelson stomped to the tent flap. "You guys are the bad luck."

It was entirely possible he was right.

ONCE EVERYONE WAS GROUPED IN my tent — and a sign detailing I would be back shortly to resume readings affixed to the flap — I laid out what I saw in the young woman's mind.

"It's Shirley and Adele."

No one reacted to my announcement.

"The old witches staying at The Overlook," I explained. "The ones excited about the dinner theater. They did all of this."

Bay wrinkled her nose. "But ... how? They're in their seventies. Heck, they could be in their eighties. How could they possibly have taken down two younger and fitter men?"

"Billy wasn't all that fit," I argued. "But that's neither here nor there. They're not doing the physical stuff."

"Rosie?" Bay rubbed the back of her neck as she considered the conundrum. "I don't see how that's possible. Shirley and Adele arrived in town after Darren died. They were on the bus that arrived that afternoon. They told me that."

"Just because they said it doesn't mean they were telling the truth," I argued. "Besides, I saw them that afternoon, too. I didn't see them get off the bus. They were with that group, but when everyone else was gathering luggage they took off without any luggage."

"But ... ." Bay trailed off, uncertain.

"Let's say you're right about that," Landon interjected, his hand resting on Bay's back. "How could those little old ladies take down two grown men? How could they have done it on the fairgrounds without anyone noticing? More importantly, how did they do it without setting off that magical trap thing that Bay told me about?"

"The dreamcatcher," I said absently as I searched for answers to his questions. "They weren't always using Rosie and some friend of hers, a girl with black hair and a nose ring."

"Stephanie Dobbs," Bay volunteered. "She hangs around with a girl named Stephanie Dobbs. She has a nose ring."

"They weren't always using Stephanie and Rosie," I offered. "They were using Lizzy and Kaley before that. They were meant to be diversions. Plus, well, they needed four people to cast the spell they have in mind.

"You said it yourself, Bay," I continued. "This comes back to the four corners. There are two of them, but they need the power of four."

"Rosie and Stephanie aren't witches," Bay argued. "They're simple girls. They just graduated from high school. I think I would know if they were witches. Both of them grew up in this town."

"Do witches recognize other witches?" Kade asked, legitimately curious.

"Not always," Bay admitted. "We would've known if Rosie and Stephanie were witches, though. They've spent eighteen years in this town. We've crossed paths with them many times."

"They might not have needed women with magical powers," Max noted, thoughtful. "They merely may have needed women they could trick into believing they had powers. That's why they went for the younger ones twice. They thought they could fool them."

"To what end?" Terry asked. "Why murder Darren and Billy? What good would that do?"

That was a good question. "I think they're trying to perform a ritual," I explained. "I saw things in Rosie's head, things she didn't understand. I think they wanted me to see because I'm capable of understanding."

"And why is that?" Kade asked, nervous. "Why would they want to tip their hands?"

"Because they need something from us," I replied simply.

"Power," Bay interjected. "They need power. They stayed at The Overlook because they heard the stories about my family and thought they would get the power from those living under our roof. Then you guys came along and they sensed a different type of power."

"But that doesn't explain the murders," Kade persisted.

"It does if you look back at blood magic spells," Bay argued. "They didn't care about who they murdered. They needed the blood. I'm sure they collected it. They covered what they were doing with the runes.

"The runes could play into the spell," she continued. "They might be necessary to whatever it is they're planning. They took the blood, though."

"It makes sense." Landon scrubbed his chin. "We said that Darren couldn't have been killed where we found his body because there was no blood. Maybe there was no blood because they collected it."

"They were pretty neat about collecting it," Kade said.

"They were," Landon agreed. "There was no blood around Billy's body either, only what was visible. To our knowledge, he never left the fairgrounds. That ground should've been saturated with blood."

"How did they cross the dreamcatcher?" Kade asked. "Why didn't it alert?"

I had the answer. "They didn't cross the dreamcatcher. I think they might have tried earlier – that's why it alerted – but they ran before we could find them. They enchanted Lizzy and Kaley to carry out the actual deed. We should've listened harder to them. They said they wanted power. They wanted the sort of power Shirley and Adele had. It was right in front of us and we missed it."

"Once we sent Lizzy and Kaley out of town, removed them from their reach, they needed other girls to control," Bay mused. "They picked locals."

"Those girls are going to be part of their spell. I can't quite see what they're trying to do, but it isn't good," I said. "Blood is only used in the absolute worst rituals, so whatever they've got planned is of the terrible variety."

"Will Rosie and Stephanie survive the spell?" Max asked.

I shrugged. "They could very well be sacrificed for an extra power boost. They're only there as pretenders. Shirley and Adele have the power."

"They're the ones who alerted on the dreamcatcher earlier," Kade noted. "It had to be them, right?"

I nodded. "They sent Kaley and Lizzy to kill Billy. The girls weren't acting of their own free will. They did the deed and departed with the blood they were instructed to collect. The girls weren't inherently evil, just under a spell. I have no idea why they tried to come back today, but I haven't seen them on the fairgrounds at all since the festival started."

"That's a little loophole in the dreamcatcher design we need to plug," Max noted.

"Definitely," I agreed. "First, we have to figure out where Adele and Shirley are. We need to stop whatever they have planned."

"Where are they going?" Kade asked me, his eyes intent. "You must've seen something that will lead us to the right place."

"I ... can't be sure. There's water around, but it almost looks as if they're walking on water. I don't recognize the landmarks. I'm not familiar enough with the area."

"Walking on water?" Bay's eyes widened as realization washed over her features. "Can you show me?"

I nodded. "Sure." I grabbed her hand and opened my mind, pushing out an image. She didn't look surprised when I shared the vision with her.

"I know where we have to go," she said, her voice heavy as she dragged a hand through her hair. "I think we should get Aunt Tillie before heading out, just to be on the safe side."

"We're talking about two old women," Landon argued. "I think we can take them. We'll have you and Poet with us. What more do we need?"

"I'm going, too," Kade said. "You'll have to kill me to keep me away."

"I need to go as well," Max said. "My people are going to be fighting a wily enemy in an unknown environment."

I knew why he really wanted to go, and it wasn't because it was necessary to stand with me. He wanted to make sure Kade was protected. He also wanted to make sure he was around to douse Kade's powers if necessary. I wasn't about to argue with more backup, so I let it slide.

"Where are we going?" I asked.

"Hollow Creek," Bay replied. "I figure that was where they were holing up when you said you saw them walking on water. It's an optical illusion. You can cross the creek easily in certain spots. They're probably setting up their stronghold on the far side."

"What's there?"

"Nothing now. It used to be a big party place for the kids."

"Ah, yes," Landon intoned. "How I miss the days when we had a huge field of pot to burn down. The entire town was stoned for forty-eight hours. It was glorious."

I smiled at the mental image he painted. "Hollow Creek is full of memory magic, too," I noted. "Several of my people have commented on it. If Adele and Shirley are trying to bolster the others enough to fake that they're witches, they need spare magic to channel. It makes sense."

"Yeah, well, all the magic flying around that place belongs to us," Bay said. "We've fought more than one battle out there."

"You're not alone today," Landon said, sliding his arm around her shoulders. "I'll be there. We'll get Aunt Tillie to be on the safe side. Everything will be okay."

He said the words in a soothing manner, but I had a feeling he was uttering them for himself as much as her.

"We'll definitely be okay," I agreed. "I think we need to end this now, rather than waiting for nightfall. They sent Rosie to me because they wanted me to know. They assumed we would come after dark. I don't think I was meant to see that part. We can't adhere to their timetable."

"Agreed." Max clapped his hands once. "We go now. They'll wish they'd never killed one of our people." His fury was palpable.

"I'll change my clothes. You call your aunt, Bay. We leave in fifteen minutes. I'm definitely ready to end this."

TWENTY-NINE

Hollow Creek was desolate, so much so that it gave me chills the second I hopped out of Kade's truck and peered through the trees to get a glimpse of the water.

"What is this place?" he muttered, his hand instinctively going out to me. "I don't like it."

I cast him a sidelong look. "Do you sense something?"

"I ... what?" He looked surprised by the question as he shifted his eyes to me. "Am I supposed to sense something?"

I held my palms up and shrugged. "I don't know. Max isn't a full mage. He's more like half a mage and something else. That means you're really only one-quarter mage."

Kade furrowed his brow. "What else?"

I didn't know the answer to that. "He never told me. He just said his father was a full mage and that's it. You'll have to ask him."

"I'm guessing now isn't the time."

I shook my head as I studied his strong profile. "You're okay, right? I mean ... if you want to wait here, I understand. You're still new to this. We have backup in the Winchesters. You can wait here."

His gaze was withering, but before he got a chance to give voice to his annoyance the sound of agitated voices filled the air behind us.

"You're not in charge," Landon barked as he strolled in front of his Ford Explorer. He looked lean and dangerous. He also looked frustrated. I couldn't tell if he was angry with Bay or Tillie.

"I most certainly am in charge," Tillie shot back, making me realize I should've known who was trying to take control of the situation before she showed her hand. "I'm the oldest one here. Do you know what that means?"

Landon nodded without hesitation as he put his hand on Bay's back and prodded her forward. "It means that we can lock you in a home if you do anything ridiculous."

"Oh, if only," Bay muttered, causing me to smile.

"Puh-leez." Tillie rolled her eyes. "You would miss me if I was gone. You would cry ... and look at my empty seat at the table and think about what a turd you were for letting me go."

Landon merely shook his head. "You're not in charge, so don't go in there thinking you are."

"Let me guess." Tillie's tone was biting. "You're in charge, aren't you?"

"No." Landon was calm as he met Tillie's challenging gaze. "Bay is in charge. She gets to boss both of us around today. How does that sound?"

Bay balked. "Oh, I don't want to be in charge."

Landon extended a finger in her direction while holding Tillie's gaze. "I don't want anyone getting hurt. Do you understand?"

Tillie shook her head. "Of course I understand. You're afraid you're inept and somehow Bay will get hurt because of it." She patted his arm in a condescending manner. "You don't have to worry. I'll take care of her when you fail."

Landon's eyes turned into molten blue slits. "You listen here ... ."

Kade coughed to cut him off, causing Landon to snap his eyes in our direction. "She's baiting you, man," Kade said calmly. "I have the same problem with Luke. He's a big, whiny baby with delusions of grandeur, too."

"Thanks," Luke said as he slapped Kade's shoulder a little harder than necessary. "I can't wait to beat you with my delusions of grandeur later."

Kade smirked. "Looking forward to it."

"We need to work together and focus on what's through those trees," Bay insisted, calm despite the tension building around us. "Don't get worked up. Just ... chill out."

Landon slowly shifted his eyes to her. "Chill out? Did you just meet me?"

Bay snickered. "Do your best." She squeezed his hand before focusing on me. "How do you want to do this?"

I shrugged, noncommittal. "I thought we would play it by ear."

"That sounds good. We don't know what to expect, so I think that's our best option."

"So ... are you ready?"

She nodded without hesitation. "Let's get it done."

BAY KNEW THE AREA better than me, so I let her lead. Landon and Kade kept close to us, but Landon's attention was split by Tillie, who kept making as if she was going to bolt into the trees so she could cut in front of the line and get ahead of our group.

Max, Luke and Nellie kept to my left — perhaps as a flanking unit — and they were focused on the job at hand. Even though Nellie kept winking in Tillie's direction, the way he gripped his ax (and who said he could bring that?) was familiar and comforting.

The second we cleared the trees, the mood shifted. A chill fell over the clearing and I pulled up short when I took in the scene.

Rosie and Stephanie were on the bank, about five feet apart, staring at us. Their eyes looked glazed, and I could sense the fog clouding their minds.

"Hello, girls," Bay called, her eyes busy as she glanced between faces. Landon and Tillie scanned the trees for signs of movement, but it seemed Rosie and Stephanie were serving as our welcoming committee.

"You came," Rosie enthused, clapping her hands as if she were a delighted five-year-old. "I'm so glad you could join us."

"Yes, we're thrilled to be here, too," Tillie drawled, tilting her head to the side as she studied the young women. "They've been thralled."

She didn't seem to be speaking to anyone in particular, so I asked the obvious question. "Thralled? What does that mean?"

"You know ... thralled."

I looked to Kade for help, but he seemed as confused as me. "I don't think that's really a word," I said finally.

"Don't go there," Landon instructed as he looked over Stephanie with a trained eye. "She always makes up words and claims they're real. Then she gets upset because she says they should've been words in the first place so she's really doing the world a favor when she coins them. After that, there's generally some portion of time dedicated to pouting."

"You're on my list," Tillie hissed, extending a finger.

"You're on my list," he shot back. "How do you like that?"

"You have a list?" Kade asked, surprised.

"Yup." Landon nodded once. "It's a to-do list. I have things like 'go to work' and 'make Bay breakfast in bed' on it. I also have things like 'see if you can make Thistle forget how to speak' and 'try to make Aunt Tillie's head spin around' on it. You learn to take your fun where you can when you're surrounded by witches."

Kade nodded as if he understood. "Good plan."

"I thought so." Landon licked his lips as he shuffled closer to Stephanie, waving his hand in front of her eyes as she continued smiling like a deranged doll. "I don't think they're in there."

"They're in there," I countered, rubbing my forehead as I tried to calm the nerves that were threatening to take over. "They're trapped. It's like ... being in a bubble. They can see what's going on, hear it, but they can't escape from the bubble to participate."

"How much danger are they in?" Bay asked.

I shrugged, unsure how to answer. "I don't have a clue. I'm not sure what kind of magic is being used, or what kind of power is being filtered through them. It's all very odd."

Bay absently swatted Landon's hand when he moved to poke Stephanie's shoulder. "Don't," she ordered, her tone telling me she wasn't in the mood for nonsense. "You could get hurt if you touch her."

"She might get hurt if we don't find a way to restrain her," Landon pointed out.

"And if there's a curse on her that forces you to attack me if you touch her?" Bay challenged, refusing to back down.

Landon sheepishly pulled back, allowing me to focus on Kade. He looked as if he was about to touch Rosie's shoulder in the same manner until Bay asked the question. The look he shot me was full of worry.

"It's okay," I reassured him. "We'll figure it out."

He didn't look convinced. "We should probably do it soon. I don't like this."

He wasn't the only one. "Where do you think Shirley and Adele are?" I asked.

Bay inclined her chin toward the sand pit on the other side of the water. "They're in those trees."

I was impressed with her instincts. "How do you know that? Can you sense them?" If so, she was stronger than me on the psychic front. The realization that she might be more powerful than me slowly sank in. "Wait ... can you sense them?"

She shook her head. "I have inside information."

"What inside information?"

As if on cue, an elderly female ghost popped into view on the other side of Bay. Even though she didn't need oxygen to breathe, she looked out of breath.

"They're definitely over there," she said, bobbing her head. "They're watching from the tree line ... and they seem amused."

I figured as much," Bay said grimly, shaking her head.

"Who is that?" I asked, confused.

"Who are you talking about?" Kade asked, glancing around.

"The ghost." I gestured toward Bay, forcing Kade to turn his head.

He stared for a long time — it almost felt too long — and then he let loose a small gasp. "Holy ... !"

"Do you see her?" I was surprised. He was moving fast when it came to acceptance of his new reality. I was proud ... and a little awed.

"I see her!" Kade gasped. "I don't understand."

"Bay is a necromancer."

"What does that mean?"

"It means we deal with a lot of ghosts," Landon interjected, his eyes flashing with impatience. "We need to focus on what's important right now. Viola is not important."

"I heard that," the ghost barked, causing Landon to jolt.

"You see and hear her, too?" I asked, surprised. "I didn't realize you were sensitive."

"I'm not." Landon briefly pressed his eyes shut to collect himself. "Bay's powers are growing of late. It used to be that she could see and talk to ghosts and I simply believed she was gifted. Now she can make me see them ... and hear them ... and occasionally smell them. It's an adjustment."

Bay's smile was wan. "Sorry. I'm keyed up."

"Don't worry about it." Landon squeezed her hand. "Just worry about Adele and Shirley. They've obviously picked what they think is a safe spot on the other side of the creek. We need to get beyond that barrier."

"He has a gift for stating the obvious, doesn't he?" Viola drawled, seemingly amused. "It's a good thing you're handsome, dude, because otherwise you'd have trouble attracting the ladies."

Landon scowled. "And I'm done talking to you."

"Focus on me, Viola," Bay ordered, snapping her fingers to get the ghost's attention. "What's going on over there?"

Viola kept her eyes on Landon for a long beat before shifting her attention to Bay. "They're talking, having a good time. They think they've already won, but I don't know what prize they're talking about. They seem excited that Tillie is here."

I snapped my eyes to Tillie out of reflex, but she was focused on the girls, her expression hard to read.

"They came to The Overlook because they heard Aunt Tillie was the most powerful witch in the Midwest," Bay mused, thoughtful. "They always wanted her. They only paid attention to you guys after the fact because ... well, I guess because they sensed something."

"Which means they're real witches," I pointed out. "Shouldn't you have sensed that?"

Bay made a face. "Shouldn't *you* have sensed that?"

She had a point ... which I decided to ignore. "How are we going to get them out in the open?" I asked, my eyes drifting back to the water. "If you're right and they set up the girls as zombie slaves of sorts, that means we can't touch them until this is over. To finish it, we need to find them."

"You said the water was shallow," Luke interjected. "Can't we just cross and find them?"

"Look around," Landon prodded, bobbing his chin. "If we try to cross the water, we're sitting ducks. We'll be out in the open."

"We're out in the open here," Max pointed out. "We're just as susceptible to attack now as we would be trying to cross."

"Except we would be closer if we did that," I supplied. "Maybe they have bad aim because they're old or something."

"Oh, that's true." Luke turned keen. "I hear old people can't see worth a darn." He looked to Tillie for confirmation. "Do you think they're blind?"

Tillie's mouth dropped open. "Why are you asking me?" She was incensed. "I'm not old. I'm in my prime."

"Yeah, you are." Nellie shot her a flirty thumbs-up.

"Geez," I muttered under my breath. I couldn't take much more of this. "We need to get them out of the trees. Do you know exactly where they are, Bay?"

Bay looked to Viola for an answer. The older ghost pointed toward a specific stand of trees.

"There," Viola replied. "They want to be close enough to hear you, but apparently their hearing isn't very good. I understand that. Before I died, I couldn't hear anything ... and that includes my neighbors listening to that ridiculous rap music people find so entertaining these days. It's not music. It's just noise."

"I agree," Tillie said, narrowing her eyes. "We need to get them out of those trees."

"I'm open to suggestions," Bay said. "How do you think we should do it?"

"Well ... ." The response fell silent when Nellie narrowed his eyes and cocked his ax.

I realized what he was going to do a second before he let it loose, but it was too late. The ax flew across the water (with a little assist from Tillie, I'm sure) and landed in the trees. The witches inside were so startled they spilled from their hiding place and splashed into the water — to relative safety — across from us.

"What was that?" Landon barked, his temper flaring. "Did someone just throw an ax?"

"That would be Nellie," Luke said. "He has impulse control issues. He's a premature ejaculator when it comes to throwing axes, if you will."

"I'm going to kick the crap out of you later, Luke," Nellie warned. "Besides, I didn't do all that myself."

"No," I agreed, my lips quirking. "Tillie helped."

"I like making things fly faster," Tillie admitted, her grin mischievous. "Now, let's focus on the troublesome witches, shall we? We'll retrieve your ax later, Nellie."

"We'd better," Nellie muttered. "I can't live without her."

"Your ax is a she?" Bay asked.

Nellie shrugged. "Maybe. Unless ... if you think it's sexist, then it's not. Now isn't the time for that anyway."

"Definitely not," I agreed, folding my arms over my chest as I met Shirley's dark glare. "Hello, ladies. How are you doing today?"

Because the water moved very slowly, my voice carried relatively well over the space.

"I see you found us," Adele noted.

"You fell right into our trap," Shirley cackled.

"Or we simply want to stop this from continuing," Max countered. "What is it you expect to get out of this little showdown?"

"We have a plan," Adele replied simply. "We're going to live forever."

"Oh, well, good," Luke drawled. "It's an original reason for doing evil. Oh, wait, it's not."

"Come on." Nellie elbowed him. "I love 'I'm going to live forever' mania. It's one of my favorites."

"I prefer 'I'm going to eat my weight in bacon' mania," Landon said dryly. "That's my favorite." He didn't look nearly as amused by the turn of events as the rest of us. In fact, he looked downright worried. "Ladies, it would be best for all concerned if you crossed the creek now and turned yourselves in."

"On what charges?" Adele called out.

"Yeah, on what charges?" Shirley echoed. "We haven't done anything ... except hang out at the creek."

"What about the girls?" Bay challenged, gesturing toward Rosie and Stephanie. "You possessed them."

"Have fun proving that," Adele challenged.

"What about the murders?" I prodded. "Darren and Billy are dead because of you."

"You can't prove that either," Shirley said. "We didn't kill them. Lizzy and Kaley did."

Something occurred to me. "No. Lizzy and Kaley might've killed Billy — that's how they crossed the dreamcatcher without it alerting us to a malignant presence — but you killed Darren. Lizzy and Kaley weren't in town at the time."

Adele narrowed her eyes, shrewd. "How do you know that?"

"Because I saw the bus they came in on," I replied simply. "They were collecting luggage that day. You weren't. You seemed to be having a good time, which is why I focused on you, but you didn't have luggage. That means you were here before then."

"They checked in at The Overlook early that day," Bay offered. "I didn't think anything about it at that time because I was focusing on other stuff — like watching you guys — but they were early. They checked in before the bus even arrived. I never considered why they did."

"That doesn't prove anything," Shirley countered, her expression momentarily shifting. I thought I saw a hint of fear. "You don't have proof that we did anything."

"I don't think that's important," I admitted. "We didn't come here to arrest you. We came to stop you."

"From what?" Adele was indignant. "People have a right to protect themselves. That's all we're doing."

"How do you figure that?" Bay asked.

"We're old ... and Shirley is dying." Adele extended a gnarled finger in her best friend's direction. "We've been best friends since we were five years old. That's seventy-five years of friendship. There's only one way to save her."

I thought about the bodies, the ritual way they were displayed. "You gathered blood," I said, puzzling things out as I went. "Whatever you have planned, you needed the blood."

"We did," Adele agreed, matter-of-fact. "We need a lot of blood for the spell we're going to cast. It can't just be regular blood. We need witch blood, too. That's where you come in." Her smile was so pleasant it was almost deranged as she focused on Tillie. "I'm sorry about this, but there really is no other way. We need your blood."

"And because we're casting the spell to save me and I can't go on without Adele, we're going to need your blood, too," Shirley said, her eyes narrowing as she focused on Bay.

Oh, well, crap. I should've seen that coming. "Wait!" I threw up my hands the moment Shirley started muttering. I couldn't tell what Tillie was about to do, but the look on her face told me she was serious. "Do you really want a war here?" I demanded. "Do you really want to kill to get your way?"

"It's not murder." Adele was sincere. "We've talked about this. We have a right to save ourselves, better our lives."

"You don't have the right to take the lives of others to do it," I argued.

"You believe that. We don't. We don't have a choice. We're saving our lives."

"You won't win," Bay said, her tone plaintive. "You can't win. We outnumber you."

"And we're stronger than you," Max added. "This is not a war you can claim victory on."

Adele's eyes narrowed as she regarded him. "What would you have us do? We're out of options."

"No, there's one option left," Max said. "You could die with dignity, Shirley. You could spend the time you have left enjoying it with your friend. And you, Adele, could let her. You could let go of this crazy notion that death is an ending rather than simply a different course."

Adele shook her head, stubbornly crossing her arms over her chest. "No. We need to stay together. We can't be apart."

"Does that mean you're willing to die together?" I asked, legitimately curious. "That's what's going to happen here. You're going to die ... and there won't be a thing we can do to stop it once it starts."

"If we're supposed to die here, then at least we'll go together." Adele was resigned. "I understand you're going to fight. You don't want to die either. You should know we're very powerful witches."

"Not really," Tillie said, taking me by surprise with her calm demeanor. I thought for sure she would be picking a fight rather than reacting with something that reminded me of ... well, sympathy. She actually looked sympathetic.

"What are you doing?" I asked when she raised her hand.

Instead of answering, she ignored me. "There is one other option, and you're not powerful enough to stop me." She briefly slid her eyes to Bay and nodded, a silent message passing between them.

"Are you sure?" Bay asked.

Tillie nodded. "It's the easiest way."

"Okay." Bay blew out a sigh as she closed her eyes. "Darren. Billy. Come to me."

I was fascinated as she whispered.

"Come to me now," Bay ordered, her voice low and demanding. In an instant, the ghosts of Darren and Billy materialized. "Distract them," she instructed. "Keep them focused on you."

The ghosts did as she asked without hesitation, quickly flying across the water. Their forms grew stronger as they skimmed the creek causing Nellie to gasp.

"What the ... ?"

Whatever he was about to say died on his lips when Tillie started chanting.

"I bind you, Adele, with all that I am and know. You cannot do harm to others, or even yourself. Your magic is done, moot and defunct. I bind you to a mortal life. May the Goddess have mercy on your soul."

She repeated the charm three times before moving on to Shirley and repeating it, adding a bit about passing with peace for the ailing woman. It showed she had a heart, which somehow softened her in my view.

When I'd dragged my eyes back to the scene across the way, both women were on the ground, sobbing as the ghosts swirled around them. They tried casting spells, but the magic never materialized. They looked exhausted. They clearly weren't the enemies we'd envisioned.

"Well, that was a bit anticlimactic," Luke complained, wrinkling his nose. "I didn't even get to make an inappropriate comment while running from danger."

"Yes, that's the true tragedy of the day," Kade drawled, shaking his head.

I ignored them as I stepped closer to Rosie. Her eyes were clearing, and she looked confused and frightened.

"What am I doing here?" She shrank away when I tried to touch her shoulder. "Who are you?"

She didn't remember anything. Er, well, at least right now. Perhaps that was a good thing.

"It's going to be okay." I meant it. "We'll get you back to town and ... well ... it's going to be okay."

I looked to Bay, who was doing the same with Stephanie. She'd called back the ghosts, who were circling her, but she appeared lost in thought. Apparently this fight hadn't gone the way any of us expected.

"It's for the better," Max said in a low voice, as if reading my mind. "Not every battle needs to be a full-on war."

He was right, but still I couldn't help feeling let down. "I guess things went as well as could be expected."

"Yes, and now we only need deal with the cleanup."

"Things could've been worse," I said finally.

"Most definitely. Let's finish it."

"That sounds like a plan."

30
THIRTY

For groups used to big fights, the relatively easy takedown of two elderly witches was a bit of a letdown. When you add to that the fact Adele and Shirley were sympathetic figures — despite being murderers, I mean — the whole thing turned into something of a downer.

Still, we couldn't dwell on that.

We left the Winchesters to clean up the mess, returning to the fairgrounds and our regular jobs for the rest of the day. Things went as normally as could be expected, the only distraction occurring when Landon parked in front of the police station and led the two women into the building.

They looked to be bitterly complaining to one another, but otherwise they were unharmed. It was the best possible outcome.

Once we closed down for the night, everyone was happy for a quiet dinner. We were well into preparations — simple burgers and pasta salad to make matters easier — when Bay, Tillie and Landon arrived.

"Hey." I wasn't surprised to see them. In fact, I'd expected them to stop by earlier. From the looks of exhaustion on their faces — except for Tillie, who looked normal — it was easy to see they'd had a long day. "Have a seat. Do you want burgers?"

"We're fine," Bay said, although she gratefully accepted the tumbler of iced tea Luke passed in her direction.

"There's bacon for the burgers," I said to Landon.

His grin was sheepish. "Oh, well ... I could eat a burger."

"You could eat a cow," Tillie corrected, taking an open spot next to Nellie and leaning closer to look at the magazine he perused. "Porn?"

Nellie made a face. "I don't read porn."

She didn't look convinced. "I would totally read porn if I could get the good stuff. Everything here is sanitized for prudish pleasures."

The look Bay shot her great-aunt was withering. "Since when do you like porn?"

"There are many things you don't know about me," Tillie replied primly. "For starters, did you know that I like square-dancing? You didn't know that, did you? I also like walks in the rain, piña coladas and irritating Landon until his head is pounding and he wants to hide under the covers."

"Well, you're excelling at that one," Landon noted, his hand rubbing soothing circles across Bay's back. "We thought you guys might like an update on Shirley and Adele."

"Of course." I gave him my full attention as I sat next to Kade. "What are they saying?"

"They're not denying anything," Landon replied. "They killed Darren in his shop and dragged his body to the spot where you found it. They drained him of blood indoors, but they thought there was a chance they might be able to deflect attention to you, so they risked transporting his body in the dark."

"How did they do that?" Luke asked. "I don't see how they had the strength."

"Apparently they used the wheelbarrow Marcus keeps at the stables, rolled the body into it, and took turns using their magic to roll it across town."

I tried to picture the scenario, but couldn't. "That sounds ... interesting."

Landon snorted. "Yeah, well, they're interesting women."

"They said they watched you that first night," Bay offered. "They tested you a few times, made noises to see how you'd react. Do you remember that?"

Something niggled at the back of my brain. "We thought we heard a wendigo howl that night," I admitted. "It threw me off."

"No, it threw *me* off," Kade corrected. "I was still jumpy."

"That means they were watching us then," I mused, concern washing through me. "Did they say anything of interest?"

Bay clucked sympathetically. "I get that you're worried they'll say something — and they did see a few odd things, like Luke taking his shirt off and staring at himself in the mirror in front of the funhouse for an hour while making his pecs bounce ... oh, and some clown wearing what looked to be chaps — but it won't matter."

I slid Luke a sidelong look. "Still? You told me you quit doing that."

"Hey, I did ... for the most part. Occasionally I'm so good looking I can't stop staring at myself. Sue me. I'm doing the best that I can."

Part of me wanted to smack him around, but I let it go. "Why won't it matter?"

"Shirley really is sick," Landon replied, tugging Bay a little closer so he could keep his arm around her. "She doesn't have much time. Prosecuting her will be a waste of time and taxpayers' money. Instead, she'll go to a hospital and live out the rest of her days there."

That sounded unbelievably sad. "And Adele?"

Landon merely shrugged. "We don't know yet. It's a difficult situation."

"What Landon isn't saying is that no one wants that woman to go before a judge and start screaming about binding spells and wicked witches," Tillie volunteered. "That's on top of the things you guys can do."

I rolled my neck as understanding washed over me. "She won't get away with it, will she? I mean ... she killed two people."

"That's the other problem," Landon said. "They are blaming Billy's death on Lizzy and Kaley. If she goes to trial, we'll have to drag them back."

"And if we drag them back, they'll be prosecuted even though they weren't in control of their actions," Kade mused.

Landon nodded. "It's a difficult situation. I called the parents, told them I was just checking to make sure the kids were okay. Other than being upset they missed the festival, the girls are none the wiser."

"They didn't know what they were doing," Bay explained. "They don't remember. Rosie and Stephanie don't remember either. How much are we supposed to tell them? It could ruin their lives."

I rubbed my cheek as I considered the conundrum. "Would you want to know?" I asked finally.

"I honestly don't know." Bay looked conflicted. "I would like to think I'm strong enough to accept it, but killing someone ... it's not always the easiest thing to swallow."

I knew that better than most. Now, so did Kade. He continued to struggle even though the woman he'd killed had it coming. "So ... what does that mean for Adele?"

"There's a chance she'll end up in the same hospital as Shirley," Landon answered. "She would be committed against her will and kept there the rest of her life. Because of the spell Aunt Tillie cast on her, she won't be able to use magic to escape. It might be the best possible outcome for all of us."

"Not for Billy," I argued.

"No, not for Billy," Landon agreed. "I don't know what to do for him."

"Is he still hanging around?" I asked. "We could ask him."

Bay slowly shook her head. "I released him this afternoon. He passed over with Darren."

"Passed over where?" Raven asked with a great deal of interest. "Where are you sending these ghosts when you release them?"

"On," Bay replied simply. "Wherever they're meant to be, that's where I send them. I didn't facilitate Darren or Billy remaining behind. They stayed on their own because their deaths were unexpected and traumatic."

"You've kept ghosts behind before?" Raven was intrigued. "That means you're powerful."

"I didn't know I was doing it at the time," Bay explained. "I try to be really careful. It's new for me."

"I know all about that." Kade flashed a small smile. "I think we can live with Adele being locked up in a mental hospital for the duration. It's not the perfect outcome, but it's better than some of the others. I agree that it's probably not smart to drag Lizzy and Kaley back just so we can explode their worlds."

Bay looked to me for confirmation and I nodded.

"I think it's a good idea," I said. "Adele can stay with Shirley until the end. After that, thinking about what she's done will have to be punishment enough."

"Okay." Bay was obviously relieved, because she exhaled heavily and relaxed her shoulders. "That's good to hear."

"Did you think we would disagree?" I asked.

Her shoulders hopped. "I didn't know. You could've tried to force things. That wouldn't have gone well for any of us."

"No, I definitely think this is the better choice." I watched her. "You don't seem happy it's done."

She was rueful. "I expected more."

I didn't want to laugh — it seemed somehow rude — but I couldn't stop myself. "It's terrible that we're so used to the idea of fights that almost kill us that we're disappointed when there's no bloodshed."

"I feel ridiculous, but I was expecting more," Bay admitted. "I'm sure I'll get over it."

"We all will," I agreed. "Things went better than they should have. We're lucky that everyone we love is safe and no one is hurt ... other than Darren and Billy."

"So, we'll take this as a win," Bay said, resting her head against Landon's chest as he kissed her forehead. "Maybe we'll all get some much-needed sleep tonight."

"That would be nice."

Silence descended for a bit, the only sound coming from Nellie and Tillie as they murmured while looking at his magazine. Bay was the first to break it.

"You leave the day after tomorrow," she noted. "Maybe we can have another meal together before then. You know, just to say goodbye?"

"I think we can manage that." I smirked. "We told the others about dinner at The Overlook. They're desperate to join us."

"We are," Dolph agreed. "I want to see the enchanted pot field. It sounds magical."

Landon growled as he glared at Tillie, who remained entranced with Nellie's magazine.

"Aunt Tillie and Nellie will want a chance to say goodbye, too," Bay added. "The dinner will be their last hurrah."

Tillie rolled her eyes. "Excuse me? Last hurrah? We're becoming online hangout buddies. We already created a forum for The Nettle, where people can learn about what to put in their kettles and Nellie can teach them how to test their mettle."

I groaned. "That sounds ridiculous."

Nellie glared. "It's genius. It'll make us rich."

"Plus, we'll get to keep up with one another," Tillie added. "I thought about joining the circus, but my family wouldn't make it without me. I can't leave them."

"We could try to make it without you," Landon suggested.

"I have a better idea," I said. "Instead of us taking Tillie, why don't you keep Nellie? I think he would fit right in with Hemlock Cove's unique makeup."

"And we would love a break from him," Luke added. "He's a lot of work, what with all the evening gowns and shoes."

Nellie's eyes filled with fire as he extended a finger in Luke's direction. "You're on my list."

The entire table erupted in laughter. Tears leaked from my eyes as I locked gazes with Bay. There was a lot left unsaid, but it wasn't necessary. In the end, her family and my family were mostly the same. The Winchesters turned out to be exactly like us.

They were almost too much like us.

In fact, Nellie and Tillie together were definitely too much.

Somehow we survived, and that's all that mattered.

Made in the USA
Coppell, TX
10 September 2020